Caroline Cauchi is an international bestselling novelist. Her writing seeks to give voice to silenced yet remarkable women, reimagining the stories of those erased from historical narratives. In 2023, her novel *Mrs Van Gogh* was published in multiple countries and selected as a 'Heather's Pick' title in Canada.

Currently lecturing in Creative Writing at the University of Hull, Caroline lives in the UK with her partner and their many children.

carolinecauchi.co.uk

X x.com/Caroline_S
instagram.com/caroline.cauchi

Also by Caroline Cauchi

Mrs Van Gogh

The Woman Who Went Over Niagara Falls in a Barrel

DAUGHTER OF THE TITANIC

CAROLINE CAUCHI

One More Chapter
a division of HarperCollins*Publishers* Ltd
1 London Bridge Street
London SE1 9GF
www.harpercollins.co.uk
HarperCollins*Publishers*
Macken House, 39/40 Mayor Street Upper,
Dublin 1, D01 C9W8, Ireland

This paperback edition 2026

1

First published in Great Britain in ebook format
by HarperCollins*Publishers* 2026
Copyright © Caroline Cauchi 2026
Caroline Cauchi asserts the moral right to be identified
as the author of this work

A catalogue record of this book is available from the British Library

ISBN: 978-0-00-878453-9

This novel is entirely a work of fiction. The names, characters and incidents portrayed in it are the work of the author's imagination. Any resemblance to actual persons, living or dead, events or localities is entirely coincidental.

Printed and bound in the UK using 100% Renewable Electricity
by CPI Group (UK) Ltd

All rights reserved. No part of this publication may be reproduced, stored in a retrieval system, or transmitted, in any form or by any means, electronic, mechanical, photocopying, recording or otherwise, without the prior permission of the publishers.

Without limiting the exclusive rights of any author, contributor or the publisher of this publication, any unauthorised use of this publication to train generative artificial intelligence (AI) technologies is expressly prohibited. HarperCollins also exercise their rights under Article 4(3) of the Digital Single Market Directive 2019/790 and expressly reserve this publication from the text and data mining exception.

*For Nathan, the boy I met in the summer of 1989.
How lucky we are to have found our way back.*

'I am not a [*Titanic*] survivor in the strict sense, but I am the daughter of Captain E.J. Smith'

Melville Russell Cooke, 4 June 1955

An Unlucky Woman

NOVEMBER 1972

The portrait had only just arrived. It leant against the wrong wall, half-shrouded in brown paper, as if the building hadn't yet decided where to put it.

Dr Catherine Haynes crouched to peel back the corner of the wrapping. The smell hit first – turpentine, canvas, and the faint, iron tang of damp stone that lived in the Ashmolean's storage rooms. A pinch of tightness caught beneath her ribs – cold air finding the weak place, as it always did. But she ignored it, steadying her breath before the porter could glance up. The overhead lights buzzed like insects. Behind her, the porter filled out his ledger in blue biro, humming something tuneless and steady.

The woman in the painting emerged slowly, the red of her headscarf burning through the yellowed varnish, the only vivid note in a storm of muted greys. Her gaze was direct, unflinching – not a pose, but a challenge. The face was leaner than Catherine expected, the expression sharpened by something lived-in rather than performed. Not beautiful. True.

A temporary label, printed on a museum typewriter, was clipped to the frame.

```
An Unlucky Woman. Oil on canvas, 1959.
Artist: R. (unknown). Sitter: unidentified.
```

Catherine stepped back.

One word. *Unlucky.* Her professional instinct noted it; something older in her recoiled. She knew that word too well – the one spoken when doctors frowned, when her grandmother prayed a little harder. Catherine slipped off a glove and turned the frame gently. A faint pencil scrawl ran along the stretcher: *Melville.*

The name pulsed with a kind of insistence. Not a common name, not one you forgot. Catherine straightened, heartbeat quickening.

'Dr Haynes?' The porter's voice carried from the far end of the room. 'You'll need to sign for that if it's leaving the gallery.'

'It isn't leaving,' she said, though her hands were still on the frame. 'I'm only looking.'

He grunted, returning to his paperwork.

Catherine studied the woman's painted face. 'You don't look unlucky,' she murmured, as if she'd caught her own reflection, arrested mid-stroke. 'Rather, unfinished with life.'

A voice came from the doorway. 'Talking to them again?'

Catherine turned. Dr Marianne Levine stood against the light, cheeks flushed from the cold, scarf slipping loose from her collar. A Canadian. A lecturer in modern art – one of only three women in the faculty.

'You'll lose your eyesight working down here,' Marianne said. 'No daylight, no heating, and none of the men ever visit.'

Catherine smiled faintly. 'That's why the work gets done.'

Marianne stepped closer, peering at the painting. 'Who is she?'

'I'm not sure yet,' Catherine said. 'The tag says "R". Looks like a David Rolt, and he never signed the personal pieces. The intimate ones.'

'The unlucky woman,' Marianne read aloud. 'Charming.'

'A temporary label. Might not be the artist's intention, so perhaps an *overly* keen observer.' Catherine's gaze lingered on the word. 'It's the same phrase I saw in a 1937 clipping. Captain Edward Smith's daughter. Melville. Her father went down with the *Titanic*. The press called it a curse – the unlucky family.'

Marianne raised her brows. 'You think this is her?'

'Look, here.' She tilted the frame forward and pointed to the name. 'There were rumours about her and Rolt, of course. The sort that cling harder to women than to paint.'

Marianne gave a low laugh. 'The British do prefer a scandal to a signature.'

Catherine didn't answer. Her pulse still hadn't settled. She crossed to the corner where her 'office' began and ended: a steel desk wedged between two storage crates, a portable typewriter beside a tea-stained mug. The wall behind was stippled with index cards, each one a thought caught mid-flight. It was a sliver of space most people walked past without seeing. She'd learned to make use of that kind of invisibility; she'd lived inside it long before Oxford. She flipped open her notebook. The title scrawled across the top of the latest page read: *Luck, Legacy and the Female Image*. Beneath it, her own shorthand:

Unlucky = cursed = burdened
Language = contagion
How myth attaches to women; how it refuses to let go

She underlined *refuses to let go* twice, the nib tearing a spot in the paper.

From the next drawer she pulled the battered index file marked, *1950s – S*. The cards rasped like brittle leaves as she thumbed through, her breath ghosting in the cold air. She paused, before she turned the next card. Each entry felt like the echo of someone else's certainty.

Then she found it.

Details of portraits of Captain Smith, his wife, his daughter. An additional note:

Press call them an unlucky family, an unlucky woman.

She sat back, the hum of the fluorescent light filling the pause. 'I have an address for Melville Smith,' she said softly. 'In Oxford.'

Marianne leant against the doorframe. 'You're going there, aren't you?'

Catherine closed the drawer with a firm, satisfying click. 'If she'll see me, yes. I think she deserves to decide what's written next.'

'Would that be ethical?'

'Probably not,' Catherine said. 'But neither were the headlines.'

'You sound like that Australian woman. Greer,' Marianne teased, but her voice softened.

'Better her than Kenneth Clark,' Catherine said.

They laughed. The sound echoed off the concrete floor. Two women in a space built to preserve other people's names.

When Marianne left, Catherine stayed. She studied the portrait until her reflection blurred into the woman's face. Two outlines, overlapping.

Every painting's a verdict. Every artist an accomplice.

She wrote those lines in her notebook, underlined them once, then added another thought beneath:

If the portrait demands a verdict, perhaps the trial hasn't finished.

The porter coughed from the doorway. 'Locking up, Dr Haynes.'

Catherine nodded, grabbing her handbag and stepping out into the Oxford dusk. The cold met her sharply, stealing a breath before she could catch it. She pressed a hand to her coat's buttons until the moment passed. The air smelled of woodsmoke and rain. Across the street, bicycles wove between buses, bells bright in the dark. Somewhere beyond the city lights, an older story was waiting – one that began not with a ship, or a statue, or a tragedy, but with what survived it.

She tightened her coat against the cold and began to walk, composing the letter she would send that night.

4th November 1972
Department of the History of Art
University of Oxford

Dear Mrs Russell Cooke,

I am studying the ways women are framed – in portraiture as well as in the public record – and how these depictions can fix a life in place, rightly or wrongly. A portrait has led me to you. If you might consider a conversation, I would be honoured to hear your own view of it.

Yours sincerely,
Dr Catherine Haynes

Find Polaris

NOVEMBER 1972

The frost had crept inside again, threading the edges of the windowpane in white veins. Mrs Russell Cooke breathed on the glass and, without thinking, drew her name with a fingertip. It blurred almost at once. Seventy-four winters, and still, she did it. Like a child marking proof of life.

Outside, a bicycle bell rang and faded down the lane. The post arrived late, as it always did. Three envelopes pushed through the door: one cream among the grey. The University Oxford coat of arms sat in the corner, precise and self-important.

She stood at the sink for a moment, the envelope in her hand, the kettle beginning to hiss. She knew that type of letter before she opened it – the measured curiosity of people who mistook her life for history. Steam clouded the window as she slit the paper with a butter knife gone blunt.

11th November 1972
Department of the History of Art
University of Oxford

Dear Mrs Russell Cooke,

I hope you will forgive my writing again so soon after my earlier letter. I wanted only to confirm that my enquiry still stands. My research concerns the ways in which women are represented when history believes it has done with them – in portraiture, in the British press, and in the public imagination. Your name, and your father's, appear repeatedly in this work.

If you felt able to offer any part of your own account, I would be deeply grateful.

Yours sincerely,
Dr Catherine Haynes

The paper smelled faintly of ink and rain. The scent of libraries and those who lived by other people's words. She folded it twice, precisely, and laid it on the hallway table beside the gas bill.

Upstairs, the room was colder. She lifted the counterpane and drew out the suitcase she told herself she no longer owned. The leather was cracked, the handle wrapped in tape, the initials – E.J.S. – dulled to a faint gleam. *Too small for the* Titanic, he'd said. He'd left it behind. When he didn't come home, she'd claimed it. Her inheritance, her curse.

The clasps resisted, as if remembering all the years they'd been forced open. Dust rose in the lamplight, shimmering like ash. Inside, lay the same small reliquary of proof:

A child's glove, soft as breath.
A toy plane with one wing bent.
A pressed lily, pale as parchment.
A White Star Line postcard: *Titanic,* Southampton Dock.
A memorial booklet for the statue's unveiling.

And beneath them, too many folded clippings:

Captain Smith: Saviour or Scapegoat?
Immortalised in Bronze.
A Family Cursed by the Titanic.
The Unlucky Woman.

She touched the headlines gently, the paper as crisp and thin as old skin. Once, she'd believed that if she gathered every fragment, she could rebuild the truth. That somewhere in the pattern, the past would confess its meaning. But meaning had never lived in the newsprint; it hid in the gaps, in everything left unsaid.

Her fingers found the initials again. E.J.S.

Find Polaris, he'd told her. *The star that never moves. On dark nights, it will show you where you are.* He had said it before he sailed, before the world renamed him hero, coward, myth.

She looked toward the window. Beyond the frost, dusk was falling, the fields stripped bare. Somewhere above them the North Star burned unseen, steady and small. Still marking its point.

The letter waited downstairs, its type neat and certain. Dr Haynes wanted her story. They all had, over the years. But Melville had learnt how a life can be thinned into something smaller the moment it is written down. She closed the suitcase, pressing until the clasps sighed shut. Dust drifted over it like a reminder. Time was closing in. She might reply. She might not. Some things were better left to end with her.

Outside, the frost began to melt. Downstairs, on the windowpane, silver water traced the lines where her name had been.

The Visiting Academic

DECEMBER 1972

The road narrowed after Woodstock, folding into the wooded lanes of the Evenlode valley. One ribbon of frost-bitten tarmac between hedgerows and stubbled fields. Dr Catherine Haynes slowed as the sign for Pratts appeared, half-hidden by ivy. The house sat behind iron gates; broad and low, its Cotswolds stone the colour of old honey. Smoke curled from a single chimney, dissolving into the grey.

She parked beside a leaning apple tree, wiped condensation from the windscreen and checked her reflection. Her face looked paler than usual; the same nervous pallor she'd worn for her viva. A faint pressure tightened beneath her breastbone – the cold, or nerves, or that familiar echo she preferred not to name. She'd told herself this was research. It felt like trespass.

The door opened before she reached it.

'Dr Haynes?'

'Mrs Russell Cooke. Thank you for agreeing to see me.'

Melville stood in the doorway, silver hair swept back, the flash of her turquoise scarf bright against her dark jumper. Her stance had the casual confidence of someone who no longer asked permission.

'After five letters, I worried you'd turn up here anyway.'

'I'm sorry—'

'You'd better come in before you freeze,' she said.

The hallway smelled faintly of lavender and coal smoke. The floorboards were polished to the colour of old tobacco. On the walls hung photographs – a man in goggles beside small aircraft, a figure at the wheel of an open-top MG, a couple on their wedding day, newspaper clippings in fading frames.

'Tea?'

'Please.'

Melville disappeared to the kitchen and returned with a pot balanced on a tray. Her movements were economical rather than slow, the kind of grace that came from habit, not frailty.

'You're from the university?'

'The History of Art department,' Catherine replied. 'I'm researching how women are represented after catastrophe. How language and image—'

'Conspire to keep them there,' Melville said, lifting the cosy from the teapot. A small smile curved her mouth. 'Pinned in place like butterflies.'

Catherine blinked, half surprised, half relieved. 'Exactly that.'

Melville handed her a china teacup. 'I've met enough historians to know their traps. The women always end up as exhibits ... or examples.' Then, poured her own tea. 'You'll forgive me if I've had my fill of being fixed in place.' She lifted her cup to her lips. 'People like to imagine the daughter of the *Titanic* crocheting away her grief. I drove cars. Flew planes. Married badly. Played worse. Does that fit your study?'

Catherine smiled despite herself. 'That's why I wrote five times.'

Melville studied her, eyes bright and amused. 'How old are you, Dr Haynes?'

'Twenty-nine.'

'Still young enough to believe the men will eventually listen.'

Catherine hesitated, unsure whether this was praise or warning. 'It's a start.'

'You'll need more than a start.' The host settled back in her chair. 'Oxford was never built for women with opinions. When I gave my first lecture there, they introduced me as *the lady pilot*. Not a soul heard a word I said after that.'

Catherine laughed softly. 'Most still think a woman's voice is decorative.'

'Or dangerous,' Melville said. 'You'll find they can't decide which. They like you better if you make the tea, not the argument.'

'That sounds familiar.'

Melville tipped her head. 'Then perhaps we've both been misfiled, Doctor. Different shelves, same library.'

They both laughed again, the tension thinning.

Melville lit a cigarette, the silver lighter flashing. 'So, what fascinates you about the unlucky ones?'

Catherine looked up, surprised. 'I suppose … I was called that once. My grandmother used to say I was born under the wrong star. Fell ill, survived, lived on borrowed luck.' She felt the old prickle of superstition along her spine.

'Ah.' Melville exhaled smoke towards the fire. 'Then you know it's a judgment dressed as a compliment.'

Catherine nodded. 'That's why I'm drawn to your story. The language of misfortune … how it sticks.'

Melville studied her again, slower this time. 'You mentioned my suitcase in your third letter. How did you know about that?'

'I found a reference to your archive in a gallery catalogue. *Private collection, Mrs M. Russell Cooke, Oxfordshire.* And then when, in the Ashmolean records, I found *An Unlucky Woman.* The artist's handwriting on the frame. It all seemed to fall into place.'

'By *the artist*, you mean David Rolt,' Melville repeated softly. 'I wondered if that painting would surface again.'

'So, it was his?'

'It was. I never owned it,' she said simply, and stubbed out the cigarette. 'You see, Doctor Haynes, people need tidy versions of grief. *Luck. Curse. Fate.* Words that make chaos look deliberate. When the ship went down, the world carried on, and those of us left behind had to live with the debris.'

Catherine reached for the tape recorder. 'May I?'

Melville gestured towards the socket. Catherine's hand trembled – the cold again – and she steadied it against her knee before plugging in the flex.

'Rolt didn't give his art that title. Someone else did. Refused to hang it in their home when they discovered I was the subject.'

'That's ridiculous.'

'That's the power of language. Of superstition, too.' A pause. 'I used to think that if I collected every word they wrote about us, I might make sense of it,' Melville said. 'The suitcase was full of their words – headlines, memorials, obituaries for people I loved. All it proved was how little they understood loss.'

Catherine glanced up. 'Do you still have it?'

'The suitcase?' she asked, and Catherine nodded enthusiastically. Melville's mouth curved faintly. 'No. It went missing decades ago. Perhaps it grew tired of being opened.'

Catherine didn't hide her disappointment. She hesitated. 'May I ask what was in it?'

'A glove. A toy plane. A pressed lily. Fragments.' She paused. 'Proof that we existed beyond the tragedy, though no one cared to look that far.' Mrs Russell Cooke leant forward, voice lowering. 'Shall we begin, Doctor Haynes? You wanted to know what it's like to live as a footnote.'

Catherine nodded. Melville reached out and pressed the start button herself, the click sharp as punctuation.

'The world called it a tragedy,' she said. 'I called it Tuesday morning. The first one after he didn't come home.'

The words hung between them. Catherine realised this was how it would be – no myth retold, no apology offered. Just the raw edge of a life reclaimed. The reels spun, the steady hiss filling the quiet.

Melville's gaze softened, as if noticing the younger woman's unease. 'They pinned a name on me before I could speak it myself. Daughter of the *Titanic*. That was the first label. Everything after that – *unlucky, survivor, curse* – only tried to explain what they'd already decided I was.'

Catherine didn't make notes. Instead, she listened as Melville's voice began to unspool the past. 'Visibility isn't the same as remembrance. To be watched isn't to be seen. That morning, May, nineteen-twelve, I was in my bedroom. I should have been getting dressed…'

A Daughter

ARCHIVE: REEL ONE

From 1912

HALIFAX BEARS TITANIC'S BURDEN – CAPTAIN SMITH AMONG THE FALLEN

Nearly a month has passed since the *Titanic* sank into the North Atlantic, and still Halifax stands as the keeper of its dead. More than 300 souls have now been brought ashore by recovery crews; sailors working in silence, their small boats heavy with loss. The city has become, reluctantly, a place of mourning.

Among those still missing is Captain Edward John Smith, long admired for his composure at sea. Some survivors speak of him in near-sacred terms: calm amid panic, clear-headed to the last. 'He remained on deck,' one woman said. 'A figure of resolve while our world tore open.'

The Halifax Gazette, 7 May 1912

The Absence

May 1912

The trunk gapes open on the floor. Its brass hinges glint faintly in the dull light creeping through the curtains. I sit on the edge of my bed, fingers tucked beneath my thighs, staring at the lilac dress folded beside me. The lace collar looks soft, delicate. Wrong. Too bright for now. I run a finger along its hem, tracing the scallops, watching the thread catch the light. It's not even a month since he was lost.

Mother's voice carries up through the floorboards. It's clipped, low, a thread about to snap. She's talking to one of the neighbours, Mrs Vaughan, perhaps – or Mrs Ellis – who keep leaving baskets of flowers we don't need. The house smells of damp petals and pity. They come and go like ghosts, slipping in with their solemn faces, gathering gossip to take away. They leave behind nothing that helps.

A knock startles me.

'Miss Helen?'

Ann peeks in, pale, her face drawn as though she's the one leaving. At twenty-eight, she's closer to my age than Mother's.

'It's Mel,' I say automatically. Helen is what strangers call me. *He* called me Melville.

'Your mother asks if you're ready.'

'I'm nearly finished,' I lie, though the trunk is half empty and I'm still in my underdress. My voice doesn't sound like mine; it's quieter now, as though even it's in mourning.

Ann's gaze drifts to the corner. To the photograph frame I've turned towards the wall. Father in uniform, serious-mouthed, the way the papers show him. I used to love that picture. Now it feels like a lie someone else has written.

'I'll let your mother know,' Ann murmurs, and leaves before I can answer.

Yesterday, I thought about how she'd never know us again. Not the real us, but then I realised that's not true. This new version of Mother and me overwrites whoever we were before. When Father lived. When the house was loud with laughter.

I stare at the lilac dress for a long moment, then push it aside. Mother's choice, not mine. From the wardrobe I pull the grey travelling dress: plain, serviceable, the colour of fog. The fabric feels coarse against my skin as I fasten it. Each button a small act of defiance. The collar sits stiff at my throat.

When I stand, the mirror catches the hem. It's practical, unlovely, safe. I smooth it flat, reach for my gloves, then I cross to the window. Outside, the taxicab waits in the rain. By the gate, another crate of flowers – roses again, red and white. Mourning colours. Reverence colours.

Reverence. The word curdles in my chest.

Mother says the papers are calling him a hero now. She reads every edition as if one of them will tell her something new. I try to keep up, but the stories fracture: one says he went down with the ship, another that he was seen boarding a lifeboat, another that he was one of the survivors who landed in Halifax. I collect the contradictions. They make it easier to believe he might still be out there.

If he were truly gone, there wouldn't be so many stories.

My chest is tight. There's a knot in my throat, my shoulder blades ache. I'm becoming someone new. Someone who must pretend well enough to keep Mother from breaking. *What if I run downstairs and refuse to go until Father comes home?* The thought dies as quickly as it comes. Mother's waiting for me to leave, and Mother doesn't wait kindly anymore. Grief has changed her shape. She's all edges now. All command.

I pull on my gloves, tugging the fingertips until they feel snug. They're too new. They're stiff, with a weak smell of leather polish. My old ones had a tear in the thumb, but I liked them better. Ann threw them away though. 'Out with the old,' she said, as if it's that easy to forget what once felt safe and comfortable. I cross the room to the trunk and kneel beside it, folding the lilac dress carefully beneath a new pinafore. Then, I pause.

Quietly, I reach beneath my pillow and pull out the scrap of newspaper I hid there this morning. The clipping that claimed Father was seen alive in Halifax. I place it into the small suitcase; the one I stole from Father's belongings. Inside are the things I can't leave behind – clippings, photos, small anchors from a vanished world. Pieces of him. Proof. I keep thinking about how I'll need them when he returns. That I'll have to show him what they wrote. I place news of the sighting alongside the postcard with the rabbit and the brass key that never fitted any lock in our last house. They're not treasures. They're evidence. Fragments of a person no one can agree on. I collect the flaws. The mistakes. The things that shouldn't be saved.

'Helen!' Mother's voice cuts sharply through my stillness. Not Mel. She doesn't need to say more. I snap the trunk shut and pull the leather straps tight. The clasps bite into place with a dull click, and I grab my hat from the floor.

Ann appears again, this time without knocking. 'Your mother's waiting by the front door.'

I nod and stand, smoothing my skirt once more and securing my hat with two pins. My thighs feel heavy as I cross the room; it's as though the weight of the house itself is pulling at me. I grab the small suitcase, too, and glance one last time at the photograph in the corner. The frame is turned slightly but still his eyes seem to follow me to the door. It's like he knows I'm leaving him behind.

Mother is pacing at the foot of the stairs. Her hands are clasped tightly in front of her. Her black dress is severe; every day she armours herself in fabric. She glances up at me. She doesn't smile. Perhaps she wants to, but it wouldn't sit right on her face. My parents were late having me. Eleven years married, Father forty-eight, Mother thirty-six. Lately, she looks older than she should. Ben, our scruffy little terrier with wiry fur and an eager bounce, rushes into the hallway. He yaps excitedly at Mother's leg. His small body quivers with energy. She tries to ignore him, gently nudging him aside with the tip of her shoe, but he circles back. He's persistent. Father brought him home for her. Something to keep her company in the quiet hours. When Mother feeds the canaries in their gilt cage by the window in Father's library, Ben's there, watching her intently, his head at a tilt. Perhaps he's always known who would stay.

As I reach the bottom stair, he bounds towards me. All bright eyes and a wagging tail that's too large for his body. I bend down and rub the rough fur behind his ears. I'm grateful for his uncomplicated devotion. Ann appears and thrusts my cloak at me.

'I trust you've remembered everything?' Mother says.

'Yes.' My voice catches, and I clear my throat.

'Good.' A pause. 'Fourteen, and leaving home.' Her fingers twist the hem of her sleeve. 'You'll write, won't you?'

I nod.

'You'll be back for the holidays.'

I nod again.

She reaches out, tucks a stray curl back into my hat, brushes something from my cheek. The gesture surprises me. Do I gasp? I lean in slightly, craving more. For a flash, I see the mother she was before – before Father sailed away on the *Titanic*.

'The taxicab is waiting.' The moment is gone as quickly as it came. She steps back. Her spine straightens like she's remembered herself.

The air outside is damp and sharp. It smells of rain and horse poo. The driver heaves the trunk. He barely glances at me. I climb in after him, settling into the corner of the seat. Mother doesn't step nearer, preferring to watch from the doorstep. Ben is back at her feet. Her silhouette looks almost fragile against our double-fronted home and the grey morning light. I know better.

As the taxicab lurches forward, I press my nose to the window. The too-big house shrinks behind us; the damp roses by the gate blur into red and white smudges. I want to feel something – relief, sorrow, anything – but my chest is a hollow place. The world beyond the glass looks too large, too empty.

It's been twenty-two days since Father's ship went down. I've counted each one. The first week was the hardest; I kept expecting his step in the hall, his laugh climbing the stairs, the sudden creak of the study door. Even this morning I listened for him, stupidly, as if the silence might break and spill him back into the room.

Mother says he's gone. Some newspapers say he's dead; others still wonder. Every day a new story – a lifeboat sighted, a body mistaken, a man rescued under a false name. The words keep changing, as though the truth itself can't decide what it wants to be.

I choose the version where he's alive. Where he's somewhere waiting. A wrong list, a missed name, a telegram that hasn't come. Believing that is easier than believing the sea kept him. Easier than living in a world that decided he was a story instead of a man.

The taxicab jolts hard over a rut, and I clutch the edge of the seat to keep from sliding. The driver doesn't apologise, doesn't even look back to check on me. His coat collar is turned up against the rain and his shoulders are hunched. The city is waking. Carriages and taxicabs rumble past, and pedestrians hurry along the pavements. A boy my age tugs a cart filled with bread loaves. Has he already forgotten about the *Titanic*? It seems impossible that anyone could forget, but life carries on. For everyone, in differing gradations.

What shade do I exist in currently? For me, it feels as though everything has stopped. Each day monotone. My world is the same grey colour as the sky and the hours blur into one another until I can't tell them apart. Perhaps I should be glad to leave Mother's house. Perhaps I should be glad for the chance to start something new. A boarding school where no one will know me. I can't shake this ache in my chest though. Do I even want that? It sits there, heavy and unwelcome, a reminder of everything that's changed.

The taxicab slows. We've reached the station. Steam curls like smoke above. The driver hops down and pulls my trunk with a thud, but I don't move right away. I sit as still as a statue. I stare out at the people bustling in every direction, their faces blurred by the rain streaking the glass. None of them notice me. None of them care.

'Miss?' The driver taps the window.

'Sorry,' I say, but his face is lined with impatience.

I take a breath. Push the door open. The damp air seeps through my dress. The driver hoists the trunk onto a trolley and gestures towards the platform. I nod, scurrying after a porter as he strides ahead.

The Second-Class Cabin

May 1912

This station is a tangle of motion and noise. Porters weave between people with caps pulled low, pushing trolleys stacked high with trunks. Steam hisses from the great iron engine ahead. It curls into the rainy sky. I clutch my ticket and suitcase in one hand, gloves in the other. Around me, passengers rush – businessmen, women in wide-brimmed hats, a sailor puffing on a pipe. No one looks at me, and yet I imagine they all know my father's name.

A newspaper boy's voice cuts through the noise. 'Captain Smith – Saviour or Scapegoat? Read the latest!'

I freeze. I can't help it. My chest tightens, sharp and sudden.

'Stayed at the helm. Died a hero, says crewman!' He shouts again, louder this time, and the words clang in my head like iron.

I can't move. People keep walking. They don't flinch, but I do. My fingers curl tighter around the ticket and suitcase, as if they could hold me together.

Two businessmen pass close, voices low but distinct. 'A disgrace,' one mutters. 'He knew there was ice. Why the speed?'

'Entirely reckless,' the other says.

'Hero, my foot. The man would've been court-martialled if he'd lived.'

The platform tilts. The gloves slip from my hand, but I don't reach for them. I can't. My fingers lock around the ticket and suitcase handle until they ache. I hear the hiss of the train at platform 2. I want to scream at those businessmen. They don't know him. They didn't see him lean out of the taxicab window that morning, waving goodbye. I grab a newspaper from the boy's stack.

'Tuppence,' he mutters. He blinks at me, surprised. 'You're her, aren't you?' he asks. 'The *Titanic* captain's daughter. One in the picture. In here.' He pats the papers enthusiastically.

I nod, unsure why. I know the one he means – the photograph the papers all ran in the days after. Me, hair frozen, mouth caught mid-word, coat too thin for grief. That's the girl they'll keep seeing, no matter how much I change.

The boy squints like he's waiting for me to say something profound. I thrust a coin into his hand, then sink onto a bench nearby. Behind me, he shouts, 'My da says your da's a fool.'

I shake my head. The headline curls through the mist: *Captain Smith – Saviour or Scapegoat?* I try to read, but the words swim. My grip crumples the paper. The whistle shrieks again, and steam pours across the platform. Everything is damp. Everything breathes grief. The wood beneath me is cold, soaking through my cloak.

'Miss?' A porter stands before me. His face is flushed from the chill and the effort of carrying trunks. 'Train departs shortly.'

I nod, following him, each step heavy. The station pulses with voices, the air thick with coal smoke and rain. Vendors shout.

'Fresh sandwiches!'

'*Titanic* news – Scapegoat Captain!'

I focus on the train: its black sides, rivets glinting in the dull light. A hiss rises. Somewhere, in it, I hear – *Goodbye, Melville*.

'This way, Miss,' the porter says, lifting my waiting trunk as if it weighs nothing.

The gap between platform and carriage yawns, dark and wide. I grip the brass handle and hesitate. Could I run back? But to what? A house that's forgotten how to breathe. A mother who won't say his name. Newspapers that keep rewriting him: dead, alive, brave, disgraced.

I step onto the train. I hold my breath. As long as I keep believing he's out there, the sea hasn't won.

The air inside is warmer, but still heavy with damp wool and tobacco. A man squeezes past. Others push towards their compartments. Boots echo. Children fog windows with their breath.

'Miss?' The porter slides open a door. 'Here we are.'

'Thank you.'

I slip inside. The compartment is narrow. A single lamp flickers. I place Father's suitcase at my feet. I unfold the newspaper again: *Captain Smith – Saviour or Scapegoat?* The train jerks forward. I look out just in time to see the platform vanish. The porter has gone. No one waves.

Lifeboats and Shadows

May 1912

A full day of travelling and now the gates of Marston House rise before me. They're tall and black, and the iron spikes catch what little light filters through the overcast sky. The taxicab jolts to a halt on the gravel drive and the wheels crunch sharply beneath us.

The porter steps forward from the boarding school and opens the cab's door. 'Miss Smith?' he asks, and I nod. 'I'll take your trunk inside.'

I step out gingerly and the gravel shifts beneath my boots. The school looms ahead; its red brick is stark, and the windows gleam as though watching me approach. There is no warmth in the architecture. The doors swing open suddenly and a tall woman strides out. Her boots land with precision, clicking against the stone steps as she moves to me.

'Miss Smith,' the woman says, her voice deliberate. 'I am Miss Bevan, the headmistress of Marston House. Follow me.'

Inside, the hallway stretches high and narrow. Its wood panelling gleams darkly; the scents of beeswax and faint coal smoke linger in the air. Miss Bevan's heels click clack against the polished floor as she leads me past a line of portraits. Some wear caps, others lace collars, all are grim-faced women. Miss Bevan stops abruptly, and I bump into her bustle.

'So sorry.'

'At Marston House, we believe in discipline and self-determination,' she says, her tone brisk, as she turns to me. 'Our girls leave here equipped for life's trials. You would do well to take this time as an opportunity to strengthen your character.'

I blink. I'm unsure how to reply.

She studies me longer than she should, eyes catching on my travelling dress. 'We do expect resilience here, Miss Smith. Resilience and discretion. It's a small community. Best to remember that.'

She strides off again. My steps feel clumsy against the smooth floor, and the grey dress suddenly feels heavier than it should. Miss Bevan stops at a narrow door. She gestures for me to enter.

'Your dormitory,' she says, but doesn't step inside. 'Given your … *lineage*, Miss Smith … you'll be under particular scrutiny here. I assume your mother told you of the letter I wrote to her?'

I shake my head. She watches me a beat too long.

'No matter,' she says. 'No space for distraction. We believe in building character. Go inside.'

She pushes my back gently and I do as instructed. The floor creaks beneath my boots as though protesting my arrival. The beds are identical: iron frames and each with heavy wool blankets, folded neatly at the foot. A shared washstand sits by the far wall. I run my fingers around the inside of the porcelain basin. It's spotless, and the water jug beside it catches the faint glow of light through the windows. Nothing here is homely. There are no personal touches. No softness. No welcome.

An older girl sits on the edge of her bed. Her long hair shines like bronze as she plaits it deftly. She looks up, her eyes narrowing slightly in assessment.

'Miss Draper, your prefect,' Miss Bevan projects from the doorway. 'This is Miss Smith. She will join your dormitory.'

The words settle awkwardly in the air between us, but Miss Draper nods. 'Yes, Ma'am.'

Miss Bevan turns to me, her sharp features softening ever so slightly. 'It is common, Miss Smith, in times of grief, to feel adrift.'

I hold my breath. *Please don't say it. Please don't say that ship's name.*

'To survive,' she continues, 'one must focus outward, not inward. If you cannot yet change how you feel, decide instead how you wish to be seen. Practise that, and the rest may follow.'

I exhale too quickly; the sound seems loud in the quiet room. Her words settle somewhere deep, where I don't want them to. *Decide how you wish to be seen.* I can do that. I already am. If they see composure, they won't ask questions. If they think I'm managing, they won't look too closely.

I glance down at the hem of my cloak. It's neat, plain, unremarkable. I like that. It hides everything.

'Thank you, Miss Bevan,' I murmur, and lift my chin the way Mother does when she's pretending not to be afraid.

She nods once and leaves, the door clicking shut behind her.

Miss Draper ties off her plait, then turns her full attention to me. 'You're the *Titanic* captain's daughter, yes?' Her tone isn't cruel, but it's not kind either – just assessing. Like she's assigned me a label and is waiting to see if I fit it.

My throat tightens, but I nod. It's easier than explaining.

'Thought so,' she says, tilting her head slightly. 'Don't worry. They'll talk, but it won't last long. The girls here always lose interest in the end.'

She picks up a book from her bedside table, opening it without another word. I sit on the edge of my bed, smoothing my dress again. Miss Bevan's advice circles in my head. *How I wish to be seen.*

'I'm Edith. Edie. What do we call you?'

'Helen,' I say quickly. I won't be Melville here. Not yet. Melville belongs to him, and if I say it aloud, someone might tell me he's dead.

'Very well,' she replies, but her expression says otherwise.

Later, after the lamps are dimmed and the dormitory settles into stillness, I sit on my bed with the newspaper. The headline is still sharp in my mind: *Captain Smith: Saviour or Scapegoat?* I search for the sections where the rain hasn't smudged the ink.

The letters to the editor are printed in small, even rows, but the words seem to shout at me. *Reckless … negligent … noble … selfless…* Each one cancels out the last, as if the truth can't make up its mind. I close my eyes, the paper crackling beneath my fingers.

I picture Father on the deck of the *Titanic*, standing tall against the cold wind. The icebergs rise around him like silent sentinels, and the deck tilts beneath his feet as water rushes in. I imagine him giving orders. His voice is steady, even as chaos erupts. In my mind, he doesn't falter. Not once.

Outside, beyond the hush of the dormitory, voices scurry along the corridor. Girls whispering urgently in the dark.

'Shot himself, didn't he?'

'No. Jumped. Swam off, someone said.'

'My uncle's paper said they found him alive, that he rowed off in a lifeboat.'

'He was captain. Should've gone down with it.'

'One of the survivors said he was shouting with a megaphone. That's the last they saw.'

'Someone said he was in New York. Hiding. Ashamed.'

'And the daughter's here now?'

'Apparently.'

My pulse rings in my ears. I reach for my diary, flipping to the back page. I write the title *Eyewitness?* and then:

They said he gave out vests without a word.
They said he lifted a boy into a boat.
They said he shouted through a megaphone – 'Women and children first.'
They said he shot himself.
They said he clung to the bridge till the sea took him.
They said he swam to a raft.
They said he's in New York, that he's hiding, that he's ashamed.

I circle *he's hiding*. I press the pen hard until the nib scratches. The ink bleeds slightly. I tuck the diary beneath my pillow, lie down, and listen to the wind shaking the windows. I tell myself the sound is the sea, and that he's still somewhere. Calling orders, waiting for the right tide to bring him home.

Icebergs and Echoes

May 1912

Morning comes too soon, and with it my first breakfast at school. Edith catches my hand and leads me inside the dining hall. Her footsteps are precise and steady. Mine catch awkwardly on the edge of the rug. Girls are already seated at the tables. Their voices mingle in a constant hum that rises and falls like the tide. I follow Edith down the centre aisle, the weight of the room pressing in on me. Are they watching? Do they whisper behind their hands?

The morning light filters in weakly, catching the glint of silver platters filled with toast, eggs, and rashers of bacon. This room is far larger than I imagined. The tall windows stretch almost to the ceiling, and the rows of dark wooden tables seem to go on forever. The air smells warm and heavy. It should be comforting, but it isn't. It feels excessive and I'm not sure I'll like it here.

'Let's sit,' Edith says, stopping halfway down the hall. She gestures to a space on the bench. I lower myself carefully.

The wooden seat is hard and cold beneath me. I fold my hands in my lap and glance around. Hair neatly pinned back, collars crisp, their identities as one. No one looks up, but they know I'm here. I feel it like a prickle under the skin. Plates and platters move down the table. I take a slice of toast without meeting anyone's eyes. My stomach is tight, like it's full of stones, but I nibble anyway.

Across the table, two girls lean in. 'Halifax,' one of them says and I stop chewing. My breath snags. 'They've been burying them there,' she continues. 'The ones they pulled from the sea. Frozen stiff. Like statues.'

'That can't be true,' the other murmurs. 'They wouldn't leave them in Canada.'

'They had to,' the first insists. 'There's nowhere else. My father said there are special ships, just for collecting bodies.'

The crust crumbles in my hand. Halifax. I can see it: the docks crowded with mourners, the long white sheets, the sea turned black with smoke. For a moment the picture feels real enough to touch. Then I close my eyes and make myself breathe, in through the nose, out through the mouth.

No. He isn't there.

He's on one of the ships, not beneath them.

He's waiting to be found, his name misplaced, his telegram delayed.

The dead are the ones with graves; he doesn't have one. That has to mean something.

I lower my head, swallow hard, and take another small bite of toast. The taste is dry, almost bitter. If I keep chewing, no one will notice the way my hands shake.

'Some of them went back to England, didn't they?' a third girl adds. 'For their families?'

'The rich ones.' That's the first girl again.

Edith shifts beside me. 'Don't listen,' she says quietly. 'They're parroting what they hear from their parents.'

I shrug, but still, the words linger louder than the clatter of cutlery. Across the hall, someone laughs. It's a high, sharp sound. I flinch.

'It wasn't just the passengers,' a new voice cuts in. A fourth girl, this one with red ribbons in her hair. 'The crew went down too. My mother says they should've known better than to sail so fast.'

'We don't know what happened,' another girl argues, quieter, uncertain.

Red Ribbons waves that away. 'We know the captain shot himself on the bridge.'

'No,' says a fifth, firm now. 'He stayed till the end. Went down with the ship.'

'He was on the first lifeboat, wasn't he? Escaped as soon as he could. Someone saw him.' A paper is pushed across the table. I glimpse columns of print but not the words.

My hands curl into fists. My nails bite into my palms. The air seems to thin, the hum of voices tilts, sharp and distant. They keep talking. Faster, louder, all of them; their chatter turns to static.

The girl with the paper glances around, conspiratorial. 'This latest headline,' she whispers, 'says he was drunk—'

'That's not true!' The words are out before I can stop them.

Everything stills. The scrape of cutlery, the clatter of dishes. Gone. A dozen faces turn.

'He wasn't drunk,' I say, softer now, but the tremor betrays me. 'He didn't drink.'

Someone breathes, 'You're the daughter.'

The word *daughter* lands like a sentence.

I drop my gaze to my plate. The toast has gone cold. My throat burns as if I've swallowed glass.

Edith's hand settles lightly on my arm. 'They'll forget by next month,' she murmurs.

I nod, though I know she's wrong. People don't forget a sinking. They just vary its ending. The thought of Father disappearing, not just beneath the waves but from the world, is unbearable. Worse still is the idea of him remembered wrong.

I smooth the folds of my dress. The fabric still smells faintly of home: coal dust, lavender polish, something ordinary and familiar. I straighten my napkin. Small things. I can do small things. They make the room stop spinning.

The bell rings, sharp and final. Benches scrape. The newspaper cuttings are nudged down the table towards me. Careless hands brushing against my sleeve.

Edith stands, composed as ever. 'Are you coming?'

I nod. I rise. I brush the crumbs from my lap. My legs feel hollow, like they might fold beneath me, but I follow anyway.

~

By evening, when the lamps have been dimmed and the dormitory smells of soap and starch, I open Father's suitcase. The paper rustles beneath my fingers. Two new articles have been folded flat inside my cloak pocket all day. Their headlines contradict each other.

CAPTAIN SMITH – CALM TO THE END, OR DRUNK AT THE HELM?

WITNESS SPEAKS OUT – LADY SWEARS SHE SAW CAPTAIN IN NEWFOUNDLAND

Each is proof of something larger: no one really knows what happened, which means he could still be out there. I smooth their edges and press them neatly beneath the others.

One day they call him a hero, the next they call him a fool. They don't know the man who took me to Portsmouth once – the brass bands, the flags, the clink of his walking stick against the cobbles. He pointed out destroyers like old friends, his voice warm with pride. Later, quieter, he said, 'A captain belongs on his own ship, Melville, not in someone else's house.'

He was right. That's why he hasn't come back yet. He's still where he belongs, waiting for the right moment to return.

I close the lid, fasten the clasp, and trace the initials on the leather. E.J.S. The suitcase hums faintly under my fingertips, as though he can feel me thinking of him.

Around me, the dormitory quiets. Breaths even out; a bedframe creaks. I draw my knees beneath my nightdress and pull my diary from under the pillow. I read what I've already written, my own record of waiting.

> *It started with – All passengers safe.*
> *Then – We were told, 'Don't worry.'*
> *Next – Then, 'All hope abandoned.'*
> *But hope doesn't abandon people. People abandon hope.*

I copy the notes again, slower this time.

> *Passenger saw him with lifeboat.*
> *Captain shot himself on the bridge.*

I circle the first, cross out the second. Lies are easy to print.

Steady voice. Handing out vests.

That one I keep. True.

Jumped at last moment. Swam. Vanished.

Yes – that one could fit.

Newfoundland sighting.

Of course.

No confirmed death.

Exactly. I underline it twice.
He isn't gone. He's waiting. Maybe injured, maybe hidden, but alive. The world will see that soon enough. There's a difference between what's printed and what's real. They write endings; I'll write beginnings.

I turn the page and title it <u>Proof</u>. Beneath it, I copy each fragment again until the ink smudges across my hand.

Then, in the smallest handwriting, a final line:

He's alive, and he'll find his way home.

The Waxwork

May 1912

A fortnight here, and already the library is my refuge. The air is thick as damp wool, the scent of polish and coal dust clinging to the dark. The storm has eased to drizzle now, but streaks of rain blur the tall windows, warping the outside world into grey ribbons. Beyond the glass, the trees and gravel paths look like a painting left too long in the sun – colours leached, outlines softened.

Rows of mahogany shelves rise around me like monuments. Their carved spines climb towards a coffered ceiling. Father would love this place. The fire is little more than an idea; a drowsy orange flicker that fails to warm even the nearest armchairs. Still, a knot clusters there of older girls, skirts brushing the cracked leather, heads tipped together in shared secrecy.

I sit alone at the far end of a long oak table. Father's copy of *Moby Dick* lies open in front of me. The paper is thin and creamy, the ink slightly raised beneath my fingertips. I haven't turned the page in ten minutes. My eyes skim the lines, but none of the words stay.

'Did you see Shaw's letter?' one girl says, her voice pitched low but urgent. I know her from chapel – she sings as if she's trying to reach heaven itself.

'"Sentimental hero," wasn't it?' another replies, folding her arms. 'As if Shaw actually knew the man.'

My hand stills on the edge of the book. The words sink through the quiet like stones. I think I'll have to find a new place to hide.

'Shaw's always like that,' a third girl says, smoothing her cuff. 'Considers himself cleverer than everyone else. As if being clever means you can't be kind.'

'I liked Conan Doyle's reply,' the first girl adds, unfolding her newspaper with a rustle that sounds deliberate. 'He called Shaw cruel. Said this wasn't the moment for mockery.'

Their voices rise and fall like a tide. Sympathy and suspicion wash back and forth.

'Still,' says another, a thinner voice, careful and precise. She's the one with wire spectacles and wrists like bird bones. 'There weren't enough lifeboats. And they were going too fast. Isn't it fair to ask?'

The auburn-haired girl straightens. 'Fair? He died saving lives. He didn't run.'

'But he made the decisions,' Spectacles says, not unkindly. 'If there were warnings—'

'He followed orders! He wasn't the architect of every mistake.'

Their words stretch and strain until they blur together. They talk about my father the way people discuss a painting hung too high on a gallery wall: admiring, critical, adjusting. As though he's a thing, not a person.

'Ladies.'

Miss Bevan's voice slices through the air like a paper knife. Even the fire seems to flinch. She stands at the doorway, all starch and stillness, her eyes sweeping the room and stopping just short of mine.

'The library is for reading, not gossip.'

The girls nod obediently, shuffle papers, open books. When she leaves, the quiet exhales.

Spectacles leans closer to her friends. 'Shaw wrote something else…' Her voice is barely audible. 'He said, "If anyone reminds me that Captain Smith went down with his ship, I'll remind them that the ship's cat did, too."'

The laughter that follows isn't cruel. It's worse; it's casual. Thoughtless. The kind that forgets it has teeth. I press both hands to *Moby Dick*. The leather creaks under my palms.

'Have you nothing better to discuss?'

The laughter dies. Their faces turn towards me in unison, colour rising. Recognition sweeps through them like a spark finding tinder.

'Don't listen to them.' Edith appears beside me, quiet as ever, her fingers brushing my sleeve.

But I do listen. I always listen. Words are what people leave behind.

The bell rings. It's sharp and metallic. Chairs scrape. The girls scatter like startled birds.

Edith stays. I stay.

'You said it would stop,' I whisper. The words feel brittle in my mouth.

'He's famous,' she says softly. 'A public figure.'

'But they talk as if he's a story someone else is writing.'

'That's what people do with tragedy,' she murmurs. 'They give it shape.'

I don't want their shape. I want the world to hold still long enough for him to walk back through it. I want quiet. I want home. I want the sound of his boots on the step.

Edith's eyes are kind, but her pity makes me look away.

'Come on,' she says. 'Let's take the long path to tea.'

'What, now?'

'Am I right in thinking you haven't heard about Tussaud's new exhibit?'

'Exhibit?'

She sighs, and the sound is somewhere between mischief and regret.

Hours afterwards, when the hallway echoes with footsteps and the girls have gone to lessons, to prayers or to write letters home, I slip back into the library. The hearth is cold now. The armchairs are empty. A folded newspaper sits abandoned by the fire.

I smooth it open.

CAPTAIN SMITH'S WAXWORK STIRS CONTROVERSY AT MADAME TUSSAUD'S

Madame Tussaud's latest unveiling, a life-sized wax figure of Captain Edward J. Smith, commander of the ill-fated *RMS Titanic*, has ignited heated debates across London. Mr John Tussaud's new exhibit, titled, 'The Loss of the *Titanic*', features Captain Smith in his full naval regalia, modelled from a *Daily Sketch* photograph taken shortly before the ship's tragic voyage.

Displayed prominently in the main room of the exhibition, the figure has provoked a strong reaction. While some admire the craftsmanship and view the effigy as a tribute to the captain's bravery, others condemn it as a glorification of a man they hold responsible for one of the most devastating maritime disasters in history.

Eleanor Smith, the captain's widow, has not offered comment on the waxwork, but sources suggest she remains horrified by the depiction. The effigy has become a flashpoint in the city's ongoing debate on heroism, failure, and how history remembers its dead.

The Times, 27 May 1912

I sink into the nearest armchair and read the lines again. The phrase *wax effigy* sticks behind my ribs like a splinter.

Modelled from a Daily Sketch *photograph…*

That photograph. The one on the pier in Southampton. He's looking slightly left, collar turned against the wind. You can't see his shoes. You can't see his hands. How did they model from that? Weeks after the sinking. Weeks after he was supposedly gone.

I tear the article free. It's mine now.

The paper softens under my grip as I fold it smaller, tighter, until the corners bite into my palm. In my diary, I write:

> *Tussaud's Exhibit – May 1912*
> *Based on photograph, 9th April*
> *No body recovered*
> *No confirmation of death*
> *Who posed? Who gave them the hands and legs?*

I stop. The next thought feels impossible, and yet.

> *What if he's the source?*

The pen digs into the page. It sounds ridiculous even written, but it also explains everything. I pull out the postcard I've kept tucked inside the diary since the day I arrived here. I couldn't bear to leave it locked away. He sent it from the *Baltic* when I was seven:

> *I could not catch a little bunny to send you in my letter, so I send you a card by this little bird. I shall soon be home. D.V. Your loving Daddy.*

D.V. – *Deo volente.*

If God wills it. But what if God has no say in it now? What if Father's still out there, quietly alive inside someone else's story?

Mr Pyral's Letter

July 1912

I lasted barely two months at school before I begged to come home for a visit. Yesterday, Mother relented, and now I prowl the house as if it might yield him back to me. Ben follows close behind, claws ticking against the polished boards. He knows where I'm heading. Father's library: the only room that still seems to breathe with him.

The smell meets me first: leather bindings, yellowed paper, a faint trace of tobacco, and something older still, steeped into the wood. The silence here hums like a held note. His presence is everywhere and nowhere. It's in the grain of the desk, the indentation of his chair, the cage in the corner where the canaries still trill as though nothing has changed.

Their song used to soothe me. Now it jars, too bright for a house that's lost its ghost.

The mourning cards remain stacked neatly on the desk. I flick through them. Their black-edged phrases repeat until they mean nothing. Mother's handwriting wavers across each one, the ink pooled, the words breaking mid-sentence. On one I read – *No son of England died a more noble death.* A phrase polished smooth by overuse, so perfect it has no weight. Is she persuading herself, or trying to persuade the world?

I shove the cards aside. Beneath them lies another pile. Thinner envelopes, some still sealed. My fingers pause on one written in a stranger's hand. The ink has bled slightly, as though caught in rain. *Mrs E. J. Smith and daughter.*

The seal's been broken, but the paper is folded tight. My breath snags. I glance towards the open door: the corridor is empty.

Daughter of the Titanic

This letter is mine as much as hers.

Dear Madam and Miss Smith,

Please forgive the intrusion, but I feel compelled to write. I do not do so lightly, nor with any wish to disturb your peace in what must be a time of great sorrow. Yet I cannot shake what I witnessed, and I believe you are owed the account.

On the morning of the seventh of May, I was travelling through Camden Station in Baltimore, Maryland. The day was overcast, a warm wind coming off the bay, and the platforms unusually crowded: a mix of businessmen, sailors, and mothers with children in tow. Amid the noise and bustle, I caught sight of a man disembarking from the Washington train. He moved swiftly, his stride purposeful, head slightly down, as if avoiding attention.

He wore a dark, well-cut suit and carried two leather valises. At first, I thought nothing of it, but something in his bearing caught me – the upright posture, the clipped rhythm of his steps. Then, as he turned towards the concourse, I saw his face more clearly. Clean-shaven now, thinner perhaps, but unmistakably him. His eyes, steady, pale, and direct, are not easily forgotten.

I served under Captain Edward John Smith aboard the Majestic *for three years. I saw him nearly every day, stood behind him on the bridge through storms and calm; I would know him in any crowd. When I called out, 'Captain Smith?', he turned for the briefest moment. There was a flicker of recognition; I am sure of it. He looked directly at me and then walked on, disappearing into the crowd before I could follow.*

I searched the station until dusk, checked every platform and café, but found no trace. Still, I feel certain it was him.

I write not to offer false hope or idle rumour, only what I saw – or believe I saw – in the hope that it may be of some comfort, or at least recorded. The captain was a man of deep resolve. If, against all expectations, he lived, I cannot imagine he would wish to remain hidden without reason.

With the utmost respect and sympathy,

Peter Pryal
Former Quartermaster, S.S. Majestic

The words blur, then sharpen. A station. Baltimore. The seventh of May. Overcast skies, crowded platforms. A man stepping from the Washington train, head down, striding quickly, two valises in hand. A thinner face, clean-shaven, but the same steady eyes. A voice in my head insists: *Father*.

Pryal. I know that name. Quartermaster of the *Majestic*. The papers called him unsound – confused by shock, they said – but this letter isn't fevered. It's measured. Careful. He dates it before the waxwork, before the frenzy of invention.

Two valises. Who carries two if they mean to vanish lightly? And the beard – gone. Why remove it unless he wished to walk unrecognised? These are not accidents. These are choices. *Patterns*. I stand there, rooted, the paper trembling in my hand. I should take it to Mother, insist she read it, insist we talk, but I already see how she'd respond. A tear. A silence. A refusal to believe.

Ben noses at my calf. A floorboard sighs overhead. The house feels unbearably alive for one missing its centre. If Father is still out there, does he not belong to me more than to anyone else?

My gaze drifts to the drawer. Writing paper. Cream, thick, embossed with Mother's name. I draw out two sheets and reach for the pen. He wrote to both of us, but she won't reply. I will.

It isn't lying, only borrowing a voice.

I practise the loops of her hand: the tall *S*, the timid *t*. I shape them slowly, then begin the draft. Longer sentences. Formal turns. *We are grateful… Yours faithfully…* Words a widow would use. Words I copy carefully until the page lies complete before me.

Dear Mr Pryal,

Thank you for your recent letter. I am grateful for the care with which you described what you saw.

Your recollection is of particular interest, not only because of your past service under my husband, but for the precision of its detail – especially your observation of his bearing. I have, as you may imagine, heard many stories in recent weeks. Few come from men who knew him; fewer still are given so plainly, without embellishment.

If you should recall anything further, however small, I would be thankful if you were to write again: the location, the time of day, the direction he walked, whether he spoke to anyone. All might prove helpful.

With appreciation for your time and sincerity.

Yours faithfully,
Mrs E.J. Smith

The lie settles quickly, like dust. I blot the ink, address the envelope, seal it. The paper feels heavier than it should. Outside, the postman's whistle cuts the afternoon air. My heart leaps. For an instant I picture Mother at the door, asking what I'm sending, eyes narrowing, but the hall stays silent.

I slip the letter beneath my cardigan. Ben pads behind me as I walk calmly to the post box. My palm presses against the cool metal slot. Gone.

Back inside, the quiet swells again. I return to the library, open my diary, and write in a firm hand.

6th July 1912

Letter sent to Peter Pryal. Maryland sighting. Used Mother's name. Asked for more detail. Clarity. Confirmation. Not desperation. Not madness.

If he replies, it will prove I was right to write.

Then, very small:

If he doesn't, I'll write again.

I underline that twice.

Shadows of the Titanic

September 1912

Two months, and no reply. Still, I hover over the post-tray like a thief – heart leaping at each foreign hand, sinking at solicitor's bills and black-edged cards. Hope makes a thief of me. Shame makes me careful.

Today the tray holds only a doctor's envelope, an advert for winter boots, and another unstamped note. I tear it open before sense catches me, but it's only Mrs Vaughan, inviting us to a garden party for the statue fund. *A tribute to Father's memory,* she writes. I crumple it hard in my fist.

The canaries sing on, indifferent. Father's chair sits angled to the light, as though he might step back in at any moment. Two months, and I still half believe he could. Pryal's letter lives folded in my suitcase, the creases thinning from rereading.

I open the drawer in Father's library: sympathy cards, dozens. Polite grief from strangers. Among them, more of Mother's abandoned replies, ink faltering mid-line. One card catches my eye:

> *Our vivacious golden-haired girl who had lost her father…*

I stare at it. That's her version of me. But I don't feel golden. I feel grey. I'm worn thin at the edges, caught between belief and mourning.

Then footsteps. The door bursts open.

'Mel—'

Mother spills in, cheeks bright, newspapers under her arm. Lavender water trails after her like a banner.

'They've published the findings,' she says, fanning the broadsheets across the desk.

'The inquiry?'

She nods. Trembling hands spread *The Times, The Mirror, The Herald*. Scripture laid bare.

'*No Negligence. Captain Not to Blame.*' Her fingers skim the Commissioner's words. '*He acted with the judgement expected of a man of his station. He could not have foreseen the scale of the disaster.*'

Her lips shape more but falter. The paper trembles. Her hand creases the edge of a mourning card. 'I told you.' She breathes. 'They see him clearly now.'

I nod, but hollowly. Truth in one column, blame in the next. Performance, not resolution.

'I'm waiting for a letter,' I say quietly.

Her eyes sharpen. 'What letter?'

'From America. I wrote to Peter Pryal.'

Her face hardens. 'Mel—'

'I only want to know if he replies. Or if he's thinking about replying.'

'Even if he does, it changes nothing.' She stabs the newspaper. 'This is what matters. Not rumours. Not ghosts.'

I say nothing. She wants an ending. So do I. But hers is in print; mine still waits, unwritten.

She sinks into Father's chair. 'They've approved the statue. In Lichfield. They'll want you to speak.'

'You mean they'll put words in my mouth.'

'It's a tribute.'

'It's a replacement.'

Her eyes flash. 'You're too young to understand what the world needs.'

I want to shout that I understand exactly. That the world needs a story, not a truth. But she wouldn't hear it. She's chosen her version, and I'm not in it.

'They'll unveil it in spring. A sacrifice remembered.'

No letter. No new sighting. No reply. I tell myself it means nothing: ships are slow, post unreliable. But a colder thought has begun to settle: *what if he is dead?* And worse – *what if I never know how? What if they bury him twice: once in the sea, and once in bronze?*

I turn to the window. The garden blazes with late-summer bloom. It's too bright, too careless. Somewhere beyond those hedges lies her version of him – a hero chiselled into permanence.

But what if she's wrong? What if the man we mourn slipped loose from the weight of paper, grief, duty, and simply walked away?

24th November 1912

> *There will be no reply. Which leaves only this: he can't answer.*
> *Whether through choice or chance, silence is all he's left me.*
> *And still, I can't let him be gone.*

Interruption One

DECEMBER 1972

The tape clicked, its reel stuttering to an end. The room seemed to contract around the sound. Neither woman spoke at once. The fire had burnt low, the coals shifting in their own quiet language. Outside, frost thinned the edges of the windowpane.

Melville exhaled. 'I went to see it once, you know. The waxwork. Madame Tussaud's, before the crowds got too much.'

'And?' The tape might have stopped, but Catherine Haynes knew she'd remember every word.

'They'd set him up behind a rope.' Melville's voice remained measured, unsentimental, a survivor narrating her own exhibit. 'Standing straight, eyes bright. You could almost imagine he'd breathe if you waited long enough.' A pause. 'That's how they like their heroes. Waxed and waiting.'

'It must have been—'

'Insensitive?' Melville smiled faintly. 'It was the neatness of it that offended me. As if tragedy could be modelled to scale. People queued to look at him; to say they'd seen the captain. They left thinking they'd paid their respects. But it wasn't respect. It was reassurance. The waxwork said: *It's all right now. He's safely dead.*'

'You think it was meant to comfort them?'

'Of course. Comfort's cheaper than truth.' Melville's gaze flicked to the recorder, now still. 'You should write that down. Academics like aphorisms, don't they Doctor Haynes?'

Catherine smiled despite herself. 'We like evidence.'

'Then shall we record this, too?' She pressed the record button again. 'Pretending he was alive … that was my evidence. Proof I could still imagine a future. Others might call it denial. I call it authorship. It was the only way to live when everyone else had already written my ending.'

The words landed cleanly, deliberate. Catherine felt them like pins through paper. She thought of the child behind the statement: a girl of fourteen, inventing a living father because the truth was too large to bear. How else could she have survived it?

She reached into her bag and pulled out paper and a pen. She then lowered her eyes, the pen trembling slightly between her fingers.

Authorship as survival. Denial as composition.

Her heart was still racing. Her fingers tightened, willing the tremor to still. It didn't. The cold had found its way deeper today; she hoped Melville wouldn't notice.

Melville leant back, studying her. 'Tell me, Doctor Haynes, do you ever wonder what happens to the women left behind in all your paintings? The widows, the mothers, the daughters?'

'I think about that constantly.'

'Good. Because no one else does.'

The words landed somewhere unsteady in Catherine's chest. Being overlooked was a familiar ache; she usually carried it quietly. Silence stretched. Catherine became aware of the sound of her own breath and the soft tick of the clock on the mantel.

'We'll stop there,' Melville said at last, though neither moved to rise. She stubbed out her cigarette, slow and precise. 'You'll come again?'

'If you'll have me.'

'I'll telephone you. And bring fresh reels. The statue comes next.'

Catherine hesitated, aware of the layers of meaning. 'Which statue?'

'Father in Lichfield. Nineteen-fourteen. Every nation needs its monuments.' Melville's smile was small, unreadable. 'Though, someone has to remember they're made of bronze, not truth.'

Evidence

DECEMBER 1972

The tape had run out hours ago, yet Dr Haynes could still hear the rhythm of Melville's voice. It lingered in her office like cigarette smoke. Thin but inescapable. In the three days since, she'd listened to the interview ten times already.

Outside, the quad of the neighbouring college was silvered with frost. Inside, the wind hissed softly through gaps, like breath through teeth. Catherine replayed the last few lines of the interview, Melville's words rasping through the old machine.

'Pretending he was alive ... that was my evidence.'

She stopped the reel and sat back. *Evidence.* In the archive, the word meant reliability, a trace you could verify. But Melville's evidence was invention, the kind that refused to die because it was the only way to live.

In the margin of her notebook, Catherine wrote:

Denial as method. Memory as argument.

Then, beneath that:

Who owns the version that survives?

A draught caught the papers on her desk and lifted them like wings. She steadied the pile with her hand and noticed the faint tremor again. It was a ripple she felt in her ribs as much as her fingers. She rubbed at her sternum, as if that might ease it, noticing now how her own handwriting had changed. It was tighter, more urgent, as though she'd already begun to speak in Melville's cadence.

For the first time, she wondered if the project was turning from study to haunting. The porter's telephone rang once, twice. She jumped to answer it, and the jolt sent a brief flare across her chest – gone almost as soon as she felt it.

Unveiling It

DECEMBER 1972

The tape clicked on.

'You've brought new reels, then.' Mrs Russell Cooke's voice again, slow and precise, the words dragged through the air like a verdict.

'As promised,' Dr Haynes replied. Her voice sounded thinner than she expected; the cold in the room always seemed to settle in her lungs first. The recorder hummed between them.

'Good. You'll want this for your monuments chapter. How sorrow hardens into spectacle. How a woman's silence gets cast in bronze.'

'The unveiling?'

'What else? That's when wax turns to bronze, and story to scripture…'

A Guest of Honour

ARCHIVE: REEL TWO

From 1914

STATUE STIR IN LICHFIELD – LOCAL HERO OR MISPLACED MEMORIAL

On the cusp of its unveiling, a statue of Captain Edward John Smith in Lichfield has attracted fiery debate for the past two years. Slated for 17 July, the monument commemorates a man with no direct ties to the city, raising questions about the appropriateness of his memorial…

By staff writer, Edward Langley;
Lichfield Gazette, 15 June 1914

What the Water Keeps

June 1914

Almost two years since the *Titanic* went down, and still the sea keeps sending fragments back. Today it comes stamped from Halifax. Ghosted across a salt-softened envelope. The corners are worn by miles of handling. I turn it over, weighing it in my palm.

For a moment, I consider hiding it. Sliding it between the pages of *Moby Dick* until nightfall, when the house sleeps. If Mother sees the postmark first, she'll burn it. Or worse, she'll open it and find it ordinary. *Let it be mine, at least for a breath longer.*

Still, I carry it to her, slow and deliberate, as though it were something volatile. She's too busy scanning today's *Lichfield Gazette* to look up. The paper trembles slightly in her hands, or perhaps that's only my eyes wanting it to.

'Oh, for heaven's sake,' she mutters. The pages fold with a sharp slap of disapproval.

'Something wrong?'

'Another piece about the statue. A provincial editor with a provincial mind. We'll not waste breath on it.'

She leaves the room in a flurry of silk and lavender. Once the door clicks shut, I retrieve the newspaper. The headline shouts in black type:

STATUE STIR IN LICHFIELD – LOCAL HERO OR MISPLACED MEMORIAL?

The words ache with the weight of argument. As if a man can be owned by place, or virtue by geography. The article hints at what I have long suspected: that Father doesn't belong in Lichfield. Doesn't belong in bronze. Perhaps he never belonged on a pedestal at all.

In the margin I write two words only – *Find Polaris*. A memory, a direction. His voice in the dark that last winter. *Look for the star that never moves, and you'll always know where you are.*

The unveiling might be delayed again. I fold the clipping into quarters and slip it into *Moby Dick*, pressed among other fragments waiting to be stored in Father's suitcase. My own private archive. Proof against forgetting.

The envelope waits on the desk, pale against the mahogany, patient as tidewater. At last, I reach for it. The wax gives under my thumb. The paper smells faintly of salt, though perhaps that's only what I want to believe.

Dear Mrs Smith and Miss Helen Smith,

I write with solemn respect as one who witnessed, in part, the great sorrow that befell the world in April 1912. Though time has passed, the memories do not fade. Halifax remains marked by that spring. The ships returned with the lost. We buried them as best we could, and we remember still.

The writer tells of Father – not the myth, but the man. He writes of cable ships, of frozen hands recorded in ledgers, of graves marked with numbers when names could not be known. *Captain Smith*, he says, *was calm to the last. Steady. Composed. Braver, perhaps, than history has credited.*

The letter folds into silence, offering no revelation, only a voice from across the sea. That should be the end of it.

But there's a second page. Smaller. Damp at the corners. Ink softened but still legible.

I freeze. Ten seconds, maybe longer. Every part of me goes still, as if movement might break the spell. This is him. Or the hand of someone who knew him too well to invent it. I've studied his signature more times than I've prayed. There are fifty-nine samples catalogued in my diary. I've traced the tails and loops until the ink thinned to ghost. Each one slightly different, and yet I'd know this hand in the dark.

It is his.

My darling girls,

If this reaches you, know that I thought of you with every breath. That I saw you in the stars. That I held firm until I could no longer.
Tell Melville she must never fear the dark.

E.J.S.

The script is unmistakable. The long tail on the *y*, the looping capital *M*. I've seen it often enough in his letters from the *Baltic*, the *Adriatic*, the *Olympic*. His initials were always a kind of drawing. A flourish that insisted upon existence.

Pinned to it, a note in another hand.

Found with personal effects of survivors. Water-damaged. Recovered from Halifax depot and delayed in processing.

I stare until the letters swim. No date. No envelope of its own. The lamp hisses, its flame low, casting amber light across the paper. The ink glows faintly, as if it still remembers warmth. I could show it to Mother, but what if she calls it false? What if she doesn't even look? Then it dies in her hands, and I can't lose it again.

Almost two years, and I still don't know where he is. Not the statue. The man. Almost two years, and the grief hasn't softened. People say the mind learns to bury; they lie. Mine only sharpens. I remember it all: the frost on the railing the day he sailed, Mother's shallow breathing in the hall as she read the telegram, the paper stiff in my hands like wood.

I slip both letters into *Moby Dick*. They'll join the archive I've created. Each one a question. Each one a door left slightly ajar before being sealed inside Father's suitcase.

～

Later, I write.

2nd June 1914

Letter from Halifax depot. Includes personal note. Water-damaged, no envelope. No clear chain of custody. No date.
Conclusion: Possibly real. Possibly not. Either way, not imagined.
Pattern: Letter arrives just before statue. Again – monument built while truth is buried.
It's a sign, not proof. Signs breathe; proof closes the door.

Outside, the wind rattles the glass panes. The room smells faintly of lavender and old paper. The statue might be unveiled next month. They want me to speak. Mother says it's a duty, that the speech is already written, but I have half a mind to say something else entirely. To stand beside the bronze and ask, 'Who decides when a story is finished?'

The Veiling of Valour

July 1914

Two years, three months, ten days. That's how long it has taken them to raise him in bronze. Long enough for the world to move on. Not long enough for me.

My gloves are damp from clutching the folds of my skirt too tightly. Overhead, the clouds threaten rain, heavy and grey. Ahead, the statue waits beneath a white veil that stirs faintly in the breeze. The sight makes me shiver. It looks less like a monument and more like a body shrouded for burial. Again. I try not to think of Halifax, of waterlogged caskets, of the weight of what was never found.

My boots catch on the uneven grass, the hem of my dress dragging against the damp ground. Around me, the crowd shifts. Hundreds of bodies jostle, all eyes fixed on the veiled figure. Not malicious, just hungry. Hungry for a story, for a daughter-shaped echo of grief. Their faces blur, but I can feel the shape of their watching. Pity arranged like portraiture. Their voices rise and fall like the wind through the trees of Beacon Park.

A man in a morning coat steps forward to meet me. He clears his throat, his gaze flicking from my face to the restless crowd. 'Miss Smith, when you're ready,' he says softly, formal as a church bell.

I turn to check Mother's still there. She stands a few paces behind, staring at the crowd. Her face is pale beneath her hat's wide brim.

'Mother?'

She nods. She hasn't said much all morning, and her silence is heavier than the speeches I've been told to expect. I face the man again and I nod, though my throat feels too tight to speak.

The mayor is talking now. His words are punctuated by applause from the gathered crowd. He speaks of duty and sacrifice. The words drone, heavy as bees. I barely hear them. My hands tighten at my sides. The seams of my gloves pull against my fingers.

'And now,' the mayor says, his tone swelling with importance, 'we call upon Miss Helen Smith, Captain Smith's only daughter, to unveil this monument to his heroic legacy.'

My cheeks burn as I glance briefly at the crowd. It's a sea of faces blurred by distance and my own rising nerves. They're not just watching the statue. They're watching me. For a slip of the tongue. A tremble. A crack. One hint that I believe the other stories: the whispered ones about speed and pride and ice. The applause is polite but restrained, and my feet hesitate before moving forward. I look at Mother, but her eyes are downward. Perhaps she's praying.

'Thank you,' I say. My voice is too quiet for this outdoor spectacle.

The man in the morning coat steps aside, gesturing towards the rope that dangles just within reach. 'Outside voice,' he demands, pointing at his mouth for exemplar.

I nod and smile, because I am polite. 'It is my honour to unveil the statue of Captain Edward John Smith. Mother and I…' Still, she doesn't look towards me. 'We are grateful for this memorial.'

As I take hold of it, the rope feels neither coarse nor rough through my gloves. My hand trembles faintly and my gaze lingers on the cloth. On the folds hiding the figure beneath. In this second, he is still just my father. Not a martyr. Not a myth. The moment I pull, I fear I'll lose him for good. Traded for a bronze version sculpted for strangers. I could walk away. I could leave the cloth exactly where it is and say nothing. Let them unveil him themselves – the version they built without us.

Still, 'I hereby declare this statue unveiled,' I say.

The wind stirs, lifting the hem of the cloth slightly. I take a deep breath. The fabric resists at first, then falls away in one smooth motion. Gasps ripple through the crowd, followed by applause that swells like a wave.

I step back. My eyes fix on the statue. It's more than seven foot tall, raised on a pedestal just as high. Lady Kathleen Scott's name is carved discreetly at the base: a widow sculpting another widow's grief. Perhaps that's what we're all doing – casting loss into shape before it consumes us. Mother liked that her sorrow, and Lady Scott's, run parallel and both turned public within weeks of one another. Perhaps this statue belongs to her husband as much as to my father.

The bronze catches the faintest light as the clouds move overhead. He stands tall, shoulders square, face set in that same steady calm from the photographs before the voyage. His cap sits perfectly.

'The wind will never disturb it,' I say. No one answers.

It is him. And not him. A captain for history. Not the man who read to me by the fire or lifted me high enough to touch the stars. This version is too tall, too certain, carved by hands that never heard his laugh, his voice, the pause before his smile. Did they guess his height? Measure from Madame Tussauds? Or simply decide how a hero should look?

The applause fades.

'Magnificent, isn't it? A fitting tribute to a brave man,' someone nearby murmurs.

'There's a fine line between bravery and recklessness. They all knew about the ice.'

I turn sharply, scanning the sea of hats and coats. So many faces, all blurred, all watching. I can't tell who said it. My hand tightens on the folds of my skirt.

Then, her touch. Mother's fingers grip my forearm.

'They didn't know him,' she says quietly.

'Will they ever stop?' I whisper. I don't turn. Her presence beside me is solid, unyielding.

'It doesn't matter,' she replies, voice low, meant for no one else's ears. 'Some will always talk. Let them. What matters is what you show them. Come, sit.'

We move together, climbing the steps to our reserved seats. Front row, level with bronze-Father.

The crowd's applause swells again as the bugles sound 'The Last Post', that ritual of finality. The Duchess of Sutherland steps forward, voice clear as she reads Queen Alexandra's message, praising the tribute to a 'good and brave man'. Others follow, their words layered with admiration, repetition, obedience.

I glance at Mother, seeking something – reassurance, perhaps – but her eyes are fixed on the statue. Her face is as impassive as the bronze figure. The knot in my chest tightens, but I say nothing more. Mother has made it clear: there are things we do not discuss. Not here. Not now.

The crowd shifts again as the final remarks begin. I follow her lead, staring at Father while the mayor concludes his part of the performance. Below us, the whispers stir like rustling leaves. I can't help but wonder how many more years they'll go on.

'Melville,' Mother says softly.

I start, realising that I've not been listening to the closing words. Her hand brushes my cheek. The fabric of her glove cool against my skin.

'They're expecting you to speak again. Here.' She passes me the paper. The words we wrote together.

The Duchess of Sutherland steps aside, giving me a small, formal nod. My fingers tighten around the page, its edges worn soft from rehearsals. I move forward, and the weight of their eyes presses against me. Too heavy, too close.

'Mother and I wish to thank you all,' I begin, my voice steady though my heart pounds, 'for joining us here today to honour my father, Captain Edward John Smith, and the many lives lost in the tragedy of the *Titanic*.'

The words taste like dust. Too polished. Too distant. The paper crackles faintly, like sea foam breaking apart.

'I am sixteen years old and do not claim to know much of this world,' I hear myself say. The crowd stills. The words are no longer hers, or ours. They're mine. 'Yet my father once told me—'

I glance at Mother. There's a flicker behind her composure. Panic, perhaps, or pride. She nods once, a small, deliberate gesture.

I draw breath. 'My father once told me that courage is not the absence of fear, but the will to act despite it. I believe he carried that courage in every decision he made.'

The words come unbidden – raw, but true. The crowd is silent now. Even the wind holds its breath.

'For me, this statue is a reminder of the man the world thought they knew. It is not a reminder of the man I knew and loved – the man who read me stories by the fire and taught me to find the North Star in the night sky. He wore a heavy coat with polished brass buttons. I remember the glint of them when he lifted me up.'

'She hates the statue,' someone mutters. The voice slices through the stillness like a thrown stone. I want to find them. To say they're right, and wrong. But I'm too tired to explain the difference.

'I don't,' I say, louder now. The sound cuts through the air. 'But consider my mother and me, too. If nothing else, today, let us be the reminder that beyond this statue'—I turn and point—'there is an adored father and a beloved husband who is missed every day. Thank you.'

When I step back, the applause begins. It's hesitant at first, then swells until it surrounds me. I glance at Mother. She's clapping, smiling, her composure intact. I allow the sound to settle against the tightness in my chest. It isn't comfort, but it's something. Her gloved fingers find mine.

The crowd sings the 'National Anthem'. Mother and I descend the platform. I kneel to place a wreath of evergreens and red and white roses at Father's bronze feet. Mother lays lilies beside them, below the plaque:

COMMANDER EDWARD JOHN SMITH, R.D., R.N.R.
BORN 27 JANUARY 1850. DIED 15 APRIL 1912.
BEQUEATHING TO HIS COUNTRYMEN THE MEMORY AND EXAMPLE OF A GOOD HEART AND BRAVE LIFE AND A HEROIC DEATH. BE BRITISH.

There is no mention of the *Titanic*.
Silence.
'It must be a great satisfaction to Miss Smith,' the Duchess of Sutherland announces brightly, 'to know that a statue of her father now stands in these grounds, where the only other is that of our late beloved King Edward the Seventh. I have the pleasure of proposing a vote of thanks to Lady Scott, who carved the statue, and to Miss Smith for unveiling it today.'

But he isn't here. Not in the bronze. Not in the words etched below. Not in this version the world has chosen to remember. They've carved a story and asked us to bow to it.

I stood because I had to, but I won't stand here again.

Yours Always

July 1914

The lilies on the dining table are split from the same bunch Mother laid at the foot of Father's statue this morning. Their scent clogs the air. Thick as fog, too sweet to be natural. I swallow against the urge to gag. It feels like breathing memory: stale, perfumed grief.

I've already changed into my afternoon dress. Grey muslin, white lace at the collar. Mother's idea of propriety, though we expect no one. She sits in her armchair by the hearth, back straight, hands folded. Black crepe, softened only by a line of jet beads at her cuffs. Her gaze remains fixed on the mantel. She hasn't looked at me once. I can't tell if it's anger or the sheer effort of composure keeping her still. The house presses in. Father's photograph watches from the mantel, naval jacket crisp, cap angled just so. The same expression I unveiled today in bronze: stern, composed, untouchable. Coal smoke drifts from the kitchen, clashing with the lilies' sweetness until the air turns cloying.

Behind me, Ann sets down the tea tray with practised care. The sound of porcelain against silver feels louder than it should. Her presence today is intrusion. She's a witness to our silence.

'That will do, Ann,' Mother says. Her voice is quiet, but the command is absolute.

Ann curtsies and leaves. I envy her swift escape.

'The statue was ... impressive,' I say at last, just to break the stillness. My own voice sounds foreign, as if it belongs to someone older.

'It was as it should be.' Mother doesn't turn. The words are smooth, polished, final.

I wait. I want her to say it looked wrong – the eyes too cold, the jaw too proud. I want her to say what I saw: not a man, but a monument built by strangers. But she says nothing. Her fingers move instead, adjusting the beads at her cuffs. Each movement neat, deliberate, and desperate in its control.

'People are still talking,' I venture, 'about the ice. About whether —' My throat tightens. 'Whether he made mistakes.'

Her head snaps towards me, eyes like a blade. 'And you thought it worth repeating?'

'I didn't say I agreed,' I stammer. Heat floods my cheeks. 'It's just … why do they still whisper?'

'Because people gossip,' she cuts in, voice cool and exact. 'It is not our business to feed them. Nor yours to dwell on it.'

I grip my skirt. 'But it isn't just Father anymore. They say it's a curse now. The fireman's widow, the steward's wife. It follows us – even at school. And if I'm asked to defend him, what do I say? That in this house we stay silent?'

'Enough, *Helen*.'

The name lands like a slap. She only uses it when she wants distance, when she means to remind me that I am no longer his. Her hands tighten on the chair's arms, breath drawn sharp. Then she smooths her skirt, reclaiming control. The silence that follows is colder than the rebuke.

'These are foolish superstitions,' she says at last, her tone restored. 'The world hunts for patterns where there are none. Don't let yourself be drawn in.'

Her dismissal stings. I search her face for doubt, for anything, but her expression is sealed. The same composure she wore for the crowd this morning.

'I just wonder if the whispers will ever stop,' I say quietly.

She rises, smoothing her skirt again. 'It is not for us to answer for him. Your father died as a man of honour should. That is the legacy we carry. Remember it.'

The knot in my chest tightens. Two years of school have taught me to measure my words, but here, at home, silence feels unbearable.

'I'm not a child anymore,' I blurt. 'I know people blame him. Pretending we don't hear it, won't make it go away.'

Her eyes narrow, assessing me. 'And what would you suggest we do? Argue with every fool who dares to whisper? Explain choices a dead man cannot defend? The world does not forgive easily. You'll learn that – if you haven't already. But there is dignity in silence. Strength in letting them see you cannot be wounded.'

She turns to the mantel, straightens Father's photograph by a fraction. 'Drink your tea. Your father's memory deserves no less.'

Her voice is steady again. She leaves the room, her steps light but unyielding.

The lilies choke the air. Father's photograph gleams in its silver frame. My chest aches, and I only realise I'm crying when a tear lands on my hand. I cross to the writing desk. Its drawers are meant for order, not grief. I open one, searching for a handkerchief, and my fingers catch on something hidden – a letter. The paper is soft at the edges, faintly scented with lavender. My pulse stutters.

I shouldn't. But I unfold it anyway.

My dearest Ted,

How strange, this wealth you have left us. It piles up in ledgers and accounts. Figures that mean nothing against the silence of this house. What use is money, when I would trade every penny for the sound of your laugh echoing in these rooms?

I sent Melville away. You would not have blamed me; you would have agreed. She needed distance from my grief – from these walls that still resound with your absence. School has been her salvation. She carries loss differently: at arm's length, as though she might tame it. Your grief has become mine alone. I wear it for us both. Yet I see the shadow it casts over her. She smiles less, though she pretends. She grows too fast, our darling girl.

In the long silences of your voyages, I was often lonely. Ben was noisy company, Mel a comfort, but still the house felt hollow. How I wish there were more of us – more shoulders to bear this weight. The burden is too vast for two.

I told myself school was for her: the gardens, the rules, a life beyond wreckage. But, Ted, it was also for me. I needed space to mourn you without her seeing me hollowed, edges sharp with anger and despair. I succumbed to heartache. I indulged it. I could not let her witness the nights when I called your name into the dark, or the mornings when dawn rose like mockery.

I hated you then. Briefly. I hated you for leaving, for going down with strangers instead of coming home. I hated the myth they made of you before your body was cold. They called you a hero, spoke of calm, of courage – as though words could erase the fact that you are gone. Their statues and speeches do not warm this house. They do not fill your chair by the fire, nor the side of the bed I still cannot bring myself to cross.

After the disaster, the crowds thronged outside the White Star Line offices. The announcement came: 'Titanic foundered about 2.30 a.m., 15th April. About 675 souls taken up by Carpathia…' The police had to hold the people back. Too many clung to hope. I hated you then, too, briefly. Hated that I could not feel that same hope. I knew you would be the last to leave your Titanic.

Still, do you hear me in the quiet hours? When the house sleeps, when the world recedes, I whisper to you the things I cannot say aloud. I tell you I am angry, and I tell you I am lost. But I also tell you I love you with a force that frightens me – for Melville, for you. You left me with too much love to bear, and most days it is heavier than I can carry.

They tell me I should be grateful for the years we had. No number of years could be enough. Till death us do part, they said – and I will die a widow, and still without you.

Yours always,
Eleanor

The words settle in my chest, the ache as steady as a heartbeat I'd forgotten was there. I fold the letter with care, smooth the paper flat, and return it to the drawer. Hidden again. Unspoken again.

For all her silence and sharpness, Mother's love for him is here. It's stitched into every line, blooming in the spaces between. The lilies catch my eye once more. They're not for me. Not for visitors, either. They're for him. They're offerings to the man she still speaks to in secret, even now. Even after two years.

He has her heart. He was her husband before he was my father.

I sink into her chair. The room feels quieter. Altered. The

photograph on the mantel is no longer the distant bronze hero unveiled this morning, but the man she keeps alive in whispers.

'Oh, Mama,' I murmur. For the first time I see her grief clearly – not armour, but a weight carried with grace. For her husband. For me.

Interruption Two

DECEMBER 1972

The recorder whirred, Melville's voice carrying through the room, though Mel herself was miles away. Catherine hadn't written a note in twenty minutes. She sat very still, hands folded, as if the voice on the tape had frozen her, too.

To call a woman unlucky is always an accusation.
Misfortune becomes moral.
Her pain becomes proof.
Every tale of female endurance requires its ghost.

She read the lines aloud, her breath misting in the cold office. On the desk lay the latest hospital letter about her illness – *Private and Confidential* stamped across the envelope. She turned it facedown, as if expecting it to speak, to force her hand, the way all unwelcome truths eventually did.

Melville's voice lingered in her mind: *Always watching. Always waiting.* The statue as sentinel. The statue as warning.

She scribbled in the margin:

The curse as method. Repetition mistaken for fate.

She switched the recorder back on. The red light blinked; Melville's voice returned – low, measured, grief trained into form. Catherine had played this section again and again, until the tape itself began to thin. That familiar sensation crept in now: someone else's story leaning too close to her own. Her notebook lay open beside the transcript. Across the margin, underlined twice.

Monuments: grief made public, women made invisible.

And beneath it:

Daughter of the Titanic

To be remembered, she must disappear.

The lines unsettled her. She had spent years doing a quieter version of the same thing – keeping small, staying safe, believing that invisibility might buy her time.

The unveiling, on tape, sounded ceremonial – applause, rustle of skirts, a distant anthem – but what struck Catherine now was the control. Every pause. Every swallow. Every polished syllable.

Inherited silence, she thought. Eleanor's composure handed down like doctrine.

She wrote –

The daughter learns the mother's grammar of mourning: stillness, correction, control. The statue preserves the father but petrifies them both.

The tape clicked. Silence. Then Melville's breath, faint, before she spoke again. 'You can still see the statue if you visit. He looks out across the park. Always watching. Always waiting. They said it was comfort. I think it was warning.'

Catherine pressed pause.

The section she'd planned – bronze, inscriptions, iconography – suddenly felt irrelevant. The statue wasn't a form; it was a message. A script for the living.

She wrote her final lines quickly.

A monument doesn't remember the dead.
It instructs the survivors.
It fixes the man in bronze and asks the women to behave like stone.

Outside, a bell marked the hour. From the neighbouring quad, students' laughter drifted into the night – loose, unburdened, untouched by the weight gathering behind Catherine's eyes. A tiredness that felt less like fatigue and more like something structural, settling in.

The Curse Begins

JANUARY 1973

It had been a month since their last meeting. The days between had frozen over with frost and convalescence. There had been the hospital appointments, too, the unsettling quiet of waiting rooms over Christmas. When Dr Haynes arrived, she was still pale, her scarf wound twice around her throat. The wool scratched at her skin, but she welcomed the pressure; it kept the faint shakiness in her neck from showing.

'This is you looking better?' Melville said, bending to light the fire herself. 'Cold or collapse?'

'A cold,' Catherine answered – though the slight pause betrayed something else. She hated how quickly the lie rose to her tongue; it had been practised long before she met Melville.

Her host nodded, amused. 'Academics always rename exhaustion as something gentler.'

A faint smile from Catherine. 'And yet you keep agreeing to see me.'

'Because you ask the right questions,' Melville replied, gesturing to the recorder. 'And because I enjoy answering them.'

The tape began to turn.

'Last time,' Catherine said carefully, 'you spoke about the statue as comfort.'

'That's what they told us,' Melville murmured. 'But comfort doesn't last. People need explanations. A ship sinks – tragedy. A family grieves for decades – curse.'

'You mean superstition?'

'No.' She exhaled cigarette smoke. 'I mean convenience. People needed a story tidy enough to print. They called us unlucky because it was easier than admitting that grief doesn't end when the headlines do.'

Catherine leant forward. 'So, the "curse" was projected onto you.'

'Stamped onto us,' Melville corrected. 'Especially the women. Widows, daughters, mothers – we were symbols long before we were people. If we remarried, we were heartless. If we struggled, we were haunted. If we coped, we were miracles. They used us to make sense of their guilt.'

Catherine made a small note –

Visibility as burden.

Melville watched her pen move. 'You asked about marriage.' She flicked ash into the tray. 'That's where the talk of curses caught me most.'

'How do you mean?'

'I don't believe in curses,' she said plainly. 'But I do know what it is to be treated as if you carry one.' She paused. 'And to make choices shaped by that expectation. I married the man who seemed safest because everyone insisted danger followed me. I mistook caution for cleverness.'

Catherine's pen hovered. 'Do you regret it?'

'Regret?' Melville gave a brief, wry laugh. 'Not particularly. I simply learnt that fear is a poor compass. If you let other people decide what shadows you carry, you end up living in them.'

A soft pop from the fire.

'Record this part,' Melville said, settling back. 'It belongs in your paper. It's about the husband I chose after the war – not out of love, but strategy. Because I thought I could outmanoeuvre the story that'd been written around me.'

The red light blinked steadily. The reel spooled on. Catherine blinked hard, willing the wavering in her vision to settle. She kept her pen poised, though her fingers felt oddly distant from it.

A Wife

ARCHIVE: REEL THREE

From 1921

MARRIAGES: Mr S. Russell Cooke and Miss H.M. Smith

A marriage has been arranged in 1922 between Mr Sidney Russell Cooke, of Bellecroft, Isle of Wight, and 12, Kings Bench Walk, Temple, and Helen Melville, daughter of the late Captain E.J. Smith, R.N.R, R.D., and Mrs Smith, of 41 Queens Gate Gardens, SW7. The ceremony is to be officiated by the Bishop of Birmingham and attended by close family and friends.

The Telegram

December 1921

The breakfast table is too long, the silence too civilised when the maid sets the telegram down like evidence between my plate and my glass.

'For Mr Sidney,' she says.

No pause, no glance. Just the efficient hush of Bellecroft. Sidney Russell Cooke's family home. Sidney's rules. Outside, the hedges are pale with frost, the iron gate rimed white, the morning mist swallowing boots on gravel.

I know the sound of a telegram by heart. I don't reach for it at once. My tea has cooled, the marmalade untouched. Still, my eye snags on the red pencil cross at the corner of the envelope. *That mark. Again.*

The envelope tears too easily. That thin, sharp crack of paper that once meant death. For a moment my chest tightens – the old sensation of snooping. It's like stepping into a room in which you were not invited. Then it passes. I unfold the sheet. The words sit plain and uncompromising, centred, justified.

```
RAVEN SIGHTED. REQUEST PISTOL.
    CAN CALL TONIGHT?
```

No address, no signature, but I know the typing. The faint tilt on the R. The heavy-footed T. The overpunched O. I've seen it before. On papers on his desk, on messages that pretended to be stock tips or weather reports. Phrases that made no sense until you saw the gaps.

I turn the sheet over. Blank.

The fire offers more light than heat. Bellecroft never warms through. The cold isn't in the bricks; it's in the tone of the conversations. I close my fingers around the telegram. Leave it? Replace it? A choice flickers. I fold it into the crease of *The Times*. Like a pressed flower no one is meant to see.

Even though he requested I stay for winter, Sidney is in London more often than he is here. When he does return, he rattles off his nouns in triple – 'a dinner, a bank meeting, a vote' – as if rhythm makes them real. What he never lists is what I already know: that something lives behind the schedule. Something coded. Something that might undo him, or elevate him. I've never seen him more alive than when he is lying, just a little. The sharpness of it. The spark behind the eyes when he thinks I haven't noticed. It isn't romance he offers, but something sharper. The thrill of secrets, the glint of risk. And part of me is tempted by it all.

I carry my cup to the window. The lawn lies brittle with frost; the yews at the gate glint like cut glass. The air smells of salt and polish. From here, the sea is a pale suggestion beyond the hedge – a boundary, not a view. Perhaps that's what he offers too: distance disguised as safety.

On the escritoire, one of his portfolios gapes open. A page has slipped free, half folded, the corner pressed like a bruise into the wood. I touch it with one finger. Not Sidney's hand: the letters are too neat, too certain. Only initials at the end – J.M.K. No date. No greeting. Just one line, clean and deliberate:

I wonder if you still keep the key. I never learnt where you hid it.

The words raise something small and electric at the back of my neck. A key. What key? I turn the page over, then back again. The ink has bled faintly, as if handled too long. Whatever this is, it isn't business. The air around it feels altered, charged.

The maid returns to clear the tray. She doesn't look up. I slide the telegram from the newspaper into my handbag. Later, I'll pretend I don't recall where I put it. The clock chimes once. A sound too elegant to be warning, but I hear it that way.

A Quiet Understanding

December 1921

New Year's Eve, almost midnight. The gramophone scratches once before settling, and a low jazz melody curls through the hush of the drawing room. Firelight licks the rug, catches the glass in Sidney's hand. He looks haloed in orange, crisp against the mantelpiece. The scent of his cologne mixes with smoke and sherry. Warmth that feels chosen. Deliberate.

'I thought you hated jazz,' I say.

'I do,' he replies, not moving. 'But it suits the mood, don't you think?'

'And what mood is that?'

'A conversational one.'

'Are we conversing?'

'We could be.'

He usually pauses before he speaks, as if deciding which version of the truth to hand me. Lately I've found the waiting worse than the lie. Tonight, though, he looks tired of trimming. He crosses to the cabinet, tops up both our glasses, and offers one to me.

'Melville,' he says, his voice lighter than the words, 'are you ever weary of being watched?'

'Constantly. But it's better than being dismissed.'

He smiles. The unguarded one, not the performance. 'That's what I admire about you.'

'What's that?'

'You don't flinch.'

'No,' I say. 'But I bruise just fine.'

The fire spits and shadows waltz across the rug. It feels like we're between acts – the others drunk on brandy in the dining room, leaving us to wait in the wings. My dress pools in green silk at my ankles; his cufflinks catch the light when he leans against the mantel. He looks more undone than usual, but not unguarded. Always watching the exits. Always cataloguing.

'Do these gatherings never exhaust you?' I ask, tracing the rim of my glass as he so often does.

'Only when the talk turns to tariffs or Lady Fenwick's niece with the eyebrows.' His smile is quick, sharp.

'And yet, here you are.' Half challenge, half invitation.

'With you, Melville, the talk has never been tiresome.'

I try not to smile. 'You're deflecting.'

'Always. But I'll allow one serious question. Choose wisely.'

'I already know the question. And the answer.'

'Say it, then.'

I meet his eyes. 'Why me? Why now?'

He doesn't answer at once. He studies the fire as though weighing a balance. Silence is our shared language; we've always spoken it best.

Finally, he says, 'Because I want a life that isn't theatre. Something constant. A household, not a mask. And I think you're tired of acting, too.'

'You mean a marriage.'

'Of a kind.'

'What kind, precisely?' My voice stays cool, though my pulse doesn't. 'The kind where I nod politely while you correspond with Maurice? Or pretend not to know what happens at Claridge's after midnight?'

John Maurice Kean. J.M.K. Cambridge, Bloomsbury, Whitehall – his name threads through all of Sidney's circles. Architect of modern economics, yes, but also Sidney's oldest entanglement. I saw the note. Heard his name at a gathering last week. Their bond was never only academic.

His shoulders shift, almost imperceptibly. 'I never meant to insult you with silence.'

'You didn't. Omission is still a kind of truth.' I meet his eyes. 'I've survived by the same method – letting silence explain what words can't.' 'And I'd rather that than invention.'

'I'm not offering a lie, Melville.' He leans closer. 'I'm offering a shape we can fill ourselves. You'll be free to write, to speak, to build a house that isn't haunted by the *Titanic*. And I'll be free to … continue my work without pretending to be what I'm not.'

The words taste strange, but not bitter. This should wound – knowing I'll never be his only – yet it steadies me. His name could be my shelter, a house unlinked to the wreck. At least this part of the story is real.

I rise and cross to the window. The winter night presses soft and heavy against the glass. Salt-laced and utterly still. Below, the grounds dissolve into hedgerow and heath, the lawn pale with frost, the sea beyond ink-dark, unmoving. Somewhere across that darkness lies the life I've already outlived. Perhaps, with him, I can invent another.

'And Maurice?' I ask at last, without turning. 'Where does he belong in this arrangement you're describing? Does he know?'

'He's part of who I am. But he's getting married.' Sidney's tone doesn't waver.

'A woman?'

'A dancer. Russian. Bold as brass. I suspect it will be war.' His mouth tilts, faintly amused.

'Two performances, then,' I say. 'Theirs and ours.'

'At least theirs is rehearsed,' he replies. 'Ours would be improvised.'

'And you?'

'What about me?'

'Are you in love with him?'

His silence is brief, but not empty. 'Yes.'

The word lands cleanly. Not apology, not plea. Just fact. The air changes – the fire dims, the room leans into shadow. I keep my gaze on the glass, but my pulse betrays me. It isn't jealousy; it's recognition. This is the truth of what I'm stepping towards: not romance, but clarity. To know the story before it begins. To choose it anyway.

'He believed in things before they became fashionable,' Sidney says quietly. 'Even me.'

'So, what is it I'd be to you? A friend? An accomplice? A shield?'

'None of those,' he says, crossing to stand beside me. Not

touching. Just there. 'You'd be the person I trusted to know the whole story … and stay.'

I smile and I nod. To be the one who stays. Perhaps that's all I've ever been destined to be. I tilt my head, gauging his tone. He isn't pleading. He never would. That's what makes it feel real.

'I'm not sentimental,' I say.

'I know.'

'I'm not naïve.'

'Good.'

'I want my own work. My own identity. A future that isn't inherited from disaster. A house that's mine – not like Mother's, with its drawn curtains and starched memory of a father.'

I think of her. How loss was stitched into the curtains, pressed into the pillows, until even silence smelled of salt. I never grieved there; I only learnt how to curate it – to keep the story tidy for others. Now I want a house that breathes, a child not born into debt. I want to stop being that girl with the ice in her hair – the photo the papers ran for weeks after the sinking of the *Titanic*: me, fourteen, mouth half open, coat too thin for grief. I've become my own headline. A relic dressed as proof.

'You'll get freedom,' Sidney says quietly. 'Your new name on invitations that matter. And you'll get to rewrite the rules.' He pauses. 'You'll also get me.'

I weigh him – not just the man, but the opportunity. Sidney is money – but not only inherited; influence – but without pomp. He moves through London like a knife: clean, sharp, rarely caught. A name beside his is both key and shield. And Bellecroft itself feels like an answer. The grandeur: the panelled corridors, the marble fireplaces, the scent of polish and old roses. This isn't the brittle pride of my mother's house. It's something alive. Sidney even met my father here once – at a garden party where the men spoke softly and I ran barefoot on the lawn with his sister, Pattie. That matters more than I'd like to admit. Sidney isn't afraid of where I come from. He saw the girl I was. He sees the woman I've made myself into.

'You remember Kamenev?' Sidney asks, unprompted.

I blink. 'From last August?'

He nods. 'He sat in this room. Right there. Complimented the roses, asked if the decanter was crystal or glass. Had a pistol in his coat the entire time.'

There's no humour in it. None of the usual wryness. A flicker crosses his face – not fear, not guilt, just calculation.

'Why would he need a pistol?'

'Because he thought someone might be listening.'

'Were they?'

Sidney doesn't answer. He drains his glass and sets it down with too much care. When he looks up, his expression has emptied.

'Some things aren't questions, Melville. They're liabilities.'

The words fall heavier than any confession. Bellecroft shifts around us: not polished wood and roses now, but steel under velvet. Mother's house was draped in mourning; this one is draped in civility. Both know how to hide a wound. He's telling me this for a reason. Secrets here are the real furniture. And marriage, I realise, might be the most elegant disguise of all.

He reaches into his coat pocket and draws out a small box. No preamble. Just the soft click as it opens: a ring – platinum, square-cut emerald, two diamonds flanking it. Exact. Controlled. A ring chosen by someone who trusts precision more than passion.

'This is a proposal, then,' I say.

'It always has been.'

He offers his hand.

For a breath, I hesitate. Is this the moment to walk away, or the one I've been circling for years? The air tastes metallic, like frost. It should wound – his truth about Maurice, about telegrams and pistols and silence – yet it steadies me. A woman can live with many things, but not with uncertainty. Better a known silence than another myth.

I take his hand.

Later, long after the fire has burnt to ash and the house has folded itself into sleep, I sit at the desk in the bedroom.

I open the drawer and pull out my diary. Writing steadies me; it turns feeling into fact.

Kamenev, pistol.
Sat in this room. Praised the roses. No bodyguards.
Sidney's tone changed.
'Some things aren't questions.'
He can now say he's told me.
Engagement before conversation ended.

My handwriting is neat. Unsentimental. I close the diary. Tuck it inside *The Times*, between the financial pages.

Bellecroft's Quiet Visitor

January 1922

A week from now I'll be his wife, and yet the days crawl as if Bellecroft itself is holding its breath. Perhaps it's waiting to see if I can disappear into it completely. At night, the house reminds me of a steamship; sound carries but never quite lands. Footsteps in the servants' passage, the clink of glass somewhere distant. Nothing you can accuse. Nothing you can name. Sidney said he'd be in his study until midnight. Parliamentary correspondence, he claimed.

Now, I walk past the drawing room, trailing one hand along the carved panelling. His study door is ajar. Light spills onto the hallway's tiles. It's too bright for this hour, too angled. I edge closer. There's a voice I don't recognise. Male. Soft. Measured. Russian, perhaps – or French, with something behind it. A vowel held too long. A consonant swallowed. The way some people wear their heritage like cologne: faint, expensive, but clinging. Sidney isn't speaking, or not yet. I tell myself this is vigilance, not fear.

I shuffle closer, breath caught just below my ribs. Through the gap, I can see the back of Sidney's head. And there's a man, seated opposite him, half in shadow. Not a servant. His coat is too fine. His posture too casual. His shoes are still damp with garden frost. There's a dark smear of something – oil, perhaps – near the heel. The man reaches into his coat. For one, taut second, I think he's drawing a gun, but it's a cigarette case. Silver. He opens it and offers one. Sidney declines.

The visitor doesn't light his. Just rolls it between his fingers. Sidney says something then. Low. Sharp. It's not in English. A clipped reply follows. The kind of answer that doesn't close a subject, only signals its weight. There's something between them. Not warmth, not trust, but something worn in. An old rhythm. Like former soldiers or men who've passed messages they never wrote down. I step back before I see more, or before they see me.

Upstairs, my hands smell of the mahogany banister. Of ink. Of paper I haven't touched. I wash my hands twice before going to bed. When Sidney enters, it's one-fifteen. He moves softly, without urgency. He smells of cold air, of fire ash, and of something faintly metallic. He doesn't speak. Just sets something on the bedside table; a book I haven't seen before. He doesn't offer it to me. It's for him, and I'm meant to pretend I haven't noticed. I lie still, eyes half-closed, but when he leaves the room again, I lean over and pick it up. Russian title. No dust jacket. It's slim, heavy with marginalia. Underlined phrases. Several dog-eared pages. One section has a word circled: *Военная разведка*. I don't speak Russian, but I've seen it before – in a letter Sidney left face-up on his desk two weeks before our engagement. I remember the shape of it. The slant of the letters. At the time, I thought it might be a name. Now I'm not so sure.

I take a sheet of notepaper from my bedside table and write in pencil.

Unknown man. Damp shoes. No coat removed.
Entered through servant's door. Not front.
Voice – accent unclear. No names used.
Sidney didn't introduce him.
Silver cigarette case. No smoking.
Russian word from prior telegram reappeared in book.

My hand is steady as I write, though the words feel like trespass. I fold the note small, tighter than it needs to be, and slip it into the split spine of my book. Hidden, but not gone. The house is silent again, but I know what I heard. What I saw. I blow out the lamp, yet the letters stay lit in my mind, sharp as steel.

Ghost of Approval

January 1922

The vestry smells of lilies, their sweetness fighting the musty hush of stone, heavy as confession. My gown is velvet – forest-green, long-sleeved, edged in gold thread. I sketched myself only a fortnight ago. It doesn't feel bridal. It feels ceremonial. Irreversible. I look less like a bride than a witness about to sign something binding.

My mother is watching me. She circles like a dressmaker at final fitting. Precise, unsmiling, adjusting the edge of the veil so it drapes just right. The pearls at my wrist were hers once. A gift from Father. The daffodils in my hands are damp, their stems leaching cold into my gloves. Their yellow is too bright. Too alive.

'The pearls will do,' she says at last. 'Sidney's associates will approve.'

I say nothing. The pearls are the least of anyone's concerns. She steps back, appraising me fully. Her own dress is black silk, high-necked, a gleam of old mourning twisted into something fashionable.

'They'll be watching everything. And they'll remember what they see.'

I hold her gaze. 'You disapprove.'

'No,' she says. 'I recognise the choice you've made. Just know this. Sidney Russell Cooke is a man who mistakes intelligence for virtue. He hides his secrets well, but not always wisely.' She checks the clasp on my bracelet. 'Keep your own counsel, and never let your silence look like ignorance, Helen.'

Helen. Still. I catch her reflection behind mine. It's composed, unreadable, looking past me already to the next impression she'll need to manage.

'He's a fine match,' she says. 'Dependable. And discreet.'

Discreet. The word lands with a softness that bruises. My grip tightens slightly on the daffodils. The word she uses when she means safe. The word I use when I mean invisible. 'I see.'

'Do you?' she asks, too evenly. 'This isn't only a marriage. It's a name. Your father would expect you to understand that.'

The mention of Father catches me off guard. I glance down, where the light catches the tiny clasp beside the pearls. 'And what do you expect of me?' My voice comes quieter than I intend.

Her gaze meets mine squarely. 'To rise.'

A knock. Ann slips in, cheeks pink, hands wringing the edge of her sleeve. 'They're ready,' she says, voice low. 'The organ's started.'

Mother adjusts my veil without comment. When she straightens again, her eyes flick over me one last time. 'You look lovely,' she says.

It isn't sentimental, but it's true. That counts for something. She takes my arm. At the chapel door, the organ surges, and the weight of the day presses in at the edges. I've never liked processions. The stillness of being watched, the slow inevitability of it. But I keep pace with my mother, step for step, until the doors open and the aisle unfurls like a green-and-gold ribbon beneath the stained-glass light.

Sidney stands at the front. He's tall, assured, his back straight, his suit immaculate. He turns as I reach the halfway mark – not too early, not too expectant. His smile is swift and real. It's like a secret only I'm meant to see.

His best man, Oswald Harker, leans in. Says something low. Sidney doesn't flinch. Only nods, once.

We reach the altar. He takes my hand – firm, dry, steady. There's no tremor. No hesitation. 'Shall we?' he asks quietly.

'We shall.'

The vows pass in elegant rehearsal. There's no quaver, no slip. We speak like people who've decided something. And we have. The ring he slides onto my hand is platinum, simple, sharp. When his hand brushes mine, it lingers. Not a romantic gesture. A signal.

I understand it.

Brahms fills the chapel during the register signing – 'How Lovely Is Thy Dwelling Place'. My mother stands to the side, back straight, already watching the room as though it belongs to her. She gave me away without blinking. I don't make eye contact with her.

When we turn to face the guests, the applause is polite. Accepting. No one here doubts the optics. *They are well-matched*, they'll say. *She's respectable again. He's settled.* The rest – what isn't said – hovers politely in the margins.

Outside, the January sun is colder than it looks. The car is waiting; its black lacquered surface gleams in the white light. Pattie, a sister, my brand-new sister, clutches her brother before he steps in beside me. Ann gathers my train with her usual quiet anxiety, murmuring, 'You did it,' as though it's something survived.

In the car, Sidney leans back, studying me. 'How do you feel, Mrs Russell Cooke?'

I pause. Let the new name settle. Smith was my father's. This one is mine. 'Like a woman who's made her choice.'

He smiles, something private behind his eyes. 'And was it the right one?'

I watch London pass: slate roofs, glass spires, the quiet wealth of Mayfair folding in around us. 'Time will tell.'

A Fine Wife

January 1922

Hours later, the solemnity of the chapel has dissolved into crystal and champagne, the vows finished, the performance shifting. Another role learnt, a new name in rehearsal. The late afternoon light filters through the tall windows of 33a Montagu Square. It spills across gilt frames and polished wood, softening the day's sharper edges. Downstairs, the reception hums – cut crystal, a string quartet in second movement, the clink of champagne glasses. Laughter drifts up the stairs, laced with lilies and expensive perfume.

I sit at the vanity table in one of the guest rooms. The veil lies over the chair back. The velvet of my gown pools in my lap, heavier than I remembered. The bodice itches. I shift, and the corset presses against skin it was never meant to hold for so long. One by one, I slide the pearl pins from my hair. Each release is a breath I hadn't realised I was holding. The woman in the mirror looks composed, but I can feel the seam between names: Smith loosening, Russell Cooke not yet set.

His note is tucked beneath the mirror's edge. It's folded neatly, addressed only to *Mel R.C.*

> *Well, we've done it – officially tied the knot, as they say.*
>
> *Perhaps not quite what you had in mind when you pictured your wedding day, but here we are. You've married your literal best friend. How glorious.*
>
> *The world might expect grand declarations, but I'll leave those to the poets.*
>
> *Still, knowing you as I do, I'm betting you're hiding in here – so*

consider this a polite push. I'll be downstairs, of course, holding our place among the crowd.

Don't keep me waiting too long, my darling. I'm already planning our escape route, should it become necessary.

Sidney R.C.

I tuck the note into my garter box. Reach for my more forgiving shoes.

The footsteps are unmistakable. Measured, clipped, the rhythm of someone who never needs permission. A knock. The door opens before I answer. Mother steps inside, the sconces behind her soften the edge of her silhouette. She's removed her jacket. Her dark silk clings cleanly to her frame: collar still high, cuffs still fastened. There's a tension in her posture I recognise, though something else lingers, unnamed.

'You're still in your gown,' she says.

'I needed a moment.'

She nods. Crosses the room. Her eyes take in the veil, the abandoned shoes, the half-drunk tea on the table.

'It's been a long day.' Her tone carries a gentleness I don't quite trust. Not softness, exactly, just absence of bite.

'I'm not hiding,' I say quietly. 'Just breathing.'

She almost smiles. A twitch, really. 'It suits you, the gown.'

'You approved it.'

'That doesn't always mean it suits.' Her gaze meets mine in the mirror. 'But yes. It does.'

The silence that follows is strange. Not cold, but not familiar either. Since Father died, there's been no middle ground between us. No silences that didn't mean something.

'I suppose this is the part where I tell you how proud your father would have been.' She doesn't wait for an answer. 'He would've admired Sidney. Quiet strength. Clarity of purpose.'

The word *clarity* settles awkwardly in my chest. As if purpose could be polished clean of cost. I say nothing.

'Ted was always watching the horizon,' she continues. 'Even when he was home. But he loved us. In his way.'

The old ache rises, uninvited. The knowledge that love, in our family, has become a quiet performance.

'And in yours?'

She blinks. Small, but I catch it. 'I did my best. I kept moving forward. For you.'

'It felt like you were moving away.'

She exhales, and for the first time in years, I see it – the cost of her control. The grief never grieved, only rearranged into routine. She reaches for my hand but barely touches it.

'I see your father in you,' she says. 'But more than that, I see something he never had. You know how to stay.'

My throat stings. I swallow. 'In what way?'

'You stayed with me. Even when I didn't deserve it.' Her thumb passes lightly over my wrist, where the pearls sit. I don't pull away. From the open window, Sidney's laugh rises – clear, sincere. It lifts above the street noise and the swell of music. She feels it too. I sense the shift in her spine as she draws back.

'He's good for you,' she says. 'Not just for what he is, but for who he lets you be.'

It's not a blessing. It's something quieter. Truer. She smooths her dress and steps away. At the door, she glances back. 'Don't keep them waiting. There are names downstairs even I couldn't have conjured.'

She doesn't list them. She doesn't have to. I know who's here: Lady Playfair, Bonham-Carter, Macmillan. Watching. Remembering. I nod.

When she's gone, I rise and face the mirror. My reflection hasn't changed. Still the daughter of a drowned captain. Still the new wife of a man who asks nothing of me. Yet the reflection stares back like someone preparing her part. A new name doesn't change the face; I'm married, with a new label, and I'm still myself. The lilies in the corner are wilting. Their scent softens as they fade. Less like demand, more like memory. Mother's choice, of course. She always believed beauty must ache a little to be sincere. As I leave the room, I touch one curling petal. It folds inward, like a hand letting go.

Harker is waiting on the landing when I come down the stairs. Pattie's new husband. Sidney's new brother. He stands slightly apart, tall and composed. The kind of man who memorises everyone's name and uses none. His stillness feels deliberate, practised. People whisper about MI5, though never with details. He carries the quiet authority of someone who already knows too much: about Sidney, about me, perhaps about both.

He raises his glass. 'Off to France in the morning?'

I nod, smile politely, and move on. In this company, conversation is choreography. Every gesture has a cue, every silence a cost.

The dining room gleams: white lilies, bone china, beeswax glossed with something far dearer. I find Sidney by the fireplace, glass in hand, tie loosened just enough to look human.

'There you are,' he says with a low smile. 'I thought I'd been abandoned.'

I glance around. 'You seem to be holding your own.'

'Pattie introduced me to a Hungarian baron who assumed I'd read every word of *Der Sozialismus*. I lied convincingly. It made him like me more.' He presses a drink into my hand.

'You slipped away earlier,' I say.

'Harker had a query. Something petty. He never could separate duty from occasion.' My husband is smooth on the surface, though his eyes flicker.

'He asked if we're going to France tomorrow,' I say.

Sidney doesn't blink. 'That's because he knows we are.'

'Missing a few names,' Harker's voice cuts across the dining room, loud enough to draw glances. Like a wasp at a picnic. Not dangerous, but impossible to ignore. 'I'd have wagered Maurice would be here. But I suppose even he knows when not to clap.'

I look at Sidney. He keeps smiling, as if nothing has been said at all. Perhaps that's how men survive exposure – by pretending it's weather.

∽

After the guests drift to cards and brandy, I see them again – Sidney and Harker in the back study behind the library. The door is ajar. I'm not meant to notice, but I've grown fluent in overhearing.

'You're not being watched. You're being remembered. Don't confuse the two.' Harker's voice is clipped, deliberate.

Sidney answers. Too soft to catch.

Then Harker again: 'Kamenev should never have set foot in Bellecroft last summer.'

A pause. Long enough to thicken the silence.

'The guest list was … curated,' Sidney says at last.

'And now it's tagged.' Harker's tone sharpens. 'You think you've drawn your line, Cookie. But I've seen lines vanish in a single night.'

I like that he calls him 'Cookie' – a diminutive that shrinks the name we now share. Then, a dull sound: glass set hard against wood.

Sidney says, 'She knows nothing.' Then, lower, 'She doesn't need to.'

I step back before my breathing betrays me. 'Sidney, darling?' I call, pitching it like I've been searching. He appears instantly at the door.

'Come quickly. The crowd's growing sentimental. I think someone's about to recite Kipling.'

He laughs, not once glancing over his shoulder at Harker left in the shadows.

We slip into the shared garden, coats shrugged over our shoulders. The air tastes clean, foreign. As if the world itself has turned the page. Still, the cold bites clean, sudden. Behind us, laughter drifts through the French doors. We circle the edge of the square, frost silvering the hedges. Sidney's breath clouds the air. Mine stays caught in my chest.

'Are you happy?' he asks.

I hesitate. Ignorance, worn correctly, is a kind of armour. 'I'm … in motion.'

He nods. 'Close enough.' Then, almost casually: 'There's a villa in Montreux. Above the lake. It belonged to a friend who died too young. He left it to someone else, but not before he showed me the view. I thought we'd stop there.'

'On the way back from France?'

'On the way somewhere else,' he says. 'Plans can be changed.'

I nod. Fix it in memory to write in my diary later. Composing a record for the day someone asks what I knew, and I'll need to believe my own handwriting.

Unseen Ties

April 1922

Three months have passed since the vows and the crowded rooms of London. Today the ferry cut clean across the Solent, the air sharp with salt and engine oil, the Isle of Wight rising like a green wall ahead of us. Father lingered at the edge of thought, but as we step into Bellecroft, it's the silence that takes hold. Not London's restless hush, but a quieter stillness, broken only by insects outside, in the grass. The sun hangs low. It settles over the island like a warm breath.

Sidney drops our suitcases in the hall. He loosens his collar as he exhales. 'Better?' he asks, watching me.

I nod. 'It's always better here.'

The house is cool despite the unexpected warmth outside. Its thick stone walls keep the heat at bay, and the scent of lavender drifts in from the garden. Bellecroft is an old house – one that doesn't change, that doesn't question. Its bones are set deep into the earth.

'A drink?' he asks, already moving towards the sideboard in the drawing room, where crystal glasses gleam under the gaslight. He pours two measures of whisky. The amber liquid pools richly against the cut glass. I watch him as he hands one to me: the way his fingers curl around the rim, the way his gaze flickers. Not quite here, not quite away. There's a new photograph on the shelf above the sideboard – a candid one, almost blurred. Cambridge, I think. Sidney and another man at a garden table, all sleeves and ink-stained fingers. It's not labelled, but I know who it must be. The frame is new.

For weeks now, I've practised the art of composure. It's almost a kind of peace. The quiet that comes from deciding not to ask.

We take our drinks onto the terrace, where the land spills down towards the cliffs. The faint call of seabirds drifts up from the cove. Sidney leans back in his chair, rolling his glass between his palms. Silence was never Sidney's weapon, but now I wonder if it's his inheritance.

'The Stock Exchange is relentless.' The words slip out as if he's trying them on.

I raise a brow. 'I imagine it's no worse than last month, or the month before that.'

'Perhaps,' he says. 'Perhaps not.'

The ice clinks as he takes a slow sip. I know better than to press. His mind is elsewhere. Not with stock prices or foreign markets, but with something more elusive. The telegrams that keep arriving, folded into his briefcase quickly. The glances exchanged at White's over cigars and brandy with Harker and Pattie. The evenings he doesn't come home as arranged, slipping into bed hours before dawn. Here at Bellecroft, I can almost believe we are simply a married couple escaping the city. Almost. But I have learnt to read him, to see the gears still turning beneath his polished exterior. He reaches across once, adjusts the fold of my sleeve, an old habit from when he still noticed small things. Then he looks past me, out towards the sea.

'You're distracted,' I say, keeping my tone light.

He glances back at me. For a fleeting moment, something flickers in his expression – hesitation, a shadow unspoken, and then it's gone.

'Not tonight,' he says. He smiles, and he's the Sidney I knew before London swallowed us whole.

In the small hours, I wake to the sound of the latch.

It's soft, so soft it might've been the wind, but something tells me otherwise. The fire has long since died in the grate. The coals are dull and cracked. I slip from bed quietly, wrapping a shawl around my shoulders. The floor is cool underfoot and the hallway is dark. Only the faintest line of light slips beneath the drawing room door. I hear nothing. But when I press gently on the door, it gives way, and I freeze. Sidney stands by the hearth, waistcoat unfastened, shirtsleeves loose. A small pile of papers rests on the grate. One already curls at the edges, ink blurring as it blackens. He watches it burn. The flames lift, and for a heartbeat I feel it. That pulse of risk I once mistook for safety.

I nearly speak, but he turns sharply. Not startled. Not ashamed. Just alert.

'Couldn't sleep,' I offer, though I doubt he believes me.

He steps away from the fire and lifts a glass to his lips. Not the one from earlier; this one's chipped, mismatched. 'Letters from a client. Private matters.' The way he says it is too measured.

I notice, then, something else. A long scarf on the chairback – not his usual style. Too patterned, too new. I'd seen it once, I think, in a sketchpad photograph of Kamenev. I blink.

'Was someone here?' I ask.

He's already shaking his head. 'No. Just Cook. Preparing for tomorrow's dinner.'

'Kamenev?'

There's a pause. A beat too long. 'Melville,' he says, voice gentler now, as if I've touched on something childish. 'You read too many novels.'

He crosses to me and rests a hand on my shoulder. 'Nothing to worry about. You're tired.'

But his hand is trembling. Just faintly. I tell myself it's exhaustion, not warning. That the trick of marriage is learning which lies to live with.

The Room at King's

September 1922

Yesterday afternoon, a clerk from a hotel in Leeds telephoned the house. There had been an overpayment on Sidney's account, he said, and they wished to return it. I told him Sidney was out. The clerk thanked me and asked when he might call again.

This morning, at breakfast, I asked Sidney where he had been these past two days. He smiled – the ordinary smile, the one he keeps for Parliament and birthdays – and said he had been in lengthy meetings, then at White's.

It was the kind of lie that required no preparation, offered as though the truth no longer needed a witness. He buttered his toast as he spoke.

That was the problem, not the content.

He promised I would always know the whole story, if not the romantic one. That was our ground: no theatre, only terms. Later, his coat draped over the bedroom chair smelt of foreign tobacco, and in its pocket a matchbook.

The Metropole Hotel. King Street, Leeds.

So, I caught the early train to Waterloo and walked the rest, and now I stand at the door of the house he keeps in the margins of our marriage. It isn't jealousy that brings me here. It's erasure. The soft shift from agreement to pretence.

The housekeeper lifts the latch. Surprise flickers, then smooths itself flat, practised as a curtsey. 'Mr Russell Cooke isn't expecting you, madam.'

'I know,' I say, light as steam. 'He asked me to fetch the ledger from the red portfolio. I've a meeting with Beecham's people in an hour. Faster this way.'

Almost true. True enough to open the door.

She steps aside. 'He's upstairs.'

The hallway is warm and underlit, the air too thick with polish. These townhouses are built for discretion: doors that won't echo, blinds that don't twitch. A man could meet a diplomat or a lover here and leave no trace at all.

The staircase pulls up and away, tightening the air. With each step, the temperature drops and a thin thread of music comes down the stairwell – Debussy, one of the Préludes. 'Voiles', I think. Sidney doesn't care for Debussy anymore; he prefers Bach's tidy certainties. Debussy is weather, not structure. It puts him on guard.

On the landing the door is half ajar. I don't knock. I don't need to. Late afternoon presses at the gauze curtains. The fire is low, but it burns. A tea tray waits on the table, untouched. Everything looks settled, arranged for the kind of comfort that doesn't need asking.

Sidney is slouched in the armchair, shirt sleeves rolled, waistcoat open. He is laughing – a careless, private sound that catches in his throat the way it used to before London learnt his edges. One hand dangles over the arm; a cufflink has slipped to the carpet and glints like a small coin. The sight tilts my stomach, not from shock, but from the terrible familiarity of it.

Across from him, sits the man from the new framed photograph at Bellecroft – the candid one, almost blurred. Maurice. He belongs to the room the way the fire belongs to the grate: not added but expected. Bare feet, a leather notebook balanced on one knee, a pen abandoned at his side. The fire lifts a sheen along his forearm.

The music hesitates and in the pause there's a stillness I recognise. Not awkward. Worn in. The measured space of two people who have learnt each other's rhythms.

Sidney says something too low to catch.

Maurice smiles. 'You always choose silence when it matters.'

'Not with you,' Sidney says. Immediate. No flinch.

The words land like weight, a clean placement in my chest. I don't step forward. I don't cough, or announce myself, or make a scene that would misname what I'm seeing. It isn't betrayal – not the kind I bargained against. It's belonging. I watch because I must. I need the moment to harden, to give it edges I can carry.

I step back, careful as a pickpocket. The gramophone hums on; the music has changed or I've missed it. My pulse has moved to my wrists.

Downstairs, the hallway has emptied of witnesses. I set my handbag on the console by the clock and draw out a slip of notepaper. It's the narrow kind kept for shopping lists and messages that don't require a reply. My pencil is blunt; the words write themselves.

I came to visit. You weren't alone. I understand more than you think.

– Mel R.C.

It isn't accusation. It's evidence. Proof that I entered the room, measured it, and chose to walk away on my own feet. I leave the note beneath the clock on the hallway mantel; the place Sidney will notice because he's trained to notice trays and clocks and the ritual furniture of power.

Later, the cab turns towards our Temple rooms. I pay the driver and climb the stairs. The house smells faintly of lilies and coal; the sort of scent that tries to make itself an argument. In the bedroom I take off my gloves one finger at a time. I listen for the telephone; it doesn't ring. I listen for my name; no one says it.

I open the wardrobe and lift my London diary from its hiding place inside the false-bottom hatbox. The pages are neat, practical, without flourish. This is what I can control: a clear hand, a record kept, a margin where the mind can move without being seen.

I knew the terms. I did not consent to invisibility.

The Boiled-Milk Incident

November 1922

The milk warms slowly over the blue flicker of gas, the pan balanced on the trivet. Bellecroft's cook once said to strain it through muslin to catch the cream skin; her voice returns whenever I do this. I've boiled milk a dozen times this week already. The doctor insists it's better for the baby.

Our Temple rooms hold their warmth; the fire has burnt low, the windows sealed against the river mist, and the air carries a faint tang of scorched paper. I've learnt to move quietly here, not out of fear, but out of habit. I can hear the tick of the hall clock, the clatter of hooves in the street below, a costermonger calling rhubarb in a voice flat with repetition. Then, from the study: Sidney's voice, raised, controlled. I lean towards the archway.

He's speaking in another language. Not French, though he's used that often enough with Maurice, as if secrecy were a courtesy. This is softer, weighted differently. Familiar now, in the way a warning becomes familiar if you hear it often enough.

And then I hear it. Clear. Named.

Kamenev.

The milk begins to tremble at the edges of the pan. I don't move to it.

Again, *Kamenev.*

The name strikes hard, heat rising in my chest. The milk hisses like breath held too long. I watch it spill. A second's delay, deliberate, as if I want to see what happens when something finally overflows. I lunge too late. The pan tips. Milk floods the stove top, and steam rises in a furious wave. A sharp crack of ceramic. My measuring cup shatters on the floor. I freeze. The voice in the study cuts off. Silence.

'Everything all right, darling?' Sidney steps into the kitchen doorway. He's composed, sleeves still rolled to the elbow. He eyes the scene without alarm. A measuring.

'I let it boil over,' I say. My voice sounds thin, even to my own ears. I crouch quickly, reaching for the broken pieces.

He crosses to the sink. 'Things escalate when you don't pay attention,' he says, as if this is about milk. He rinses the saucepan with cold water, and for a moment the only sound is the rush of it against metal.

'I thought I heard you on the telephone,' I say lightly, wringing out the cloth.

He nods. 'Redmayne. Trouble with a shipment in Vienna. Or possibly Dover. The line was poor.'

I turn to look at him. 'Was that Russian?'

He doesn't blink. 'Redmayne?' He laughs. 'He can barely manage Sussex vowels. God help the continent.' His smile is charming. Entirely insincere.

I nod, because that's what's expected. We clean in silence. I sweep the glass; he mops the spill. There's a rhythm to us, even in this, or perhaps especially in this. The choreography of trust, learnt by repetition. Our understanding built on implication, on unspoken lines neither of us dares test.

'Shall I bring up the trunk from the laundry cupboard?' he asks suddenly, too casually. 'If you've things to send to Bellecroft in preparation.'

He's finally agreed that we'll move there nearer the birth next year. Have the baby on the Isle of Wight. The doctor said I ought to be somewhere quieter. The choices were Bellecroft or a place near Oxford – a cousin of Mother's, all draughts and geese and curtains that would make me weep. The island won.

The baby was always part of the arrangement. Proof for him; protection for me. He wanted lineage. I wanted cover. What happens between us has never been complicated. Occasional, practical. A kind of punctuation, not feeling.

I nod as he talks, but my mind is still on the telephone call. The name. The tone. The way he didn't blink when I said Russian. There are codes everywhere we stay, I'm beginning to see – phrases tucked into ledgers, telegrams that pretend to be nonsense. He speaks a language I'll never be permitted to learn. I tell myself it doesn't matter.

The Question of the Pistol

February 1923

By February, the snow has thinned to slush, and I've begun to move slower – one hand always pressed to the small of my back, the baby restless inside me. Fog clings to the Inner Temple like a stain, collecting in corners of the rooms.

I step into the study in my slippers, expecting silence. Instead, Sidney sits at his desk, sleeves rolled to the forearm. A square of cloth is spread out across the mahogany like a dinner napkin, and on it lies the pistol. Black. Compact. Civilian issue, but not the kind one keeps for show. The barrel glints in the weak afternoon light. He cleans it like my mother used to polish the brass. Something to busy the hands when the mind was elsewhere. He doesn't look up as I enter. Instead, he runs a cloth through the barrel, his motions practised.

'Still sleeping with it under the bed?' I ask, trying for lightness. My voice comes gentler than I mean it to.

Usually, that earns a smile. Today, nothing. His jaw tightens. 'Not since Moscow.'

I stop in the doorway. He doesn't elaborate, and I don't ask. We've long passed the point of clarifications. But the way he says it – as if it's not a memory but a mark left behind – makes something low in my chest constrict.

I cross to the bureau where the letters sit in a neat stack, unopened. One from Mother. One from a children's outfitter I don't recall ordering from. I shuffle them absently, eyes still on the pistol.

'I thought you said we were safe here,' I say, turning the letters in my hands.

'I said we were safe enough.'

The cloth winds through the barrel again. Click. Slide. A part slots back into place with a sound too intimate, too final.

'Is it something new?' I ask. 'Or something old returning?'

His fingers still. 'Old things don't stay buried.'

There's no need to say more. We both know what he means. *Kamenev.*

'Maurice used to say revolutions begin in ledgers, not streets.' He runs the cloth through the barrel again. 'Now, I wonder if he meant it as a warning.'

'But—'

'It's precaution,' he says at last. His tone returns to its usual register: crisp, faintly bored. 'Like wearing a good coat in bad weather.'

I move to the window. The Thames is hidden behind a curtain of fog, the sound of traffic distant and muffled. 'I'm tired of fog,' I say.

'You'd rather I didn't carry one?'

'I'd rather you didn't need to.'

He folds the cloth carefully, each motion deliberate. The pistol disappears back into the drawer with a soft clunk. Like a closing thought. I turn to watch him, my hand resting against the swell of my stomach. The baby moves sharply, a pulse beneath my ribs. Not pain, exactly, but insistence. I envy its certainty. It doesn't know what fog means yet.

'I want our child to grow up somewhere else,' I say, resting a hand on my stomach. 'Somewhere ordinary. Somewhere people don't clean guns before dinner.'

Sidney leans against the edge of the desk. His eyes are unreadable. 'There's no such place. Not for me. Not anymore.'

A silence stretches. The gaslights flicker. Then he moves, gently, deliberately, and presses a kiss to the top of my head. 'Come to Paris with me,' he says. 'After.'

'After what?'

He doesn't answer, and I stand still until the lock of the drawer clicks. The sound stays with me. Small, final, certain.

A Letter Without a Name

April 1923

The fire in our bedroom has burnt down to a bed of coals and the poker rests idle by the fender. I haven't the strength to stir it. My spine aches from the weight of this belly, each breath pressed awkwardly by a rib or a lung. The rug is rough beneath my feet, Persian, its colours faded and edges worn. Everything in Bellecroft feels as though it is waiting: the house, the air, and me with it.

I shift in the armchair, the one Sidney brought from London. I never asked who else had sat in it before me. The upholstery has softened with use but tonight it gives no comfort. The silk of my gown pulls tight across my stomach; skin stretched to a taut drum. I run a hand over the swell and speak into the stillness.

'Surely there are three of you in there.'

The child shifts, deliberate as a thought turning over. It unsettles me more than a kick. I press both hands to the curve and wait, listening. The gas lamps flicker with a draught along the skirting. Outside, the island holds its quiet: the churn of tide below the cliffs, a cart creaking along the lane, a dog barking once before silence again. A clock chimes the half hour somewhere beyond the hedgerows. Half past seven.

Sidney is late. Not unusually, but late all the same. I try to distract myself – the knitting basket waits by my chair. I lift the yellow bonnet I began a fortnight ago, but my fingers cramp, a stitch drops, then another. I abandon it.

The post came this morning. Mrs Ellerby set it neatly on the bureau: a parcel from Harrods, something from the pram company, a letter from Mother. And one other. No crest. No return address. Only

Sidney's name in slanted black ink. The paper stiff, expensive, continental. A man's stationery.

I left it untouched until the silence grew unbearable. By afternoon I slid a finger under the flap and lifted the seal. The handwriting was precise, restrained. And the first line of many.

Does she suspect? I still taste you in my mouth.

I stopped there. I didn't need a signature. The words themselves carried the breath of the writer. I pressed it back into the envelope, resealed it, left it on the mantel. But the words took root beneath my ribs.

The fire hisses tiredly. I stay seated, heavy, anchored. When the door opens, Sidney steps in, shaking rain from his coat. His suit is pressed, his collar sharp, his eyes bright with wind. A smear of damp darkens one cuff. He kisses me, brief, habitual, before nodding to the sideboard.

'Letters in here?'

I smile as if nothing stirs beneath the newspaper. 'One from Mother. A parcel from Harrods. Something from the pram company. And one other.'

'Opened?'

'Not yet.'

A pause, slight but measurable. He crosses to the hearth, lifts the poker, coaxes flame from the coals. I watch the movement of his shoulders, how lightly he carries himself, while I sit swollen and breathless. Bound by my own body.

'I've been thinking,' I say.

'Dangerous habit.'

'I want to go away. Before the birth. Somewhere that isn't old. Somewhere that's mine.'

'Paris?' His smile is half amusement.

'Not that far. I can barely get down the stairs.'

The words stretch, vague as smoke. He pours two glasses of port. I leave mine untouched. When his gaze shifts, I tip it into the hydrangeas. They've bloomed unnaturally since I stopped drinking. It feels like a small victory.

'Sidney,' I say softly, 'do you think this will ever feel ordinary? Not the baby. Us.'

He doesn't question the meaning. He sits on the arm of my chair and lays his hand over mine.

'What we have is more real than most,' he says. 'Better than ordinary.'

The child turns again, slow and insistent.

∼

Near midnight, the house holds its breath. Sidney sleeps soundly in the bed, his breathing even, while I shift again in the armchair, trying to ease the pressure against my ribs. Sleep won't come; the weight of this body won't allow it. The envelope waits on the mantel, too, impossible to ignore. I rise, hands steady.

This time I read it through. One line, then the second:

Our trips to Paris are never long enough.

I tear the paper into strips and feed them to the fire. They curl, blacken, vanish. The air smells faintly of scorched cologne. I can't convince myself I imagined it. The fire settles. I watch until only the embers remain – steady, red, waiting.

Interruption Three

JANUARY 1973

The tape clicked off. For a long moment neither of them moved. Heat from the fire pulsed unevenly, rising and fading like a tired lung.

Catherine lifted the reel before it began to hiss. 'So ... that brings us to the end of the first part of being a wife,' she said quietly. 'The arrangement. The pregnancy. Maurice.'

'A neat arc,' Melville replied. 'Academics do love structure.'

'Structure isn't neatness,' Catherine said. 'It's containment.' She heard the word land too honestly; it was how she managed anything that threatened to spill.

'Containment,' Melville repeated, amused. 'Women like me mistake it for safety.'

Catherine hesitated. 'You never went to Paris together, then?'

'No.' Melville's answer carried the weight of a door closing. Then, lightly: 'Would you put more water in the teapot?'

Catherine rose. Pouring steadied her. These sessions always lulled her into thinking she understood the landscape – until Melville nudged a trapdoor open beneath the conversation.

'What I keep hearing,' Catherine said, returning to the hearth, 'isn't superstition, at all. It's pattern. The way women learn to survive threat.'

'Survive it,' Melville said. 'Not banish it.'

'You adapted.'

'That's the word people prefer when they don't want to say endure.'

A small pause. The flames brightened.

'Falling pregnant,' Catherine continued carefully, 'you make it sound—'

'Practical?' Melville finished. 'It was. I built a marriage that looked unbreakable from the outside. Cold enough to be safe. Logical enough to keep tragedy at bay. That's what people meant when they whispered "curse", you know. Not fate – pattern. The repetition of damage.'

Catherine set her notebook on her knee but didn't open it. Earlier she'd written a line:

The curse is not misfortune; it is repetition mistaken for destiny.

A sharp hollowing opened beneath her breastbone, sudden and disorientating, as if the floor had tipped. Something cinched inward – precise, internal. Her hand rose to her sternum before she realised she'd moved.

Melville's gaze sharpened. 'Still pretending you've only got a cold?'

Catherine stilled, lowering her hand to her lap. For a moment she felt exposed, armour slipped; illness was the part of herself she rarely named, even in private. 'I'm fine.'

'Fine,' Melville echoed, gently mocking. 'The most dangerous word a woman uses about herself.'

Heat flushed Catherine's cheeks. The fire spat softly. 'You think this work is about me?' she asked.

'Everything is about the person who asks the questions.' Melville leant back, smoke curling from her cigarette. 'You study women who survive because you recognise the shape of it.'

The words landed too close; Catherine wasn't ready to admit the recognition, even to herself. She swallowed, steadying her breath. For a heartbeat she saw herself reflected in the window behind Melville: two blurred figures, layered like a double exposure – one woman framing the other.

'Shall we continue?' she managed.

Melville nodded once. 'This next part begins with the birth. The doctor thought there was one child. There were two.' A beat. '"Luck," he said. I wasn't sure whose.'

Catherine pressed *record*. The reels spun, gathering the next story into their coils.

'Bellecroft, June, nineteen-twenty-three,' Melville said. 'The house breathed differently…'

A Mother

ARCHIVE: REEL FOUR

From 1923

BIRTHS: RUSSELL COOKE

On 18 June 1923, at Bellecroft, Isle of Wight, to Mr and Mrs Sidney Russell Cooke (née Helen Melville Smith) – twins, a son and a daughter. Both mother and children are doing well.

Glass and Silk

July 1923

The twins are asleep.

Priscilla's hands are tucked beneath her chin, as if she's cradling a thought in miniature. Simon lies looser, flatter, his chest rising with an almost careless rhythm. Watching them brings the kind of joy I don't need to rehearse. The sort that arrives unbidden. Complete. It frightens me, a little, to feel something that isn't practised. Love that doesn't require permission. I lean towards the nursery window, and my breath leaves a soft oval of mist on the glass. I don't wipe it away. I note these things like a steward, or a witness. Not because anyone will ask, but because memory is unreliable and I've learnt not to trust what vanishes too quickly.

Their christening gowns hang on the armoire doors. Ready for next month, worn today. The lace – Belgian, antique – was sent by my mother, who believes that tradition is a kind of moral instruction. They shimmer oddly in the gaslight. Not quite white. Not quite real. The photographer positioned us stiffly this morning. An official portrait for the newspapers. Sidney was at my side, the babies in my arms, the lilies behind. The man barked orders at us in a clipped rhythm, like a sergeant.

Sidney leant in as the shutter clicked. 'We are blessed,' he murmured.

Not quite a statement. Not a prayer. Almost a staging note. His hand came to rest at the base of my back. Not with tenderness, but intent. Adjusting the line of my shoulders, as if I were an object to be correctly angled.

'You're very composed, Mrs Russell Cooke,' the photographer said.

'Thank you,' I murmured. I smiled, because I was meant to. That small, untroubling smile I've practised since girlhood. Smile, tilt, stillness. The babies stirred briefly in my arms then. They felt warm and real against the stiffness. That part no one could stage. When the photographer stepped back, we were silent, arranged, devotional. A family on display. The camera took us as evidence, not truth. Something to be printed, archived, interpreted by strangers who will swear they knew what we were. Afterwards, I pulled off the gloves and let them fall into the sink. The silk collapsed at once, soft and slack – like someone else's skin.

The lilies, which my mother insisted belonged in the portrait, slump now in their cut-glass vase on my desk. Their edges already brown. She called them 'a symbol'. She didn't say of what. A floorboard creaks below. Ada. Always measured, always in motion. Wiping, boiling, turning keys, straightening frames by half inches. She arrived a month before the twins, on my mother's recommendation: 'A girl like you can't manage a child alone.' Her tone had made refusal juvenile. Now Ada's presence has settled into the house the way starch settles into linen – shaping it, holding it. She moves the way I have learnt to breathe: quietly, without calling attention to the effort. I no longer imagine the rooms without her.

Now, the nursery is warm. The twins sleep in their cots, soft breaths rising and falling in unison. I move carefully, not to disturb the air. My diary waits on the small desk, next to the vase. Blue leather. Thick paper. A christening gift to myself. I sit. I untie the ribbon. I write, very slowly:

If Sidney dies before me, what story will they tell about us?

I don't believe he'll die soon. I write it only because too much in this house has begun to feel pre-arranged. The ink pools. I blot it, but the words remain. I stare at them longer than I mean to, aware of how quickly thoughts become record. How easily record becomes evidence. For a moment I consider slipping the book into Father's suitcase. It's beneath my bed. The brass clasps are dulled by dust and time. I haven't opened it in weeks, but sometimes, even silence needs filing.

There's a knock. Soft. Ada steps into the nursery. 'Are they still, ma'am? Both of them?' She glances at the window. 'Might be best to leave it cracked. Fog's lifting.'

I nod. 'Thank you, Ada.'

She leaves as quietly as she came, the door ajar. I still know almost nothing about her – only that she was once employed by someone at the Foreign Office. Mother had said it offhandedly, as if it were a character reference. There's an efficiency to that kind of silence though, and a usefulness too.

Back in my bedroom, I slide my dress fully off. The silk of my slip clings slightly to the heat of my skin. No one sees me undress. That, at least, is mine. *There must be more than this*, I think. More than ribboned gowns and someone else's smile pressed into baptism photographs. A clock chime from below – nine. It belonged to Sidney's grandfather, and I wind it every Sunday, as his father did, as his grandfather did, though none of them seemed to have questioned the lag. Three minutes each week. Without fail. Sidney hasn't come up. He'll be in his study. I no longer ask whether it's the campaign or the accounts. I no longer need to.

The night before last, he didn't come home at all. Said the train had been delayed. A London engagement. Liberal men, foreign guests, too much brandy. His voice held a new caution when he said it. Deliberate, weighed, measuring what would be remembered. He said a name in his sleep last night. *Varvara*, or something close. Maybe I misheard. Maybe I didn't.

A sound from below. Loud. A raised voice that isn't Sidney's.

I move to the bedroom door, pulling it open further. Male. Clipped. Foreign, maybe. The cadence is more than the content. Not danger exactly, but recognition. A language that has passed this way before. Not English. Educated, but not local. It's the kind of rhythm Sidney once said meant 'St Petersburg, not Paris'. I move onto the landing. Tiptoe walking. I listen.

Another voice. Sidney's this time. It's lowered but unmistakable. A pause. A laugh. Not his usual one. Then silence.

I remain still, one hand on the banister.

'Melville?'

I freeze. I hold my breath. Sidney and his guest move back into his study. The heavy latch creaks as the door is shut. I return to the bedroom. I turn the page in my diary, and I write.

Baptism at Carisbrooke

August 1923

The sun presses down on the lawns outside Carisbrooke Castle, the stone walls throwing long, sharp shadows across the grass. Beyond us, the Isle of Wight rolls away towards the sea, bright with summer haze. Yet no one looks outward today. All eyes are fixed here, on a baptism no one thought they would see. It's been more than a century since a child was christened within these walls. Today there are two. Priscilla and Simon. Their lace gowns shimmer in the August light, but they are asleep, untroubled by history, unburdened by expectation.

I hold my daughter close, and her breath feathers the silk at my collar. My son shifts against Sidney's arm; one small fist curled stubbornly into his father's palm. They are mine. Ours. And, in this moment, I let myself feel joy without condition. I hadn't expected motherhood to arrive like this. Not as duty, but as astonishment. A label I didn't have to negotiate.

Princess Beatrice stands near the chapel entrance beneath its Norman arch. The black folds of her mourning dress move faintly in the breeze. Since the war took her youngest son she's lived in retreat, yet today she's here, and her presence lends the gathering a gravity that no newspaper notice could match. Mother, of course, is nearest her. Immaculate in black silk, her expression perfectly pitched for admiration. She carries the moment like a coronet. Sidney stands between us, measured and correct. He looks every inch the father, the husband, the statesman. Around the lawns, flags lift lazily in the warm air. I wonder how many eyes here watch for more than the sacrament. Sidney once said the island is thick with watchers. I didn't believe him. I almost do now.

The officiant clears his throat. 'If you could all move inside.'

The chapel is a cool refuge. Its Norman walls hold the scent of stone, beeswax, lilies – always lilies. I've stopped asking Mother not to send them. The officiant's voice carries through the hush, his words of blessing steady and familiar. I barely hear them though. My attention is fixed on the soft weight of my daughter against my shoulder, the small twitch of Simon's hand in Sidney's grasp. Their bodies know only warmth and breath. No arrangement, no performance, no curse. Do I envy them their unknowing? I shake my head. *This is my family*, I think.

Sidney leans closer, his voice low. 'We are blessed.' The words fall like a refrain. I search his expression, but even now his gaze flickers. Always scanning, always half elsewhere. He looks like the proud father, but I know he's mapping faces and calculating allegiances.

Princess Beatrice steps forward. 'May they be raised in strength and in faith.' Her voice is softer than I expect, yet it carries through the stone. Her eyes meet mine. Not approval, not pity exactly – something weightier. Recognition, from one mother to another. A reminder that joy and loss are never far apart. Those who survive tragedy recognise each other by scent alone.

We bow, we curtsy, the twins sleep on.

The reception spills across the castle grounds. Champagne glitters in cut glass, children run wild through the crowd, and the twins are passed from one pair of arms to another. My mother moves through the reception like a conductor, and the crowd tunes itself to her key. I recognise the technique. I learnt performance from the master. Yet her gaze lingers on me with that familiar assessment: not of my happiness, rather my performance.

'I see you've kept your composure,' she says.

'I was raised well.'

Her lips twitch. Almost a smile. 'It is an honour. That the princess came.'

'I know.' I sip champagne. It tastes too sharp. Still, I let her words stand, because this is her way of saying I've succeeded.

Sidney appears at my side. His hand is steady at the small of my back, his presence sure. For a moment, I lean into it, surprised to find comfort there. Yet his eyes still stray. They catch on a man I don't recognise: uniform cut sharp, cane angled neatly against his leg. Something passes between them. Not recognition, but instruction. No name is given, no insignia I can see. Just Sidney's jaw tightening, remembering I'm watching.

'You should enjoy yourself,' I murmur.

He turns back with a smile. 'And I am.'

I thread my fingers through his. His hand is steady, his smile convincing. Perhaps he even means it. The sun lowers over the battlements, casting the castle in gold. The twins lie in their bassinets, safe and sleeping. Their small fingers twitch in dreams. Around us the reception hums. Glasses clink, laughter rises, silk skirts brush stone.

A Harvest of Expectations

September 1923

The voices blur into a warm hum: greetings, laughter, children weaving between stalls. The air is thick with rosehips and earth turned for winter planting. September is holding its breath. Not summer, not yet autumn. I stand still a moment and breathe it in. I've come to recognise that scent is memory before thought.

Last week, I paused outside a small gallery window in Newport. Nothing grand – only local oils in crooked frames. But I recognised one of the names. A girl I once sat beside in school, both of us bent over charcoal and newsprint. For a moment, I saw myself as I had been then: hands stained, intent, certain I would make something worthwhile of my own. That possibility wasn't taken from me in a single moment, but in a series of small, well-mannered expectations: Mother's grief, the wedding fittings, two babies and the quiet narrowing of my days.

Now, as I pause beside a table of late harvest – apples polished to a waxed gleam, carrots still dusted with soil, plums dark as bruises – something stirs again. Mrs Finch adjusts her sheaf of wheat with a quiet, satisfied pride. A thing that's hers.

'A fine turnout this year, Mrs Russell Cooke,' she says with a nod. 'And you to open it! Quite the honour.'

'It certainly feels that way.' I smile, softly enough that it won't be remembered. I have learnt how to be visible without leaving a mark.

Near the marquee, a group of elderly men debate the weight of their marrows. One insists the frost last year ruined everything. Another attributes success to sheep dung. A girl tugs at her mother's sleeve, pointing towards the cake stall. Priscilla will do that, one day.

There's fresh bread, blackberry tarts, beeswax and honey – the smell of a childhood I never lived. I smooth my gloves against my skirt. My fingers tremble. The steward clears his throat.

'Ladies and gentlemen...' His voice carries above the crowd. 'We're honoured to welcome Mrs Russell Cooke to open this year's show.'

Applause rises. It's both gentle and well-bred. I step onto the wooden platform beside the rector. The crowd stirs below: ladies in hats, farmers in Sunday coats, children fidgeting in stiff collars. Somewhere among them, my mother watches. I spot Mrs Lane. The new nanny that Sidney insisted we needed. Her presence is like Ada's – composed, permanent, disapproving of weakness in any form. She's holding Simon. Priscilla sleeps in her pram, her face half-shadowed by a folded lace bonnet. I glance at the church again. The light catches on the leaded glass.

'Thank you for inviting me,' I begin. My voice is steady, trained. 'It's a pleasure to join you for such a tradition... A reminder of the richness of the land, and of those who tend it.'

There's a ripple of approval. I hear it rather than feel it. My fingers find Mother's brooch. I watched Ada lay out the jewellery for me – paste gems, mother's brooch, a string of pearls I never asked for. She placed them on the counter like offerings to a woman I hadn't agreed to become.

'It has been some time since I've spoken publicly... Not since the unveiling of my father's statue in Lichfield.'

The words surprise me. They hover, heavier than I expect.

'I'm honoured to be here today.' I steady my voice. 'This event, and all who make it possible, are the heart of our community.'

Applause again. Firmer. I step down.

'You spoke well,' says Mrs Talbot, the vicar's wife, folding her arm into mine. 'More than well.'

'I only said what was expected.'

She smiles, kind and clever. 'Your father would have been proud.'

The words land gently. I allow them to.

The afternoon drifts on: rosettes pinned to jars of jam, ribbons tied around dahlias. An elderly beekeeper accepts his award with great seriousness and tells me honey is the key to longevity. I nod, though

I've never cared for honey. There's talk of fundraising for the church roof. I'm already being volunteered. That's how things are done here. Quiet insistence. No refusal permitted.

Lately, though, I've been reading the circulars Ada leaves near the stove. They're quiet newsletters no one talks about, filled with minutes from Women's League meetings and dry amendments to things most men ignore. I don't attend, but I make notes in my diary. Sometimes I write in the margins of old speeches. Not just correcting grammar, but intentions. There's something steadying in it – drawing a firmer line through vagueness, tightening what's weak.

Sidney finds me at the edge of the marquee, his hat tipped back, his smile measured. And yet, when he leans to kiss my cheek, there is a softness – unguarded, unperformed – that startles something living in me. His hand brushes mine just long enough to make me catch my breath. He asks after the vicar's arthritis, comments on the weather and smiles when our twins are praised. For a moment, we're simply husband and wife, proud parents at a village fair. Then he turns, his attention already elsewhere, and the moment slips. The man with the falcon cane appears again. I saw him at the baptism, and now here. His nod to Sidney is rehearsed, deliberate. Not quite respect, not quite threat. Their conversation is short. His voice carries a Slavic drawl over French vowels. Sidney doesn't introduce us. The man walks away. His appearance isn't coincidence. Sidney knows it. I know it. The island knows everything before anyone speaks.

I glance at Sidney. He's already turned. Watching something else. 'Where's Maurice these days?' I ask, too lightly.

Sidney's brow lifts. 'Still in London, I believe. We don't see each other now. Not since the twins were born.'

I nod, but I know my husband is lying. Sidney's coat still smells faintly of Maurice's cologne – something herbal and sharp. The scent clung to the lapel when he leant in too close. Still, we walk the grounds together. We smile where needed. We pose when asked. I know how to hold myself. The right incline of the head, the curated stillness. I've been doing it for years already.

I smooth Priscilla's bonnet as she stirs, the lace falling across her cheek. Simon kicks against the pram's blanket beside her. For a moment, joy is simple. Two children, a village fair, sunlight soft on the church walls. It belongs to me. This island has accepted me. This life has grown around me like ivy: ornamental, quiet, trained.

∼

Later, as I flick through the afternoon post, one envelope catches my breath. Cream paper, the slant of a familiar hand. I slide it beneath the folds of my sleeve and read it alone in the scullery.

I shouldn't post this, not now. But I think of you daily. I think of the orchard last week. I think of what we might have concluded if we had time.

J.M.K.

This letter isn't meant for me. Yet it reaches me all the same.

I stay up restlessly, leafing through old pamphlets I've hidden in the linen cupboard. Birth control, housing, reform. Small words that feel larger when I write in their margins. A quiet proposal for my life is forming. I'll ask to speak at the Women's Circle next month.

A House in Winter

December 1923

Snow arrives overnight. Not thick enough to bury the garden, but enough to soften its edges. The hedgerows blur into white, and the yews at the gate gleam like iron under frost. Bellecroft looks almost gentle in this weather: stone smoothed to pearl, chimneys breathing slow smoke into a pale sky.

The twins are six months old already, and newly fascinated by everything that shifts or shines. I sit with them on the nursery rug, their quilt spread beneath us. Priscilla is propped against a bolster, solemn as an empress, watching her own fingers curl and uncurl. Simon presses his palm to the windowpane, gurgling at the snowflakes. His breath fogs the glass, and he squeals at the shape it makes. Ada says he'll have strong lungs. I think he simply has a taste for the world.

Sidney came down from London two nights ago. No telegram. He walked in with the cold still clinging to him, and the twins reacted before I did. Simon flung out both arms, Priscilla blinked once and leant towards his voice. Something in him loosened then, almost imperceptibly, as he gathered one child, then the other, murmuring nonsense in a tone I've never heard him use elsewhere.

And it's continued. This quietness. This nearness. I'm almost afraid to look directly at it, in case it vanishes. Sidney sits cross-legged on the nursery floor now, too. Not as a husband, but as something nearer: a man without performance.

'He'll have the world in his mouth if we're not careful,' he says, tugging a curtain tassel free from Simon.

'Let him start with Bellecroft,' I reply.

My husband laughs. It's a small, unguarded sound. It changes the room more than the fire does. Priscilla lets out a soft coo, a noise almost startled by its own existence. Sidney pauses, entirely, to listen. His hand stills. His face, too. It's not sentiment, that's not in his nature, but it's attention. And attention, when it comes from Sidney, is its own form of devotion.

The house smells festive: of spruce, apples baked down to sweetness, and the faint mineral tang of cold air seeping in at the sash. This isn't a grand celebration or event. No guests. No staged tableau. Just warmth and a room large enough to hold it.

'We could stay here together,' he says, eyes still on the twins. 'Through winter. Through January. Perhaps longer.'

Not London. *Here. Together*. The words land like a door opening a fraction. Enough to be seen but not yet stepped through.

'I would like that,' I say.

His hand brushes mine as he reaches for Priscilla's fallen rattle. Our fingers touch, lightly. Not for show. No audience to receive it. A small, ordinary contact, but I feel it all the way to the ribs.

∼

Later, once the twins sleep, I write.

> *Today, we were a family. No performance. No glass. No audience.*

And then, quietly:

> *I let myself hope.*

The Season of Return

January 1924

The telegram arrived at breakfast on New Year's Day, placed beside the jam as if it were no more than a tradesman's invoice. He read it once. Folded it twice. His expression didn't change, and yet the room altered around him.

'I'll only be gone two or three days,' he said.

'You said you'd stay through winter. Through January.'

No response. He kissed Simon's forehead, adjusted Priscilla's blanket, touched my wrist. Not rushed. Not guilty. Practised.

But the train didn't return him two, three or four days later.

The days stretched. Letters came, careful and brief. No explanations. Only assurances. And now, three weeks later, we're finally reunited at Lady Fenwick's dinner table in Mayfair. We act as if nothing has shifted. The table glitters with silver: pheasant glazed in port, carved oranges studded with cloves, the faint sweetness of almond tarts. The room is warm, but the warmth feels borrowed. A fire that belongs to someone else. Sidney speaks easily. His charm is intact. His presence is whole.

He looks like a man who has resumed a life I was never permitted to see.

Lady Fenwick turns to him, her pearls trembling faintly at her throat. 'It must have been an eventful return to London. One hears the House was lively those first days of January.'

Sidney smiles. It's the mild, diplomatic one, built for drawing rooms and inquiries. 'Necessary business. Nothing more.'

Not a lie. Just omission of detail, which is a lie's older, more elegant cousin. I lift my glass. The wine is too warm.

Across the table, Harker – always too watchful – says casually, 'I hear Maurice came back from the continent on New Year's Day. Apparently, he left half his sleep in Moscow.'

The name slides into the room like a key finding the right lock.

Sidney's gaze – taut, alert, alive – shifts. Just enough. Just once. Not towards me. And I see it instantly: Christmas wasn't a turning point. It was a pause. A place for him to stand, quietly, while waiting for the reopening of the world he belongs to. Like a fool, I'd mistaken stillness for intimacy.

The soup is cleared. The fish is served. Conversation deepens into the soft, expensive kind of laughter that floats rather than lands. I say nothing. That, too, is a choice. When the ladies withdraw to the drawing room, I take a seat near the hearth. The fire casts gold across satin and lace. I fold my hands with the ease of someone long accustomed to being observed. Lady Fenwick settles beside me. Not unkindly.

'The island must have been peaceful,' she says. 'Such a sweet first Christmas for the little ones.'

I nod, once. 'It was.'

She hesitates, just long enough for truth to flicker. 'Men returning to London often forget the hush of holidays,' she adds, soft, precise. 'One shouldn't take it personally.'

I turn my head slowly. 'I don't.'

The men enter. Cigar smoke follows. Sidney stands a little apart, listening to Harker. His posture is both easy and attentive, as though he never left this city at all. As though I was the foreign country.

When the coats are brought, he offers me his arm. I take it. Not as wife. As witness. Outside, the fog presses close, muffling carriage wheels and gaslight. Our motorcar waits.

Before he can speak, I do. 'You weren't planning a quick return when you left the island.'

He doesn't deny it. He doesn't apologise. He simply exhales, barely acknowledging a truth shared rather than discovered.

'Have you been with Maurice since you left Bellecroft?'

His stillness is answer enough.

The driver opens the door. Sidney waits for me to step in, and I do.

Daughter of the Titanic

Later, in my diary, I'll write only one line.

Hope is the most elegant stage direction, still I mistook rehearsal for permanence.

Shadows and Silhouettes

May 1924

Nine months since the baptism, yet the days haven't slipped away; they've settled – sediment, not air. The twins grow. The garden finds its rhythm. Bellecroft folds itself into habit.

Some mornings brim with laughter and porridge spilled down pinafores. Simon tugs at the curtain rings until they clatter. Priscilla curls against me, thumb tucked beneath her chin, her breath soft against my collarbone. Other mornings are quieter: work done with hands and breath – feeding, washing, soothing, hushing. No applause. No record. Yet these hours steady me more faithfully than any vow.

Now, night gathers. The fire burns low. A single log glows, throwing red across the hearth tiles. Shadows stretch along the panelled walls, thin and reaching, as though the house itself is listening. Bellecroft always feels watchful after dark; it remembers more than one kind of silence.

Earlier, Ada warmed the bricks for the twins' beds – wrapped them in flannel and slipped them beneath the blankets exactly nine minutes before I carried the twins upstairs. She learnt that trick in a house near Portsmouth, caring for a naval officer's children. She never volunteers such details; they surface, like everything from her, through practice rather than confession.

The lilies Mother sent have browned at the edges. Their scent has thickened – funereal, even now. I lift the vase and carry it to the farthest window. Some symbols are better kept at a distance.

The door opens without a knock. A draught stirs the curtains. Sidney steps in, closing it softly behind him. No apology, no attempt to disguise his lateness. His coat is rain-dark at the seams, the wool steaming faintly where the heat catches it. He drapes it over the chair nearest the fire.

'You're late,' I say.

'The train lingered at Southampton.'

Not an excuse. Barely a sentence. His cufflinks catch the light: the Viennese pair. Maurice's gift. I watch the flicker of silver, and something – something old, something I have been holding still in my chest – shifts. I once told myself I wanted protection, not love. Stability, not longing. I thought that made me pragmatic.

Now I realise that it's made me quiet.

'Did the twins settle?' he asks.

'I put them down at seven. Priscilla kicked the blanket off twice. I think she enjoys being rescued. Simon turned to the wall and chirped.'

A faint smile touches me. Those details are mine. Unwritten. Unobserved by him. But real.

He pours a whisky. No water. He warms the glass between his hands. 'The boy dreams of birds,' he says.

'Yes.'

Simon does. There's something uncatchable in him. Even in sleep. It's a freedom I don't want to flatten out of him. I see my father's precision in his fingers. No one else does. That's my inheritance.

'Did you speak to anyone useful?' I ask.

He sits, angled slightly away from the fire. Always half-turned. Always facing the door.

'Maurice sends his regards.'

The air changes. Not sharply, just enough. A reminder of where his loyalties were forged, and where they return. I nod. The log cracks. Sparks dance, brief and bright.

'Ada's staying?' he asks.

'Another week. Mother worries I'll unravel without supervision.'

'She may have a point.'

'She always thinks she does.'

A flicker of a smile. Gone almost before it forms.

We settle into silence. Once, I mistook that silence for elegance – a mark of maturity, restraint, intimate understanding. Now I see it for what it is: choreography.

He checks the mantel clock. It's lost one minute already this week.

'If only you could have married him,' I say, and he doesn't pretend not to know who I mean.

'You should have married no one,' he answers gently.

I laugh, quiet and small. Not unkind. Not forgiving. 'We were already remade before we met,' I say. 'You by the war. Me by the water.'

'We're not flinching,' he says.

'No. We're carrying on.'

He stands. Crosses to the bookcase. His fingers skim the spines without seeing them.

'I'll sleep in the study.'

Not distance. Arrangement. Preservation. A way of maintaining shape without acknowledging why it must be maintained. He leaves. The latch clicks with care.

I kneel at the hearth. Shift the embers. Coax the flame back to life. I open the window by an inch. Sea air threads the smoke. I take up my diary. My fingers rest on the stitched spine. Then I write one sentence.

Carrying on is simply another name for not choosing.

Wind rises outside. A gate clatters once, metal against post. Then a knock at the front door.

Three raps.

Silence.

I freeze.

Ada calls from the hallway, but her voice is swallowed by doorways. I step out onto the landing just as Sidney crosses the hall toward the door.

Ada's voice, composed: 'A man to see you, Mr Russell Cooke. Says he's come from Zurich.'

Interruption Four

JANUARY 1973

Catherine paused the tape before the next reel clicked in. The afternoon light had thinned to the colour of bone; beyond the window, the garden was nothing but silhouettes. Melville sat motionless, her gaze fixed on the hearth's black grate rather than the recorder.

'You move differently in this part,' Catherine said, surprised to hear her own voice. She'd meant to keep her distance, but the story seemed to draw her in before she noticed herself leaning 'We're skipping over months.'

Melville didn't look up. 'The months were only repetition. By then I was no longer a wife.'

'But still married,' Catherine said.

'Which isn't the same thing.' Melville's tone held no bitterness. 'Marriage is a structure; wife is a part you learn to perform. You can stop performing long before the structure collapses.'

Catherine noted the sentiment, though not the words. Silence gathered between them.

'Memory folds time,' Melville said at last. 'There were years I thought were solid. When I revisit them now, they lie flat – pressed flowers, colour without scent.'

'Did you realise then,' Catherine asked, 'that the marriage was ending?'

'Not ending,' Melville said. 'Unmasking. We began as allies, then companions, then I became the echo he preferred to the sound itself. That's what no one warns you of... How easily devotion can be mistaken for silence.'

Catherine felt the line land somewhere physical, beneath the collarbone – a small, interior ache that had nothing to do with illness. 'And you stayed,' she said quietly. She hadn't meant it as a question;

it slipped out like something she'd been asking herself for years – why she remained in the life she'd built out of fear rather than choice.

Melville turned, assessing her with a cool, unhurried eye. 'A marriage doesn't fail by accident,' she said. 'It fails in patterns. Women call it bad luck, or sacrifice, or duty. I called it endurance. But endurance is only repetition with better manners.' The fire shivered in the grate, though no one had moved.

Catherine reached for the next reel. Her hand hovered above the recorder.

'Shall we go on?' she asked.

Melville nodded once. 'We go on.'

Catherine pressed the button, though her pulse quickened – not from exertion this time, but from the sense that she was no longer only recording Melville's story. She was brushing against the edges of her own.

A First Trespass

April 1925

The twins are almost two now. They're small tempests.

Priscilla stamps when she wants something; Simon points at gulls and crows as though he can summon them with sound alone. Their presence holds me to the world, yet nanny's also given me an unexpected escape: time that is mine, however narrow.

Perhaps that's why I came here. I hadn't planned to, but I put on the gloves anyway.

The studio smells of linseed and turpentine. The tang is softened by the faint damp of old newspapers lining the skirting boards. Light falls in long, pale bands from the high north windows, pooling over the easel and across the bare floorboards. I sit in the plain wooden chair, hands still gloved and folded.

'You can remove them, if you'd rather,' he says.

The room is clearly *worked in*, not curated. His boots are scuffed, and his shirt cuffs are stained with graphite. His name is Cummings. Not the Shanklin postcard painter; younger, sharper-edged, the kind of man who looks directly and then looks away without apology. He's preparing a series – portraits of women in quiet positions, to be shown in Cowes for some hospital fund.

'I prefer them on,' I answer.

He nods, already lifting the charcoal. No flourish. No performance. Just work.

It was Ada who left the leaflet beneath the bread tin. Not mentioned aloud. A permission, disguised as an oversight. She's still with us – neither formally retained nor dismissed. Hers is a presence that has settled like furniture: quiet, necessary, unassuming. There's comfort in a loyalty that requires no naming.

A moth brushes the air near the window. Light glances off the glass jar of brushes. Cummings sketches with swift economy, glancing up only long enough to register a shift in posture or breath. His gaze isn't hungry. It's practised. Observing shape, not story.

'You're not local,' he says at last.

'No.'

'Locals fill the silence to feel polite. Outsiders do not, because they know the cost of giving too much away.'

I don't answer. My stillness is not performance here. It's simply mine.

When he turns the sketchpad, I brace for some version of Sidney's world – softened, flattered, composed. But what I see is something else entirely.

My shoulders held tightly. My chin slightly raised. My hands at rest, but tense. I'm waiting for the next request, the next role, the next demand. I look neither kind nor cold. I look both present and withheld. A woman occupying space without apology.

Had I not realised how rarely I'm seen?

He steps closer, slow, deliberate. Not towards my face – towards the loose strand escaping my hairpin. 'May I?'

I nod.

He lifts the hair back into place. His fingers never touch my skin. There's no suggestion of intimacy. Only recognition. The kind that invites, not takes. Permission. And release.

Outside, the rain begins with a soft hiss across slate. I rise, fasten my coat, and thank him. He doesn't walk me to the door, and I step out into the downpour without lifting the umbrella. The lane is slick with spring run-off, hedgerows bowing under water. A ferry horn sounds faint across the Solent: long, low, unanchored.

∽

Later, with the house still and the twins asleep, I carry the sketch into the bedroom. I asked to keep it, and I asked to return for another sitting. Under the lamplight, the charcoal lines hold.

A woman who isn't waiting to be chosen. A woman who's already begun choosing.

I lift Father's suitcase from beneath the bed, and I place the sketch among the paper and history. A record of who I was for an hour when no one expected anything of me. I close the lid lightly.

At my desk, I open my diary and write.

I have spent years arranging myself inside the frames others built. Today, I was not arranged, and I admired myself better for it.

A Distinguished Husband

October 1926

Morning light cuts across the breakfast table, catching the mess the twins left behind: jam smears, a paper hat folded from yesterday's broadsheet, Simon's toy-boat collection. Their boots are drying on the rack by the stove, mud from the orchard still crusted along the soles. I always mean to scrub them before Mrs Lane notices, but I never do. They're three now. They're full of certainty, tugging the world their own way.

My cup of tea is untouched. Last night's *Portsmouth Evening News* sits beside it. The headline seemed harmless at first glance, but I've learnt to read what sits underneath.

Fortunate in securing Mrs Russell Cooke's services…

My eye halts before the sentence ends. As if not finishing might stop the meaning from settling.

…as they would also secure interest and association with her distinguished husband.

So neatly dismissive, I almost admire it. Sidney's name is the currency. I'm the receipt. I tear the article out, fold it, then unfold it again. My name appears three times. My husband's actual name once. But everything still belongs to him. The thought unsettles me – that one day even my grave might read *and Melville, his wife*. A small life, reduced to a footnote. But what I feel isn't sadness, it's recognition. Old, familiar, wearying. The world won't hand me a name; I'll have to claim it. I think of that art room again – charcoal smudging my hands, the teacher leaning close to say, 'You see angles other people miss.' I believed that once. What unsettles me now is how easily I forgot to keep believing.

The pen is in my hand before I realise.

I begin a letter to the editor. It's clipped, precise. I note the omission, without anger, but with emphasis. A paragraph on the Women's Health Bill. A line about the canvassing I led in the spring. Then I stop. The letter rests on the blotting paper. I read it twice. Set it aside.

Another version begins.

Not for the editor – for a room I haven't entered yet. A drafty hall. Women seated in rows. Chalk dust on the floor. Their hands folded, expectant.

We are tired, I write, *of being folded into our husbands' footnotes.*

I pause. Cross it out. How quickly a woman learns to edit herself.

A draught lifts the edge of the newspaper. The coal grate ticks as it cools. The silence of the house presses as tangibly as a hand. I glance back at the article. No mention of the winter meetings with no heating. No mention of the speeches I wrote alone, or the fact that others paid someone's son to write theirs. No mention of the letters dictated by candlelight with one twin coughing down the corridor. Sidney hadn't asked to be included. He hadn't even known I was being profiled. That's the point. In our world, men don't have to show up to take credit. They only need the right surname and the quiet benefit of assumption. *Her husband, a vastly successful...* It always drifts back to him.

'Mummy!'

Simon bursts in like a well-dressed cannonball, aeroplane in hand, shoes still wet from the garden. Priscilla follows close behind, dragging a blanket like a cape. Her curls stick up on one side.

'Careful—' Too late. Simon crashes into the leg of my chair. The newspaper slips to the floor, its pages scattering like dropped cards. My son looks up, all open face. I gather the sheets. He climbs into my lap. His breath smells faintly of apples; they must have been in the orchard again.

'No, no, that's not for you,' I murmur, gently pulling the front page from his grasp. He waves the plane in protest.

Priscilla eyes me closely. 'Why is this sad, Mama?' She pokes a finger at my cheek.

'I'm thinking,' I say, which is close enough to the truth. 'Just cross with some men who forget that ladies can do things better than them.'

She frowns, and I kiss the crown of her head.

'And sometimes silly men are the ones who get listened to. So, we must be louder. And cleverer.'

She nods. She doesn't know why, but she likes the sound of it. Simon has begun folding part of the paper into a hat. His plane nosedives into my teacup. I fish it out, pop it in my cardigan pocket and set him down with half a crumpet. Mrs Lane appears in the doorway with a letter.

'Post for Mr Russell Cooke, ma'am. Their coats are dry if you're going out.'

I take the letter. The seal is familiar. The handwriting isn't. It's firmer, sharper than I expect.

'Thank you, Mrs Lane.'

She nods. Pauses. Her gaze lingers on the envelope for a beat too long. Then she retreats. I don't open it. I leave it on the table beside the torn article. This house is divided now. My husband and I move through the same rooms, but not together. A marriage can hold two lives. It can also hold two exits.

The twins squabble over the butter. Priscilla wins – by logic, not force. Simon sulks. I don't intervene. He lines up his toy boats across the table. Smallest to largest, their sterns tipped upward. One lies on its side.

'Boats fall in water,' he tells his sister.

I reach out, too fast. I right the boat without thinking. 'Not all boats sink,' I say.

My son frowns and I slide Sidney's envelope into my cardigan pocket, alongside Simon's aeroplane.

Chasing the Eclipse

June 1927

The airfield heaves with anticipation, necks craned, voices low. Five years ago, I'd have stood in that crowd, waiting for something extraordinary to arrive. Now I understand that nothing arrives. You either step toward it, or you don't.

The light is flat and uncertain. Grey clouds hang low over the horizon. The papers warned that visibility would be poor. They said that the three million people who have travelled for the eclipse might see nothing at all. Yet, Sidney doesn't believe in disappointment. He refuses it. He bends reality to his will – and today is no different.

'No point standing in a field with the rest of them,' he said last night, unfolding a telegram with a flicker of satisfaction. 'We'll watch it from above the clouds.'

And now the de Havilland DH.50's polished struts gleam in the uncertain light. My husband has secured it, as he secures most things – with quiet confidence and an unwillingness to hear the word 'no'. Sidney speaks with the pilot. His posture is easy and his hat is tilted at that familiar, insouciant angle. He glances back at me – a flicker of a smile, the one he wears in photographs. For a moment, I allow the picture: a couple, unremarkable, unobserved, belonging to one another without explanation. It's gone almost as soon as it forms. The imagination is a dangerous muscle; it remembers the hungers we learn to silence. The wind ruffles the edges of Sidney's flying jacket. Its leather is still stiff with newness. I wonder, fleetingly, if he had it ordered the moment he decided on this scheme. When was that though?

I draw my own jacket tighter and glance back at the scene behind us. The airfield is crowded. Desperate figures crane their necks skyward. Perhaps they're willing the clouds to part. Men in tweed coats and felt hats pace anxiously, while women pull their shawls tighter, clutching at children already restless from the wait. The hum of conversation carries a current of doubt – *what if the clouds don't lift, what if the journey north was for nothing?*

'Nervous?' he asks, now by my side.

'Not remotely.' I fasten my gloves with deliberate precision. 'But if we die in pursuit of scientific wonder, I shall never forgive you.'

The pilot gives a short nod and gestures towards the aircraft. My husband grins. He takes my hand. 'Noted. Come on, then.'

Sidney climbs in first, ducking beneath the wing to reach the narrow cabin. He turns, offering his hand to steady me as I follow. Inside, the air smells of oil and damp canvas. The seat is cold beneath me, the space close and intimate; it's less adventure than awkward proximity. Still, my pulse thrums with exhilaration.

I pull the flying helmet over my hair, fastening the strap beneath my chin. Through the small window ahead, I can see the pilot in his open cockpit, shoulders hunched against the wind, goggles already in place. Sidney adjusts his own with the ease of a man accustomed to control.

The pilot checks his instruments, then raises a gloved hand to signal the ground crew.

The engine catches with a deep, chest-filling roar. The world trembles. The propeller blurs into motion, and the aircraft lurches forward. Wheels bump over the grass; a breath later we're airborne. The airfield drops away, its edges softening to green and brown patchwork. Above us, the sky widens into an impossible blue. I breathe it in – the sheer, dizzying lightness of it.

'Well?' Sidney watches me, his mouth twitching.

The laugh rises before I think. Not for him. Not to please him. For me.

Higher and higher we climb. The earth falls away, swallowed by a lid of cloud – thick, grey, endless. The light dims: the air feels close, pressing from every side. Then, with a sudden shudder, we break through.

Sunlight pours across the cabin in shards. Blue opens above us.

Raw, unbroken. The sun burns at its centre. Brilliant and whole. The aircraft hums steadily. It's indifferent, as though nothing remarkable has occurred, yet time itself seems to hold its breath.

I think of Maurice – briefly, intrusively – and of Sidney's talk of patterns and forces larger than us. I remember his expression then, searching for something that wasn't there.

My husband shifts beside me, turning his head. Our eyes meet. His hand finds mine. Not affection, not apology. Recognition, perhaps; that we are bound, if not joined. The strap tightens beneath my chin, and I realise I'm grinning. Not because of him, but because I'm here, rising above the ordinary at last. I hold his gaze.

It begins.

The light shifts. An eerie silver bleeds across the sky. A false twilight, unnatural and absolute, deepens around us. The air grows cold. I press the small rectangle of welder's glass to my eyes, just as Sidney does the same. We shield ourselves from the sun's final moments before it vanishes completely.

Then, the world exhales.

A perfect black disc hangs in the sky. The corona flares in tendrils of ghostly fire. The stars burn bright, scattered across a sky that should not hold them at midday. The aircraft hums beneath us. Steady. It's indifferent to the miracle unfolding beyond its wings.

I lower the glass. My breath catches.

Sidney does the same. He watches with something unreadable in his expression: part calculation, part wonder, perhaps. His fingers tighten briefly around mine. A rare moment of stillness. We exist in a world suspended beyond time. Beyond reason. Just us, the machine, and the sky.

The first sliver of sunlight reappears far too soon. A burst of blinding radiance – the diamond-ring effect – flares through the atmosphere. Sidney jerks his gaze away first.

'Glasses.'

I snap mine back into place. I blink against the sudden brilliance. The temperature rises instantly. The golden wash of daylight floods back into the world. Did we imagine the darkness entirely? The pilot steadies the aircraft. He tilts us slightly as we begin our descent. The land below stretches out once more.

I turn to Sidney, grinning. 'Let's do that again.'

He chuckles. He shakes his head. 'You're insatiable.'

'Perhaps,' I say. The exhilaration still hums through me. It's as tangible as the thrum of the aircraft beneath us. 'I want to fly,' I say. 'Not as a passenger. Not beside someone. Alone.'

He looks at me then – truly looks – as if realising something too late.

Architects of Bloomsbury

September 1928

For all my post-flight bravado, I haven't figured out my path back to the sky. Sometimes, though, I feel the echo of it – that thin, bright air where I wasn't anyone's wife. Ahead, Woolf's house glows faintly. The façade is stark, softened only by the amber spill of a lamp in the upstairs window. Inside, the rooms will already be alive with voices, laughter rising and falling like a tide. A meeting ground dense with argument, wit, and the relentless pursuit of art. Virginia is genuinely interested in what I have to say, and that's one of the many reasons why I like her. Sidney takes my arm, but it's my pace that carries us forward. We've found a kind of equilibrium again, he and I. Not closeness. Not estrangement. A *draft of peace* that holds so long as no one looks too closely.

There's a figure on the front steps. He's perched with an air of casual possession and exhales a long plume of smoke.

'Good evening, Maurice,' I say – calm, measured – the way one greets a shadow they've finally turned to face.

For years he's lived at the edges of our marriage, in silences and in half-truths. We've met before but tonight is sharper. The stakes have shifted recently into his demands. Now he's flesh and voice, the tilt of his head, the glint of intellect sharpened by mischief. Handsome, yes, but magnetic in a way that makes people bend towards him without realising. I'm not here to bend.

Maurice flicks ash into the night and grins. 'The Russell Cookes. Late. That never bodes well for a currency.'

'Currencies survive volatility. What matters is whether they hold their value,' I reply.

'You've kept *our* husband from me, Melville. He owes me an evening.'

'If Sidney owes anything,' I say, 'he settles it privately. We've no need of witnesses.' I brush us past him and into the hall.

Maurice stills for a heartbeat, amused but caught. Sidney laughs – too quickly, too loudly. His grip on my hand tightens. More performance than possession.

The hallway is narrow, and rich with scent: Turkish coffee, beeswax, cigarette smoke clinging to velvet. I graze the deep green walls with my fingertips. The paint is cool and clean. A landscape by Roger Fry looms, the strokes thick and impatient. I feel that way sometimes too. Beyond, the sitting room flickers with movement. Virginia's voice, quick and sardonic, threads through layered conversation. Sidney slips ahead. He belongs here, among the clever, the untethered. I used to consider myself an interloper in rooms like this. Over the last year I've recognised something simple: we belong where we speak, not where we're invited. And tonight, I'm claiming my seat.

The room is grand and cluttered, austere and intimate. Books rise in uneven towers. Virginia reclines, dark hair pinned haphazardly. Lytton sprawls. Forster murmurs. Leonard hovers. I've stepped into a living manuscript.

'Good,' Virginia says, spotting us. 'Cookie, we need your rational mind. We were just about to arrive at a conclusion, and that simply won't do.'

Sidney bows with mock solemnity. I stay standing until Virginia gestures. 'Melville. Sit. You're the only one here still capable of objectivity.'

'I wouldn't be so sure,' I say, settling opposite her.

'Then we are doomed to bias. No matter. The question is this – *Is the pursuit of change more intoxicating than the change itself?*'

'The chase,' says Lytton. 'Once you catch the fox, it's only a carcass.' He winks at Maurice.

'Charming.' Forster sighs.

'Progress demands motion,' Maurice interjects. 'We never really catch the fox. We just convince ourselves we have.' Lytton bats at his arm.

'Markets or love?' Leonard asks.

Virginia turns to me. 'And you? Do we chase, or do we build?'

The fire crackles. I hold their gaze 'We chase to feel alive,' I say. 'But we build so the feeling doesn't vanish when the chase ends.' I smile at Maurice, and he nods before looking back at Lytton. I see the eye roll they exchange.

'And what have you built, my dear?'

Sidney leans closer, brushing my hand. A motion for the room, not for me. I let it rest but keep my eyes on Virginia.

'A life,' I say. 'A life that's mine. One not defined by Father's *Titanic*, or by anyone else's surname.' I smile at my husband, and he feigns injury to his heart.

Virginia raises her glass. 'To life. And to the architects of it.'

Glasses clink and the fire shifts.

Cold Floors

November 1928

The cold has a way of seeping into old houses. Through window frames, under doors, up through the floorboards. I feel it now, pressing into the soles of my feet as I stand barefoot outside Sidney's study. The slate tiles are unforgiving beneath me.

Since Bloomsbury, the house has carried a different gravity. Not in the rooms themselves, but in him. Sidney met Maurice the morning after and came home to a letter. He's been changed since – brittle, watchful, like something he thought was secure has been quietly taken from him. It's persisted and deepened since.

The door tonight is ajar. A cry, or an oversight. I can't tell. I see the slope of Sidney's shoulders, the glass in his hand, the pipe cooling in its rest. The room smells of smoke and something metallic underneath.

'Sidney?'

His head lifts too fast. The flicker of guilt is brief, but unmistakable.

'I didn't hear you,' he says. He straightens, preparing for scrutiny. 'What time is it?'

'Past ten.'

'You should be in bed.'

'I might say the same.'

I cross the threshold. My diary is tucked under my arm – ballast, yes, but also witness. The fire in the hearth casts a dull orange light. It doesn't touch the cold between us.

'You're writing again,' he says.

'Still,' I correct. 'Someone needs to remember what actually happened. Not just what was convenient.'

His mouth hardens. 'You always did prefer narrative to people.'

'My narratives don't lie.' I don't raise my voice, but the words land hard anyway.

Silence. Heavy. Familiar.

Finally – too casually – he says, 'Maurice wrote again today.'

'I saw the envelope.'

A beat. The room holds its breath.

'He wants me in Cornwall this time. A month. Perhaps longer. There's work that needs … alignment.'

'Will you go?'

He studies the amber in his glass as if it might give him permission.

'Would it trouble you?' he asks.

'What would trouble me,' I say, 'is if you pretended you didn't want to.'

He blinks – and there it is: not desire, not longing – shame. 'You think I've grown distant.'

'I think you're trying to live two lives in the same skin.' I sit. I don't look away. 'And only one of them has room for me.'

He turns sharply towards the window, his silhouette thin against the frost-silvered glass. 'You think this is about him.'

'It always was.'

He flinches, barely, but the movement is real.

'I don't ask for confession, Sidney,' I say, rising. 'But I won't be made into a shadow of your indecision. If you're leaving me for him, leave honestly.'

The fire shifts. A log splits with a soft collapse. I've heard rumours of John Maurice Kean's other affairs and the trail of tragedy that follows.

My husband doesn't answer. He doesn't need to. I step back into the hall. The floor is still cold beneath my feet, but I walk taller.

Hunting at Naseby

November 1929

The ground is iron beneath its frost; each hoofbeat rings sharp against it. The sky is a pale, unsparing blue. The kind that refuses warmth. Breath hangs white in the air. Another year married, and again Sidney has gone to Cornwall as the leaves begin to fall. He calls it compromise. I call it arrangement. Maurice has his schedule of lovers, each assigned their weeks or months, and I pretend not to mind when my husband is summoned. Down there, on that southern coast, he belongs to Maurice – who has a habit of claiming time the moment my husband remembers to offer me any.

The scent of damp earth and horseflesh drifts through the countryside as I step down from the motorcar. The Pytchley Meet at Naseby is already in motion. Riders gather in small knots, red hunting coats flaring against the browns and greens of late autumn. Horses shift, breath pluming in the chill. I adjust my stock tie and smooth it beneath the lapels of my dark riding jacket. The bowler sits firm, with its brim shielding my eyes from the weak morning sun. There are glances. Curious, but not unkind. A woman arriving alone by motorcar remains a novelty here, but it isn't the vehicle they're watching. It's me.

'Mrs Russell Cooke,' a voice calls. Warm with familiarity. Davenport, already mounted, approaches. His dapple-grey stands square and still beneath him. His coat is faultless. His expression carries its usual irreverence. He finds the entire performance both absurd and amusing.

'Davenport,' I return.

A groom steadies my bay gelding: recently acquired, good-tempered, sure-footed. Riding has become a quiet obsession. One that tends to favour good weather. Yet the first time the horse gathered beneath me, I experienced a comparable lift to how I felt above the clouds during the eclipse. A body answering its own momentum. Something new to master. Sidney laughed when I insisted on proper lessons. He forgets I don't take up anything idly. This is my first hunt, though. I nearly turned back home, but I didn't.

I gather the reins and mount. The shift of weight, the readiness of the animal – it steadies me.

Davenport watches. 'Marvellous seat. I imagine your parents would be scandalised. Or delighted.'

'Both,' I say, settling my gloves. 'My father never shied from opportunity. Neither do I.'

He nods. 'A woman of enterprise among a sea of inherited fortunes. Quite the thing.'

'As is your presence,' I counter, easing my horse to move beside his. 'A man of finance with no patience for the machinery that funds your peers. You're meant to admire them, you know.'

'I do,' he says, dryly. 'For their ability to preserve whole empires in mahogany writing desks while lifting barely a finger.' He gestures at a group of gentlemen in crimson coats, deep in conversation. 'Some are still puzzling over what Sidney and I mean by "Imperial Finance" in our latest paper.'

Sidney's name feels oddly abstract out here. I laugh – brittle, involuntary. 'He's in Cornwall again,' I say, before Davenport can ask. 'His time with Maurice.'

Davenport tilts his head, the trace of a smile forming. 'Still taking turns, then?'

'Apparently,' I reply. 'And I gather the rota's expanded again.'

'Ah,' he says lightly, adjusting his reins. 'So, the faithful must queue.'

'Something like that.' I keep my tone even. 'It's been their arrangement for more than a year now.'

'And does it hold?'

'For them, perhaps,' I say. 'For the rest of us, it depends on the weather.'

I glance ahead. The Duke of York has arrived and is speaking with the Master of Hounds. He catches my eye and tips his hat. I incline my head in return.

'I don't wait, though,' I say. 'Not anymore.'

Davenport studies me with something between admiration and concern. 'You've built quite the life. President of the Newport Women's Liberal Association. Fluent in old money and new politics. What's next? A yacht?'

I smile. 'Why not? I've learnt not to wait for invitations. I make my own.'

'Then you must come to Cowes next summer. I'll see you placed on a fast boat, with someone clever at the helm.'

'Tempting. Though I'm quite capable myself.'

He chuckles. 'Yes. I rather think you are.'

Beyond the rising conversation, the hounds lift their voices. The start is near. Riders shift into place. Saddles creak, breath clouds, and the field hums with anticipation.

'There's a ball tomorrow evening, if you haven't heard,' Davenport says. 'You'll come?'

'I will now.' I draw in a breath. The cold stings, bracing and clean. The horn sounds. We move forward, into the wild. 'But first, let's ride.'

The field opens. The hounds surge forward. The horse beneath me gathers itself, and I let myself go with it.

A Living Masterpiece

March 1930

The backstage air is thick with powder and perfume, sharp under the gaslights. A glint of gilt paint clings to the air. It's still drying on the great wooden frames that will house us. Beyond the curtain, the Prince of Wales Theatre murmurs with expectation. The night's guests – baronets, ambassadors, curious duchesses, their bejewelled necks craned – await a parade of spectacle in aid of the Italian Art Exhibition. Not a single painting on canvas. Instead, flesh rendered still. The world's finest Renaissance works made live. Tableaus. For sixty seconds at a time, a portrait steps from the wall.

I stand beneath a fluted mirror, unmoving as a dresser adjusts my headdress. My gown is impossibly heavy: brocade lined with stitched gold, its hem puddled in a circle at my feet. Painted skin, perfumed hair, a neck stiff with jewels. Tonight, I'm Pharaoh's daughter. I don't fidget. I breathe slowly. I've learnt to carry weight well.

'Melville Russell Cooke, you look imperial,' says Cecilia Fairburn, gliding past in Titian red. Her pearls wink with every turn of her head. 'Utterly fit for worship.'

'Perhaps I am.' I extend a gloved hand and examine my fingers as though born to such pageantry. 'Though I imagine Simon and Priscilla might have something to say about that.'

'Only if they saw you,' says Lady Anne Latimer, tucking a wimple around her golden hair. 'Which they won't, of course. Mothers don't dress up as Moses's saviour every evening.'

'Not unless they're lucky,' I murmur. It's only half a joke. I think of the children briefly, left in safe hands with Mrs Lane. Simon, who already loathes being watched and flinches at applause. Priscilla, who insists on orchestrating elaborate tea parties for dolls. She performs and would revel in it. There's something of the stage in her already.

'And Sidney?' someone asks. I don't bother to check who. It's always the question.

I smile into the mirror, smoothing my gloves. 'He's in Vienna. Or perhaps it was Rome. No … Trieste. Something diplomatic.'

'Always in motion, that one,' says Cecilia. 'Are you sure he's not leading some secret mission for His Majesty?'

The room laughs. I don't. I'd thought all that finished – or perhaps I only hoped.

If they'd seen the brown envelopes left open on his desk, or the names threaded in cipher through his journal, they wouldn't be laughing. But of course they haven't. They don't know my husband is coming apart, that he's somewhere at sea on a so-called health cruise, far from me and the children. Even his handwriting has changed – the lines tilt upward now, as though trying to climb out of something nameless.

'At least it leaves you to shine,' says Elizabeth Harcourt, fastening an earring. 'You've become quite the figure in your own right, Mel.'

There was a time that sentence would have wounded. Now it's accurate. I nod, accepting it. It's no longer new, this attention. I've cultivated it. I was the stranger in this world once. The girl with a dead captain for a father. Now I move among them without asking permission. On stage, in parliament rooms, in editorials. Mrs Russell Cooke, champion of reform, figure of grace.

'One minute,' a stagehand calls.

We move, not rushed. Trained. Each woman steps into her frame. We hold our breath as though preparing to sink beneath water. I take my place in the centre of the *Finding of Moses*, arm outstretched, eyes tilted skyward. Somewhere in the theatre's front rows, a man with a pencil will draw me. Another will remember the exact shade of my skin in the footlights.

The curtain lifts. Gasps. The hush is total. In this moment, we're not women. We're myth. We're artefact. We're untouchable. The tableau holds. I steady my balance, quiet my breath. And I think, for the smallest second, of my father. Still lost beneath ice. Of the telegram that never came. Of the life he wanted me to build. I wonder if he'd recognise me now.

The curtain falls. Applause blooms like a struck match. We breathe again.

'That,' Cecilia says, reaching for my hand as we step into the wings, 'was glorious.'

I incline my head, still half within the role. 'Let's see if they remember us tomorrow.'

Unravelling Threads

June 1930

He came back thinner from the health cruise to Lisbon. Not in body, but in outline. Something essential had been scraped away. Since then, he's not been right. Two months of silences, of late nights, of study doors locked when they never used to be. He won't tell me why. I've stopped assuming the reason is singular. Lisbon? Maurice? The Foreign Office? Or something darker still.

The door creaks faintly as I push it open further. My footsteps are hesitant on the worn rug. The curtains are drawn, though the morning is already well underway. The room smells of cold ash, tobacco burnt to its bitter end, and yesterday's brandy left unfinished. It's the scent of withdrawal. Not from drink, but from the world itself.

'Sidney?' I call softly. My voice barely carries over the muffled tick of the clock on the mantel.

He doesn't respond. I find him slumped in the chair by the hearth. His dressing gown is pulled tightly around his chest, bracing against a cold only he can feel. His face is pale, his cheeks gaunt in the early light, and a shadow of stubble darkens his jawline. A familiar weight settles in my chest. It's been weeks since he's truly engaged with the world. Barely speaking to the children, avoiding visitors, retreating into this room as if the outside has nothing left to offer him.

'The twins want you,' I say softly. 'They've built a tower in the playroom. Taller than Simon. He's itching to knock it over, Priscilla's guarding it like a fortress.'

I wait.

His fingers twitch slightly against the armrest, but his gaze doesn't shift from the grate. The fire's long since gone out.

'You're disappearing,' I say. Not an accusation – a fact. 'They miss you. I miss you.'

Nothing. Then, at last, he looks up. His eyes are dull, sunken.

'What's the point?' His voice is not dramatic. It's the voice of someone describing the weather. 'What's the point of any of it?'

I crouch beside him, the floor cold against my knees. I rest a hand on his sleeve. His skin is clammy beneath it.

'I don't know what's happened,' I say, barely above a whisper. 'You won't tell me. You won't speak of Lisbon. Or Maurice. Or why the Foreign Office has rung twice in three days. You wake from dreams already exhausted. I don't need everything – I never have. But you must speak to someone.'

He lets out a quiet, humourless laugh. It doesn't reach his eyes. 'You've always been better at knowing what things mean.'

'That's not true.'

'Isn't it?' he murmurs. 'You belong in this world. You've built something. With or without me. I…'

He shifts his gaze to the desk. It's covered in letters, most unopened. A few names are circled in red. The blotter is stained with ink, the pattern of someone writing, then crossing out.

'You're their father, Sidney. You're still their centre.'

'You've seen how they look at me now,' he says, with a flicker of something near grief. 'As though I've disappeared but forgotten to tell them.'

I reach for his hand. He flinches. Doesn't pull away but doesn't return the pressure.

'Do you want me to arrange another health cruise?' I ask gently. 'Just another couple of weeks. Warmer air. Quieter skies.'

'I need to think,' he mutters, moving toward the desk.

A dull gleam – not polished, not cared for – the kind of metal kept close out of habit, not need. Half-hidden beneath papers. The sight jolts me colder than the morning floorboards. My breath catches, a sudden chill running down my spine.

'Sidney,' I say slowly, rising to my feet. 'Why is that there?'

He hesitates, his hand brushing the edge of the desk. 'It's nothing,' he says after a moment, his tone dismissive. 'I meant to clean it. Just haven't got round to it.'

'Then put it away.' My voice steadies – quiet, but firm. 'Now, please. The children might consider it a toy.'

For a moment, I think he might argue, but then he nods. He slides the revolver into the desk drawer with a clunk. He doesn't meet my eyes as he locks it and slips the key into his pocket.

'Who knows?' I ask quietly. 'Who knows where you are, truly?'

'Nobody.' The word bursts with anger.

I hold his gaze. 'Then someone should.'

That stops him. He looks away first. 'I'll come down for breakfast,' he says quietly, though I can see the lie in the set of his jaw. 'Tell the twins I'll join them soon.'

I nod, not trusting myself to speak, and step back towards the door. My heart is too heavy. It's weighted with all the words he won't let me use. As I leave the room, I glance back once. I catch a glimpse of him leaning heavily against the desk, his head bowed. I've seen men vanish before. Into water, into duty, into myth. This time, I'm watching it happen in the same room.

A Room of Her Own

July 1930

The operation was scheduled, though they said it couldn't wait. Now I lie propped against white linen, stitched and sore, while the city carries on beyond the window as if nothing has been taken.

The room is never still. The ceiling fan ticks at the end of each slow turn. Down the corridor, a trolley squeaks past at steady intervals. The window is open just enough for a thin breeze and the faint rattle of traffic from the Embankment. The air smells of antiseptic – sharp as soap, without its mercy.

A book rests in my lap, unread. Each breath pulls at the stitches; not agony, just insistence. I haven't seen the children since Sunday. I sent word that I was only resting, that I'd be home soon. I didn't want them to see me like this: pale, hollowed, hemmed in by stiff hospital sheets, with tubes at my wrist and a needle in the crook of my arm.

Sidney lingers in the doorway too long, imprinting the room, committing it to memory. Once, he'd have crossed the room immediately. Now, he waits to be invited into his own life. I heard that he returned early, two days ago, from the latest health cruise. Now he's arrived without fanfare. No flowers. Just a folded newspaper under his arm and his own flask of coffee, as though determined to frame it all as ordinary. As though I'm not lying here, sutured and stitched and shivering.

'You're awake,' he says, finally.

'You're back.'

He pours the coffee into a cup and hands it to me without comment. His hand trembles. Only slightly, but enough to make me pause. It isn't the tremor of travel fatigue or guilt. It's deeper, lodged in the bones, and that unsettles me more than the incision at my side. Whatever has haunted him these past weeks is still here, breathing through him. His skin is thinner. His eyes more sunken. His mind seems to spin behind his gaze, darting ahead of the room, searching for a way out.

I take the cup deliberately, steadying both our hands. The gesture surprises him – and settles me. 'I'm glad you came home,' I say. Not softly. As a statement.

'Of course,' he replies, but his voice is already elsewhere. 'Maurice isn't taking my calls,' he says, eventually. 'Apparently he's … unavailable.'

It's the closest he's come to saying: *I am no longer chosen*. Like someone ashamed of once needing another man too deeply. Whatever thread bound them has been stretched too far – or severed. I say nothing.

'You've had your procedure,' he says, glancing at the chart.

'Don't make it sound so mechanical,' I answer. 'They cut me open. They removed something. I'm held together with twine and prayer.'

He flinches – not visibly, but in the tightening at his jaw and the hard blink that betrays more than he intends. He sets the newspaper on the chair beside him without unfolding it.

'I'll be in Portsmouth next week. They want to inspect Davenport's *Coralyn* before Cowes.'

I nod, fingers pressing into the edge of the sheet. 'And after?'

'There's talk of a lecture series. Cairo. Possibly Athens.'

'So vague, and yet already planned.'

He exhales through his nose. 'You can't expect me to sit beside a bed and wait.'

'I'm not asking you to wait,' I say. 'I'm asking whether you remember how to be here.'

No reply. The silence stretches thin. A nurse enters, checks my temperature. Her eyes flick between us, politely unreadable. When she leaves, Sidney stands and adjusts his sleeve – a nervous tic, brushing at dust that isn't there.

'The children will visit tomorrow,' he says. 'Morning or afternoon?'

'Neither. I'll be home soon.'

He nods. Once. Then again, slower. Our eyes meet for a moment that might have been something – recognition, apology, return – but it isn't.

As he turns, the door catches against the air. For a second, I think he'll glance back. He doesn't.

TRAGIC ACCIDENT AT A TEMPLE FLAT

The sudden death of Mr Sidney Russell Cooke, 38, was reported yesterday following a tragic accident at his residence in King's Bench Walk, Temple.

Mr Russell Cooke, a distinguished figure and the husband of Mrs Helen Melville Russell Cooke, formerly Miss Smith, daughter of the late Captain Edward J. Smith, notably of *RMS Titanic*, succumbed to an injury sustained while attending to his firearm in the privacy of his study.

The accident occurred late on Friday evening, and despite immediate medical attention, Mr Russell Cooke's injuries proved fatal. It is understood that the firearm discharged unexpectedly during routine maintenance.

Mr Russell Cooke was widely respected for his contributions to local affairs and was known for his intellectual pursuits and connections to notable figures in British society. He leaves behind his wife and their two young children, Simon and Priscilla.

The family has requested privacy during this period of bereavement. A private funeral service is to be held later this week at St Mary's Church, with close family and friends in attendance.

The Times, 4 July 1930

7th July 1930

They say I'm not well enough to leave hospital. They mean watch her, not heal her. The incision aches, but it's clean. They check my pulse as if that's the thing that might break.

Sidney is dead.

The words still feel foreign in my mouth. As if a truth spoken too early hasn't yet settled into the world. He was here the day before. He brought his own coffee. He was already departing.

They found him in our Temple rooms.

Shot in the stomach.

Not quick.

It's the not quick that holds me by the throat.

There was order to the room: his shirt laid out, his papers stacked, the curtains drawn against the river light. No note. Just the shape of a man who had already stepped away.

Before the bullet ever struck.

He had been fading for months. I saw it in the pause before he spoke, the slackness of his hands, the way laughter left him too soon. He stopped reading to the children. Stopped calling me by my name. He moved through rooms like a man rehearsing how to vanish.

And there were the other things – the coded cables, the midnight callers, the sense of being watched. I told myself it was nerves. Exhaustion. The residue of whatever he and Maurice had unravelled between them. Now I wonder whether he chose the only exit he still believed he owned.

The children don't know. Simon will ask whether Papa has gone to Cowes. Priscilla will press her face into Mrs Lane's collar and wait for me to explain.

I don't yet know how to explain a silence that will not end.

Mother will come. She'll say grief can be managed. Contained.

Tamed. I remember how her hands shook when she said it back then, though she believed she was steady.

I swore I wouldn't become her.

And yet I lie here, fists closed against the shaking. Did I love him? Yes. Even in the half-life we made. Even when I knew I wasn't his only tether. Love isn't innocence. It's persistence. He wasn't always kind. He wasn't always present. But he was mine to lose.

Our children are his continuation. And now I must carry both them and the weight of how he left.

I wanted to break the pattern.

The captain taken by the sea. The husband taken by silence. The children left to inherit absence like an heirloom.

But grief, once it has chosen a house, doesn't knock. It remembers the way in.

Accidental Death

July 1930

Someone has removed the crossword from this morning's *The Times*, as though blank squares might remind me of unanswered questions. I read what they left:

CLEANING MISHAP – VERDICT OF ACCIDENTAL DEATH IN RUSSELL COOKE INQUEST

An inquest was held yesterday at the Westminster Coroner's Court into the sudden and tragic death of Mr Sidney Russell Cooke, who was found at his London residence on the morning of Thursday, July 3rd, suffering from fatal gunshot wounds. The proceedings were presided over by Dr F. J. Waldo, with a jury in attendance.

Mrs Russell Cooke, who remains indisposed in a London nursing home following an operation, was not in attendance. However, the family was represented at the inquiry, which examined the circumstances surrounding Mr Russell Cooke's untimely passing.

A double-barrelled sporting gun, a bottle of oil, and various cleaning apparatus were brought before the court as evidence, suggesting that Mr Russell Cooke had been engaged in the maintenance of his firearm at the time of the incident. Testimony was heard from Mr Frederick Archibald Hugo Pitman, of Mulberry Walk, Chelsea, who stated that he had last seen the deceased on Wednesday evening at the offices of Rowe & Pitman, 43 Bishopsgate. He remarked that Mr Russell Cooke had recently made arrangements for a grouse-shooting weekend in Scotland, which he had anticipated with great enthusiasm.

Further evidence was provided by Mr Oliver Paget who assured the court that the deceased was of sound financial standing, happily married, and had exhibited no signs of distress or despondency. He noted that Mr Russell Cooke had been working particularly hard in recent months but dismissed any notion of undue strain. He further remarked that the deceased had a long-standing aversion to blood, an observation which appeared to cast doubt on the possibility of self-inflicted injury.

Dr Westerman, who conducted the post-mortem examination, gave his medical opinion regarding the nature of the wounds, describing a gunshot injury approximately one inch to the left of the abdomen, with a secondary wound two inches below. The immediate cause of death was determined to be heart failure and haemorrhage. Dr Westerman stated that the barrel of the gun must have been between two and six inches from the skin at the time of discharge. While he initially considered the possibility of self-infliction, further examination of the position of the body and weapon led him to favour an accidental cause.

During the inquiry, one juror inquired how Mr Russell Cooke, if seated at the time, came to be found lying on his back. This prompted a dramatic demonstration in court with the sporting gun in question, allowing the jury to assess the plausibility of an accidental discharge while handling the weapon. The positioning of the firearm and the nature of the injuries were deemed consistent with the misfiring of a gun in the process of being cleaned.

At the conclusion of the proceedings, the jury returned a verdict of accidental death, a finding in which the coroner concurred. Dr Waldo, in summing up, joined the jury in expressing their deepest sympathies to Mrs Russell Cooke and the bereaved family at this most distressing time.

They say *accidental*. They must. The alternative is too disruptive to their order.

I'm too tired to argue with the world today.

Funeral Attire

July 1930

Grief has settled into the house like damp. Seeping into every wall, every breath. The muffled sounds of Ada setting the breakfast table reach me from the dining room, but I have no appetite. The smell of egg makes me retch. The parlour is dim, the thick curtains barely letting in the grey July light. Outside, the rain clings to the leaves in uneven drops, and the garden is overgrown. The stitches pull when I breathe too deeply. The doctor said I was mending well. People like to say 'well' when they mean 'surviving'. I've learnt to hold myself carefully, as though my own body might bruise at the slightest thought.

Priscilla mimicked Sidney this morning. Same tilt of the chin, same clipped reply. 'That's not a question for the children,' she said, when Simon asked about the moon. I watched her face for a long time. We teach more by accident than design. She's learning how to close doors before they're knocked upon. I recognise the gesture. That's the inheritance I fear most.

It's my husband's funeral today. Once, I'd believed marriage was a harbour – that I'd stepped off the deck of my father's sinking world and onto steadier land. But I see now I didn't outrun the tide. I chose a man already half-claimed by it.

I sit in the armchair near the hearth. Newspaper cuttings in my lap. My hands twist the black gloves I should already be wearing. Across the room, the twins' shoes lie neatly by the door. Their tiny scuffs are a reminder of how fast they've grown over the past seven years. Priscilla asked me yesterday why Papa wasn't coming back. I couldn't find the words to explain again. How do you tell a child their father is truly gone? Not just gone – lost to something so dark and consuming that even love can't pull him back. The notion of *accidental* doesn't soothe me.

The sound of footsteps on the stairs jolts me from my thoughts. Mother appears in the doorway. Her figure is as imposing as ever. She's dressed in black crepe. Her hat casts a shadow over her pale face. She holds Simon by the hand, his hair still damp from a hasty wash. She surveys me with the same assessing gaze she's used all my life.

'You're not dressed yet,' she says, her tone clipped. She considers grief something to be managed, like a stray thread on a hem. 'The car will be here shortly.'

'I'm almost ready,' I say, though my voice sounds small and uncertain. My fingers tighten around the gloves in my lap.

'It matters how we present ourselves,' she says. Her voice wavers – very slightly – and I realise she's afraid, too. She remembers what it is to be the woman left behind.

Simon shakes free of her grasp and runs to me. He climbs into my lap, the clippings falling to the floor, and presses his face into my shoulder. Pain shoots up my side, but I hold him close. I feel the warmth of his small body against mine. He's quieter than usual. His boundless energy is subdued these past weeks. I don't know if he fully understands what's happening today, but he knows enough to sense the weight of it.

'You will spoil his suit,' Mother says sharply. Her gloved hands adjust the hatpin at the side of her head. 'And Priscilla's hair is unruly. You will need to see to it before we leave.'

'Their father has just died. You want dignity? Let it be in truth, not in crepe and polished shoes.' The words escape before I can stop them. 'Does it matter if her hair isn't perfect?'

Mother's eyes narrow and the faintest wrinkle forms at the corner of her mouth. 'It matters how we present ourselves,' she repeats. 'There will be people watching. Whispering. You know what they will say if we don't hold ourselves with dignity.'

I glance down at Simon, stroking his hair absently. 'What they say doesn't matter,' I mutter, though I don't quite believe it.

'Of course it matters,' she counters. She steps further into the room. 'Have you forgotten the whispers after your father died? The speculation, the blame? And yet we endured. That's what we must do now. Endure.'

The mention of Father sends a chill through me. The familiar knot tightens in my chest. The *Titanic* is never far from any of us, no matter how many years pass. It lingers in every conversation and in every headline. Now, in the shadow of Sidney's death, it's closer than ever.

'You think this is a curse, don't you?' I ask quietly, my voice trembling. 'That the *Titanic* is still pulling us under. Even now?'

Mother's expression hardens. Her lips press into a thin line. 'Superstition is for the weak,' she says firmly. 'This family has endured enough without succumbing to such nonsense. Your father's death was a tragedy, and so is Sidney's, but neither of them defines those who remain… Us. Do you understand?'

I shake my head. 'I think grief repeats itself when we are taught silence,' I say.

I glance at Simon's shoes on the floor, the scuffed toes a stark contrast to the polished black of mine. I want to believe Mother. I want to hold onto the strength she so easily projects, but I can't ignore the fear gnawing at the edges of my mind. *If the* Titanic's *shadow still looms over us, how can I protect the children from it?*

'I need a moment,' I say, my voice barely above a whisper. Mother gives a curt nod, gathering her skirts and turning back toward the hallway. Grief is her domain. She's determined to guide me.

'Don't dawdle,' she calls over her shoulder. 'The car won't wait.'

I hold Simon a little tighter. His soft breath is warm against my neck. I close my eyes, trying to steel myself for what lies ahead. Today isn't about me, I remind myself. It's about Sidney. About showing the world that we love him, no matter how many shadows now linger at our door. I wonder if the twins will stay quiet during the funeral. Simon's barely spoken since Sidney's death, but Priscilla… She'll ask questions. They always come at the worst moments.

The faint creak of the car on the gravel reaches me from somewhere beyond the heavy curtains.

'Go and find your sister,' I say and my boy does as I ask.

I bend carefully to pick up the articles. I'll put them in the suitcase under my bed before I leave. Through the gap in the curtains, I catch sight of Ada crossing the garden. Her black cap bobs as she speaks to the driver. For a moment, it's almost comforting – something normal in a morning that is too far removed from ordinary life. But the air shifts. The unmistakable sense of something approaching that you've no language for until it stands in front of you.

And then I see him.

Maurice. Motionless at the car, rain streaking down his face until it's impossible to tell where the weather ends and grief begins. He's holding something under one arm, a hat, perhaps, and his stance is rigid. His head is slightly too bowed. He's familiar.

The air in the room tightens around me. A chill moves up my spine. For a moment, I can't move and he doesn't step forward. He doesn't wave or call out. He just stands there. Still and solemn, like a statue in Lichfield. I glance at the clock on the mantel, at the black band around its face marking the hour, count the three minutes it has lost, and then back at the window. The rain streaks down the glass, blurring his outline further. Ada takes his hand and guides him towards the front door.

The sound of the latch pulls me back to the room. Ada speaks to him – quiet words I can't make out – and then the heavy sound of boots on the entryway floor. My stomach knots. The footsteps approach. Slow and deliberate.

And then he's standing in the doorway. Soaked through with his hair damp, curling at his temples. His face is pale, with deep shadows under his eyes. My breath stumbles. Not from longing, from recognition. He's the only other person alive who knew the building of Sidney, brick by brick, and the unravelling too. We're not allies. We're not enemies. We're the witnesses left standing.

'Melville,' he says. The sound of my name is like a stone dropped in water. It ripples through me, scattering my thoughts.

'Maurice.' The word comes out barely above a whisper.

'I'm sorry,' he says. 'I ... wasn't sure if I should come here.'

Simon has returned. He's curious. Maurice ruffles my son's hair. 'Go and find your sister,' I repeat, sterner than necessary.

I grip the arm of the chair, grounding myself. The fear subsides slowly, replaced by an overwhelming sense of unease.

'You're soaked,' I say, my voice sharper than intended. 'Ada, fetch Mr Kean a towel.'

Ada hesitates for a moment, her gaze darting between us, then scurries off. I rise from the chair; my legs unsteady beneath me. Maurice doesn't step further into the room. Instead, he watches me carefully, waiting for permission to exist here.

'Why are you here?' I ask, the words tumbling out before I can stop them.

'I came because … Sidney … there is no one else who understands what has been lost,' he says. 'Not entirely. Not cleanly.'

The way he says Sidney's name, quiet and deliberate. It's like a thread pulling at an old wound. I glance away, focusing instead on the rain streaking the window. My heart's pounding, but I don't know if it's anger, sorrow, or something else entirely.

'Was he shot by the Russians?' My words rush. Unspoken until now. The absurdity of the question strikes me even as it leaves my mouth. Grief loosens logic before it loosens tears.

'No.' Topic closed. 'I'd seen him. The night before,' he continues, his voice faltering.

'Did you rejoin?' I ask and he shakes his head. I see his sorrow, his guilt, his regret.

'Do you think it suicide?' he asks.

'Inexperience cleaning guns,' I say, quietly but firmly.

'He was unravelling,' Maurice murmurs.

'And no one speaks of loneliness until it's too late,' I say.

My voice is harsher than it should be. The sound of the twins upstairs – their footsteps thundering across the ceiling – breaks the tension. Maurice glances up instinctively, his expression hardening.

'They'll be down soon,' I say, my tone firmer. 'The car's here.'

He nods. 'I won't keep you,' he says. 'I just … I wanted to say how sorry I am.'

I study him for a moment, searching his face. I see his weariness, the same kind that's been pressing on me since Sidney's death.

'Thank you,' I say finally.

I watch the rain blur his figure through the glass until he's gone. The children thunder above, loud and alive, and I cling to that sound as proof we're not yet pulled under.

Interruption Five

FEBRUARY 1973

The post was pushed under the door, paper rasping against the floorboards. Catherine rose slowly. The radiator was still cold, the flagstones biting at her feet.

Her makeshift desk waited exactly as she had left it: ordered transcripts, black-spined notebooks, the reel-to-reel poised in its stillness. The curtains were half-drawn, the early light flattening the room into muted grey.

Before she dressed, she pressed play.

Melville's voice unfurled: low, measured, certain. Today's section was the Mayfair dinner. Catherine had heard it before, yet it landed differently now.

I'd mistaken stillness for intimacy.
I'd mistaken rehearsal for permanence.

She stopped the tape. She didn't underline the line; she felt it. A quick, unwelcome tightening beneath the ribs.

Her notebook opened under her hand.

> *Notes –*
> *A life built in negotiation, not surrender.*
> *Endurance ceasing to function as identity.*
> *What they called a curse = repetition mistaken for fate.*

Her handwriting was neat, stripped of excess. Outside, a bicycle skidded, followed by laughter – students running late, untouched by whatever was tightening inside her.

She rewound the tape a few seconds and pressed play again. She closed her eyes. She hadn't anticipated this: that listening might begin rearranging her, line by line.

She wrote:

Daughter of the Titanic

To understand her, I must face the part of myself that lives by rehearsal.
The part that fears what begins when the performance ends.
The part that mistrusts the body – as though illness were inherited logic.

Her breath caught. She had never written the thought aloud before. On the page it looked too much like confession. She waited for the feeling to settle.

The envelopes rested on the floor. One was official paper, the medical seal stark even upside down. She stepped around it on her way to the window. Not yet. She wasn't ready. She had grown skilled at postponing herself – a habit forged in childhood wards and never quite shaken. Even now, it was easier to ignore the weight of test results than to open them.

Outside, winter dulled the river to pewter. She imagined walking there later, letting the cold steady her spine. Stillness unnerved her; it left too much space for the thoughts she tried to outrun.

Listening was no longer academic. Melville wasn't merely recounting a life – she was charting refusal, survival, the work of not disappearing. And in the small, frost-bitten room, the instruction settled somewhere deep, somewhere difficult.

Catherine sat again. She pressed play.

Two Widows

FEBRUARY 1973

The drawing room at Pratts was overheated, the coal fire working too hard. Warmth pooled in the carpet and rose through the wood panelling. Melville Russell Cooke sat near the window, shawl drawn close despite the stifling room. She looked smaller than she had at Christmas – not frail, merely stripped back to her essentials.

Catherine set the recorder on the table between them. Melville's eyes flicked to it, then to her.

'You've been listening again,' she said. 'You always bring her back with you.'

Her. Not *me*.

Catherine felt the correction land with more force than it should. She wasn't entirely sure anymore where the recordings ended and her own thoughts began. She took the opposite chair. Her hands were steady through will alone. Outside, the February light thinned against the fogged glass.

'You're paler,' Melville observed.

'I've been working.' It wasn't untrue. Still, work was the easiest explanation, the one no one questioned.

'On the Mother years.'

'Yes.'

A quiet formed – not tense, simply aware of itself.

Catherine opened her notebook but didn't yet touch her pen. 'You keep saying that everything that mattered went into the suitcase.'

Melville looked over, gaze level. 'That was before.'

'Before Sidney?'

'Before I understood the cost of being remembered.'

The line struck Catherine low in the chest, the familiar tightening she had begun to dread. She breathed through it.

'It would help to see it,' she said softly. 'For context, not scrutiny.'

'No.' Melville's refusal was gentle and absolute. 'Some things are kept intact by being unseen.'

Catherine nodded. A different answer. It wasn't lost? She didn't push further. The work had taught her that pressure only distorts what it seeks to reveal.

Melville turned back towards the window; the grey light caught along her jaw. 'You're reaching the part where I live as a widow,' she said. 'Be careful.'

'Careful of what?'

'Of turning grief into shape. It doesn't have one. It spreads. It colours what we remember – the dead, and ourselves.'

Catherine hesitated. 'And the curse? You've mentioned it less lately.'

Melville's smile was thin, almost amused. 'Because I never believed in it. Other people needed the word. It made the pattern easier to stomach.'

'And now?'

'Now I'd say this: naming it a curse is just another way of avoiding the truth.'

A log in the grate shifted, sending up a deeper glow. Catherine switched on the recorder.

'This next part isn't about tragedy.' Melville's voice settled into the room, measured and unbroken. 'It's about aftermath. They call it widowhood, as if it belongs to the man who's gone. But it's really about who remains.' She paused. 'There are two widows in this part…'

A Widow

ARCHIVE: REEL FIVE

From 1931

According to *The Times*, the estate of Mr Sidney Russell Cooke, of Bellecroft, Newport, Isle of Wight, who died under tragic circumstances at the age of 37, has been valued at £120,098 gross and £91,369 net. Probate of his will has been granted to Mrs Helen Melville Russell Cooke (née Smith), his widow.

The Widow's Watch

March 1931

Sidney's boots are too big, but I wear them anyway. The leather slaps loose at my heels, the laces frayed where his fingers once tied them tight. Each step along the garden path is a dull scuff and drag, as if Bellecroft's ground itself remembers him. At the lane's end, near the red post box, a figure lingers. A dark coat. Collar high. Too far to recognise, close enough to notice. I blink, and the space is empty. Some might call that an omen, I call it tiredness. The wind stirs, nothing more.

I turn back to the border. The daffodils are late this year – two weeks at least. Rows of green shoots stand stalled, like a sentence paused before its verb. I crouch and brush aside damp leaf mulch. The bulbs are intact. Waiting. Hesitant. Eight months from his death and I know how they feel.

Inside, the house is still. I climb the stairs, careful to soften my step. Simon's arm is flung above his head, his blanket kicked into a half-gesture. There's a line of dirt beneath his thumbnail, from the trench he dug for pretend soldiers this morning. Priscilla is a tangle of limbs and knitted blankets, sock half off, heel exposed. She always wriggles free before midnight. I pull the blanket back over her feet and pause. Watching them breathe is the only time I feel sure of anything. They sleep as if the world can't reach them, and I envy that.

The fire downstairs has burnt out. Only a thin plume of smoke drifts from the grate, the ash collapsed into itself. I don't relight it. The cold sharpens things. The magazine is still on the arm of the chair. *Life*, March 1931. The page is creased down the middle from where I folded it earlier, meaning not to come back to it. I do, though.

The article covers one page. Three columns. Two photographs. The first shows a cluster of men outside a railway siding in Ohio, most of them looking past the camera. The second is closer – a body: bare chest, slack jaw. The words Rock of Ages are tattooed in blue ink above the ribs. No name. Just what the locals called him – 'Silent Smith'. Lived rough on the edge of Lima, worked odd jobs, slept in boxcars. Said once, long ago, he'd captained a ship. A British ship. '*Titanic* sank,' he told a nurse. Said no more about it. The article claims he died in the rain, mid-February. Age uncertain. Mid-sixties, the coroner guessed. Possibly older. No documents. No family.

IS THIS OUR LONG-LOST CAPTAIN SMITH?

That's the headline.

I run my finger along the edge of the page. The tattoo. Rock of Ages. Father's hymn. He'd hum it when winding the hall clock. Said the rhythm steadied his hands. The man in the photograph isn't him. Logically, I know that. Father was born in 1850. He'd be eighty-one now. This man – the nose is too broad and the mouth sags. Still, there's something in the brow – the angle, perhaps? – that makes me pause.

Mother used to say the dead find their way back in fragments: a voice in a corridor, a shadow on a stair. I never believed her, but grief has its own gravity. It pulls you towards what you know is impossible, then dares you to look again. I stare until the image blurs. Then I tear the page from the magazine, fold it twice, and press it flat. It'll join the others in the suitcase. I open to a blank page in my diary and begin to write.

15th March

Cutting about Lima, Ohio. Wrong age. Wrong continent. And yet, I keep it. The tattoo has never appeared before. That makes twenty-four plausible sightings of Father.

I know the exact number, even though I pretend not to count. Twenty-three was the waiter in Montreal. Wouldn't give his name, but said Father always sat at the edge of the room, watching the door. Twenty-one was the Belfast woman who told a journalist she saw the captain stepping off a train, dry as dust and calm as stone. He didn't speak. Just looked straight at her, like he knew her name before she did.

That's just the sightings. There are other claims. Like the boy in Salt Lake City. Arrested last month, nineteen, thin as a fence post. He tried to pawn a suit that wasn't his. Said his name was John Smith. Said his life ended when his father, Captain Edward John Smith, went down with the *Titanic*. I sent away for the newspaper clipping, pretending to be a cousin. The face looks nothing like ours, but the weight in it – that I recognise.

I don't think I believe Father lived. Not truly. Not anymore. Believing that would sit alongside a possibility that he chose to stay away. Still, I keep the sightings, each one pressed flat in the suitcase. Not hope – I've outgrown that. It's order. A way to make loss behave, to stop it spreading. If others called it a curse, I call it containment. The diary, my ledger, never leaves this house.

Upstairs, a floorboard gives beneath the rug. I don't move. The fire stays cold, my hands fixed to the arm of the chair. Only now does it strike me: the *Life* magazine hadn't come with the post. No envelope. No note. Just lying on the hall table when I came down yesterday morning. The mat by the door was damp. As if someone had already stepped inside.

I close the diary and carry it to the suitcase on my writing desk. The clasps resist before snapping open. Inside, the clippings lie in their careful stack. I lift the top layer to settle my diary among them. That's when I see it. A postcard, slipped between two letters. *White Star Line*. Titanic, *Southampton, morning light on the hull*. The back is blank. No message, no name. Not mine.

Something placed here when I wasn't looking.

I slip the card into the diary and press the cover flat, though my fingers tremble. I bought a new one after Sidney died. A fresh ledger. I called it 'Widow'. Not as a title. A label awarded to me. Something to file this version of me within. Perhaps grief is easier when it's categorised. I used to think survival meant outlasting what haunts you. Now I know it involves learning its language.

I glance out the window. The garden bends eastward in the wind. The orchard gate knocks once. Pauses. Then again – like someone deciding whether to enter.

The Hallway

March 1931

'I saw him again,' she says – flat, certain, as if she were naming the weather.

My hand freezes on the hearth brush, knuckles grazing the heat. 'Who?' I ask.

Mother doesn't answer. Just stares at the hallway. Behind us, the wireless crackles, half swallowed by static. She insists on leaving it tuned to the *Light Programme*, though she never listens. A world still going on, she says. But I know she can't see the dials anymore. Not properly. I set her tea down on the small table beside the fire and adjust the lamp. She blinks into the new light and winces.

'Too bright?'

'No,' she says quickly, though she turns her face away.

I crouch to poke at the fire. It's low again. It never seems to take anymore. Not unless I start it from scratch. I don't say anything – just reposition the logs and wait.

'The milk's fresh,' I offer. 'I bought it from the man this morning.'

'Hmm.'

She's not really listening. Her hands, liver-spotted and fine-boned, rest in her lap. Idle. A blanket covers her knees but has slipped to one side. I lean over and pull it straight. The fire lets out a reluctant hiss and finally catches. A small flame licks up around the edges of the coal.

'I saw him again.'

'Who?'

Still, she doesn't answer. Her eyes are fixed on the doorway.

'Mother?'

Still nothing. Then, without turning her head, she says, 'He was in your hall. I felt him there. Watching.'

A pressure builds at the base of my spine. I glance over my shoulder, expecting nothing, and fearing something all the same. The hallway is empty of people: coat stand, sideboard, the little silver tray where Sidney used to keep his pocket change. The light bulb above the stairs hums faintly. Nothing out of place.

'I didn't hear anyone.'

'He wouldn't make a sound,' she says. 'Not him.'

There's no fear in her voice. No wonder, no strain. Just the quiet confidence of someone stating a fact. That, the calm in her voice, unsettles me most. It sounds like memory, not madness. The phrasing almost identical to what she said immediately after Father's death. A rhythm inherited, not remembered.

I return to the armchair opposite and sit. Her face has settled back into its usual expression – soft lines drawn by time and habit. Her hands still tremble slightly as she reaches for the teacup. She misses the handle the first time. I reach over to help her, but she waves me off, trying again more slowly.

Mother used to have such sharp eyes. Could spot a chip in the china from across the room. Everything has softened around her. Frayed edges. Blurred contours. The world no longer quite holds still. She doesn't say it, but I can see the frustration in her mouth when a button won't fasten or a key won't line up. Maybe the ghost is clearer than the cup. Easier to see something unreal than something slipping away. She's naming absence the only way she can. Perhaps that's what belief becomes in the end – a grammar for what refuses to stay. Mother sips once, then lets the saucer rest in her lap.

'Was it Father?' I ask.

The fire snaps. She doesn't answer.

'Did he speak?'

'No,' she says. 'He never does.'

On the table beside her, that postcard from last week sits tucked between the teacup and a receipt. I don't remember leaving it there. I don't think she could've found it in the suitcase. Weak eyesight and her fingers don't grip so well now. Still, it's turned face-up: *White Star Line. Titanic, Southampton, morning light on the hull.* We sit like that a while. The radio muttering. The fire sighing. Her breath slow and shallow, eyes half-shut. I stay longer than I mean to, watching the way the fire outlines her jaw. She has aged more in this one year than in the ten before. Her eyes are cloudy now. The hands that sewed hems and shelled peas without falter tremble if she lifts a cup. She wears Sidney's grief as if it were her own coat – too heavy, dragging her shoulders down – and I have let her carry it for me.

She drifts off around half past ten, chin dipping to her chest. I fetch a pillow from the sofa and wedge it firmly behind her head. If she won't admit to needing help, I'll give it anyway – quiet acts of care, like prayers said beneath breath. The living tending the nearly gone. The blanket has slipped again; this time I tug it tight and smooth it flat, as if order might hold her together a little longer. I stay beside her, but not idly. My eyes don't leave the hallway. I'm listening for it: the step, the shift, the thing she swore she saw. Part of me dares him to come.

The light above the stairs flickers, quick as a blink. I rise, take two steps towards the door, ready to prove it false. The bulb steadies. Empty air. Not tonight. Upstairs, the children breathe in their private rhythms. Simon curls his hand beneath his chin like a soldier at rest. Priscilla sprawls across both pillows; I slide one free and settle it beneath her head, my hand lingering a moment in her hair. They deserve a world without hauntings.

In my room, I open the drawer and lift my diary. The act feels deliberate, almost defiant. If there are ghosts in this house, I'll set them down in ink before they undo me.

~

Before I sleep, I creep down once more. Mother's still there in the chair, head tilted to one side. The fire's burnt low again. Her mouth slightly open. The wireless just static now. I pull the blanket tighter around her. Something in me wants to ask again – *Where was he standing, exactly? Was he never gone to begin with?*

I don't ask though. I just whisper, 'Night, Mother.' She doesn't stir. Tomorrow she'll return home.

The floorboard creaks – slow, deliberate – not beneath her, but from the hallway, just out of view. The space she'd pointed to. The place he'd been. I straighten, half step towards it. The air holds itself. The shadows wait, patient, just beyond the doorframe.

Fading Light

April 1931

The *Daily Telegraph* is already on the mat. Folded neatly. The corner is soaked through, the rain having crept under the porch overnight. I bring it into the kitchen, place it on the table, and set it aside.

I won't read it straight away.

Instead, I slice an apple. The peel falls in ribbons to the floor, curling like red shavings from a carpenter's plane. She always wanted them that way – skins off, slices neat, laid flat in a white bowl. Last month she couldn't manage the knife herself. Her fingers wouldn't obey her; her eyes blurred the blade to water. I peeled it for her, though she insisted it was nothing. Just a stiffness. Just the light.

She used to hum as she worked, tuneless, more vibration than song. I never asked what it was. Now the silence tells on me. The blanket on her armchair remains folded. The house has been holding its breath again, and I with it. People have begun to speak of us – the Smith women. 'Unlucky', they say, as though loss were catching. They already lower their voices when I pass, but I still hear the word. *Unlucky*. Like a verdict.

I open the newspaper. Third page. Second column.

TITANIC CAPTAIN'S WIDOW – ACCIDENTAL DEATH

Two days ago, Mrs Eleanor Smith, widow of Captain Edward John Smith, commander of the ill-fated *RMS Titanic*, died tragically in what authorities have deemed a traffic accident. Mrs Smith, 69, was struck by a taxicab while crossing Regent Street during a heavy rainstorm.

Witnesses describe the scene as sombre yet sudden. Mrs Smith, who was holding an umbrella and appeared preoccupied, stepped into the road at the same moment a London taxicab was approaching. Despite the driver travelling at no more than five miles an hour due to poor visibility, the collision proved fatal. She later died in St Mary Abbot's Hospital, having sustained severe head injuries.

The accident is being ruled as a misstep caused by both limited visibility and Mrs Smith's partial blindness, yet the symbolic weight of her passing has not gone unnoticed. Mrs Eleanor Smith is survived by her daughter and two grandchildren. A private funeral service will be held on May 1st. In lieu of flowers, the family has requested donations to maritime welfare charities, a cause Mrs Smith quietly supported in honour of her late husband.

I read it again. And again. Then I fold the page into quarters. I smooth the crease with my palm, as though pressure might force truth into the words.

They call her the *Titanic* captain's widow. Even now, they fold her back into the legend. The *Titanic* captain's widow – as though no other name remains. Perhaps that's what people mean when they call us unlucky: women remembered only for the men who vanished first. But even in this short column there are errors. They say she carried an umbrella. She never used one. Said it closed out the air. They call her blind. Her eyes had dimmed, yes, but in good light she could almost thread a needle. Small mistakes. They shouldn't matter, yet I can't let them go.

The line that stops me though is this: *She appeared preoccupied.* Preoccupied with what? With whom?

The photograph is not hers but Regent Street at night, headlights smeared by rain. She's been reduced to a caption. Dignified. Finished. Neatly contained, like the peelings at my feet. But my mother lived more than that. And the longer I stare, the more the words unsettle. *Was she crossing the street, or was she following someone?*

The Titanic Captain's Widow

April 1931

The envelope comes on the fifth day. Thick, cream, weighted – tucked between a sympathy card and a parcel of biscuits I won't eat. My name loops across it in a hand I don't know. Sussex postmark, sent to Mother's address. I sit in her armchair, in her home. The cushion still remembers her shape. The fire has gone out, my fingers are stiff with cold, but steady. I open the envelope. A cutting from *The Times*. There's a discipline to mourning – a choreography of stillness – and I follow it as she did.

ELEANOR SMITH, WIDOW OF TITANIC CAPTAIN, DIES IN LONDON AT 69

Eleanor Smith (née Pennington), widow of Captain Edward J. Smith, master of the ill-fated *RMS Titanic*, passed away following a road accident in Regent Street last Saturday. Known for her quiet dignity and enduring devotion, Mrs Smith lived most of her later life in seclusion in the South of England...

I stop reading. The obituary contains nothing about the woman who sharpened pencils with a knife. Who left concerts halfway through. Who refused to speak to a neighbour for a decade over a misdelivered letter. Nothing about the way she hummed while washing up, or how she sliced apples so thin they looked translucent. What's written is only what the world made of her. What they needed her to be. I let the paper fall to my lap.

I never lived in this house and now I'm trespassing. I'm not sure what I'm looking for. Something that isn't smoothed over, perhaps. Something real. Her dressing table still smells faintly of lavender oil and old powder. I open its drawer and under sachets, stray buttons, and a crystal jar of hairpins, there's a large envelope.

I pull out paper. It's yellowed at the edges. Marked in pencil: *Ohio, 1931*. Inside, a newspaper clipping. *The Lima Gazette.*

WHISPERING SMITH CLAIMED TITANIC PAST

The same photograph. Same tattoo. Rock of Ages, faint but visible. But this article is longer than the one I found. Local print, smaller column. Less edited. I skim for the detail. Then stop. There's handwriting in the margin. Mother's. A name underlined.

> *He said he saw the ship break. Said he surfaced near a lifeboat but no one pulled him in. Said no one would ever believe he lived, so he stopped trying to prove it.*
>
> <u>*Thomas O'Connell*</u> *might recognise him?*

Not a name I recognise instantly, but it's familiar. I remove the next clipping, and then the next. Stacked carefully beneath the first are more: Halifax, Liverpool, Galway. Notes in the margins. Some typed. Some pencilled. Each connected by a thread that tightens with every fold.

Thomas O'Connell appears again. Mother considered him important.

> *Liverpool, 1926 – naval pension claim under false credentials. Man disappeared before questioning.*
>
> *Halifax, 1928 – disturbance outside shipping office. Witnesses say man spoke in 'nautical language'. Refused to give name. Limped.*

My throat tightens. The phrasing – the rhythm – is hers. Even in the margins, she speaks as though transcribing confession. There are quotes, too. Marked with faint lines.

Said he worked for the White Star Line. Wouldn't take money. Just wanted to know if anyone remembered the fourth officer.
Told a child in Galway the ship had left without him. Then vanished.

There's a sketch on a piece of paper – a quick pencil outline. Did Mother draw this? The angle of the jaw, the slope of the shoulder. I bring it closer to my eyes. It's him. The man from the lane's end, near the red post box. At Bellecroft. I see him clearly now. The stillness. The watching. Underneath the sketch.

He knows the truth.

I drop the paper. My pulse pounds. Then pick it up again.

At the bottom of the drawer, folded flat, is a postcard. Blank on the back. No message. No stamp. Just the White Star Line crest, and a photograph of the *Titanic* at dock. Mother was collecting them, too. Not casually. Not sentimentally. Systematically. She had her own ledger. We've both been keeping the same vigil. Two women searching for the truth of a man the world decided was myth.

I place Mother's findings back into the envelope. Carefully. As if they might bruise. Downstairs, the house is thinner somehow. The kind of quiet you feel on your skin. Outside, something knocks – a loose panel, perhaps, or the gate. Then again. Once more. The sound insists. I don't move to the window.

The Watcher

May 1931

'I see you,' I whisper at the glass.

Along Bellecroft's lane, across the street, by the post box, he stands exactly where he has before. One hand on the railings, coat collar turned high. He doesn't move. Doesn't glance up. Solid as a statue awaiting orders.

'Look at me,' I say.

My breath fogs the pane. He refuses. That's what unsettles me: the discipline of not looking up to my window. I count to twenty. Then again. He never shifts, never scratches, never checks his watch. He's a breath held too long. He wants me to go to him.

By that time, I realise that my coat is already on. I need to see him closer. To prove he's flesh and not the echo of the grief everyone expects of me. The buttons fasten under my hands.

'Just going for a walk,' I mutter, though I don't believe it.

The driveway's gravel crunches beneath my shoes. A boy bounces a ball somewhere near, the sound hollow and regular, marking my nerves. Near the gates I stop, scanning the street. There. Same coat, same stance, half-hidden by the yew hedge. Watching. I step off the kerb fast.

'Wait!' My voice carries, sharp as a crack. He turns, not startled, not hurried, and slips between two houses. By the time I reach the corner, he's gone. Only pigeons rise, feathers drifting down like ash.

'Coward,' I spit, though the street is empty.

Back at the house I slam the door harder than I mean to. 'Still watching, Father?' I whisper. The words sound absurd in the quiet, but they steady me. Not by name or ghost, but by the silence he left behind.

Upstairs, Simon's train lies derailed on the carpet. I set it back on the track. In the room Mother stayed, the lavender sachets catch at my throat. The dressing-table mirror holds me too sharply. I pull open the top drawer. Buttons, tape measure, a jar of pins, her Bellecroft diary and more clippings.

'Let's see what you knew.'

The spine cracks under my thumb. Birthdays, shopping lists, sea temperatures. Then:

17th February 1929

Same man again. Outside the grocers. Too still. Didn't buy anything. Waited. Then gone.

6th March 1930

Limp on the right. Gloves even in sunshine. No one else seemed to notice him.

'Why didn't I notice more?' I say. Perhaps because I've learnt not to look too long at what unsettled me – the habit of our stance: endurance mistaken for strength.

More notes.

18th March 1930

Men at the club went quiet when I entered.

7th September 1930

Regent Street too busy last week. Rain. No umbrella.

My finger traces the line. 'What does this all mean?'

'Lunchtime, Mama?' Simon's voice carries from the landing.

'In a minute,' I call back, snapping the diary shut. My hands shake. I press them flat to the cover. 'In a minute, darling boy,' I repeat more softly.

At the table, Priscilla pushes her apple aside. 'Sour?' I ask.

She shakes her head. 'Different.'

'Different how?'

She shrugs. I slice another piece, thinner, neater, the way Mother did. 'Try this.'

'I like Grandma's way best,' she says.

I slice more pieces. Priscilla smiles. The knife flashes in the window light and I remind myself to keep my attention on the living, not the silence they'll inherit.

After lunch I go to my writing desk. 'Thomas O'Connell,' I say aloud. The name fills the quiet. I dip the nib, write steadily:

How do I already know your name?

The children thump down the hall, laughter bursting, then fading. Anchors, both of them. I close the diary and set my hands flat on the desk.

'What does this all mean?' I ask the room, the silence, myself.

At the window I part the curtain. The post box stands red and certain. The railings gleam with rain. Nothing moves. Still, I watch until my eyes sting.

The Curse, Rewritten

June 1931

Two months on, Father's suitcase has become our archive – mine and hers. Most days, I kneel beside it, half hoping the clippings might have shifted in the night and reordered themselves. Offered something new.

Today I don't hesitate. I spread the papers across the rug. The carpet's worn thin beneath them – the weight of what I've looked at too often. Inside, Mother's handwriting trails along the margins – light, precise, pressed too hard:

> *Check with registry*
> *Ask Ruth about this date*
> *Same tattoo?*

Mother was better than me at collecting.
A clipping from Salt Lake City:

**YOUNG MAN ARRESTED FOR PAWNING STOLEN SUIT.
CLAIMS FATHER WENT DOWN ON TITANIC.**

His age fits. Was my Ted unfaithful?
The photo is blurred, but the mouth, the jaw. Too familiar to dismiss.

I begin connecting the pieces. Halifax to Dover. New York to Montreal. Sightings. Corrections. Second-hand stories. The evidence spreads outward like roots. I trace their pattern with my fingertips, as if they'll spell something I've missed.

'Mama.' It's Priscilla.

'Not now,' I shout, regretting it instantly. She sobs as she scurries away. 'I'm sorry, my darling. Mama's busy.'

I don't go after her, though. Instead, I glance at my writing desk and a folded copy of the latest *Life*. I meant to throw it out last week, but instead it taunts me.

THE CURSE OF THE SMITH LINE – A LEGACY OF MADNESS AND MYSTERY

Beneath it, a grainy photograph of Father and a smaller one of me at sixteen – proof that even a daughter's face can be made to serve a myth. They've turned my family into a headline again. Made him into lore, a fable in uniform. They diagnose madness as if it were an heirloom passed from father to widow to daughter. They never saw the man – not in his boots, not at his table. They never knew what was taken from him. Or from us.

I read the article's words again and feel the poison of them settle in my bones. Sidney, too, reduced to whispers of instability and being cursed through marriage to the daughter of the *Titanic*. Eleanor reduced to an old widow in the rain. As if grief itself is proof of weakness. As if silence is madness. I press my hands flat against the writing desk, forcing myself to breathe. I won't let them make a curse of us. Not for me, not for Simon, not for Priscilla. My children won't inherit doom in print. They'll inherit me: my steadiness, my sharpness, my refusal. But still the words thrum at the back of my skull, steady as a pulse: *madness, mystery, curse.*

I pull a fresh sheet of paper and begin a letter to the editor. The nib bites the page, moving quicker than my thoughts.

Sir,

Your recent article confuses grief with hysteria and remembrance with spectacle. You mistake silence for madness, and I will not permit it—

The nib falters. Ink pools. I stop. What am I doing? Arguing with strangers who've already decided who we are? The world has always preferred its version. A *Titanic* curse is easier to print than a family's grief. I fold the page, but not neatly. I don't align the corners. I feed it into the fire and refuse to watch it burn. My words aren't for them. Not yet.

For a moment, I imagine the shape of what I could write: an essay, a case study, cool and precise. *Unfiled Histories: Testimonies and Reappearances, 1913–1931*. There would be maps, diagrams, postmarks. No sentiment, just the weight of facts. Something no editor could dismiss. Something Simon and Priscilla could point to one day and say, *This is who we were. This is what we carried.* One day, perhaps, another woman might read it and recognise the pattern – how truth survives through those willing to catalogue it.

But not tonight.

Instead, I return to the suitcase. Our family's suitcase. The clippings, the gaps, the unfinished noise of it all. Once it felt like chaos. Now there's comfort in the disorder – proof that nothing fits cleanly, that no notion of curse can be so neatly traced. The fire cracks in the grate. Upstairs, a laugh bursts from Priscilla. It's quick and bright, gone in an instant. I cling to it like a promise.

That's when I see it. A sealed envelope inside the case. Was it there before? Lighter than I expect. I break the seal carefully. Inside: a single photograph. Sepia, edges lifting. A man half-turned, already leaving the frame, as though refusing capture. His face obscured.

On the back, in Mother's hand—

March 1925. Not the first time. Lichfield in 1914, too.

Not the first time for what? And suddenly I'm back in Lichfield – July 1914. Sixteen years old, the statue shrouded in cloth, the crowd restless. Mother's voice low enough for only me – *Not here, too. Stop following me.* At the time I thought she meant the sun, her health or even the press of mourners. *Was she watching someone?*

I slip the photograph back into its envelope and steady my hands.

Whispers in the Rain

September 1931

Three months of quiet – no watcher by the post box, no midnight creaks pretending to be footsteps – and for a moment, I almost believe we've been left alone. Then Simon streaks past the doorway, curls flying.

'Not the curtains!'

The sharpness in my voice startles us both. His head pops out, chastened. 'Sorry, Mama.'

I beckon him over. He hesitates, then pads across the rug and leans against me, warm and restless, fingers picking at the seam of my blouse. I smooth his hair and the heaviness in my chest softens under the weight of him. 'It's all right. Just be careful, my love. That's all I ask.'

He nods, but his eyes linger on mine longer than they should. It's as if he's searching for something I can't give.

The floorboards creak. Priscilla appears in the doorway, hands on hips, chin lifted in mimicry of Mother. 'Simon cheated,' she declares, her voice high and sure.

'I did not!' he protests, spinning to face her.

'Did too!'

Their voices clash, too loud, too close. I close my eyes. 'Enough,' I say, gentle but firm. They fall quiet. Priscilla shoots one last look at her brother before sliding beside him. I draw them both in, wrapping my arms around them, holding them close. I've promised myself that laughter will be louder here than the past – that they'll inherit noise, not dread.

The house settles into stillness. For a moment, it feels like peace.

'Will we always live here?' Priscilla asks suddenly, her voice muffled against my shoulder.

The question startles me. I glance toward the window. The skeletal trees cast long shadows across the floor. 'Why do you ask that?'

She shrugs. Her little fingers tug at the buttons on my cuff. 'Ada says Bellecroft is too big for just us. She said we'll move one day.'

I force a smile. 'Ada talks too much,' I say, brushing my daughter's hair back. 'This is our home. We'll stay as long as we wish.'

Simon looks up. His brow is furrowed. 'Even with the ghosts?'

The word stills the air.

'What ghosts?'

'The ones in the attic,' he says simply. 'They whisper when it rains.'

'Ada told you that?'

He shakes his head. 'She said not to listen. But I heard them.'

I force a smile too quickly. 'Ada reads too many stories. There are no ghosts, Simon. Only echoes – the kind we make ourselves.'

He nods, but his eyes don't leave mine. I wonder if, even at his age, he knows the truth: ghosts don't need attics to haunt us. The clock chimes from the mantel. The children slip from my arms and vanish back into the hallway, their laughter echoing behind them. A melody I can't quite hold onto. The space they leave behind isn't empty; it waits, as if listening for the next sound to fill it. Outside, the first drops of rain tap against the glass – soft, deliberate, like fingertips searching for a way in.

Red and White Roses

September 1931

The storm hasn't let up in two days. Rain lashes the windows with the steadiness of a drumbeat – the kind that makes the very walls seem to draw in. At the desk, my pen drags to a halt. Ink smudges where my hand has pressed too heavily, the words already blurred past saving. There's nothing else I need to write tonight. I cap the inkwell and push the page aside.

On the desk, lies the letter. Heavy cream stock, deliberate folds, the wax of Southampton glinting red. I almost left it sealed. I should have. The mayor – a man I've never met – writes with courtesy, almost apology, with gratitude, and then a request:

Will you continue your mother's tradition?

He wants to know if I will send, on St George's Day, the buttonhole of red and white roses – just as she has done every year since the *Titanic* sank. I read the letter twice when it came. Once more now. The words haven't changed, but their weight feels heavier than it did earlier. For him, remembrance is a civic duty and not a private wound.

Mother never spoke of it. Not once. Yet every spring she prepared the same parcel: tissue folded in sharp triangles, florist's ribbon, a tag no bigger than a thumbnail. *Sixteen mayors*, he wrote, *wore her grief in silence*. She made sure of it – duty disguised as honour, memory dressed as decorum.

And now they want me to continue that honour.

My hands curl into fists. I don't need a tradition to remember what I can't forget. I rise from the desk. Cross to the hearth. The fire is out, but still warm. I open the iron box beside it, take a folded taper and light it from the candle on the mantel. The flame flutters as I lower it towards the edge of the letter. My hand pauses. Not from doubt, but from something colder. Anger. Not at the mayor. Not even at Mother. At the assumption: that inheritance is obligation, that I must carry what she carried, simply because I can.

I let the flame catch. The paper curls and blackens. *Duty.* It flakes in on itself. *Decorum.* I drop it into the grate and let the ashes fall where hers never did. It's done. Let that be the end of ceremony for other people's comfort. I return to the desk. The room is quieter now. No sound from the hallway. The children are upstairs. The house settles into itself and I think of Sidney, of Mother, of Father. The *Titanic* threads through them all like a vein – invisible but pulsing. *Do the children feel it, too?*

I shake my head, trying to clear the thought. The word that others whisper – *curse* – seeps into me, slow as water through stone. I dismiss it as Mother would have – *Superstition is for the weak,* she used to say. We endure. But endurance, I'm learning, erodes quietly, grain by grain.

That's when I see it.

Another envelope. On my desk. Not there a moment ago. I blink and lift it. The paper is faintly warm, as if a hand had only just released it. The ink gleams green-black. No wax seal, no return address, no stamp. Only a single horizontal line where a name should be.

The Brass Button

September 1931

Morning breaks grey and low, damp light crawling into the bones of the house. In the kitchen Ada clatters at the stove; the children's voices rise and fall like seabirds on a restless tide. I stay at my writing desk.

The letter lies exactly where I left it, pale against the wood, daring me. I watched it through the night. Sleep never came. Unopened, it already spoke – the silence of it, the wrongness of the paper, dry as if it had been kept in some cold cellar. Now my hand hovers. The house holds its breath with me. And finally, I open it.

Miss Smith,

> *My name is Thomas O'Connell. I believe your father saved my life. I am in town until Thursday. I hope you'll agree to meet. I'll be at the bench near the churchyard each day at nine in the morning.*

– T.O.C.

No embellishment. I read it twice, then fold the letter and slip it into my coat pocket. Ada calls that breakfast is ready, but I wave her off and return to the window instead. Outside, the garden is glazed in wet light. The rose beds are beginning to curl at the edges, autumn pulling them inward. I press my palm against the glass and breathe out. The warmth fogs the surface. The children's laughter has returned, loud and bright as a bell. Still, behind it all, the weight of the letter anchors itself in my chest.

I don't tell Ada where I'm going. Only that I need air. The old path to town remembers Sidney's steps as well as mine. All those afternoons when silence was the only language left to us. Now the hedgerows are thinning, brambles brittle, the seeds gone.

And still I wonder: *is this a trap? The Russians he swore were watching?* Some nameless enemy who recognises my weakness – this desperate hunger to know whether my father is dead or alive.

By the time the church spire spears the sky I'm sweating beneath my coat and my pulse is a steady drum. At the gate, I falter, one hand on the iron. Just getting air, I tell myself. Just walking off the thought. But the letter presses against my ribs like proof, and I know it's too late to turn back.

Then I see him.

He's on the bench, exactly as the letter promised. His cap is folded in his lap and his hands are laid out flat and waiting. He's a man who has rehearsed patience. He doesn't see me at first. I don't hesitate. My steps are quick, deliberate, my coat brushing the iron gate as I pass through.

'Thomas O'Connell?' My voice is steady, louder than I expect, carrying across the churchyard.

He looks up, startled by the force of it. A pause, then a small nod. 'Miss Smith.'

'Once. Mrs Russell Cooke now.'

We study each other. His beard is greying, and his coat hangs loose, but something in his bearing is solid – as if the years have weathered him, not worn him down. The smell of pipe smoke clings to him; ordinary, human.

He shifts, clears his throat. 'Didn't feel right just turning up.'

'You've followed me. I've seen you.'

'I'm not best proud of that. I—' He stops. His shoulders lift, apologetic. 'A letter seemed the least intrusive way. Wasn't sure you'd want to hear what I've got to say. For years I tried to pluck the courage to tell your mother, but I left it too late.'

'Got to say?'

He pulls something from his coat. A square of linen, folded. He opens his mouth, closes it again. Looks down at his hands. He opens it with care. Like it's something fragile. Inside, there's a brass button that's dulled with age. He holds it out.

'He gave me this. Said it would bring me luck.'

I don't move. I can't. My stomach flips. My hand grips the bench before I can stop it. The chill runs up my arm. 'He?' It's a whisper.

'Your father put me in the last lifeboat. Said my name aloud. Told them who I belonged to. My brother, too. Both of us. Kept us together…'

'Father?' I ask. It's another whisper.

'He was tall,' Thomas says. 'Had a steadiness to him. Not panic, just … purpose. I never knew his name at the time. Only later, in a newspaper photo. That same mouth. Same kind eyes.'

'You saw him?'

'He was there till the end. Said he'd not leave his ship.'

'Do you believe he lived after that?' The question leaves me before I can weigh it. It sounds childish even to my own ears – the kind asked by someone who still half-hopes for rescue.

He shakes his head and pushes his hand out again. 'I want you to have this. Might bring you luck, too.'

I step closer and I take the button from his palm. Turn it over. E.J.S. The engraving is shallow, but still there. I used to watch him polishing the brass buttons on his uniform. A ritual he never rushed.

'Kept it for nearly twenty years,' he says. 'Thought it ought to come home.'

'Why didn't you speak to my mother?'

'Your father could have saved himself.'

We sit in silence. Around us, the wind moves through the yews, and the early light flickers in the trees. I hear the distant peal of a bell. Somewhere, someone tending to graves.

'He saved you instead of himself,' I say at last.

Thomas nods. 'How do I apologise to you when I'm grateful to him?' he says. 'I've never forgotten him. Named my first son Edward, the second one John.' He stands then, brushes his coat smooth. 'That's all I came to say.'

He doesn't ask for anything. Doesn't linger. The button presses into my glove. I feel its shape settle into my hand like something long missing. I hadn't realised I'd been holding my shoulders so tight.

Later, the house is quiet. The twins have fallen asleep curled against each other. Books open in their laps. I leave the door ajar and return to the fire, where the coals are still warm.

I take the button from my pocket and place it on the hearthstone.

My father saved two brothers. Two boys once lost. That's the truth I'll keep – not the rumours, not the curse others made of us. Instead, there's a legacy carried in silence, passed from one family to another, and now it's home again.

Interruption Six

FEBRUARY 1973

The last of the light had thinned to nothing. Only the coals in the grate glowed, a low, patient heat. The tape clicked itself to a stop – a small, final sound in the stillness.

Catherine closed her notebook. She didn't immediately rise.

'You've gone quiet,' Melville observed.

'I was thinking,' Catherine said.

'About me?'

'About the word they stuck on you,' Catherine answered. 'Unlucky.'

Melville gave a soft, dismissive breath. 'A useful shorthand. It saves people the trouble of asking what actually happened.'

'It appears everywhere,' Catherine said. 'In letters, in the papers, even in the museum files – "Unlucky widow", "unlucky daughter" – as if misfortune were a vocation.'

Melville's mouth curved – not quite amusement. 'That's the trick. Call a woman unlucky and you never need to ask what she endured, or who failed her.'

Catherine nodded. 'It freezes the story at the point of survival. You and your mother become proof, not people.'

'Exactly,' Melville said. 'The curse wasn't what happened. It was the name they gave us afterwards.'

The coal shifted with a soft crack. Catherine wrote the sentence down before it cooled in the air.

Melville reached for her shawl. 'Same time tomorrow?'

'If you're able,' Catherine said. Her voice was steady, but she felt the familiar tightening low in her abdomen, brief and folding inward.

'I'll be here,' Melville replied. 'Bring cake this time.'

Catherine nodded, then smiled. 'And the transcripts from the Mayfair interviews. I'd like to look again at the phrasing around the "curse". It shifts tone after 1931. The press moves from superstition to pity pieces.'

'Mmm.' Melville's eyes sharpened. 'Pity outlives truth.'

Catherine gathered her satchel. The act steadied her more than the fire. At the door, a thought caught and held.

'What replaces pity?' she asked quietly.

Melville did not hesitate. 'Will.'

Outside, rain began in a thin, deliberate thread along the windowpanes. Catherine wrote one final note and underlined it before slipping the book into her satchel and stepping out into it.

<u>*Unlucky: a label that preserves the story and erases the woman.*</u>

The Research Fellow

FEBRUARY 1973

Catherine unlocked her office with the stiff, familiar turn of the key. The storage room was colder than the corridor – dust, old varnish and stone hanging in the stillness. The scent of things kept, not lived with. She stepped inside and shut the door behind her. No windows, no heating; just the low hum of the dehumidifier and the thin fluorescence that flattened everything it touched. Her desk sat exactly where she had left it, now wedged between two crates marked *FRAGILE*, the chair turned slightly askew as though someone had been about to sit and thought better of it.

On her desk lay the morning's post. She recognised the first envelope by its weight and its discreet seal – the hospital again. Her work address this time. She set it aside without opening it.

Beneath it, another piece of paper. Lighter. Folded once.

Dr Haynes—

If you're free later this week, perhaps a coffee?

M.

She stared at the initial for a moment before sitting down. Michael. The new research fellow in History – brilliant, awkward, unexpectedly shy. She'd met him at a departmental drinks reception in December, where Marianne had nudged her twice in his direction, whispering, 'Try letting yourself be seen.'

Catherine hadn't known how to answer him then; she knew even less now. She had never been on a date. Never allowed anyone close enough to see the fault lines. Illness had taught her early that people worried, then retreated, then treated you as though you were already half gone. Better, she'd decided, to keep the distance herself.

She folded the note and placed it beneath her blotter.

The office hummed weakly with the sound of the antiquated pipes in the wall. Across the quad, laughter drifted into the grey morning – light, unburdened, belonging to lives that seemed to move forward without her.

She turned to her notebook. The page she had left open the night before was headed:

Aftermath as Identity.

She added, beneath it:

Fear of ending = fear of beginning.
Impermanence mistaken for destiny.

She paused, pen suspended. She closed the notebook.

On the chair beside her, the reel-to-reel waited with its usual patience. Catherine threaded the tape through the spools, her fingers steady from habit rather than calm. Melville's voice filled the office at once: measured, deliberate, unafraid of the dark corners of her own story.

Catherine sat back. Listening. Letting someone else's survival steady the places in herself she still refused to touch.

The Motorina

FEBRUARY 1973

The reel clicked, stuttered, then began its low hum. A fragment of static, followed by Catherine's voice – quieter than before, but more assured.

'*The Times*, third of October, nineteen-thirty-one,' she read aloud, paper rustling. '*Daring Damsels or Dangerous Drivers?*' A short pause. Then, half to herself, half to Mrs Russell Cooke: 'They always find the headline before the history.'

Melville gave a soft laugh. 'At least this one gave us engines instead of obituaries.'

'You liked it?' Catherine asked.

'I cut it out. Put it with the others. I liked the way it sounded – *daring damsel*. I thought, perhaps, they'd written it for me.'

The reel caught, the room breathed. Somewhere beyond the recording, a door shut softly, as though the house itself wished to listen.

'Was it a rebellion?' Catherine asked. 'To drive?'

'Not rebellion,' Melville replied, as if her mouth were full of a soft food. 'Rebellion requires someone left to defy. By then, they'd already turned their backs. I was the unlucky woman, the widow, the cursed daughter. What freedom they left me was silence… So I filled it with the sound of an engine.'

A small shift – the faint scrape of a chair, a breath near the microphone.

'And did it feel like freedom?'

'Not at first. More like velocity. But sometimes velocity is enough.'

The tape hissed, then steadied. Catherine's voice was fainter now, almost a murmur: 'That's where we'll begin today, then. With the speed that comes after survival.'

Melville: 'Yes. And their curse that couldn't keep up.'
The reel turned on.

A Driver

ARCHIVE: REEL SIX

From 1931

While many still believe the motorcar a man's domain, a growing number of so-called 'motorinas' are taking to the roads, and, more alarmingly, the racing tracks, with a zeal typically reserved for war heroes and fools. Women drivers, once confined to gentle Sunday outings in borrowed Austins, are now purchasing Bentleys, oiling engines, and flying past policemen with the abandon of barnstormers. One society matron was reportedly spotted at Brooklands donning goggles and lipstick in equal measure, her children cheering from the pits…

The Times, 3 October 1931

A Study in Green

October 1931

Jacques Lemare circles Priscilla like a sculptor about to strike the first cut.

'Chin up just a little, *mademoiselle*. Yes, *parfait*.' His French accent curls around the words like silk.

She obeys without hesitation, head tilted, hands folded in her lap as though she has done this a hundred times. My daughter – my impossible daughter – holds herself so still. The lamps blaze hot against the studio's heavy curtains, muting Piccadilly to a faint murmur. I tug off my gloves, fold them in my lap, and watch. Her expression is calm and composed beyond her years. She's always been like this: watchful, self-possessed, already learning to hold her course when others might pull the brake. Today, in her green linen dress, the fabric neatly tied in bows at each shoulder, she looks older than eight. Too old, perhaps. I resist the urge to step in; to adjust the way her too-smooth hair falls over one ear, to ruffle the hem of her skirt.

She doesn't need me to.

I'm not the only mother in the room. Lady Diana Cooper – radiant even in the half-light of the studio – kneels beside her young son, John. She murmurs softly whilst straightening his collar. He's restless. All energy and impatience, tugging at his cuffs with a child's easy defiance. Diana clicks her tongue. She smooths a wayward curl from her son's forehead before catching my eye with an amused smirk.

'Children,' she says. Her voice is honey and mischief.

'Incorrigible,' I agree. Simon sulks in the corner, his fingers busy dismantling a mechanical toy. He'd never sit still long enough for a portrait, or a life like this.

I watch as Jacques moves to John and attempts to coax him into stillness. Diana and I both know it's a futile effort. Jacques is patient, though. He shifts his focus back to Priscilla, who has barely moved. He circles her again, adjusting the light with the care of a painter mixing pigments. I remind myself she's not marble. Not portrait. A child who deserves to be seen by me before she learns to be looked at by everyone.

'Look past me,' he instructs. 'As if thinking of something far, far away.'

The pose is familiar. I've seen it before. In another studio, in another lifetime. The same wistful gaze, the same quiet elegance. My own portrait, taken when I was barely older than she is now. *Has she seen it tucked away among my things, or is there simply something in her that mirrors me without trying?* I should be proud, and I am. But somewhere beneath that pride, something colder presses at me. It's like watching a portrait hang itself. *This is where the fracture begins*, I think – the moment a girl mistakes composure for strength. I won't let her inherit that confusion from me as I inherited it from Mother.

The camera clicks. The bulb flashes. Priscilla doesn't flinch. *Was this how it began?* A girl posed just so. A camera's flash. A mother watching her daughter and thinking, *don't become me*.

'*Très bien*, Mademoiselle Russell Cooke.' Jacques steps back, satisfied.

My daughter blinks, the spell breaking, and turns to me. I see the question in her eyes – the unspoken *Did I do well?* I push off my chair and stride over, tilting her chin up with a finger. 'You were exquisite, my love. If I didn't know better, I'd say you've done this a thousand times before.'

She preens just a little and her lips twitch at the corners. 'Perhaps I have,' she says, and I laugh. I tug one of the bows on her shoulder playfully.

'*Monsieur* Lemare, you've made a dreadful discovery. She's got a taste for it now.'

Jacques grins, but his attention is already shifting back to his equipment.

As we gather our things, Diana watches Priscilla with the keen eye of someone accustomed to knowing who'll rise and who'll fade. She tilts her head, her lips curling in amusement.

'Watch out, Mrs Russell Cooke,' she says lightly. 'She'll cause a stir one day.'

Diana's words settle like perfume: flattering, lingering, and slightly poisonous. I reach out to smooth Priscilla's hair, then pause. She's already perfect. Already composed. But perfection is brittle, and I won't let her carry it alone. I take her hand instead, warm and certain in mine. She is still only eight. Still my girl. My impossible, enchanting daughter.

'Come along, my heart,' I say.

28th October 1931

The money came quickly – Sidney's, then Mother's. The efficiency of it sickens me: grief converted into ledgers, loss assessed like property. Houses, silver, heirlooms heavy with other people's wants. None of it chosen. All of it inherited.

Enough.

The conclusion is clear. Not born of tears, but of the hush that follows them.

I need something that's mine. Entirely. Unequivocally.

What I need is movement. Noise. A machine that answers only to me. Not a chauffeur's eyes in the mirror. Not a carriage upholstered like a coffin. I want a car that snarls when I touch the accelerator. Something alive.

They think my family unlucky. They whisper curse as if misfortune runs in the blood like a tint. Let them. If superstition grants me space to behave as I please, I'll take it. There's a strange power in being quietly dismissed.

Tomorrow, I go to Oxford. I'll choose something British. Something audacious. They may call it reckless, unfeminine, unwise.

They've said worse.

Chasing Shadows

November 1931

The Bentley waits in the drive, a dark green defiance against the morning frost. Beyond it, the trees stand stripped and still. There's no breeze, no birdsong. Just the quiet, and my car. I pull on my gloves. The leather is stiff with the cold. The air smells of petrol, of distant woodsmoke, and something else – not real, just memory. Behind me, Bellecroft looms, unchanged. Still curtains, silent hall. Neighbours who lower their voices when they speak my name, as if misfortune runs in blood rather than in newspapers.

This morning, Ada asked whether a fresh start somewhere else might help. I brushed it off immediately. The idea felt absurd – as though grief could be wrapped in paper, packed with the china, and sent on ahead.

I said, 'It's the silence I'm fighting, not the bricks.'

But now, standing here, I'm not so certain. The silence inside the house has begun to feel structural, something I live around, not with. I climb into the driver's seat: key in ignition, press the starter. The Bentley stirs and then growls. Its voice is deep and full of promise. I grip the wheel. The grain of it presses through the leather and into my palms. A small, steady pressure. Something to hold.

The gravel crunches as I guide the car down the drive. Each turn feels deliberate, considered. At the end of the lane, by the post box, I hesitate. Then I turn left. Away from the church, away from town. The road opens. The engine finds its rhythm. A low, throaty hum.

The wind slips in at the edges, tugging at my scarf. I let the car gather speed. Thirty. Forty. Fifty. The hedgerows blur. The fields pull away. *The Times* would call it reckless – the papers always do when it's a woman's hands on the wheel. Let them. Reckless is better than still. Besides, a woman dismissed is a woman unobserved, and there's freedom in that.

The countryside feels unfamiliar at this pace. Trees become streaks. Crows scatter at the sound of the engine. The world grows narrower, simpler. I like that it's reduced to lines and turns and the sound of the machine.

Then, without warning, the memories rise. My mother's hands, folded in her lap. Sidney's slippers beside the bed. My father's cough catching in the dark. They come as they always do – uninvited, insistent. I blink, but they stay like footnotes I never wrote.

A bend in the road. The tyres bite too hard, the wheel bucks in my hands. For a breath, the car owns me, not the other way round. Then it steadies. I steady. We hold each other upright. I ease off the throttle.

Up ahead, a church spire breaks the sky – pale stone against a pale morning. I pull to the verge. The engine ticks as it cools. My breath mists the air, and I sit with my hands still on the wheel.

They're never far, the dead. They wait at the corners, in the fields, in the spaces between thoughts. Sometimes I think they're sewn into the very air I breathe.

The Bentley idles beneath me, steady now. I put it back in gear.

'Let the memories keep pace,' I say. 'I'm not slowing for them.'

The Taste of Speed

March 1932

Four months of learning what the Bentley can do, and still the sound of engines catches in my chest. Brooklands is alive – a temple to speed and daring. Mechanics swarm, adjusting carburettors, shouting over each other in a constant low buzz. The track stretches wide, grey and banked. Its surface is scarred by the passage of countless tyres. The hum of engines saturates the air. It's a ceaseless, rhythmic growl that reverberates through my chest.

My Bentley gleams in the sunlight, dark green and unapologetic against the scuffed machinery around it. A jewel, yes, but one with teeth. It sits in the paddock like it already belongs, and for once I feel the pulse of that belonging in myself. I stand beside it, hands in my pockets, not hiding but measuring the moment. Men glance, recognise me, and glance away: the *Titanic* daughter, the widow, the unlucky girl. *Let them.* Their distance is a freedom of its own.

These women, though – quick, relentless, entirely themselves – aren't another species at all. They're a version of what I could be. The papers call them 'daring damsels', as though speed was borrowed plumage, but the air here tells the truth: petrol, hot tyres, ambition. No apologies. No permissions. This is a world that rewards nerve, not lineage.

A laugh cuts through my pity and the drone of engines. I turn instinctively towards the source and see her, Kay Petre, leaning against her car with the easy grace of someone completely at home here. The red Daytona Wolseley Hornet Special behind her looks like it's seen its fair share of battles, but the way she runs her gloved fingers over its bonnet is almost affectionate. She's animated. Her voice rises above the din as she speaks to two other women, and they appear to hang on her every word. There's something magnetic about her, as though the world itself leans in just to listen. I like her instantly.

I linger by my Bentley. But hesitation won't teach me a thing. Standing still never has. Kay notices me, or my car. Her sharp eyes narrow slightly and then recognition softens her gaze.

'You must be Mrs Russell Cooke,' she calls, breaking away from her conversation and moving towards me.

I step closer, the gravel crunching beneath my boots. 'Only to men who think names matter. To everyone else, it's Melville.'

Her smile deepens as she offers her hand. 'Kay. Kay Petre. A pleasure.'

Her handshake is firm; her gloves are soft but worn, carrying the faint tang of oil. Up close, she's smaller than she first appeared, but her presence makes her taller. Her pale-blue silk overalls look like armour, her hair set in neat curls, a streak of oil darkening one cheek. She doesn't notice – or doesn't care.

'That accent's not British.'

'Canadian,' she says, sly grin returning. 'Toronto born and raised.'

I picture snowbound streets, a city half a world away, and marvel that it's brought her here, to this patch of Oxfordshire earth. 'What made you cross the ocean?'

'Curiosity,' she shrugs. 'And the need for something bigger. Toronto's fine, but it isn't the centre of the racing world. I came to England to see what I could do … and I haven't left.'

There's a tone I recognise: quiet determination, the refusal to let circumstance dictate a life. Perhaps Kay knows what it means to carve out space where none was offered.

'And have you found it? What you were looking for?'

Her eyes spark with mischief. 'Sometimes. Other times, I invent it.'

I laugh. Kay's confidence is infectious, a spark striking against something long buried in me.

She points to her motorcar, and we move over to it. She leans against the car with the casual ease of someone who knows every bolt and rivet by heart. The other drivers mill about, some adjusting goggles or gloves, others engaged in animated discussion about tyre pressures and gear ratios. Kay nods towards a tall woman with a cropped hairstyle, clad in grease-streaked overalls.

'That's Margot,' she says, lowering her voice as if sharing a secret. 'Watch her on the corners. She's got a knack for finding the racing line before anyone else even sees it.'

Margot glances up, sensing the attention. She flashes a quick grin before returning to the delicate task of tightening a bolt. Beside her, another driver – Evelyn, Kay tells me – adjusts the brim of her leather flying helmet and lights a cigarette with a practised flick. Evelyn's car, a sleek Riley 9, gleams in the sunlight. Its paint is polished to perfection.

'It's not just about speed,' Kay adds, her voice carrying over the din of the paddock. 'It's about knowing your machine, trusting it to respond when you need it most. Doesn't matter if it's a Riley or a Bentley, you're the one in control.'

Her words hang in the air as a mechanic fires up a nearby engine. The roar momentarily drowns out everything else. Kay's eyes flick to the clock tower at the edge of the paddock. Time is ticking. The air is thick with anticipation, and a restless energy ripples through the crowd. I wasn't sure what I expected. A curiosity, perhaps. Something to admire and walk away from. But as I watch them – women in overalls, hair tucked back, hands black with oil – something tightens in my chest. They're everything the newspapers swore I could never be: unburdened by a story that isn't theirs.

A question, unformed but insistent: *Why not me?*

Drivers pull on their flying helmet and goggles. I see how their movements are precise and almost ritualistic. 'Where are they going?' I ask.

'You'll see,' Kay says, pushing off the car. She leans into a small compartment behind the seat. She pulls out a lipstick in a case, a stopwatch, cigarettes, hairpins and various other beauty supplies. 'Need to ensure I'm transformed back to perfection after the race,' she says and climbs into the car.

It strikes me that the lipstick isn't vanity, at all. It's armour. Proof for the men in the stands, for the reporters with their sly jokes, that a woman can thunder round a track at eighty miles an hour and still reappear powdered, polished, unmistakably 'ladylike'. Survival comes in many forms. Some women survive by fitting the script. Others, like Kay, survive by driving straight through it.

'Let's see if all those blokes with their fancy motors can keep up with a Wolseley Hornet,' she says.

There's a spark in her eyes, a challenge to anyone who might doubt her or her machine. The growl of the engine swells around us. Brooklands has already taken its toll: drivers flung from the banking, machines overturned, lives ended in an instant. Everyone here knows the risk. It hangs in the air with the petrol and the smoke. It's sharper than perfume. The danger isn't hidden. It's part of the allure.

Kay's eyes are fixed on the track, not the crowd. She doesn't wait for permission. I watch her go and, for the first time in a long time, I truly want something. Not a purchase or a name or a man. I don't even just want excitement anymore. I want knowledge. Ownership – the kind that begins under the bonnet, not just behind the wheel.

19th April 1932

Sidney's cufflinks turned up today, hidden beneath a wicker basket. Small, bright, familiar and sharp in the way grief still knows how to cut.

I should have put them in a drawer. Instead, I took the Bentley out. The road did what it always does: pared everything back until there was only the engine, the wind, and the ache pressed thin by speed. Not healing. Not even solace. Just movement.

When I came back, Simon was sitting on the stairs, watching the dust shift in the sunbeam. He said he wants to fly. Said there's nothing up there but sky to explore.

I laughed – too quickly – and he frowned, the way Sidney once did when he thought I wasn't listening.

The Banking

April 1934

'Hold your line, Mel!' Kay's voice rides the air as she darts past in her Wolseley, scarf snapping like a banner.

Two years of work – racing lessons, engine failures, and every condescending smirk the paddock could hurl – have led me here. The borrowed Riley 9 bucks beneath me as the tyres bite into the curve of the banking. The concrete rises steep, sun glaring off its worn surface, and the wheel kicks hard in my hands. My arms burn, but I don't yield. I push harder.

This is what I came for.

I press my boot down and the car growls. Eager. The scarf at my throat slaps against my chin. Breath stings my teeth.

A red Riley looms on my right, its driver edging close. Too close. He thinks I'll lift. That I'll give him the line. I bare my teeth. I don't. The cars skim side by side, metal shivering in the heat between us, until he flinches first and drops back.

I laugh, but the sound is torn away by the wind.

The straight opens ahead. Kay glances across, goggles flashing, grin wild. She raises a gloved fist in salute. I answer by pushing harder. The Riley stretches, engine screaming, air punching through the gaps in the bodywork. For a moment it feels like flight. The car and I are suspended. There's nothing beneath us but speed.

The crowd is a smear at the edge – trilbies, parasols, smoke curling above the pits – but I know where to look. Margot waves her goggles high, grease streaking her face. Evelyn tips her cap back just long enough to holler something I can't hear, cigarette still balanced at the corner of her mouth. Their presence is louder than the jeers from men behind the rail. We keep each other here.

The next bend comes fast. Too fast. The wheel judders, the tyres scream. The Riley lurches an inch too wide. The banking tilts me towards the sky. For a breath the car tests me. I answer. The tyres catch. The grip returns. I steady. We steady.

Lap after lap, the rhythm builds: engine, breath, hands. My gloves are slick with sweat, the wheel scalding. My jaw aches from holding it tight. But this is mine – every turn, every risk. Not Sidney's legacy. Not Mother's silence. Not Father's infamy. Mine. Behind the rail, men mutter the word they always reach for – *unlucky*. I take the bend higher, faster. Let them whisper.

The flag rises, white against the haze. One more lap. I lean low, teeth clenched, every nerve singing. The Riley hurls itself forward, engine straining. My body braces in the seat as though welded to it. The world narrows to a line of concrete and sky.

The flag drops. I take the finish behind Kay.

I pull up in the paddock. My goggles are streaked with grit and my hair is damp beneath my cap. My arms tremble. It's from triumph, not shock. Kay is already there, her Wolseley ticking as it cools, and a thin thread of smoke curling from the bonnet. She claps once. Sharp. Certain.

'That's it,' she says, grin fierce. 'Now you're racing.'

I swing out of the Riley, boots crunching gravel, the tang of petrol still burning my throat. Dust sticks to my lips. Kay fishes in her pocket, produces a silver lipstick case, and presses it into my palm. Woman to woman, driver to driver.

'One for the photographers,' she says with a wink.

The metal is warm from her body, slick with oil at the hinge. I twist it, the red bullet rising smooth as silk, and catch my reflection in the Riley's polished bonnet. My mouth is cracked, raw, but I paint it anyway: crimson against the grey grit of the track.

Kay grins wider. 'Now you look the part.'

I laugh, breathless, and cap the lipstick with a click that feels like punctuation.

Spanners and Siblings

June 1934

I know the rhythm of engines now, the lean of corners, the quiet satisfaction of overtaking men who never imagined I'd choose their line. Two years of turning up at Brooklands – rain or shine, crowd or no crowd – have carved this into me. Here, on the lanes of Newport though, the new Bentley saloon hums beneath me, eager rather than obedient. I prefer it that way. No machine is ever truly tamed. Not at speed. Not on a track. And not on these roads, where control is earned mile by mile.

Simon and Priscilla are quiet in the back seat. That, in itself, is a novelty. Simon leans forward, elbows on his knees, eyes bright with anticipation. Priscilla sits upright, hands folded, gaze locked on the passing scenery as though memorising it.

The island looks much the same, though everything's different. Now we're visitors, ghosts at the edges of our own memories. Once, this place rang with Sidney's voice, with the clamour of our children running barefoot through fields. I pull over near a sloping field where the grass blows in gusts off the coast. Gravel crunches beneath the tyres as I ease the Bentley to a stop. The engine ticks and settles. I exhale. Oil and salt mingle in the air, sharp and grounding.

'Out you get,' I say, more command than invitation. My heels grind into the gravel as I circle the bonnet. I lift it cleanly – the gesture practised, purposeful. Not so long ago I'd have needed a mechanic's hand, but now I can strip and rebuild half this engine myself. Racing teaches you that: if you can't fix it, you can't trust it.

Simon is out before the words have landed. He cranes forward, eyes alight. 'Are we fixing it?' he says.

'Not today.' I throw him a glance. 'We're learning it still, remember? There's a difference.'

Priscilla steps out more slowly. She dusts her skirt and hesitates, unsure if this is a game or a lesson. I slap the side of the engine casing gently.

'This is the engine – the heart of the car. Everything starts here. If you don't understand it, you don't drive. Simple.'

I narrow my eyes. I want them to know how things work. How to take hold of something and not flinch. That's the only defence I can give them. Not softness, but skill.

'People will tell you certain things run in families,' I say, my voice sharper than I intend. 'Fear. Fate. I don't believe in any of it. What you can take apart, you can master.'

Simon points instantly, jabbing at a metal curve. 'What's that bit?'

'Carburettor. Remember? It mixes air and fuel, so the engine runs right. Too much of one and not enough of the other, and the whole thing chokes.' I crouch so he can see properly. 'It breathes for the car – just as you breathe for yourself.'

Priscilla edges closer. Her fingers drift over the leather tool roll, brushing spanners and screwdrivers as if they're relics in a museum.

'Does it break?' she asks.

'Everything breaks eventually.' I pluck a spanner from the roll and hand it to Simon. 'That's why you learn to fix it yourself.'

He grips it with both hands and sets to the bolt I show him, his tongue poking from the corner of his mouth. His grip is wrong, but he doesn't ask for help. He's stubborn. That, he gets from me. Priscilla crouches, inspecting the tool roll more closely now, no longer wary. She's measuring it, cataloguing. She always does.

'Why do you love cars so much?' Simon asks, voice muffled under the bonnet. 'I like planes better.' His arms stretch out like wings. For a moment I see it: the boy, the man he'll become. Too brave. Too weightless.

I want to laugh. I want to correct him. Instead, I look away – at the horizon, the pull of it. The same pull Father once had. 'Because they answer only to skill,' I say. 'Not to rumour, not to history. When I drive, I'm exactly who I choose to be.'

The words land with more weight than I expect. Priscilla's gaze snaps to me. Her eyes – too knowing for her age – hold me there. She understands more than she says.

'Planes go in the sky!' Simon shouts, lifting his arms and spinning until he collapses, breathless, beside the front tyre.

'Watch the spanner!' I laugh despite myself. I take it from his hand, still warm and smudged with oil, and slide it back into the roll.

'Back in the car,' I say, closing the bonnet with a firm click.

They climb back in, and I take the wheel again. The engine fires, and the Bentley answers with a low growl. The road curls away ahead, narrow and familiar. The children chatter now, their voices climbing and falling like birdsong. I love them fiercely, but they remind me daily of what I've had to outlive – and what I refuse to let define them. I can't change what came before, but I can show them how to move through the world without flinching.

I take the next bend with purpose. The engine answers. The road unfolds.

Falling from the Sky

July 1934

'She'll climb if you let her,' Flight Lieutenant Christopher Clarkson calls over the engine's roar, hand light on the stick.

The biplane's wheel still hums in my bones, but now the sky carries me. Wind claws at my flying cap, the cockpit rattling as if it might splinter apart. I grip the seat edge and let out a laugh – raw, involuntary. The air stinks of fuel and hot metal. Nothing but blue stretches ahead, vast and endless. Clarkson adjusts the controls, sleeves rolled, a slim leather watch catching the light on his wrist.

'This is the only way to travel, Mrs Russell Cooke,' he says. He turns his head just enough to flash me a grin.

I smile, tucking a stray curl beneath my flying cap. 'So you've said, Flight Lieutenant. Repeatedly.'

He chuckles and shifts in his seat. 'And yet you keep coming up here with me. Either you're reckless, or you like my company.'

I glance out at the clouds below us, swirling like silk. 'A bit of both, I expect.'

The truth is, I've given much thought to the risks. Amy Johnson made it to Australia alone. Jean Batten bettered her time. Even Croydon's airfield is full of girls training now; the papers call them 'aviatrixes' as though it's a novelty, not skill. I envy their certainty. I'm only just learning what it means to leave the ground. Women have been proving their place in the sky for years now. Still, for me, flying is a new pursuit. It's not yet about proving anything. I'm not the one in control. But I promised Simon I'd learn more about flying. Something bold, something my mother would never have dared.

Tilford's rooftops flatten beneath us like pressed flowers. Clarkson glances at the fuel pressure gauge and frowns.

'That feed's dropping,' he mutters, tapping the glass. The needle shivers. Slips.

A cough judders through the engine – a sharp, metallic stutter that punches through the cockpit. The RPM falls. Not catastrophically, but enough to make the whole frame tremble.

I straighten. 'That's not promising.'

'Fuel starvation,' he says. 'Line's choked. Hold on.'

The engine coughs again, louder this time, then falters into a thin, uneven splutter. The propeller spins, but slower, the note flattening. We're losing power.

The nose dips. Not a plunge, but a slow, inevitable bowing to gravity. The aircraft begins to descend in a long, unwanted glide. Clarkson trims the nose up slightly, buying us seconds, not safety. Wind tears at my goggles. My breath fogs the glass.

'We're making a forced landing,' he says. His voice is tight but calm. 'Field ahead. Keep your shoulders back.'

The engine coughs once more, then almost quits entirely. Without thrust, the wind's noise changes: less roar, more howl. I feel the shift in my bones. We're gliding now, dead stick, the wings doing all the work. Trees rise beneath us, hedge-lines rushing closer.

'A little more space—' I gasp.

'I see it.' Clarkson coaxes the stick, trying to hold our glide as long and flat as possible. The airframe shudders under the strain. Fabric rattling. Wires singing with vibration.

The field is too near. Too narrow. We're coming in fast.

'Brace,' he says.

The wheels clip the top of a hedge. A shock ricochets through the fuselage. We bounce once – a vicious, teeth-snapping jolt – then skid. Wood splinters. Metal groans. A spray of earth erupts ahead of us. The wings tilt, then catch, and—

We slam to a stop.

My harness bites deep into my collarbone. Dust fills my mouth. A cloud of feathers erupts around us. Pain sparks sharp across my nose. There's only stunned silence. My breath is a ragged thing. My chest rises and falls too fast.

A squawk. Then another. Suddenly, the air is alive with the furious flapping of wings.

A farmer's wife screeches from the yard, apron flying. 'Lord save us. My hens! The coop!'

Clarkson turns his head towards me. He's dazed but alive. 'I don't think we'll be invited back.'

I press a hand to my face, wincing at the sting of a fresh cut. My fingers tremble slightly. I'm scraped, shaken, dust-covered, and more alive than I've felt in months.

'I'd say we made quite the entrance.'

Clarkson sighs, flexing his wrist with a grimace. 'You all right, Melville?'

I nod. I'm rattled, bruised. The sky is above me, the earth behind. We came down and I didn't shatter.

'I want to do that again,' I say, breathless, dust still in my teeth. 'But next time, I'll take the stick.'

15th July 1934

Clarkson says a licence will take six months. I told him I'd do it in half. Not bravado – a promise to myself.

Taking Flight

September 1934

'You're set on this, then, Mrs Russell Cooke?' Andrews calls across the grass. His cap is tugged low against the wind, his wiry frame angled into it. He's checking the Cadet's propeller with quick, practised movements, but his eyes flick to me, measuring.

'I am,' I answer, pulling my gloves tighter. The leather creaks against my fingers. My scarf whips at my shoulder, tugged by the breeze that carries the sharp sting of aviation petrol and trampled grass. Flying isn't a whim. It's the next step – the only one that makes sense.

'Shall we?' he says, in a voice that's clipped but clear.

The airfield stretches wide and bare, edged with hangars like bleached ribs. Ahead, the Avro Club Cadet waits – silver skin catching the sun, its Genet engine ticking over, impatient. Smaller than the machines I've trained beside – but no less capable. My boots leave faint imprints in the soft earth and my jacket is heavy across my shoulders. Perhaps it's weighted by expectations – Simon's, mine, and everyone else's. Flight Lieutenant Clarkson laughed at my determination to do this today. Called it inevitable. I run my hand along the fuselage as I pass. The metal is cool beneath my fingertips, and its surface is rippled with tiny imperfections. It's a machine that doesn't pretend to be more than it is and, for that, I trust it.

Andrews climbs into the rear. His movements are quick and practised. I follow into the front cockpit. I settle into the seat as the straps pull tight across my lap. The wind is louder here. It's pressing against the fabric sides of the plane. A reminder of how small we are against it; it grounds me in this fragile thing we are about to hurl into the sky.

The engine roars, rattling the plane to life. The vibration travels through my body.

'Let's see what you've got,' Andrews says over my shoulder. His voice is carried away by the slipstream.

I push the throttle and feel the resistance give way under my hand. The plane rolls forward. Its wheels bounce slightly over the uneven grass before catching a smoother rhythm. The acceleration is quick. It's sudden. There's no space for hesitation, only instinct.

The moment the ground lets go, everything inside me tightens. The air catches the wings and lifts us. Sudden, fierce, clean. I grip the stick tighter, every instinct screaming not to flinch. The wind tears at the scarf at my neck, and the field falls away beneath us. No woman in my family has ever flown a plane. None were given permission to do anything this free.

I move through the sequence Andrews has drilled into me: a steady climb, the engine thick in my ears, the nose of the plane tilting skyward as the air thins. The fields below flatten into pattern and colour; hedgerows reduced to the finest of threads. I level out, as instructed – not too soon, not too late – easing the controls until the pressure steadies, and the machine hums with something like contentment. There's a lightness to it. It's as though the plane itself recognises we're aloft now. We're part of the sky.

The shallow turn comes next. I bank us gently, careful to keep the horizon line just so; not too high, or we'll climb again, not too low or we'll lose height without meaning to. I'm aware of my own breathing. How it's slowed to match the motion, how each adjustment in the stick answers something instinctive. We cut through a pocket of air that jolts us slightly, but I correct for it without thinking. The correction feels earned – the sum of every hour spent learning what machines do when they're trusted, not feared. There's a rhythm here. It's one that exists beyond the instructions Andrews has given me. It's beyond the levers and dials. Something felt, rather than known.

Below, the land continues to unfurl: distant farms, a ribbon of river, smoke rising from a chimney that seems impossibly small. Above, the sky stretches with its bright, unsparing blue. There's nothing soft about it; it demands your attention. It's a place that insists you stay present.

I begin the descent. Slow and careful. Letting the nose dip by degrees. The plane doesn't fall; it leans into gravity with a kind of controlled grace. I think of the first time I tried this – how my hands trembled, how the earth seemed to rush up too fast – but now there's calm. There's a quiet certainty. Andrews remains silent. That silence is not disinterest; it's a form of trust. He's letting me have this.

We cross the line of trees that border the airfield. The runway draws into view. It's solid and narrow. I hold my breath. A soft kiss of rubber against tarmac, and the plane settles into itself like a creature returned to earth. I taxi to a halt and the engine ticks as it begins to cool. The stillness is oddly loud after the wind and noise.

Certainty is there before he speaks, pulsing beneath my ribs like a second heartbeat. I've crossed some invisible line. Not just between air and land, but between who I was and who I get to be now. This isn't just a skill. It's a new axis.

'Congratulations, Mrs Russell Cooke,' he says as we climb out. His tone is neutral, but there's a glint in his eye. 'You've done it.'

I take off my gloves and let them dangle from one hand. I turn back to look at the plane. It sits quietly now. 'I can't wait to tell my son.'

Andrews nods, accepting the answer without question, and walks toward the hangar.

Between Sky and Earth

June 1935

The bonnet of the Bentley saloon stands open like a hinged jaw, catching the morning sun. Heat shimmers off the metal, carrying the familiar mix of petrol, oil, and something faintly sweet from the nearby lilac bush. Simon circles the car with the deliberate energy of a boy becoming something else – no longer small, not yet grown, limbs all angles and intent.

He crouches, then rises, then drops to one knee again. He can't seem to stay still for more than a breath. At twelve, movement is thought; motion helps him reason.

I pass him a spanner. He takes it without looking at me, checking the tightness of a bolt with a certainty that surprises me still.

I didn't plan to say yes to Clarkson.

The thought comes as I lean over the engine, running my thumb along a frayed wire. I chose to. Not for him, but for what saying yes pushed against: the widow, the dutiful mother, the woman whose life is neatly contained by other people's expectations. With Clarkson, I glimpsed a lighter version of myself – not shaped by loss, not hemmed in by responsibility, not required to be sensible. In another country, I could slip those labels for a whole week and see who truly remained beneath them.

'Mama?' Simon calls, wiping an oily hand across his nose and leaving a streak of black.

I straighten. He's bracing one foot on the running board, elbow propped on his raised knee. His posture is almost adult – until the wind lifts his curls and he blows at them impatiently.

'Yes, darling?'

'When you're away next week … you'll be flying most days, won't you?' He tries for nonchalance, but his fingers tap a rapid rhythm on the metal. He wants the truth, not comfort.

'Most days,' I admit. 'That's the plan.'

He nods, gaze drifting back to the engine, but he's no longer studying its parts. He's gathering courage. After a moment, he drops lightly to the ground, kneels, stands again, wipes his hands, abandons the rag, picks it up once more – movement betraying thought.

Then, quieter: 'Do you think I could do it?'

I rest a hand on the side of the bonnet. 'Do what?'

He looks up at me properly. His face is narrowing with adolescence, but the eyes are the same – wide, searching, hungry for the horizon.

'Fly.'

The word lands with weight. He isn't dreaming; he's preparing.

'Yes,' I say, and the answer is so clear it surprises even me. 'You could.'

He doesn't beam or blush. At twelve, he evaluates. He absorbs. He measures possibilities. Then he wanders a short, restless circle around the car, dragging his fingertips along the warm metal. He stops near the rear door, rubbing a smudge of grease between his fingers.

'Flying isn't only freedom,' I add, moving to stand beside him. 'It takes patience. Practice. Responsibility. The sky doesn't forgive mistakes.'

He's silent for a long moment. The garden hums around us – the low murmur of bees, a distant clatter from the kitchen. Simon turns the spanner in his hand, testing its weight, then tucks it into the toolbox with a decisive clunk.

'You'll teach me?' he asks – not tentative now, but steady, as though he's asking the world to confirm what he already knows.

I meet his gaze. 'When you're ready.'

He nods slowly, a thoughtful dip of the head. He's imagining it, calculating routes, requirements, risks. Already assembling himself towards it.

Then, just as suddenly, he breaks into a half-run across the drive, vaults the low stone edging, and returns triumphantly with a handful of washers he'd forgotten earlier. Boyish again, breathless and careless with his limbs.

'We should finish this,' he says, all business once more. 'If Priscilla comes out, she'll only complain we've ruined her morning with the smell.'

His voice cracks slightly on the last word, but he carries on as though he hasn't heard it. I watch him duck under the bonnet again, face intent, curls falling into his eyes.

Homeward Bound

July 1935

'Steady as she goes,' Clarkson shouts over the slipstream.

I don't answer him. I've learnt enough by now to trust my own hands more than his instructions. I tighten my grip on the stick, and the Gypsy Moth answers to my hand. Below, the French coast falls away, the Channel restless and grey. England waits ahead; its fields are sharpened by distance.

The sun still lingers warm on my shoulders. The burn of it has settled into my skin, darkening it more than I'd expected. It's a reminder of days spent on the beach: of bare feet in the sand, salt on my skin, passionate embraces. That world moved slower without obligation. Now, England rises through the haze.

Flight Lieutenant Christopher Clarkson shifts behind me and stretches out his legs as much as the cockpit allows.

'I'll miss the sun,' he says, his voice half lost to the wind. 'And the wine. And the way you looked in that blue dress yesterday evening.'

Once, I might have flushed at the attention, now I recognise it for what it is: a man mistaking admiration for ownership. 'You'll miss being away from England, you mean.'

'That, too.' He pauses. 'But I'd fly anywhere with you.'

It's flippant, meant to charm, but I feel the tug beneath it. Something heavier than either of us agreed to. The words aren't a proposal, but they suggest a path. One I've already veered from.

I adjust the throttle. The biplane responds, steady beneath my hands. The wheel of the Bentley, the stick of the Cadet, now this – it's all the same. Power taken in my grip. Direction chosen by me. Not passenger. A driver. Below us, the French coast recedes into memory. In Biarritz, I chose ease. I chose being wanted. I chose a life that demanded nothing of me but pleasure. To be no one's widow, no one's mother. Just Melville. But names, like gravity, reclaim you. Now the sky stretches out ahead, and England waits with its hedgerows and consequence.

Clarkson leans closer. 'Looking forward to seeing your children?'

He'd called me lucky earlier – lucky to walk away from that landing, lucky to have children, lucky to have means. If only he knew me. 'Of course,' I say, tightening my grip on the stick. 'I've had my freedom, and now I want them back.'

He chuckles, but I don't think he quite hears it. Not the contradiction. Not the truth of it.

'So,' he says. 'No regrets?'

There's a power in ending things on your own terms. 'None,' I say, and mean it. 'But I always knew when it would end.'

I know he watches me, something unsaid caught behind his expression. 'We could go further. South again. Or east. Just you and me,' he says.

I think of Simon's curls, Priscilla's tilted head. They're my compass. Not him. Clarkson doesn't see that side of me. He only sees what the sun brings out.

'One day,' I say eventually, guiding the plane towards Heston.

Not with you, is left unspoken. It's understood. The English coastline sharpens beneath us. Sussex fields, orderly and green. The sea behind us now, the sun weaker, the air less forgiving. My skin still hums with warmth but already, I feel it fading.

Clarkson shifts behind me. 'I don't like goodbyes,' he says, almost soft.

'Then don't say it.'

He doesn't.

The runway appears, narrow and pale against the grass. I bring us down gently. The wheels kiss the earth, and we roll, the engine easing, the wind softening. He helps with the ropes, glancing at me from under his cap. There's charm in his smile, but something quieter now. A man who suspects, perhaps, that this has been a detour for both of us.

'I'll write,' he says.

I nod. Let him write. The sky has already answered me more clearly than he ever could. I offer nothing more. He walks ahead towards the hangar.

Number Sixteen

August 1935

'Number sixteen to the line!' the marshal shouts.

The demonstration has begun. A staged exhibition of skill and sound. The crowd watches, detached and dutiful, as each machine takes its turn: growling, spinning, flaunting its muscle. A Bugatti skims the perimeter of the track with theatrical flair. Polite applause.

I walk to the single-seat Austin Seven and smooth the front of my slim black trousers. They're sharp, deliberate. I chose them because they make people look twice, and because they let me move the way speed demands. I'm a minor scandal, which is part of the point. My cropped leather jacket is softened at the edges with wear. A silk scarf at my neck is my only nod to the event's formality. Eyes follow me. Some curious. Some amused. Some appalled. I let them look.

The other drivers – tall, broad-backed men – lounge beside their gleaming machines: Bentleys, Lagondas, a solitary Bugatti. They're bold, expensive declarations of status. My Seven, light and efficient, says something else entirely.

'Mrs Russell Cooke,' one of them calls out. His tone is silked with condescension. 'Quite the outfit. Here to make a statement?'

I pull on my gloves. 'Only with the wheel in my hands.'

He smiles, but it falters. That flicker of uncertainty; I've seen it before. It's the moment they realise I won't apologise.

'Number sixteen to the line!' the marshal shouts again.

'Okay, okay,' I say.

I slide into the Austin Seven's seat, the leather hot from the sun. My gloves creak on the wheel, and for a breath I hear nothing – not the clink of champagne glasses, not the hum of engines, only the hush before movement. I steer to the line as the starter drops his arm.

We move. The first turn comes fast. I downshift and take it close, brushing the inside edge. A cone topples. I don't slow. The Seven bites into the tarmac like it wants to prove something, too.

On the straight, I let her go. The speedometer creeps towards its limit. It's modest by comparison, but that's not the point. It's about control. About knowing exactly what to do with the space you've got.

A Bentley lumbers ahead. I catch it at the slalom. He falters, late on the brake. I slide through. Tight and clean. I've watched men misjudge that high-banked corner for years. It feels good to take it the way it was meant to be taken. The crowd gasps. That ripple – surprise, interest, something harder to name – presses me forward.

The final corner demands more than skill. It needs instinct. I brake gently, hold the line, feel the car settle. The tyres grip. I come out of the bend with just enough push to carry me clean to the end. I brake hard. The Seven shrieks once, then stills. We stop just short of the barrier.

Silence.

Then the applause comes. It's uncertain at first, then louder. Longer than any before. I climb out. Peel off my gloves. Let the pause settle. Let them watch. I hadn't realised how much I wanted this. Not the approval, but the acknowledgment. Not to be pitied, not to be whispered about, but recognised for what I can do.

Still, among the faces: a woman in a fur stole. Her mouth is tight. Her eyes don't move from me. 'Such wild behaviour,' she says to her companion, not bothering to lower her voice. 'She's hardly respectable.'

I walk toward her, slow, deliberate. Let her see me properly. 'Respectable?' I say, meeting her gaze. 'Respectability never saved a woman like me. Remarkable might.'

Interruption Seven

FEBRUARY 1973

Dr Haynes hadn't meant to applaud. Academics didn't clap for tapes, and certainly not while seated in a windowless office lit by a single buzzing strip of light. Yet when the reel clicked to its end – Melville's voice still bright with the thrill of the Austin Seven cutting through the slalom – Catherine's hands had come together before she could stop them. It was as if the body recognised something the mind had not yet caught up to.

A quick, startled burst. Then stillness.

She exhaled. Pressed *stop*. The machine settled into silence.

Something had shifted – she could feel it. For weeks she had been handling the same materials, circling the same questions: unlucky, cursed, widowed, marked. The language repeated itself in every archive box, every clipping. A system. A shorthand. A set of boundaries Melville never agreed to.

But this section – the racing, the grit, the flying, the refusal to yield – unsettled that tidy taxonomy. It widened it.

Not tragedy. Not curse. Not survival.

Authorship.

Catherine stood, pacing once across the narrow room. Her reflection wavered faintly in the glass of the door: pale, drawn, but with some new alertness beneath the exhaustion. She recognised it – the afterglow of witnessing a woman step cleanly outside the shape history had insisted upon.

She returned to her desk. Her notes waited – methodical, obedient, suddenly too narrow. She uncapped her pen.

> *Speed was not escape; it was authorship.*
> *She wasn't 'unlucky' – she refused the meaning others made of her.*

Her chest tightened. Not pain, exactly, but a full, bracing awareness. The paper would need reshaping.

Catherine rewound the tape a few seconds and pressed play. Melville's laughter spilled back into the room, reckless, uncontained. She felt herself smile.

'Remarkable woman,' Catherine murmured.

Then she wrote:

This is why the paper must be written: because the frames remain, and women still learn to live inside them. Melville didn't escape hers — she simply refused to stay framed.

The tape turned. She kept writing, no longer sure whether she was documenting Melville – or herself.

Mr Rolt

FEBRUARY 1973

Dr Catherine Haynes: could we talk about him now? David Rolt?

Melville Russell Cooke: (Soft laugh). I wondered when he'd appear.

DCH: accounts make it seem as though he arrived from nowhere. Your papers suggest otherwise.

MRC: he didn't arrive. I moved towards him. He just happened to be seventeen years younger, which made society pay attention.

DCH: and you?

MRC: I paid attention for different reasons.

DCH: was it sudden?

MRC: no. Desire rarely is. I'd been gathering speed for years — engines first, then the sky. He was simply the next risk I chose.

DCH: (Quietly). What was he like when you first saw him?

MRC: curious. Sharper than he let on. And amused by me, which is rarer than you'd think.

DCH: and what did you want from him?

MRC: (Laughs). To be looked at cleanly. Not as a widow, not as a captain's daughter. Just as myself.

DCH: someone who saw you.

MRC: someone who didn't look away.

DCH: in what sense?

MRC: I was his muse…

A Muse

ARCHIVE: REEL SEVEN

From 1936

A new wave of portrait painters is making itself known in Oxfordshire studios. Their work leans towards truth rather than flattery, with a rawness some find uncomfortably intimate. One critic remarked that such portraits 'seem to look back at the viewer'.

Oxford Mail, 10 May 1936

Moby Dick

May 1936

The smell of turpentine greets me the moment I step inside. It's sharp and acrid, mingling with the subtler scent of beeswax polish. This room feels alive with texture: scuffed floorboards, canvases leaning in uneven rows, and the faint ghost of past conversations caught in the grain of the wood. It's not just an artist's studio; it's David Rolt's world. It's chaotic and raw, yet somehow deliberate.

I pause just inside the doorway and glance at my boots, checking I've not brought half the lane in with me. We'd agreed on this – though 'agreed' might be overstating it. He'd suggested I see his work properly, his words fumbling somewhere between confidence and uncertainty. His eyes, though, they said something else entirely: a challenge, veiled in curiosity.

David hasn't noticed me yet. His back is to the door. His shoulders are slightly hunched, with his right arm steadied against the edge of an easel. His left hand hovers with a brush, suspended mid-thought. His movements are deliberate. His frame tall but slightly off-balance, favouring his left leg as if the right might betray him. Still, there's a tension in the way he stands. Purposeful, but guarded.

'You're late.' His voice cuts through the stillness.

'You didn't strike me as the type to care about punctuality,' I reply, stepping further inside.

'I don't. But you do,' he says, turning to face me.

The unruly shock of dark hair, the sharp, intelligent eyes that seem to see too much. He's young, twenty-one, but there's a weight to him. There's a quiet defiance that makes me linger. He takes me in, from the leather of my jacket to the scarf tied loose at my neck. His gaze lingers briefly on my hands: bare and resting lightly at my sides.

'How do you know what I care about?' I ask, arching an eyebrow.

He sets the brush down and shrugs. 'I don't. But I'm learning already.'

The words are simple, but his gaze holds something weightier. As though he's testing my reaction. I glance past him at the canvas – a swirl of restless colour that draws the eye in without offering it a place to settle. Greens and ochres bleed into muted blues. It's alive with movement but resisting resolution.

'You're prolific,' I say. My fingertips twitch against my thigh. It's a small thing, but I feel it.

'All of them remain mine.' He gestures to the canvases crowding the walls. 'Until someone decides they're worth taking home.'

'You don't sound bitter about it,' I say, stepping closer. There's a faint trace of tobacco and something citrus beneath the paint. Clean. Unexpected.

'I'm not.' A smile. 'It's just the way it is.'

His honesty is disarming, and, for a moment, I'm not sure how to respond. Instead, I let my attention wander, taking in the room: the jars of brushes, the worn chair near the window, the small desk cluttered with charcoal sketches. It's a life distilled. It's messy and unapologetic.

'You're not what I expected.'

He raises an eyebrow. He brushes a strand of paint-streaked hair out of his face. 'And what did you expect?'

'Someone more polished,' I admit. 'Less … genuine.'

He laughs. It's a low, warm sound that feels like a ripple through the air. 'You're not what I expected either.'

'Which is?'

'Not someone who looks like she belongs in a society portrait.'

'Careful,' I say, tilting my head. 'Flattery is dangerous.'

'Only if it's insincere.' His smile widens just slightly.

We stand there for a moment. The silence between us is charged with something I can't quite name. He shifts his weight. My eyes flick to his leg before I can stop myself.

'Does it hurt?' I ask, my voice quieter than I intended.

His expression flickers – surprise, then something softer. 'Not anymore. I've had it all my life. Doctors called it a defect. I call it perspective.'

'Good answer.'

His gaze sharpens, perhaps he's deciding whether I'm mocking him. Then he nods, the faintest trace of amusement returning.

'Melville?' he says, as though testing it.

'After Herman Melville. My father's favourite novel was *Moby Dick*. My friends call me Mel, though.'

He smiles. 'Have you decided what you want from me, *Melville*?'

I hesitate, glancing at the storm-tossed canvas behind him. 'A portrait,' I say. It lands heavier than I expect and I realise, too late, that I mean it.

That makes him pause. His expression is unreadable. 'Of you?'

'Yes,' I say, meeting his gaze.

'And what should it say?'

I falter for a moment. The weight of the question. 'I don't know yet,' I admit. 'Something true.'

He watches me, his expression thoughtful but still distant. Then, without a word, he picks up a charcoal pencil from the desk and gestures towards the chair by the window.

'I thought you didn't paint from sketches,' I say. I'm resisting the urge to fidget under his scrutiny.

'I don't. But sometimes it helps me understand what I'm looking at.'

It isn't flattery. It's scrutiny. I should bristle, but instead I let him keep looking. That unnerves me more than any compliment could. His gaze doesn't roam, it *pins*. Maybe that's why it's already disarming me. He isn't looking at me through a male gaze. He's looking at me as an artist. Somehow that's worse.

'You're restless,' he says after a moment, the charcoal moving across the canvas.

'What makes you think that?'

'People who are still don't grip the air like it might get away from them.'

I laugh, though it's softer than I intended. 'Is that how you see me?'

'It's how you are.'

The words linger, unexpected and raw. He doesn't break eye contact. I look away first. That annoys me more than it should. For a moment, I forget that he's younger, forget everything except the way he speaks. Not just as someone observing me, but as someone unafraid to say exactly what he sees. I laugh softly.

'I used to find stillness on the bridge of ships. Strictly off-limits to passengers, but my father…'

'Father?'

'He was…'

David's charcoal stills. 'Go on,' he says.

'Captain Edward Smith.' The name doesn't land lightly. It never does. 'He was the captain of—'

'The *Titanic*.'

I nod. 'Last time I saw him: April the tenth, nineteen-twelve. Seven o'clock.'

David's eyes soften. 'And after?'

'The papers lied at first. Passengers safe. Then, *Ocean Catastrophe*. My mother knew. He wouldn't leave the ship until everyone was safe.' My voice catches. 'Then came the incessant headlines. Over and over. Saying he was drunk, that he shot himself. That he was responsible. Travelling too fast…' Deep breath in and out. 'Never once considering what we lost.'

'Keep talking,' he says, without turning to me. I shift to see his canvas, but he shakes his head.

'In the days after the disaster, my mother was overwhelmed with letters and telegrams of condolences,' I say, and David's charcoal dances. His movement is confident. 'Each day brought two or three hundred new messages, each one a reminder of the world's eyes fixed upon us.'

He freezes, charcoal hovering, his expression thoughtful. 'That's an incredible burden.'

'She still found the strength to contribute to the *Titanic* Relief Fund.' I hear a note of pride in my voice. 'It was organised by the Mayor of Southampton… On just one day, the nineteenth of April, they raised thirty-five thousand pounds.'

'A significant sum,' David comments, resuming his sketching.

I nod, feeling the weight of the memory heavy. 'I remember a report, in *The Washington Times*, suggesting that had my father been saved, his career would have been over anyway.' I shake my head; the absurdity not lost on me even now. 'As if his career mattered more than his life.'

'Ignorance,' David says softly.

'I've learnt about many of his true acts of heroism over the years, though. I cling to them now…' Another nod to continue. 'Emma Bucknell from lifeboat number eight said he placed her there himself. When men nearby became desperate, he demanded, "Can't you behave like men? Look at all of these women. See how splendid they are!".' My attempt to mimic Father's voice is awful. I giggle softly. '"Women and children first." That's what he said. Used a megaphone to be heard over the chaos.'

The room is quiet. 'You carry all of this with you,' he says.

It unnerves me, the way he says it. Like he's found a bruise I didn't know I still had.

'Just as you carry that leg,' I say, and he laughs. 'I don't know if I like you enough yet,' I add lightly, though the weight in my chest betrays me.

His lips quirk upward. Not quite a smile. 'That makes two of us.'

There's no malice in the words. Instead, there's an honesty that cuts through the air between us. And, as he leans back and studies the beginnings of his sketch, I feel a pull. Not to be liked, but rather to be understood truly.

Maybe that's more dangerous.

Irish Waves

August 1936

'It's angrier than last week,' I tell him, arms folded as I stare at the new painting.

Salt seems to hang in the air, though the sea is only here in oil. It rises from the vast canvas dominating the room; deep, tempestuous blues streaked with foam so vivid it feels alive.

Behind me, David leans against his easel with his cane propped nearby. His stance is easy, but every detail of his presence feels deliberate. Already, I know the way he stands now, leaning his weight on a steady surface as though it were habit rather than need. His right shoe – polished leather with a thick cork lift hidden inside – stands firm against the uneven floorboards. A testament to his quiet refusal to let anyone see what might be perceived as weakness. Already, I've learnt that the streaks of paint in his hair last longer than the scent of turpentine in his clothes.

'Angry or alive?' I hear amusement threading through his tone.

'I suppose that depends on how it ends.'

His grin is quick. It flashes white against his olive skin, tanned deeper by the summer sun. I feel it low in my stomach; a ripple, small but insistent. I fold my arms tighter, as if I can press it back down. He leans into his step as he approaches.

'The ocean never ends,' he says finally. 'That's the point.'

I take his left hand. Not firmly, but fully. His fingers twitch beneath mine, surprised. He doesn't pull away. I turn back to the canvas. I let my gaze follow the waves he's brought to life. Each brushstroke is a testament to something relentless. They crash against unseen cliffs.

'It's Ireland, isn't it?' I ask, the familiarity tugging at a distant corner of my memory.

'Donegal,' he says, his voice closer now. I catch the faint, earthy scent of his tobacco pouch as he shifts beside me. The worn leather is hooked in his right hand. A subtle sleight of hand that masks its limitations.

'Sketched it years ago. Took me until now to figure out how to paint it.'

'Why now?'

He pauses, releasing his hand from mine. His fingers brush the rim of a paint jar before shrugging lightly. 'Maybe because I finally understand it. You don't paint something like this until you've lived it.'

Those words hang in the air. They're heavy with a meaning that neither of us attempts to untangle. I step closer to the painting, as if proximity might reveal the storms etched into the waves.

'It's untamed,' I murmur. 'Refuses to be anything less.'

'Like someone else I know.'

I turn to him, sharp, but there's no teasing in his expression. His brown eyes hold steady on mine. They're unflinching, they're certain.

'I mean it,' he continues, his voice low. 'Do you even know how rare it is? To see someone so … wholly themselves?'

'That's a kind way of saying I'm difficult,' I reply, though my pulse quickens.

'You're not difficult.' He steps closer. His presence coils through the room. It's quiet and anchored; it's laced with heat. My breath catches low. The air between us feels thick enough to touch. 'You're defiant. And maybe that's why you're here … to remind yourself that you can be.'

The truth of his words catches in my chest, but I laugh softly. I shake my head. 'I came for a portrait, not a lecture on the state of my mind.'

'And you think they're different?' His grin sharpens. It's playful yet disarming.

I let the moment linger. The charged stillness settles over us like the hush before a storm. Turning back to the painting, I trace its restless edges with my gaze. The waves seem to watch me. Perhaps they're daring me to look away.

'I'm not used to this,' I admit, the words heavy but unguarded. 'This … freedom.'

'Because you've never had it.' His voice is quiet, but his words land with force. 'Here, you're not Mrs Russell Cooke the mother, or Mel the widow or even Helen the daughter of the *Titanic*'s captain. You're just my Melville.'

The room feels smaller, the air denser, and I can't bring myself to meet his gaze. Instead, I step even closer to the canvas. My fingertips brush its edge.

'You'll let me keep it when it's done?'

David laughs. The sound is warm and unrestrained. 'You're not serious.'

'Why not? It would look lovely above the fireplace.'

'It's priceless.'

'Then you'd better finish it before I take it anyway,' I shoot back, and my smirk dares him to challenge me.

He shakes his head, but he's grinning. 'You're impossible.'

'Untamed,' I correct. I turn to face him fully and wave a finger towards the canvas. 'Like that.' *I want to take up space here*, I think. I want more than to be looked at. I want the wind. I want the kind of recklessness that leaves a mark. Then, 'Will you fly with me?'

The moment stretches, the room brimming with something raw and undeniable. His gaze dips briefly, catching on the curve of my jaw, the tilt of my shoulders, before returning to mine.

'I can't.' His voice is low. 'I plan every aspect of leaving here. I check the stairwells, locate toilets, even how many steps to the street. I don't like not knowing.'

I say nothing. Instead, I take one step closer, slow and deliberate, until the space between us narrows to breath.

'You don't have to control everything with me,' I say, quiet but clear. 'Let me take some of it.'

The words hang there. I want to disrupt him, unsettle him, as much as myself. He looks at me then – properly. Not the way he studies a canvas, searching for what he can master. But as if I might be the one thing he can't.

'That's the part that scares me,' he says.

I hold his gaze. Let the silence stretch until it's taut. Then. 'Good. It should.'

~

Later, as I watch him work on my portrait, his movements are unhurried but deliberate. They're like the waves he's captured elsewhere. His right hand steadies a jar of turpentine while his left moves the brush in slow, calculated strokes.

I am seventeen years older than this artist, who paints like a man taming storms. And perhaps that combination is what unsettles me most. I don't want calm seas. I want to be broken open by the tide.

13th August 1936

The waves in Mr Rolt's painting haven't left me. They rise in my chest. Waiting. I once thought desire looked like ruin. Perhaps it simply looks like appetite.

I went back to the studio this morning. Not for the canvas, for the shift I felt inside it.

He didn't touch me. I didn't touch him. Yet everything was altered. I felt the shape of his attention as he passed behind me, the warmth grazing my back, the catch of breath before he said nothing.

For years, my body has belonged to other people's stories: to grief, to duty, to photographs I never chose. A wife, a widow, a captain's daughter, a footnote. Now I'm here: flesh, wanting, uncertain.

He looked at me as though he could see that. As though he sensed I'd been keeping myself folded up for too long, as though he was waiting for the moment I'd open.

I let him look. I let myself be seen. Not as evidence, not as inheritance, simply as myself.

I think of the so-called curse – the word others clung to when they couldn't explain our grief. How easily it's served me. A shield to stay cautious, to make my hesitation sound like fate rather than choice. But it was never in my blood. Only in the hesitation I mistook for safety.

I'm done hesitating.

Now, with the window open, the air tastes of salt and smoke. I think of his hands, his mouth, the look he gave me when I stood too close and didn't move. I picture what it would be to choose – not to be chosen, but to choose – and the thought is enough to keep me awake.

Leaving Pratts

September 1936

His trunk waits by the door, brass clasps gleaming in the dim hall. Simon straightens his collar again, as if the uniform can make him older than thirteen. This house – *my* house chosen, not inherited – feels too still, too unbroken. It doesn't yet know us fully. It doesn't know the cadence of my daughter's careful footsteps or the sharp thud of Simon's hurried ones. It doesn't yet know our silences either.

Pratts, they call it now. *Pratts House* and *Pratts Cottage*. It was Ivy Dene before, though the old name lingers like a ghost in the stone. The house is solid; Cotswold rubble pressed into walls thick with other people's lives. I chose it for its remoteness, for the way it turns its back to the village and to the world. I chose it because it's as far from the sea as I could find. Here, I told myself, the children would be safe. Rooted. Out of reach of tides, of wars, of headlines.

And yet the quiet doesn't reassure me. It feels watchful, unsettled, as if even the air is holding its breath. I walk the halls, and the house resists me still. Its rooms echo with a kind of emptiness that won't yield to warmth. I've begun forcing it into shape: tearing out the mean spiral staircase, insisting on something solid, manageable. I won't live in a house that makes movement difficult. The servant's bell remains. Though Mary Moss, who came with the house, mutters she'll take her wages elsewhere if it rings too often. She hasn't left. She knows what it is to root yourself against a storm. Ada is with a naval family these days; I miss her more than I miss any house I've lived in.

Now, Simon stands too straight next to his trunk. He's adjusting his tie for the third time, ensuring it sits just so beneath the stiff collar of his uniform. Determined to master the small rituals of adulthood before he's even left. The navy-blue blazer, the polished shoes, the crisp white shirt – it all looks oddly foreign against the unfamiliar walls. I touch his sleeve.

'It'll be fine, Mama,' he says, though his fingers betray him, worrying the edge of his blazer cuff.

It's the last thing I can fix for him. A fold. A wrinkle. The rest, he'll have to navigate without me. I spent years trying to outpace grief by keeping my children close. But the world's cracking open again, and all I can do is let my son meet it, not shield him from it. I've taught him motion; the rest must be his own.

By the hallway's fireplace, David watches with a kind of detached amusement. A pipe rests on the mantel. Instead, one of my cigarettes hangs from his lip, and the ivory of a matchbook flicks open and closes in his good hand. My children have accepted that Mama has a friend.

'You'll be fine, old man. The first few weeks are tedious, but you'll find your set soon enough.' David's voice carries an effortless polish. It's the sort that doesn't rush, doesn't beg either.

Simon straightens under the praise, folding his grin into the pocket with his handkerchief. 'Can't believe I'm in E House, Morshead's,' he says, for the seventh or eighth time since yesterday. 'Rowing trials are soon. And the air squadron of course.'

He tells it like it's inevitable, like the sky is waiting for him. I feel a pull of dread beneath the pride. Boys his age don't yet know what the world does with their eagerness – how it takes it, sharpens it, and throws it into battles they can't yet imagine.

David exhales a slow plume of smoke. He considers before speaking. 'The squadron's a good lot. All terribly keen, of course. I knew a chap from Cambridge who ended up in the RAF. Practically married to his machine by the end of it.'

Simon's eyes flash with interest. 'I'd like that. Not to be married to it,' he corrects, 'but to fly.'

David chuckles, lazily amused. 'Of course.'

At the end of the hallway, Priscilla is silent. She's curled into the corner, all small and contained. She's watching but not engaging. She doesn't like David. He's polite to her, but he doesn't soften for her the way he does for Simon. Equally, she's too much *my* daughter to warm to someone who doesn't try. I step to her and reach out, smoothing the sleeve of her dress.

'You'll write to your brother, won't you?'

She shrugs. 'If he writes first.'

Simon snorts. 'You'll miss me, Pris. Don't pretend.'

She scowls, but it lacks real venom. I know, because I feel it too.

Mary Moss appears in the doorway from the kitchen, wiping her hands on her apron. 'The car's out front, Mrs Russell Cooke.' Her voice is softer than usual. Perhaps she too feels the weight of this morning.

I nod. 'Thank you, Mary.'

Simon doesn't hesitate. He grabs his cap, hoists his trunk, and strides for the door as though he's done this a thousand times before. He barely glances back. I follow. My breath catches. This is the part I've been dreading.

Outside, the morning is brisk. The sky is a pale, watchful grey and the air is edged with the first whispers of autumn. The car is waiting with an engine purring faintly. Its presence breaks the stillness of the gravel drive. The house looks wrong in the cool light: too bare, too new. It hasn't yet earned the right to be the kind of house where a mother watches her son leave for school.

Simon adjusts his cap. He tilts it at an angle.

'Do you have everything?'

'Yes, Mama.'

I touch his sleeve, smoothing a different imaginary wrinkle. 'Your letters should be detailed.'

He laughs. 'I'll tell you all about the planes and the boats, don't worry.'

But that's not what I mean. I mean the things in between. I mean the moments I won't be there for – the cold mornings, the whispered secrets, the quiet before lights-out, the loneliness that might creep in when he doesn't expect it.

David has followed us out. He's standing just behind me with his hands in his pockets. 'You're a lucky boy,' he says, tone idle but sincere. 'A fine school, and a mother who'll spoil you with letters.'

Simon grins. 'I'll keep them all in my desk.'

A lump rises in my throat. He's so young. Thirteen. His father's age when he went away to school. I stand on my tiptoes. I press my lips to his forehead. My fingers tighten on his sleeve before I let him go. 'Be good.'

'I will.'

'Take this. For luck.' I place a button in his palm. He turns it over. E.J.S. The engraving is shallow, but still there. 'I used to watch my father polishing the brass buttons on his uniform. A ritual he never rushed.'

'It's the button he gave to the brother he saved?'

I nod. 'Thought it ought to travel with you now.'

The trunk is lifted, placed in the back, and the car door swings open. Simon climbs in. He waves, his face bright with expectation. I manage to lift my hand, but my stomach twists. I hate this. The leaving. The part where I'm to stand still and they drive away. The fear that one day they won't return. *Father, Sidney, Mother.*

He waves without fear, though. Like someone who doesn't know he's already had his safest years. Priscilla tugs at my sleeve. 'He'll be back at Christmas.'

I nod, but the ache in my chest doesn't loosen.

David, now at my other side, exhales through his nose. 'Brave boy.'

He doesn't ask how I'm feeling. That's not David's way. I glance at him, but his eyes are on the car as it pulls away. I wonder if he's thinking of his own school days, of the parents he barely mentions.

'Come inside,' I say. My voice is tight.

He flicks the cigarette into the gravel, and I watch the embers flicker and die. As I turn, Priscilla hesitates on the step. I reach for her, wrapping an arm around her thin shoulders. She nestles in without a word. Simon's gone, and we'll count the days until he returns.

Above Oxfordshire

May 1937

'Bloody hell,' David shouts as the biplane jolts forward, his knees jutting awkwardly against the cockpit walls. The Genet roars, the air claws at my scarf, and I grin into the slipstream.

He's in front of me, uncomfortably folded into the forward seat. His legs are too long for the cramped space. I can see his head tilt slightly as he scans the dials and his shoulders are set with tension. His hands are tucked beneath his thighs, braced against what's coming. Perhaps he's worried about accidently hitting one of the controls, too.

'Nervous?' I call.

'Should I be?'

I smirk and ease the throttle forward. 'Only if you don't trust me.'

A beat. Then, 'Do you?'

Before he can answer, we're rolling. Wheels bumping over uneven grass and the whole machine trembling with promise. The rush of air grows louder. It pulls at us. Then, suddenly, the ground lets go. The weight drops away. The sky opens.

'Bloody hell!' His voice carries in the slipstream. I watch the set of his shoulders tighten – the only part of him I can see from back here.

'Relax,' I call over the engine. 'You're not going anywhere but up.'

The horizon tilts as I bank us gently. Below, the countryside unfolds. Its soft-edged fields are stitched with hedgerows and rivers coiling like silver thread. Far off, Oxford's spires catch the sun. They're sharp and golden. The Genet hums. The air is crisp against my cheeks.

'You can breathe now,' I tell him. I hear the laugh in his exhale.

He shifts slightly. Just enough that I know the grip is loosening.

'You do this often?' he calls. 'By choice?'

'As often as I can,' I reply, trimming the rudder, adjusting the stick. 'It's better up here. No clocks, no noise, no one telling you who you're supposed to be.'

He doesn't reply right away. I watch the line of his back and the slight tilt of his head.

'This is freedom,' he says at last, more to the sky than to me. His voice is quieter now.

'Exactly. No one owns the sky.'

'It's … disconcerting,' he admits. 'I don't like surprises.'

There's something in the way he says it – not defensive, just honest. It's taken months to convince him to fly with me.

'Not used to letting someone else take the reins?' I ask.

'More than that.' He doesn't turn. His gaze must stay fixed on the horizon.

Below, the landscape glows with the late light: spires and riverbanks and rippling green. His good hand rests on the edge of the cockpit, but the other stays drawn in, close to his side.

I lean forward until my breath brushes his ear. The smell of tobacco and turpentine clings faintly to him, carried even up here. If I reached just an inch more, my shoulder would press against his. 'Do you want to try?'

He twists just enough to glance back. 'Try what?'

'Flying. The controls are right there in front of you… Stick, throttle, pedals. I've got mine here, too. I won't let us fall.'

He laughs, uneasy. 'You're serious?'

'I don't offer things I don't mean.'

A pause. He hates uncertainty. He's built a whole armour of carefulness around it – every step measured, every weakness masked. But up here, there's no way to script it. That's why I offer him the stick. To see if he'll risk letting go.

'Go on,' I say gently. 'I'm right behind you. You're safe.'

His good hand hovers, then settles on the stick. The plane dips, a sharp lurch that throws his shoulder back into mine. The touch is brief, accidental, but it sends a shiver through me sharper than the drop.

'Not too tight. Let her move. She'll tell you what she wants.' My voice stays low, steady.

He listens. His grip softens, his shoulders loosening as though the machine is unknotting something inside him. I watch the line of his back shift, less rigid now, and it feels like I've coaxed not just the Cadet, but him, into trusting the air.

'That's it. She listens to you. You're gentler than I thought.' A pause. 'It suits you.'

He breathes out a laugh. 'This is … extraordinary.'

I smile where he can't see. For a year I've been the one to follow his gaze, to let him frame me in his charcoal lines. But here, in the sky, it's my hands that steady him. My gift. My freedom, lent to him for a moment.

'I told you. She's forgiving.'

We fly like that for a while. Him with his hand on the controls, me shadowing his movements, the air stretching out in all directions. There's something easy in the silence. There's something new in the rhythm of us. When I take back full control, the sun is already dipping and the spires of Oxford are shrinking behind us as we begin our descent. I note that the shadows are long and blue across the fields.

'You did well,' I say as the ground rises to meet us.

'You're just saying that.'

'I'm not. I was right there with you. I'd have known if you weren't.'

He says nothing, but I catch a flicker of something in the set of his shoulders.

The engine ticks as it cools, the airfield hushed in the last gold light. When he steps down, he favours his left leg, but he masks it with a shrug. David stretches stiffly, brushing paint-streaked hair from his forehead.

'Next time, I'll let you land us, too,' I say, resting a hand on the biplane's silver flank, still humming with flight.

He laughs, startled. 'You're serious?'

'I'm tired of being the only one who runs the risk.'

He steps closer than he needs to, close enough that I feel the warmth of him through the cooling air. My pulse jumps. For a moment, it feels like gravity has shifted.

'You're impossible,' he murmurs.

'Good,' I say. 'I've had enough of being safe.'

10th June 1937

His restraint is its own seduction. Not coyness. Not shyness. Control. It makes me ache. I've spent years arranging myself to be proper, to be safe. With David, I want to be seen. Not just understood. Desired.

He's seventeen years younger than me. Old enough to paint storms onto canvas, young enough that the society would call me indecent. Perhaps I am. But what if decency is just another word for vanishing?

I could have kissed him today. I didn't. He didn't ask. That's the danger of him; he waits. And in the waiting, I unravel. Each silence coils tighter until even my breath feels like a surrender.

I'm not grieving anymore. Not like before. Desire is louder than grief now, and I never thought that would be true again.

Tomorrow I'll return to the studio. I'll wear red. Let him look.

The Portrait's Progress

June 1937

The brush slips. A streak of paint cuts across the canvas where it wasn't meant to. David curses under his breath, low and impatient. I'm already in the room, though he hasn't turned yet. His shoulders are hunched, his weight balanced unevenly, his focus so fierce it almost hurts to watch.

The studio smells of turpentine and beeswax, but underneath it, I catch something else – tobacco, and him. The light is different today: golden, unapologetic, pouring across the floorboards and catching on his hair. He glances back when he realises I'm here. The smile that breaks across his face is unguarded, sudden, like he hasn't learnt to hide what I do to him.

'You're late.'

'Or you're early,' I reply, tossing my coat aside. 'Which is worse?'

'What a dilemma,' he says. His voice is light but teasing.

'I thought you could use the head start,' I reply. 'Or did you get lost in your genius again?'

David chuckles. It's a deep, warm sound that fills the space. 'Flattery doesn't suit you. Unlike that red dress…'

'Who said it was flattery?'

'There's coffee in the pot.'

I move towards the small kettle on the cast-iron stove. The faint strains of a gramophone float through the room, a melody somewhere between wistful and defiant. 'What's the occasion? A bribe to keep me here longer?' I tease, pouring myself a cup.

He doesn't answer immediately. His focus returns to the canvas.

'Maybe I just like having you around,' he says eventually. His tone is almost too casual.

I pause and the warmth of the cup grounds me. His honesty is attractive. It's a reminder of how differently we move through the world. Where I've spent years guarding myself, David seems utterly without armour.

'You're lucky I like your company.' I settle onto the stool nearest him. I watch his hand as he paints. The brush trails vivid strokes across the canvas. His movements are deliberate. I find its rhythm strangely soothing.

'What's it like?' I ask, breaking the silence.

He glances at me, one eyebrow raised. 'What's what like?'

'Seeing the world in lines and colours. Finding the truth in all of this.' I gesture vaguely at the half-finished painting, at the chaotic beauty of his studio. There are two new portraits of me here, too.

David leans back slightly. His brown eyes narrow in thought. His fingers brush the pouch on the table; it's a gesture as familiar as breathing. 'It's about the bits people don't know they're hiding,' he says. 'It's about revealing them.'

I tilt my head, letting his words settle. 'And what have you found in me?'

His gaze doesn't flicker. 'A woman who wants to be known but doesn't yet know what that costs.'

I laugh. It's a sharp, quick sound. 'That's one way to spin stubbornness.'

'You can call it whatever you like,' he says with a shrug. His gaze is steady. 'It's still there.'

I stand and move toward the window, aware of every inch between us. The glass is streaked from earlier rain and, beyond it, the sky glows faintly with the last light of the day. I press my fingers to the sill; the cool surface grounds me.

'You see more of me than I'm comfortable with,' I admit, my voice quieter now.

David's uneven gait is audible on the floorboards. He doesn't reach for me – not quite – but I feel him behind me, close enough that the heat of his body raises goose bumps at the back of my neck. If I moved back even an inch, I'd touch his chest. I think about it. The space between us feels charged: no movement, no sound, just the long pause between decision and desire. I want him to reach for me. I want to not stop him. I keep my fingers pressed to the sill. His breath stirs the nape of my neck. I don't move. I don't speak. My whole body listens. His hand rises. Not touching, not yet. Hovering just above my hip. The distance between us is measured in heartbeats and I feel every one.

'Maybe it's time to get comfortable,' he says softly.

When I turn to face him, we are too close. His eyes hold mine. Unflinching. My fingers brush his wrist – deliberately, this time. His breath catches. I know, in that second, that I could kiss him. I don't. But I let the silence between us burn.

I let him see me want.

'You scare me.' The admission lands heavier than I mean it to. I regret it instantly and yet want him to hear it. To hold it.

He nods, slow and sure. 'Then let's paint through the fear. Let's see where it leads.' His voice is calm, but his eyes say something else entirely. The air between us shifts again. Charged. Waiting.

I turn back to the window, heart thudding too fast. My skin is aware of him in ways I haven't felt before. The glass shows us both: me, rigid and waiting; him, steady and unflinching. His reflection doesn't waver. He doesn't step away.

The air is charged with everything we haven't said.

The tension between us pulls tight. Not breaking but holding. Stretching. I lean back, just slightly, into the space where I know he's standing. He doesn't move. Neither do I. We're past the point of pretending it means nothing.

Then, a shift.

The faint scrape of his boot on the boards. The warmth of him presses closer. His hand comes to rest at my waist. Deliberate. He's claiming the space we've circled for months. His other hand finds my wrist, slow but certain, and he turns me towards him. The move is careful, but there's no question in it. His touch is warm. Decisive. Not a test. A decision.

When his mouth crashes against mine, it isn't gentle. It's hungry. Like we've both been holding our breath for too long. Heat floods low and fast. It twists through me before I can steady it.

I grip his shirt, fist tight, dragging him closer until there's no space left. The taste of smoke and salt is on his lips. Sharp. Unrefined. He deepens the kiss, and it steals whatever thought I had. My back hits the cool glass, and still, I want him closer.

Closer still.

Every line we've pretended to draw between us snaps in an instant. It's reckless. It's consuming. It's indecent, and I don't care.

17th June 1937

I could ruin him.
God help me, I want to.
Seventeen years between us and every one of them is a rebuke. Yet he looks at me when I undress as though I'm the one untouched.
The danger is not in his youth, but in how willingly I would surrender my years. I want the indecency of it. I desire his fingers.

Interruption Eight

FEBRUARY 1973

Catherine Haynes switched off the recorder. The room settled into its usual hush, but something in Melville's story still shimmered – the heat of the studio, the unfurling of desire, the unmistakable sense of a woman choosing herself.

'There's one thing I've been meaning to ask,' Catherine said, clearing her throat. 'The portrait, *An Unlucky Woman* – I found different correspondence about its disappearance.'

Melville's eyebrows lifted, not in surprise but in recognition. 'Ah. That old superstition dressed up as taste.'

'The buyer loved it,' Catherine went on. 'Until someone told him who the sitter was. Then the renaming, the refusal to keep it, the insistence it "cast a shadow".' She hesitated. 'They said it had *an ill-luck air*.'

Melville gave a soft, dismissive hum. 'People prefer a curse to a conscience. It spares them from admitting their fear is their own invention.'

'You didn't try to reclaim it?'

'Why would I? Let them hang their dread wherever they please. The truth rarely changes minds.' She turned towards the fire, watching the flames shift. 'If a portrait unsettles them, that's the artist's triumph, not my burden.'

A beat passed. The warmth from the grate felt patchy; Catherine rubbed her thumb across her knuckles, suddenly aware of an ache that hadn't settled in weeks. She adjusted her sleeve, a pointless, delaying gesture.

'Did you ever…' Catherine began, then faltered. 'Did *it* ever feel … dangerous, to be desired like that?'

Melville smiled – not unkindly. 'Are you asking about David, or about yourself?'

Catherine inhaled sharply. 'I only meant—'

'You're flushed,' Melville said gently. 'That's not from the fire. Something's unsettled you.'

For a moment Catherine couldn't meet her gaze. 'It's nothing.'

'It isn't nothing,' Melville said, eyes narrowing with a knowledge that was almost maternal. 'You ask about love as if it's a concept. It isn't, not for you.'

Catherine swallowed. Her hand drifted, unconsciously, to her sternum. 'I can't … offer certainty.' The words escaped before she could temper them.

'Because you're frightened of your body,' Melville said simply.

Catherine stiffened. 'I never said—'

'You didn't need to.' Melville leant back. 'You mentioned it when we first met. A childhood illness. Borrowed luck, your grandmother called it.' Her voice softened. 'And now it's returned.'

Catherine looked over her satchel, as if her unopened correspondence could have found its way out and onto her lap. The latest small, rectangular weight she carried with her.

'I can't open it,' she whispered.

'What?'

'It's the results. Test results.'

'You're afraid of a curse,' Melville said. 'Borrowed luck.'

Catherine nodded. 'If I name it, I make it real.'

Melville's expression shifted – not pity, something closer to recognition. 'Then let me tell you something about curses,' she said. 'They don't run in families. They run in what we leave unsaid.'

The fire hissed. Outside, evening pressed its weight against the windowpanes.

'Come back tomorrow,' Melville murmured. 'We'll continue. And you can decide when to open your envelope.'

Catherine nodded, her throat tight.

Avoiding Pratts

MARCH 1973

She hadn't meant to stay away so long. A week slipped into two; two weeks blurred into four. She told herself she was marking essays, planning for a conference, waiting for the term to settle. But when she finally returned to Pratts the truth followed her across the threshold like a shadow.

Dr Haynes knocked only once before letting herself into the drawing room.

Mrs Russell Cooke didn't rise. She looked up from her chair by the fire with the calm of someone who had already decided what to say.

'You stayed away,' she said, as Catherine set her satchel down. No accusation. Just fact, and that was somehow worse.

'I had work to finish,' Catherine replied lightly, though her throat tightened around the lie.

'You were frightened,' Melville said, watching her closely. 'Not of me. Of yourself.'

Catherine wanted to argue. Instead, she wrapped her scarf more tightly, as if the drawing room were draughtier than it was. Melville's gaze moved, almost idly, to the envelope tucked beneath the flap of Catherine's satchel.

'Did you read it?' she asked.

'Not yet.' Catherine kept her voice level.

'Borrowed time is still time,' Melville replied. 'But it burns faster when you pretend you can't see the fuse.'

Heat rose up Catherine's spine. 'That isn't why I stayed away.'

'No,' Melville said gently. 'But it's why you came back.'

Catherine didn't deny it. She felt its truth land, quiet and exact. She looked at her host then – properly – and felt the knot in her abdomen loosen almost imperceptibly. She moved to the chair opposite. 'Shall we continue?' she asked, reaching for the recorder.

'Yes,' Melville said. 'It's time.' She shifted, settling her shawl, and something in her posture changed. It was a small alignment she always made before speaking history rather than opinion. 'You'll want the war years next,' she said. Not a question.

Catherine nodded. 'If you're willing.'

'Willing,' Melville murmured, leaning back. 'But not patient. You've made me wait a month.'

Catherine flushed. 'I … needed time.'

'You think I don't recognise it?' Melville said softly. 'Borrowed time has a gait. You come to know the walk after enough years beside death.'

Catherine felt the breath leave her – not with panic, but with a sense of being seen too clearly. She steadied herself and asked, quietly, 'And during the war? Did you feel it then?'

Melville's expression changed. It sharpened, as if memory required precision. 'The war made everyone aware of their hours. Mothers most of all. You didn't live on borrowed time then you rationed it. You counted it. You prayed it stretched far enough to keep your children whole.' She paused. 'Some prayers were answered. Some weren't.'

The tape caught the faint crackle of the fire in the hearth.

Catherine swallowed. 'Is that where we begin?'

'Begin with nineteen-forty-three,' Melville said. 'The year the telegrams multiplied. The year the world asked every mother to pretend she could survive whatever news arrived.'

She drew a long breath, as though bracing herself against the memory's chill. She leant forward, her voice dropping into the slow, steady rhythm she used only when the past was heavy enough to shape itself.

The tape spun on.

A War Mother

ARCHIVE: REEL EIGHT

From 1943

The Ministry of Information reminds families that the quiet endurance of mothers and widows is among our nation's greatest strengths. While their sons serve at sea, in the air, and on distant battlefields, their steadfastness at home is a contribution no less vital to victory. From ration queues to fire watching, to the long nights listening for the All Clear, the nation depends on the unbroken courage of its women. 'They keep the heart of Britain beating,' a spokesman said yesterday, 'often unseen, but never unneeded.'

The Times, 17 May 1943

A Modern Philosophy

June 1943

The room crackles with a restless kind of energy. Not joy, but something sharpened by scarcity and danger. Conversations veer wildly: surrealism, syphilis, war. Somebody is talking about the Dambusters raid, all precision and glory, but I can only think about the lives not named in the papers. How many won't come back? A woman in green silk raves about antique spoons, another insists she saw Dylan Thomas eating powdered eggs in Soho. Even here, even in wartime Marylebone, the war seeps in – through the whisky, the silk, the powdered rouge smuggled through Lisbon. We wear defiance like perfume: invisible, intoxicating, already fading by morning.

David circulates, of course. He's brilliant at this now. He moves like an actor hitting their marks. He's deliberate but unhurried. His head tilts as he listens, his dark eyes catching the light and drawing people in like moths to a flame. People orbit him as if proximity might catch them some of his light. I see it happen every time: the way they lean in, wanting to be nearer to something extraordinary.

Simon's letter burns in my bag. I can almost hear his voice between Bosie's barbs and David's charm – *P.S: Tell David I've taken up charcoal again*. A boy in uniform writing about charcoal sketches. I can't pass on the message. If I do, I'll break the room's spell.

My boy is so far away from this decadence.

I follow David into the fray, but not behind him. I learnt long ago how to take my own space in a room like this. I've my own gravitational pull, even if it's different. I catch snippets of conversation, throw in a sharp comment here, a knowing look there. People notice. I'm the daughter of the *Titanic*, after all. That label still carries weight, though it's more ghost than glory these days. The newspapers may have stopped calling me unlucky, but the room still hasn't forgotten the headline. They don't always know what to do with me, and I like it that way.

'Melville Russell Cooke, in the flesh.' A voice cuts through the air, sharp and melodic, and the room seems to pivot toward its source. Lord Alfred Bruce Douglas. Bosie. He stands by the fire, one elbow resting on the mantlepiece, the other gloved hand gripping a cane he doesn't seem to need. Even his waistcoat looks pre-war, or handmade by someone clever with blackout curtains. His face is finely drawn and pale. His thinning hair catches the flickering light.

David doesn't hesitate. He strides toward Bosie with the kind of confidence that makes me smile. He reaches out his good hand.

'David Rolt,' he says, his voice even. His smile is warm but sharp at the edges. 'A pleasure to meet you, Lord Alfred. Your reputation precedes you.'

Bosie's eyes flick over David like he's appraising a painting. He takes his time. 'The rising star,' he drawls, lazy with entitlement. 'I've heard talk. They say you're the war's new darling. They say you've captured the death of the empire in oils.'

'I paint people,' David replies. 'Empires are beyond me.'

'Quite right,' Bosie says, lifting her glass. 'Empires are men's work. Art is ours.'

David smiles, unflinching. 'The world doesn't sit still,' he replies. 'You just have to see it as it is.'

The corner of Bosie's mouth twitches. 'Well said,' he murmurs. 'But the world is fickle, Mr Rolt. Fame even more so. I wonder … will you adapt when yours turns away?'

'*If* it turns away?' David says. 'It'll have to catch me first.'

That earns a real laugh. Low and sharp. Bosie shifts slightly, turning his gaze on me. 'And you, my darling Melville! How very bold to show your face again among the decadent.'

'And here you are,' I say coolly, 'still chasing Wilde's echo.'

A ripple of laughter.

'The daughter of a legend, wife of a spy and the companion of a genius. Tell me what it's like orbiting such luminous figures?'

Someone turns to listen. I raise an eyebrow, my smile slow and deliberate. He looks older now, his beauty faded to pallor, but his words still land with the cut of good tailoring.

'It's easier to orbit brilliance than live in the dark,' I say, then regret it. Too honest. Too near the truth. 'Some burn too bright and leave nothing but ash. Others create light for everyone around them. David's the latter.'

Bosie's eyes narrow and, for a moment, I think I've caught him off-guard. Then he laughs again, shaking his head. 'Touché,' he says. 'You've still got claws, then.'

I take a step closer. 'And you've still got a reputation,' I say, my voice smooth.

The room pauses. The fire pops loudly in the silence. Bosie pulls me into the tightest embrace. 'I've been thinking about young Simon,' he whispers and I nod in appreciation.

'And you,' he says slowly, releasing me and turning back to David, 'are an interesting one, Mr Rolt. Let's hope the world doesn't ruin you.'

'The world ruins those who let it,' our host, Marie Stopes, says. She's been sitting silently on a sofa nearby. Now, her voice is crisp and certain. Her gaze locks on David. 'I've seen genius wrecked by war, Mr Rolt. Paint while you still can.'

David doesn't flinch. 'Discipline has its place,' he says, his voice calm but firm. 'But inspiration doesn't follow rules. And the best art comes from letting it lead.'

'A modern philosopher,' she says with a clipped tone. She glances at me, as if expecting me to disagree, but I just smile.

'Your fellow has quite the way with words.' Bosie leans toward me again, his voice low. 'Does his art hold the same weight?'

'It carries truth,' I reply, not bothering to lower my voice. 'And truth doesn't fade.'

Bosie straightens. His smile is sharper than before. 'Well, then,' he says, lifting his cane as though in toast. 'To truth.'

The air-raid warden's whistle from outside cuts the room in two for a moment, then conversation resumes. The crowd shifts. Someone spills champagne. A woman in peacock feathers gestures toward David's lapel and asks whether he has met Augustus John. David deflects, gently. I watch his movements, the slight drag of his foot, the precision of his distance from the table. He's in pain, but he'll never say so.

Instead, I move through the room, listening to scraps of conversation. Churchill and Roosevelt. Ration points and black-market oranges. The latest casualty list from Tunisia. One woman whispers that her cousin flew with the Dambusters. Another mentions evacuation from Sicily. The war is everywhere, and yet never quite here – not in this room with its brandy and borrowed feathers.

Duty and Skylarks

September 1943

'We'll begin in just a few moments,' Lady Dunmore says. I watch her weave through the gathering.

The blackout curtains are drawn. They pool at the floor in heavy folds, and the gas lamps flicker with the movement of the crowd. On the back wall, a map of the Eastern Front is pinned beside a list of sugar allowances and the names of local boys who haven't come home. It's not the first war meeting I've attended, nor will it be the last. I speak at these things because I must. Silence, now, is suspect. The war effort is insatiable: always needing more, always asking for what has not yet been given.

I glance down at my gloves, smoothing a crease in the kid leather. A woman stands near the hall's doorway. She's twisting her hat in her hands. It's as if she might wring out the worry that's settled in the seams of it. There's something familiar in her posture – in the way she turns her head towards the door every few minutes, as though expecting someone to walk through it. The posters outside call this a *Rally for Courage*. The local newspapers have taken to calling me a model of wartime resilience. They say it like it's a compliment. I say yes to these things because it would feel cowardly not to. And, perhaps, because when I speak, I can pretend that the words make something solid out of what I'm living.

We are all waiting. In one way or another.

At the front of the hall, Lady Dunmore clears her throat. She's an indomitable woman. She's always worn black, but wears it differently now. Less for fashion, more for the permanence of loss. She scans the room, and her eyes settle on me.

'Mrs Russell Cooke, would you care to say a few words before we begin?'

I hesitate for the briefest second and then walk to her. I feel the heaviness of my own name as I do.

'I wear my lipstick, my hat, my gloves, because I was taught to dress for the weather, and this war is a storm.'

There's a communal laugh that's soft and sad. They don't want jokes, though, not really. They want something to hold.

'We speak often of sacrifice,' I begin. My voice is steady. 'It's a word that has become woven into the fabric of our daily lives, but I wonder how often we allow ourselves to feel the true weight of it. Sacrifice isn't just in ration books; it's in the way we lay three places instead of four. In the silence when the post is late. In the way a mother irons a shirt she knows may never be worn again. Sacrifice is not only what's given … but what's lost. And, in war, loss doesn't wait for our permission.'

The room stills. They know. They all know.

'My son is twenty. Last week, he flew his fifteenth operation. In his last letter, he joked that I should knit him a luckier scarf. I cannot predict what will become of this world when peace returns,' I continue, 'but I do know that we owe our sons and brothers more than memory. We owe them a future worthy of what they have given.'

A murmur ripples through the crowd. There's a shifting of feet against the wooden floor and the rustle of cloth as people nod. I don't name Simon, but he's in the words. My knees buckle slightly as I descend the platform steps. No one notices. Or if they do, they look away. He's in the pause before I sit, in the way I fold my hands in my lap.

I long for my son to come home.

~

The evening stretches on in a series of quiet handshakes, murmured thanks, and polite farewells spoken in low voices. A woman grasps my wrist for a moment too long. Her fingers are cold through her gloves. She searches my face as if I might have answers. Another man, older, balding, pushes a donation into the tin by the door. His lips press into a thin, grim line. People part around me. They're reluctant to leave, yet eager to escape the weight of the conversation.

Priscilla's standing near the doorway. She's half in shadow, but her arms are crossed over her chest.

'How long have you been there?' I ask, though I already know.

'Long enough.' She steps forward, heels sharp on the boards. 'I didn't know you were speaking tonight.'

'It's expected of me.'

Her eyes flick to the blackout curtains. '*Expected*.' The word lands heavy. 'It sounded … neat. As if you were talking about milk rations, not people.'

'They need something to hold on to,' I say carefully. 'That's why I do it.'

Her mouth hardens. 'Simon isn't something to hold on to. He's not a number.'

The name cracks between us. I nod. 'I know.'

Priscilla swallows, eyes glistening but hard. 'Are you afraid?'

It's an impossible question. 'Of course I'm afraid,' I say. 'But fear doesn't change anything.'

She exhales sharply and her hands flex at her sides. 'I hate it that we don't know where he is half the time. I hate it that when there's a knock at the door my stomach twists. And I hate it that—' She stops herself, her breath uneven. 'I hate it that we must be brave. I don't want to be brave, Mama. I just want my brother back safely.'

The words land like a blow. I reach for her, pressing my fingers against the curve of her shoulder and feel the tension coil tight beneath the fabric of her coat. 'I know,' I say. Inadequate words.

'Do you?' She takes a step closer. Her voice is low, urgent. 'Sometimes I think you like it. The speeches. The way they look at you. It gives you something to do.'

The words sting, because they're too near the truth.

'I miss him too much.'

I can't make this easier, or better, or go away. We want the same things, we simply voice it differently. The room is quiet except for the faint sound of a chair scraping somewhere at the back, and the shuffle of the last few people leaving. Beyond that, someone outside is whistling – a soldier's song, something half-forgotten from the war before.

I draw breath, steadying. 'Write to him. Tell him about the garden. The skylarks in the fields.'

She lets out a brittle laugh. 'Do you think he cares about skylarks?'

'I think he cares about hearing from you.'

She presses her fingers against the doorframe, grounding herself. Finally, she nods, though her eyes stay distant.

'Come home with me,' I say softly.

She exhales. 'Yes. Let's.'

I reach for my daughter's hand, and we step out into the cold night. The air is crisp with the promise of rain. The streets are dark. The blackout holds the road in silence, but the stars blaze, fierce and countless. Skylarks in the fields, stars in the sky, my son somewhere between them. I have to believe he'll find his way home.

A Study of Boldness

November 1943

The parquet flooring gleams as if the Blitz has never touched this street, though the sandbags at the basement doors tell the truth. Only last week an incendiary fell three streets away; one of the gallery girls lost her husband at Salerno. Yet tonight the quartet plays as though none of it belongs to us. The glasses are full. The smiles are practised.

I step further inside and claim the space as though it's mine. Emerald silk clings before flaring at the hem: bold, unapologetic. Simon's last letter ended with, *Don't let the world forget how to be beautiful.* I wear the dress for him. The fox fur at my shoulders carries its own weight, heavier when I think of his thin RAF scarf, but the sheen catches the light, and my ivory gloves – pearl buttons glinting – draw every eye to the movement of my hands.

Faces turn. Some familiar, some curious, all gilded by the paintings on the walls. David's work dominates: portraits that look back too directly, landscapes that refuse to explain themselves. His brushstrokes are fearless, almost unruly. Around me, the polite chatter of wartime London frays at the edges: jokes about powdered eggs, shoes stuffed with newspaper. The perfume, the pearls, the pretence: none of it disguises the war clinging to the hems of our coats.

David stands slightly apart, as he always does. Someone has tried to tame his hair for the evening; it hasn't worked. The suit sits on him like an idea he hasn't yet agreed to. And there, on his cuff, a thin smear of paint – his refusal to be polished, even for this.

'Darling, you're turning heads again,' Lady Agnes Montague

murmurs, nodding toward the knot of women whispering behind their gloves. Their eyes flick to me, then dart away.

'Good,' I say. 'I'd be disappointed if I didn't give them something to do.'

Agnes's chuckle carries admiration. 'You do have a way of making them swallow their spite. Still, it's not every day one sees a woman like you with a man like him.'

I smile, slow and deliberate. 'You mean I'm widowed. And he's scandalously younger.'

She meets my gaze. 'I mean, you are a woman whom death hasn't soured and he is still young enough to mean what he feels.'

The words settle like a verdict, and across the room, David catches my eye. His expression softens, though he doesn't smile. Instead, there's a steadiness in his gaze. It's a quiet acknowledgement of my presence, and it feels more intimate than any gesture. The young woman at his side – one of his many admirers – follows his line of sight and visibly falters. I feel no animosity toward her. She's a child. She's swept up in the thrill of his success. Dazzled by the man without knowing the sacrifices that forged him.

I take my time crossing the room, weaving through the crowd with practised ease. Smoke and damp wool hang in the air, tempered by perfume and polish, but none of it matters. David's gaze doesn't wander. It fixes, holds, and I feel the weight of it between each step.

When I stop before him, he tilts his body just slightly, opening a space that wasn't there a moment ago, and the cluster around him adjusts as if obeying an unseen cue. The air feels narrower, sharper, carrying the faint scent of turpentine from his cuff and the warmth of champagne on his breath. He doesn't touch me, but the closeness is enough: the scrape of his sleeve against mine as someone brushes past, the near-silent intake of his breath when I pause too close. The gallery hasn't rearranged itself for us, he has. And I fit into the space he's made, as though I've always belonged there.

'You've outdone yourself,' I say, gesturing toward the nearest painting. It's a windswept treescape that feels almost alive, its branches twisting like a dancer caught mid-spin. It's storm-battered. Raw. Like the sea holding its breath. I see my fear in the brushwork and wonder if David knows.

'You sound surprised.'

'I'm not,' I say, meeting his gaze. 'But I'm allowed to be impressed.'

He chuckles at that; the sound is like the brief spark of a match. 'And here I thought you only came to make a scene.'

'Oh, I came for that, too.' I let the corner of my mouth lift into a sly smile, my glove brushing his sleeve as I lean closer to the painting than necessary. 'Though it seems your work is doing most of the heavy lifting tonight.'

Behind us, a woman in a severe black dress murmurs something about our age difference to her companion. The words are faint, but I catch them, nonetheless. David hears them, too; I can tell by the way his fingers brush his tobacco pouch.

'Ignore them,' I say, touching his cheek.

'If only they were capable of discussing the paintings with as much passion.' His tone is dry but not bitter.

'They're clearly in need of good company themselves,' I say. I'm louder this time. Enough that the woman glances sharply in my direction. I meet her gaze directly; my expression is unyielding until she looks away, flustered.

David watches me for a moment. He shakes his head, but a faint smile tugs at his lips. 'You're impossible.'

'And yet, here I am,' I reply, lifting my glass in a mock toast.

He raises an eyebrow but says nothing more. Instead, he turns back to the painting. I watch as his fingers brush lightly against the frame. There's a tension in his shoulders, but it seems less pronounced now. Can I hope that my presence will temper whatever unease the evening might hold?

~

The gallery begins to quiet as the evening wanes. The crowd thins. Someone mentions the war in hushed tones: Malta, ration points, the boys who won't be coming back. Another voice, lower, says what most won't: that some men never went at all. That they were broken beforehand, marked out of the fight before it began. The words hang, careless and cutting, and I feel them find David across the room, even if no one else does.

As the last of the guests begin to filter out, David and I linger by the door. He's still holding the glass of champagne someone handed him earlier, though he hasn't taken a sip.

'You know,' he says after a long moment, his voice barely above a whisper, 'sometimes I wonder if they'll ever see me for more than this.'

'More than what?' I ask, though I already know the answer.

'The crippled artist,' he says simply. It's without self-pity but with a weight that presses against my chest.

I step closer and place a hand lightly on his arm. 'Let them see whatever they want,' I say. 'You already know who you are. That's the only truth that holds.'

He looks at me then, his expression unguarded in a way I've only seen a handful of times. 'And who are you?' he asks, his tone quiet but insistent.

I hold his gaze, and the weight of the question settles between us. 'Labels don't last. They tear with each war, each grave, each beginning. I sew a new one on every time.'

For a moment, the noise of the gallery fades entirely, and the world seems to shrink to just the two of us. David smiles. Together, we step out into the cold November night and the lights of the gallery cast long shadows behind us. The last time I wore this dress was the farewell dinner we held for Simon – a lavish little defiance with just the four of us. I wonder if David remembers.

5th January 1944

The house is colder tonight, despite the fire burning steadily. Blackout curtains cling to the windows, sealing me in. Simon's letter lies on the desk, his ink faint where the nib faltered.

I've read it enough to know every line, though it says almost nothing.

'I'm fine. Don't worry. It'll be over soon.'

Fine. As if anyone could be fine in a world like this.

He writes nothing of danger, but it hums between his words. Italy. France. The South Pacific. The papers say enough for me to imagine him in all of them, though I wish I couldn't. The wireless speaks in its endless monotone: more sorties, more missing, more names folded into silence. Each report is a rehearsal for the moment I dread.

David would call it melodrama. He doesn't mean cruelty; he simply doesn't know. To him, Simon is a uniform, another figure on a canvas. To me, he's the boy who pressed grease into his curls as he leant under the Bentley's bonnet. My son. My daughter's twin. The child who taught me what it meant to be split open by love.

I told my son that bravery wasn't the absence of fear but purpose in spite of it. I wonder now if I was teaching him or trying to steady myself.

The fire cracks sharply, and I start. I shiver. I've waited for news before; my body remembers how. But this waiting is worse. It's stretched thin between letters, between breaths. It isn't absence – it's anticipation.

I fold his letter carefully back into its envelope, as though neatness could ward off fate. Tomorrow I'll write again. I'll tell him what mothers always tell their sons at war.

'I'm fine. Don't worry. Come home safely.'

Words to steady him, even as I pray he lives long enough to read them.

A Faint Chance

March 1944

Where else could I go?

    I stand in his doorway with the letter crushed in my hand. The paper is already fraying at the edges. My gloves are soaked through, the leather stiff, but I can't take them off yet. To strip them away would be to admit the truth squeezed in my grip. David's at the easel, bent into his work. The scratch of charcoal on canvas is steady, deliberate – the sound of order, of control. The studio smells faintly of turpentine and rain. It should comfort me. It doesn't.

'You're soaked,' he says without turning.

His voice is calm but alert. He glances over his shoulder and his hair catches the light. I don't move. A statue. Afraid even to breathe. Terrified he'll ask. His eyes narrow slightly. He notices the paper in my hand. He sees me entirely; I see the shift in him at once. The charcoal stills in his fingers. He straightens.

'It's nothing,' I say quickly, but I hear the lie in it.

It's everything and my voice betrays me. It's thin. It's brittle. It's as unconvincing as the pale smile I force onto my lips.

David takes a step towards me. His limp is more pronounced on the studio's uneven floorboards, but he doesn't falter. He knows.

'Melville.' He says my name softly, as if it were honey on his tongue. His gaze flicks between my face and the paper in my hand. Recognition flares in his eyes.

My throat tightens as I hold out the letter to him. I swallow hard. The room is smaller. Heavier. The walls press in. He takes it from me. He unfolds it carefully. Reads. Brow furrows. Emotion swings over his face. His eyes scan the words with quiet deliberation. The only sound is the rain. Each drop is a drumbeat against the glass.

Finally, he blows out his emotion. '"It is with deepest regret that I have to inform you that your son, Simon, is missing as the result of air operations on the twenty-third of March, nineteen-forty-four."'

His voice is steady, but I hear the hesitation.

'"He was the pilot of an aircraft taking part in the successful operation against enemy shipping off the Norwegian coast. He had established himself to be one of the best and most reliable pilots in the squadron."'

David stops reading. He gulps. Swallows his feelings.

'You don't have to—' I begin, but he holds up a hand. He isn't done.

'"It is believed he was killed. However, there is always a faint chance that he may have escaped from the crash and been picked up."'

A flicker of something unfamiliar passes across David's face. Raw. Honest. Grief. He looks up at me slowly. Searching. I don't know what he expects to find. I can't make this better for him.

'They don't know,' I whisper.

David exhales slowly. 'No. They don't.'

Is that the torment of it? Perhaps that's the weight I can't set down. This is an echo. Worse. More. *If they'd written to say he'd died, would that have been easier?* I hate myself for that thought. If they had said he was safe, I could have begun to hope. Instead, they've given me nothing but a limbo of maybes and faint chances. I can't protect my heart if I hope. Still—

'I won't believe it,' I say, shaking my head. 'Not until they tell me otherwise. Not until there's proof.'

David doesn't argue. He watches me. His fingers tap lightly against the letter, as if the paper itself might reveal some hidden truth.

'I thought if I came here, it wouldn't feel so real,' I admit finally. My voice is barely above a whisper. I don't know if he can hear my words. 'With you, it's always been … safe.'

David doesn't move closer. He won't comfort me with empty platitudes. He leans against the edge of the workbench and his arms cross over his chest. 'It's still safe,' he says.

'Is it?' I ask. My hands tremble as I pull off my gloves. The wet leather lands with a soft thud against the wooden table. 'It doesn't feel that way anymore. Everywhere I go, the curse follows. Father. Sidney. My mother. And now Simon…' My voice cracks. I press my lips together, willing myself to stay composed.

'Melville.' David's voice is firm but quiet. 'You're not cursed.'

'Am I not?' I snap, the words sharp and bitter. 'They'll call it that soon enough. They always do. Tell that to my son, to my mother, to Sidney—'

'Stop.' The single word is calm but unyielding. It silences me instantly. 'We don't know, yet…'

David's eyes meet mine. Steady and grounding. I want to be angry at him, at anyone, but I can't. I won't. Not yet. He's the only thing in this room that isn't unravelling. He's giving me the permission I need to cling to that hope too. Not delusion, but logic. He doesn't lie.

'You're not cursed, and Simon isn't gone. Not yet,' he says.

'We don't know,' I whisper. My voice is hollow.

'You're right. We don't. I'd be the first to dismiss foolishness.'

The room feels unbearably quiet. The weight of silence bears down between us. Thick and oppressive.

'I couldn't stop him joining the RAF. By then it was already decided … long before call-up papers. He'd been in the school squadron at fourteen, polishing propellers, learning formation drills, tugging at the rudder pedals as though they were made for him,' I say. 'It gave him a taste, and once he'd had it, there was no holding him back. He thought it was destiny … but he's only twenty years old.'

David doesn't respond immediately. Instead, he moves to the easel. His fingers brush lightly over the canvas. It's unfinished – a stormy seascape with waves that seem poised to spill off the edge.

'You see this?' he asks. He nods toward the painting. 'It's not done yet. I don't know how it ends. But that doesn't mean it won't be beautiful.'

I blink at him. The weight of his words settles somewhere deeper than I expected. For the first time since I arrived, the tightness in my chest loosens just enough to let me breathe.

'He's lost,' I say and David nods. The words are hollow, but I'll tell them to stick.

'We won't mourn a rumour,' he says.

'Thank you,' I murmur. A faint smile tugs at the corner of my mouth. It won't form into anything.

The rain outside begins to ease, the steady rhythm fading into a softer patter. I let my gaze drift to the painting. Perhaps the stormy waves mirror the turmoil in my chest. I reach for the letter again. Press out the creases with my fist.

Later, I'll place it in my suitcase.

1st April 1944

The rain hasn't stopped. It beats against the windows, relentless, as if the sky itself is mourning. I've grown tired of its persistence. No confirmation. Neither dead nor alive. This liminal space persists.

David came today – uninvited, but steady as ever. The house felt less hollow with him in it, and I didn't resent that. He brought tea, and a book of poetry. I touched neither. I think he hoped to anchor me to something beyond this waiting, but I couldn't quite look at him.

I've tried to keep him clear of this darkness. David was meant to be escape – light, appetite, the version of myself that could want again. He was never meant to shoulder the weight of what I cannot name.

Yet grief has a way of seeping into every room; now I hear it in his voice. He avoids Simon's name, but it hangs between us, heavy and unavoidable. He feels it too – not as I do, but enough that I see the shadow in him when he thinks I'm not looking.

Priscilla hates everyone. The whole world is the enemy now, and I can't blame her.

Your Simon

April 1944

The letter arrives on a Wednesday. I find it buried between details of the village fete and a circular from the Ministry of Food. A thin envelope. Airmail. Addressed in Simon's hand.

I steady myself on the hall table. Not out of grief this time, but something sharper, stranger. Hope. Joy. Then, disbelief. This letter is dated before the one that told me my son was missing. This timeline isn't linear. I wish it were. Grief makes patterns out of nothing.

David hears the silence from the hall and appears beside me.

'It's from … Simon.'

David doesn't speak, but he takes the letter from me. I focus on how his fingers tremble. It anchors me. For a moment, I'm the steadier of us both.

20th March 1944
RAF Station

Dearest Mama,

We're due to go up again tomorrow. It's a big one, they say. The chaps are pretending they're not nervous, but you can feel it. The silence before mess. The cigarettes smoked down too fast. Everyone's shaving more carefully than usual, just in case they end up in someone else's newspaper photo.

I've kept the new scarf. It still smells like home. Do tell David he was right. Green suits me more than I thought! I tried to sketch him last week, though I mucked it up something awful. He makes it look so easy. I miss you all terribly. I want this over.

If something should happen, which it won't, still I need you to know: flying has made me feel alive in a way nothing else could. It was never about glory. Only about the sky.

I'm not afraid. Truly. I carry your voice with me, Mama. Give Pris a hug from me and remind her that I'm your favourite child. We both know how much she likes that fact.

All my love, always,
Your Simon

David hands it back to me. A tear on his cheek. I fold the letter twice. Then once more. He sits. His head bowed.

'He wrote this three days before…' I say.

David nods. 'He knew.'

I nod, too, not in surrender but in recognition. My son faced the sky the way I once faced the track. The clock ticks. The coals shift in the grate. A plane passes low overhead. The vibrations feel like they move through my ribs.

'He wasn't afraid,' I whisper. 'He said he wasn't afraid.'

David closes his eyes. I don't ask what he sees.

I go to the writing desk and take out an old photograph: Simon, aged eight, a wooden plane in each hand, his hair windswept from the beach. He wrote his name on the back in red pencil.

I tuck the letter behind it. A shrine of paper. A boy in flight. Arranging these fragments is the only part of this I can shape.

Later they'll be archived in my suitcase, too.

~

Priscilla comes shortly. She doesn't speak at first. Just sits beside me, her hand resting near mine but not touching.

'I wish I'd written to him,' she says finally. 'I meant to.'

'He knew,' I say.

We sit there. Two women suspended in the space between knowing and not. Between telegrams and photographs and ink fading with each rereading. Outside, the sky is bright. April bright. The kind of day that forgets its own context.

My boy flew. He's gone. He left words behind.

Grin and Bear

April 1944

Your son has not been found. We can but presume that he is dead.

The letter lies folded in my lap, edges worn from my fingers. Ink blurring where I keep pressing my thumb, as if pressure might change it. *Presume*. The word offends me. I refuse a presumption dressed as certainty. Outside, rain drums on the glass. Relentless. The magnolia buds swell against the grey, blind to everything.

'I don't want to believe in curses.' I say it aloud. Perhaps I urge the words to stick. I know it's only a pattern my mind reaches for, a story to contain the unbearable, but what if I'm wrong?

David looks up from his chair, wanting to come closer but held back by something – grief, respect, or fear of breaking me. He's wearing his painting cardigan, sleeves rolled, a charcoal smudge near the hem. He doesn't speak. We share a glance. Not a conversation, just a silent exchange between people who once knew how to comfort each other. Lately, I exist more in my head than in this house. I move through it like a ghost. Startled by my own reflection, finding myself standing in doorways without knowing why.

Priscilla walked past me earlier, eyes fixed ahead, fists clenched hard enough to mark her palms. She didn't say a word. *Twins lose differently*, I think. They lose the mirror, not just the brother; I've lost my only son. I recognise her look, though. I wore it once, when the telegram came about my father. She leaves the wireless on, lets the static run. That's how she keeps him near.

Yesterday, the council sent a letter of condolence. Neat, typed, impersonal. As if the loss of my son could be common. They will call me a 'war mother' now, as though grief were a civic duty. Another title I never chose. Another box to make my grief useful. I'm one of many, and that's supposed to bring me comfort. It doesn't.

David moves to the kitchen. The kettle rattles, the cups clink. He's still alive, still carrying on. For a moment I resent him for it – not him, exactly, just the fact of his breath when Simon's is gone. He's upright. Breathing. Not touched by war. Still busy with the business of being alive. It isn't his fault, but resentment rarely cares for accuracy.

This bloody war has stolen too much from too many. Why should I tell myself my pain is not unique, that grief is somehow lighter because it's carried collectively? War does that. It dilutes sorrow into something shared and expectant. Private devastation becomes indulgence. *Grin and bear it*. That's what they tell us. That's the blasted lie they feed us, served with tea and clipped sympathy.

I drift to the hall. Simon's coat still hangs by the door. The wool is cold and smells of dust now, but I press my face into it anyway.

'Do you want me to look in on Priscilla?' David asks when he returns, tea in hand.

I shake my head. She doesn't want him. He's only here because Simon isn't. He nods, but the hurt flickers across his face. He turns away, letting the silence close again.

I carry the tea back to the sitting room. The rain has lightened to a fine mist, and the clouds have thinned, their edges torn. I stare at the sky, wondering if Simon ever looked at it like this: grey, endless, holding more questions than answers. I glance down at the letter again.

The Storm Above

April 1944

The rain doesn't fall – it assaults. It hammers the hangar roof as if it means to flatten me, to drown out thought itself. Tonight, I almost welcome the violence. Inside would be warmer, safer, but I can't stay there. The airfield is near-deserted. Most of the aircraft grounded or claimed for the war. But I need this. I need to climb. To rise above it. To get away.

In my pocket, a letter is folded so tight the paper has begun to tear. £360 8s 6d. The War Office's calculation of my son's worth, set down without regard for age. His laughter, his stubborn streak, the way he hummed when he brushed his teeth – all closed out like a bank account. Paid in full by cheque.

Nothing. Less than nothing. A full stop pressed onto Simon's life.

I drag the biplane out into the rain. Its wings buck under the wind. Each gust feels like resistance, as though the earth itself is warning me back. I push harder. If the storm means to stop me, it will have to take me, too. Staying still is worse.

This morning, Priscilla barely spoke. I told myself she was tired, but I know she's waiting. Waiting to see if I return.

The engine sputters, then catches. A raw, defiant growl. The vibration judders through me as I climb into the cockpit. The cold bites through every layer. I shove the throttle forward. The wheels skid through standing water. Spray lashing up. To the east, a crater scars the hill; the wreck of a training plane still buried there since February. They never found all the pieces.

The Cadet lifts. The rain streaks across the glass, turning the ground into a smear of grey and green. I force her higher, through cloud and dark, until at last, we break into the light.

For a moment, silence.

Above the storm the sky is limitless. Pale gold at the horizon. Endless. And for one mad instant I see him; Simon, curls plastered damp, hands outstretched as if he might catch the sun.

£360 8s 6d.

I shake my head. They reduced him to a figure. A sum. A clerical detail.

But he was more.

He was my stubborn streak made flesh. The boy who perched on my knee with a wooden toy plane, arms outstretched as though the room itself were sky. The teenager who spent hours carving balsawood, coaxing wings into shape with hands that should have been restless but were always steady for flight. He could never keep his shoes polished, but he could read the wind, trim a sail, make a boat skim faster than it should. He was twenty. Too young to die.

I will never know where he fell.

I grip the controls tighter. My knuckles are white beneath my gloves.

Missing in action.

The phrase loops in my mind. Cold and clinical. It's as though it were a logistical detail instead of a sentence passed down from the heavens. He flew because I did. Because I taught him to believe the sky could be his. I gave him the dream, and the sky collected the debt.

The plane lurches as another gust of wind catches it. I steady her. Hands firm on the stick, I force my focus back to the present. I'm struggling to maintain control.

Priscilla.

She needs me, too. Below, the land will reveal itself in pieces: roads like dark ribbons, fields pockmarked with craters, a village too small to name. The war is written into the earth, as much as it is written into me. I don't want to go back down. Not yet. Not ever. For a breath, I almost let the Cadet tip. Almost surrender to the storm.

Priscilla.

I begin my descent, cutting through the thickening grey. The rain returns as I drop below the clouds. It hammers against the plane, blurring the outlines of the field. The wheels hit the ground too hard. We skid through the sodden grass before the aircraft finally slows.

I kill the engine and climb out. My legs are unsteady. My breath is sharp in the damp air. David is waiting. Just beyond the edge of the hangar. His coat is pulled tight against the rain. His hair is plastered to his forehead. He takes one look at me and knows not to speak.

'It's still safe up there,' I say.

David's eyes don't leave mine. 'And down here?'

'The sky may have spared me, but the ground never has.'

His Exhibition

June 1944

The invitation is tucked beneath the morning post. Between a gas bill and a letter from the Red Cross. Ivory card, thick, perfumed faintly of turpentine. It smells of permanence. Of something that might last longer than any of us.

DAVID ROLT – RECENT WORKS
Portman Gallery, Fitzrovia – Opening 16th June

I hold it a moment too long. A reminder that exhibitions continue even in wartime – art carrying on where everything else fractures. It's tonight, though, and he hasn't mentioned it. Not once. Not in passing, not in his sleep, not in the long quiet evenings when we drink whisky and pretend we don't count the days since the final letter. Why am I surprised? We've both been skirting around anything that might feel like a future.

I find him in the back garden, kneeling by the stone trough. He's pruning the lavender. It's too early, too cold, and he's doing it badly.

'You didn't tell me,' I say.

'You found it, then.'

'It's tonight?'

David doesn't look up. 'I wasn't sure you'd want to come.'

'Is Simon in it?'

He straightens. Shrugs. 'He's in all of it.'

We don't speak for a while. A robin hops near the rose bush. Somewhere on the street, a boy whistles a tune I can't place.

'I painted him from memory,' David says. 'I shouldn't have. It wasn't enough. So I painted the grief instead.'

∼

The Portman Gallery is a narrow, white building tucked just behind Charlotte Street. Its windows are blacked out for security, but its entrance is crowded with war paint and well-fed critics. Ration books haven't touched this gallery circuit. There's sherry being poured into polished crystal, women in fox fur with their seams inked straight, officers on leave, in creased blues, their cap badges glinting like medals.

Inside, the lighting is cautious. Bulbs are hooded to protect against air raids, but enough to illuminate the canvases. The walls are bone-white and hushed. There's a weight to the air that isn't just the war or the crowd, but the work itself.

David's style has evolved. The brushstrokes are looser, more muscular, entirely furious in places. He's always drawn comparisons to Augustus John and Orpen, but there's something now of Soutine in the flesh. There's a near-violence to the way the light falls. He's titled the collection *After Silence*. It's less a name than a confession.

The first portrait stops me. There I am, unmistakably, but not softened or flattered. I remember the sitting: a grey January morning, just after a fundraising rally. I'd worn my mother's hat, gloves too tight, a jacket too formal for the weather. In the painting, I sit rigidly upright, hands folded in my lap, mouth set in that almost-smile I use when I'm too tired to be gracious. My eyes are sharp. Not cruel, just watchful. As if I'm daring someone to challenge the weight I carry. The background is spare, the palette cold, and yet there's something alive in it. He's caught the way I hold myself together. Not elegance – endurance. The brushwork catches the set of my jaw, the rigid press of my hands in my lap. I see what he's done: turned weariness into armour. A portrait built to outlast me.

The label reads: *The* Titanic *Captain's Daughter* A woman beside me leans in and whispers, 'It's so very British. So very … contained.'

I smile without answering.

Further on, I find a study of hands. Knotted, expressive, blurred at the edges. Simon's, I think, or a memory of them. Another canvas: a figure in RAF blues with his back turned, walking into smoke. The palette is muted; umbers, greys, a single glint of green that might be the scarf.

Then, near the rear wall, a small but commanding canvas stops me. It is Simon. Entirely imagined and yet utterly him. A three-quarter profile, the tilt of his chin just so. There's no uniform, no plane, no war. Just my boy in blue, as he was at fourteen – clear-eyed, unfinished. I move closer. My fingers hover at the line of his jaw, the boyish slant of his shoulders. For a heartbeat I almost hear his voice, almost see the grin beginning to lift. But the canvas holds still while memory stutters. Paint endures where flesh fails. And that truth almost undoes me.

David appears beside me. He hasn't shaved. His coat is worn at the elbows.

'Your memory is exquisite.'

'Thank you,' he says, and we move around the gallery together, in silence.

The last portrait is the one I don't expect. Me again, though taller somehow. More sculpted. My hands are folded tightly in front of me, not demure but deliberate, as if I'm holding something in. The blouse is dark, nearly severe, the skirt pale, almost spectral. Behind me, a tall mirror and an open window: one reflecting the past, the other letting in too much light. He's caught the stiffness in my posture, the press of grief against composure. My expression is set, but not cold. Watchful. Wary.

The label reads: *Melville*.

I raise an eyebrow. 'You should have asked.'

'I couldn't,' he says. 'You'd have held back.'

A woman nearby pretends not to listen. A man with a pencil moustache mutters something about emotionally brutal realism. I ignore them.

'You made me look strong,' I say.

'I made you look real.'

The gallery crowd is thinning. Outside, the evening sirens wail once – a test only. No one flinches.

David pours two glasses of sherry and hands one to me.

'I wasn't sure you'd come,' he says again.

'Curiosity,' I say.

We drink in silence. He studies the final canvas the way a man watches a cliff he's just climbed: unsure if he made it or merely survived.

I look once more at my boy in blue. Simon. Not as he was. As he's been remembered.

The lights dim slightly. The room hushes. A painting cracks in its frame. It's a small sound, but I hear it as a reminder – *nothing holds forever*. Not flesh, not canvas, not memory.

Interruption Nine

MARCH 1973

Catherine let the tape run a few seconds longer than necessary. Not because she feared the silence that had shifted, but because she needed the sound of the spooling reel to steady her, to anchor her body before her thoughts scattered. When she finally pressed stop, the room seemed to inhale with her.

Melville watched, hands folded loosely, waiting with the poise of someone who refused to rush another woman's thought.

'After your son's death,' Catherine began, her voice low, 'the language they used. The newspapers returned to – "cursed", "ill-omened", "unlucky" – as if grief required a pre-existing label.'

Melville's mouth curved slightly. 'The shorthand spared them from looking directly.'

'But that specific loss wasn't unusual,' Catherine said warily. 'Not in nineteen-forty-four. Every street in Britain held a mother waiting for a knock at the door. Yet they didn't call all of them cursed.'

'No,' Melville replied softly. 'Just the women they'd marked early. Patterns are comforting, even when they're invented.'

Catherine opened her notebook but didn't write. 'I've been looking again at the Imperial War Museum's portraits of mothers and widows after the first war – Orpen, Tonks, the Ministry commissions. They're almost devotional. Blanched, serene, dignified. No one is allowed to look furious or unmade.'

Melville gave a knowing hum. 'Grief edited for public consumption.'

'Exactly.' Catherine looked up. 'David's private portraits of you don't resemble those at all. They unsettle. They confront. You never look … tidy.'

'Nor did I feel tidy,' Melville said. 'David painted the truth of a woman standing upright when she had every reason not to.'

Catherine hesitated, then, 'You don't look cursed in them.'

'Do I ever?' Melville asked dryly.

'No,' Catherine admitted. 'You look … undiminished.'

A flicker of joy crossed Melville's face. 'There it is. That's what unsettled them.'

Catherine felt something align in her – quiet, decisive. 'So, when they called you unlucky, they weren't describing you,' she said slowly. 'They were naming what frightened them.'

'Precisely,' Melville said. 'A mother who survives visibly becomes a mirror. And people don't like mirrors when the world is cracking.'

The flames in the hearth whispered against the grate. Catherine lifted her pen at last, steadier now.

'This helps,' she murmured. 'It moves the argument away from myth and into structure – how grief, when embodied by certain women, gets rewritten as fate.'

Melville nodded once, satisfied. 'Good. Write that. Not the story they told about me. The one we both can see clearly now.'

Catherine bent over the notebook. The room held still while she began to put the truth into shape.

The Framing

MARCH 1973

The Ashmolean's storage room felt warmer than usual when Catherine stepped inside – close, almost. The strip lights hummed overhead. Dr Marianne Levine was already there, leaning over a packing crate with a pencil tucked behind her ear, sorting through a folder of loan forms.

'You look different,' she said, glancing up. 'Not tired. Just ... altered. Did you ever reply to that historian chap? The research fellow.'

Catherine deflected with a small smile and a flick of her hand. 'Change happens in archives.'

Her attention had already moved to the portrait propped against the far wall. *An Unlucky Woman*. The same canvas she had unwrapped months before, though it seemed changed now – weighted not by superstition but by everything she had learnt. Melville's story had given the varnish a darker cast, the posture a kind of intent.

Marianne followed her gaze. 'Still unsettling?'

'Not the painting,' Catherine murmured, letting her fingertips rest lightly on the frame. 'The naming. "Unlucky" became the only story she was permitted.'

'Hardly unusual,' Marianne said. 'Think of the post-Great War portraits. Grief made decorative. Mothers posed as emblems so that the nation didn't have to face the cost.'

'Exactly.' Catherine straightened. 'I've been looking at the Imperial War Museum examples again – the lifted chins, the devotional poses. Women turned into symbols of endurance.' She nodded towards the portrait. 'But she won't take that stance and refuses to be arranged. Rolt painted her meeting loss head-on, not smoothing it away.'

Marianne tilted her head. 'You sound very sure of her.'

'I am,' Catherine said quietly. 'More than I expected to be.'

There was a pause before Marianne spoke again. 'I read the cuttings you flagged,' she said. 'They reused the same word after her son. As if one woman could be appointed to hold a country's grief.'

'Or to hide it for them,' Catherine replied. 'That's what keeps striking me – misfortune becomes a public convenience. It lets everyone else feel absolved.'

Marianne studied her for a long moment. 'So, what do you do with that? With her story?'

Catherine pulled her notebook from her satchel, her other hand still on the frame. 'It isn't just about the portrait anymore.' She sighed. 'I keep hearing her voice long after I leave. It's about the narratives she resisted – and the ones still clinging on.'

She looked again at the painted face beneath. Not unlucky. Not cursed. Simply a woman refusing the posture she was meant to hold.

'I'm going back to see her tomorrow,' she said at last, feeling both the pull and the fear of it. 'There are things I still need to ask. About her daughter, Priscilla, this time.'

A Bride's Mother

ARCHIVE: REEL NINE

From 1945

MARRIAGE: MAJOR J.C. PHIPPS AND MISS RUSSELL COOKE

The forthcoming marriage is announced between Major John Constantine Phipps, Coldstream Guards, eldest son of Sir Edmund Phipps, C.B., of 21, Carlyle Square, Chelsea, and the late Lady Phipps, and Priscilla Russell Cooke, daughter of the late Sidney Russell Cooke and Mrs Russell Cooke, of Pratts, Oxfordshire.

The Times, 25 July 1945

Lemonade in the Garden

June 1945

The scent of roses drifts across the garden. It's sweet and heavy, it's almost enough to disguise the smoke that still lingers from distant chimneys. Early summer clings to Pratts like a fragile promise: cut grass, wet earth, the hum of bees, a lone cabbage swaying in the breeze where roses used to bloom. The war has left its thumbprint here, too: the greenhouse with its cracked panes, hedgerows stripped thin, flowerbeds claimed by the victory patch we planted in defeat.

David moved out yesterday. It was always meant to be temporary. A shield against the sharpest edge of grief. His absence isn't an ache, but a shift in balance. Life is a series of readjustments now, and I'm learning to keep stepping forward.

And yet today the sun warms my shoulders. And for the first time in months, I let myself feel it without guilt, as if light itself might be a kind of defiance.

Priscilla sits across from me at the wrought-iron table, her hands folded neatly in her lap. Her pale blue dress skims her ankles, seams mended with faint, careful stitches. I wonder if she keeps the dress out of habit, or for Simon. If she believes wearing it long enough might let him see her again. The colour suits her, but her posture is brittle, as if even breath might splinter her composure.

I pour lemonade into our glasses and the ice clinks softly. It's a fragile note in the stillness. 'You're pensive,' I say, sliding her glass across.

She curls her fingers around the crystal without looking up. 'I've been thinking.' Her voice is lower than usual.

'Dangerous,' I tease, hoping to coax a smile.

It comes, but faintly. She sets the glass down, worrying at her cuff. 'I met someone.' The words are careful, like she's testing them in the air.

I raise a brow. 'Did you now?'

'At a gathering,' she says. 'One of those dreary war socials. Everyone pretending to be cheerful while quietly counting what they've lost.'

The quiet bite in her voice startles me. I wait.

'His name is John Constantine Phipps,' she continues. Her cheeks flush as she avoids my eyes. 'He's a lawyer. Thirteen years older than me.'

'Is he dull?' I ask lightly, as though we are back in a world of small jokes and easy talk.

She gives a startled laugh and swats at the air. 'No. He's not.'

'That's something.' I tilt my head. 'What else?'

'He's kind,' she says softly. 'And steady. He listens. Really listens. He doesn't look at me like I'm … broken.'

The confession hangs in the air like a moth in sunlight. It's both delicate and heavy at once. Since Simon's death, she's been the quieter twin turned quieter still. Her silence has thickened into something I couldn't breach.

'And what else do you see in him?' My voice is gentle now.

'Someone who doesn't ask me to forget,' she whispers. Her hand trembles faintly on the glass. 'But he makes me believe there might still be something worth holding onto.'

Sunlight glances across her profile, and my chest tightens. There are flashes when she is so like Simon, and I feel that old ache pulse through me: love and loss tangled together.

Footsteps crunch on the gravel path. Priscilla's head lifts and, for a moment, I see a light I thought gone from her face.

'John!' Her voice wavers with sudden joy.

He comes into view: tall, dark-suited but understated, hair combed neatly, though the breeze has teased a strand free. He pauses at the garden's edge, scanning the scene with a quiet confidence. He carries the air of a man used to order, to precision, one who has built walls around himself – but not too high. When his gaze meets Priscilla's, a wide smile softens his features.

'This must be him,' I murmur, and my daughter blushes as she rises to greet him.

He approaches, and I stand, smoothing my skirt. 'Mr Phipps, I presume?'

'Mrs Russell Cooke,' he says warmly, extending a hand. His grip is firm but unforced.

'Please, call me Mel.' I motion to the table. 'Join us.'

He glances at Priscilla, who nods, and then sits beside her. His movements are deliberate but unselfconscious.

'So, Mr Phipps—'

'John,' he corrects with quiet ease.

'So, John,' I continue, 'what's a barrister doing in our quiet corner of Oxfordshire?'

'I'm staying nearby with family. A cousin hosted the gathering where Priscilla and I met,' he says. His voice has the even cadence of a man who speaks in rooms where words matter.

'And what impression did my daughter make?' I ask, though I already see the answer in the way he looks at her.

'That she's someone worth adoring,' he replies without faltering.

Priscilla blushes deeper, and for a moment, I see it – the flicker of hope in her that's been gone for too long.

We speak for a while, my questions gentle, his answers careful but never false. He's steady. Unpretentious. Perhaps that's what she needs: something solid, something that will not disappear into the sky.

When he rises to leave, I walk him back to the path, giving Priscilla a moment to herself.

'You seem like a good man,' I say softly.

'Thank you.'

'She's been through a great deal. She'll need more than kind words to feel safe again.'

'I know,' he says, and his expression tells me he means it. 'My intentions are honourable.'

As he walks away, I return to the table. Priscilla is tracing circles on the rim of her glass, her cheeks still faintly pink.

'I approve,' I say, settling into my chair. 'He seems solid.'

Her lips lift into the smallest of smiles. 'Thank you.'

The garden hums around us. Bees drift lazily between the roses and the wildflowers, and the soft warmth of June settles on my skin. For the first time in months, my daughter looks as though she might belong to tomorrow.

A Union of Hope

September 1945

The bells of St Mark's chime with clarity and purpose. I hear them not just as today's music but as an echo of my own wedding day. A different church, another life. Their echo weaves through the patchwork hum of London's streets, a city breathing again after years of silence and sirens. The scars are still visible – crumbling walls, bombed-out buildings – but for once, the air carries relief instead of dread. Today the city feels alive again. It's a day of beginnings, not endings.

Inside the church, sunlight pours through the stained-glass windows and casts fractured rainbows onto the stone floor. The air smells faintly of beeswax polish and old wood, mingling with the floral sweetness of the bouquets arranged carefully along the pews. Priscilla insisted on lilies and wildflowers. Nothing too ostentatious, she'd said. In their simplicity, they're perfect; their pale petals catch the golden light. Somehow, Mother, Father, Sidney and Simon are here. Not ghosts, but stitched into the lilies' scent, into the hush between organ notes.

I turn and Priscilla stands at the end of the aisle. My girl is beautiful. Her gown catches the soft light like a whisper of satin. The fabric is plain – rationing still clings to us all – but it has been cleverly refashioned from one of my own dresses. Elegant in its simplicity, with long sleeves tapering to her wrists and a modest train that swishes softly as she moves. It carries both thrift and grace. The veil is sheer, edged with delicate embroidery, and a nod to the tradition she's kept just enough of. Around her neck are the pearls I gave her this morning; my hands trembled slightly as I fastened the clasp.

She catches my eye. It's a fleeting glance that steadies me. Her smile is subtle, reserved, but her cheeks are flushed. For a moment, I see the little girl she used to be, running barefoot in the garden at Bellecroft with her twin. The years have reshaped her into something altogether more poised, but her spirit hovers under persisting grief. This girl is the bravest, and the love I feel for her bursts from me. What a privilege to be her mama.

The organ begins. A familiar hymn fills the church with its stately notes. I rise with the others. My hands smooth the folds of my navy silk dress. Priscilla takes her first step forward. She wanted to do this alone. She connects eyes with me again and I nod. It's the smallest gesture, but in it I hear her say, *Don't let go*, and I answer, *I never will*. It should have been Sidney, or Simon; she wears her loss in the soles of her feet today. Her stride is steady, but I notice the faintest hesitation in her second step. A mother knows. She's nervous, though her face gives nothing away.

John stands at the altar. His back is straight and his morning suit is impeccably tailored. His hands rest loosely in front of him, but his fingers twitch slightly. They betray his nervousness. He looks older today, more serious, but there's a steadiness about him that reassures me. He turns. I observe him watching my daughter approach. His gaze doesn't waver. He looks at her as though she is already his compass. My girl has chosen well.

'Dearly beloved, we are gathered together here in the sight of God, and in the face of this congregation, to join together this man and this woman in holy matrimony, which is an honourable estate, instituted of God in the time of man's innocence.' The vicar's voice carries through the church. Solemn but beautiful.

Each word of the vows is deliberate, anchoring the couple in their promises. Priscilla's voice is clear, though her hand trembles slightly as she slides the ring onto John's finger. John's voice is softer, but steady, his gaze fixed firmly on her.

When they turn to face the congregation, applause ripples through the church: gentle, dignified, yet full of warmth. Outside, the air is crisp, the sky a patchwork of clouds and light. Handfuls of dried petals and scraps of coloured paper flutter through the air, catching in hats, and laughter rises from the crowd. Priscilla shrieks softly as a handful lands in her hair, and John brushes them away with a fond smile. The sight catches at something deep within me; a joy so sharp it almost hurts.

Today, we're normal. This is the ache I will carry when joy feels impossible again.

I step back slightly and let the crowd press forward. The women are radiant in their floral tea dresses, the hemlines falling just below the knee, their hats perched at precise angles. The men are polished in their suits, a few tugging at their collars as the afternoon warms uncharacteristically. Cigarettes are lit and the thin tendrils of smoke curl into the air. I catch sight of David near the church door. His shape and height are unmistakable, even from a distance. He leans slightly on his cane, his smile faint but genuine as he watches the scene unfold. When his eyes meet mine, he tilts his head in a quiet acknowledgement, and I nod back. I feel the quiet companionship of someone who understands both joy and loss. The last of the confetti settles on the stones. The bells fade. I wonder, briefly and foolishly, if joy is something the world will allow me without exacting its price. Old habits of thought. Old superstitions. I shake my head. I remain for a moment longer, letting the happiness wash over me, imprinting every detail – the flowers, the light, the sound of her laughter – because I know how rare it is.

Priscilla and John climb into the waiting car. Its black paint gleams even in the muted light. Tin cans tied to the bumper clatter merrily as the car starts and the sound carries down the narrow street. Priscilla leans out of the window, waving, her gloved hand catching the light.

'Goodbye, Mama!' she calls. Her voice is high and clear. It's tinged with the excitement of a new adventure.

I lift my hand in reply. My smile is wide but my throat tight. The car pulls further away. The sound of laughter and tin cans fades into the distance. The guests begin to disperse, their voices low and companionable as they exchange parting pleasantries. The churchyard empties slowly, but I linger. Pratts will feel even quieter tonight.

Emptier.

This emptiness is gentler. It is the space a mother makes when her child steps into her own life, not the void war carves out by force. One

I can bear. One I must. Priscilla is married, stepping into her own life, her own story.

Buttercups Beneath the Chin

May 1946

The Bentley Mark VI hums beneath us, steady and sure as it takes the winding country roads. It's brazened, really; every mile is borrowed from the ration books folded in my handbag. Petrol is still meant for necessity, not indulgence. But today I choose to call joy a necessity. The car, one of the few luxuries I've allowed myself since the war's end, feels almost scandalous. It's a brand new and gleaming rebellion against years of queueing and coupons.

My daughter sits beside me. Her hair is unpinned and catching the wind like golden threads. She wears one of her old dresses – a light cotton with faded blue flowers – though she's knotted a scarf at her throat in an attempt at elegance. It's a futile effort. The breeze tugs at the scarf, threatening to unravel it entirely.

'You're pushing her too hard,' she says, though her grin belies the protest.

'The Bentley or you?' I quip. I shift gears with practised precision.

'Both!'

I hear her laughter as I press the accelerator. The car surges forward and the open countryside stretches wide before us. Golden fields flicker with the movement of wildflowers in the wind.

'The Bentley can handle it,' I say, glancing at her sidelong. 'As for you, my darling girl, you've always been sturdier than you let on.'

She scoffs, but her cheeks flush pink. Whether from the breeze or the compliment, I can't tell. The road dips. It's a shallow curve that allows the car to glide as though we're skimming the earth. A hay cart lumbers past in the opposite direction. The driver tips his cap in bemusement at the sight of us: a woman and her daughter, unchaperoned, laughing at the wind. His cart smells of coal dust and cabbages, and this countryside still wears its war years in patches: hedgerows hacked for fuel, cottages with blackout scars on the windows.

'John would be terrified,' Priscilla says. She leans out slightly to feel the rush of air against her hand.

'Your husband is a dear man, but he takes life far too seriously.'

'And you don't?'

I shrug. 'I've learnt when to be serious. But this? This is not one of those times.'

She tips her head back and giggles again. The sound is light and unburdened. It's been too long since we laughed like this. Alone, without ceremony, from our bellies.

Ahead, a grove of beech trees marks the turnoff to a stream we used to visit when she and her brother were younger. Without asking, I slow the car and pull over. The tyres crunch on gravel before settling into the soft earth.

'Why here?' she asks as we climb out. Her dress catches on a stray bramble and she tugs at it. We hear the rip.

I glance toward the stream. Its waters glint in the late afternoon sun. 'Because it's quiet,' I say, 'and because I want to show you the stream.'

We walk to the edge of the water, where the scent of damp earth mingles with the faint sweetness of wild mint growing along the bank. Priscilla picks a buttercup and holds it beneath her chin. The light reflects gold against her skin. We used to test one another like this when she and Simon were small, holding flowers to their chins to see who 'loved butter most'. That memory presses between us now – childish laughter spliced with absence.

'What does it say about me?' she asks, her tone playful.

'That you're radiant, and love butter most.'

Her smile falters slightly, and she looks at the water. 'Do you think we'll ever stop missing him?'

The question catches me off guard. It shouldn't; I wish it wouldn't. Still, I crouch by the stream, running my fingers over a smooth stone. I focus on its surface; it's cool and slick.

'In my experience ... no,' I say finally. Inhale. Exhale. 'Grief changes. Doesn't go away, but it shifts. Becomes something you carry instead of something that carries you.'

Priscilla sits beside me. She pulls her knees to her chest. 'Grandmother never spoke about her grief, did she?'

I shake my head. 'She trapped it inside.' I tap my palm against my chest. 'Buried it under duty and decorum until it rotted away in her. I don't want that for you.'

'And for you?' she asks. Her voice is softer now.

'I've tried to release it,' I say. I toss the stone into the stream. It skims twice, splashes briefly, then disappears beneath the rippling surface. 'To let it move through me instead of poisoning my core. Some days, I manage. Others, I don't.'

I could add that naming it aloud, instead of locking it away like my mother did, feels like resistance. Like choosing life over silence.

My daughter reaches over, taking my hand in hers. Her grip firm and warm. 'Mama, I'm grateful for you. Every single day.'

The words are simple, but they settle somewhere deep. They ease a weight I hadn't realised I was carrying. This girl is my gift for surviving.

When we return to the car, the light is fading. It's painting the fields in soft golds and muted greens. Priscilla ties her scarf properly this time, tucking the ends securely beneath her chin.

'Let's take the long way home,' she says as I start the engine.

I glance at her, surprised, but I nod. 'As you wish.'

The Bentley hums beneath us as we take the winding roads. The countryside unfolds like a painting. The air is alive with the scent of spring, and, for the first time in a long while, it feels as though the past is not chasing us.

The Edge of a Canvas

July 1946

By the time I reach David's studio, I know he's no longer mine to lean on. Still, the smell of turpentine and pipe smoke greets me like an old coat. It's familiar, worn, but no longer warm. The windows are open slightly to the summer air, but the heat clings to the room as though reluctant to leave. Light slants through the glass, catching on frames and canvases in various stages of completion; some leaning against the walls, others propped in purposeful shafts of gold.

'Don't touch anything,' David calls from behind the easel before I've even stepped over the threshold. 'You're late.' The old tease. His voice has that playful edge he reserves for me, a reminder that he knows exactly how little I care for rules.

'How presumptuous,' I say, peeling off my driving gloves and feeling the air settle over my skin.

'I know you.' He emerges, sleeves rolled to the elbow, forearms streaked with paint. His hair is damp with sweat, untidy, a strand clinging to his forehead.

'You should open the windows wider,' I say, scanning the room. 'The fumes will kill you.'

'Not before you do.' He leans his cane against the table and wipes his hands on a rag, the movement slow and deliberate.

My eyes catch on the largest canvas, and I'm drawn across the room before I think to ask permission. Bold strokes. Sunlight fractured against sea. A solitary diving board juts out above the swell, suspended in air as though daring someone to leap. The cliffs loom beyond, sheer and immovable, their shadows bleeding into water that shimmers with restless light.

'It's different,' I say at last, tilting my head.

'Good?'

I don't answer immediately. The painting unsettles me. It's not the sea as it is, but the sea as it feels: vast, indifferent, alive. The diving board pulls my eye, not the water. It's a place of pause. A held breath before the fall.

'Is it Spain?' I ask, searching the cliffs, the play of ochre and black.

'Los Gigantes,' he says. 'Tenerife. I stood there once. Couldn't forget it.'

His words hang between us. Distance. Memory. A moment caught and held.

'And the board?' I gesture to the stark line of it, suspended over nothing.

'It's where the choice happens,' he says simply. 'Jump, or retreat. You can't stay there forever.'

My fingers graze the canvas. 'It feels like loss. The instant before something vanishes.'

'Perhaps. Or the instant before something begins.'

I laugh softly, though it catches in my throat. 'Trust you to find beginnings where I see endings.'

He shrugs, wiping his hands on the rag. 'Someone has to.'

'I haven't heard from you in four weeks,' I say, not quite keeping the accusation from my tone. His absence used to wound me; now it only confirms what I already know; we're pulling in different directions.

'Perhaps I was busy.'

'Perhaps you only remember what you want to.'

He steps closer, enough that I feel the heat radiate from him. 'Perhaps.'

For a moment, the room feels charged: the scent of oil and turpentine mixing with something unnamed. My pulse ticks in my throat. I force myself to study the painting instead of the man. 'It's good,' I say finally. 'Unsettling, but good.'

'Unsettling is exactly what I wanted.'

I move towards another canvas propped near the window. Two figures on a riverbank, their faces turned away, the water behind them blurred but alive.

'You've grown softer,' I say, letting my fingertips graze the edge of the frame.

'Softer?' He leans against the table, his expression unreadable.

'Still bold,' I clarify. 'But quieter. More … intentional.'

He gives a small, surprised smile. 'Quieter? I didn't think that was possible for me.'

'It suits you.'

Once, his work had the same recklessness as our nights together. Now both of us are steadier, less hungry. Survival has smoothed our edges. His success has settled into him. Sunlight slides across his forearms, picking out the paint-stained hairs and the faint sheen of sweat. He studies me as intently as any canvas.

'Why are you really here?'

'To see you.'

'And?'

'And to remind you not to forget who you are. Even when they try to make you someone else.'

'You think I'd forget?'

'No. But I think you like the reminder.'

He laughs softly. 'You're impossible.'

'Untamed,' I correct.

The moment holds: tension and familiarity, memory and something unspoken. But I feel the edges of it slipping. Things have shifted since Simon. We're casual now, tethered by habit and history, not by the same restless hunger.

I gesture to the painting. 'Don't let them tame you, either.'

He laughs softly.

'I keep thinking,' I say, eyes still on the cliff-face, 'that if I lean on you too long, the rot that follows me will seep into your life even more.'

'You're not cursed,' he says, too quickly.

'No,' I agree. 'But I'm marked. And you know it.'

He doesn't deny it. His silence a kind of gentleness. 'Dinner at Pratts?' he asks, leaning on his cane now.

'Eight o'clock.' I turn towards the door. I don't look back, but I feel his eyes on me, warm as the July sun.

Not Quite Extinct

December 1946

The house hums with warmth and voices, the air thick with mulled wine and beeswax polish. Cigarette smoke curls upward in slow silver ribbons. The men stand in small knots, leaning closer as they talk. The women tilt their heads towards the firelight, their pearls catching the glow, their tea dresses in coloured prints despite the chill that presses at the windows. Wine is scarce still, but I've saved enough for tonight. Some celebrations need substance, not substitutions. Laughter rises and falls like music, reckless now, as though we're all testing the weight of freedom. I linger near the window, half in shadow. Through the shifting warmth of the room, I watch my daughter.

Priscilla is curled on the sofa with John, one leg tucked beneath her. She has a glass in her hand and a faint pink flush on her cheeks. Her head rests against his shoulder as he leans in to murmur something, and she laughs. It's soft and unguarded. It's the sound of a girl who has remembered how to breathe. I grip the window frame. I keep checking myself, testing whether sorrow still radiates from me. Whether I'm safe to stand close to her happiness. This is survival, too. Laughter stitched back together from loss. My chest tightens with a warmth so fierce it almost hurts. For a fleeting moment, I imagine Simon standing behind her, smiling that crooked smile of his, and the thought settles like snow. It's somehow cold but clean.

David is by the hearth, his cane propped against the stone, his drink in his left hand, a cigarette burning in an ashtray. He looks at ease, though the tilt of his body towards the firelight marks him as someone who doesn't quite belong anywhere for long. People still orbit him though, drawn to his quiet magnetism; it's the way he listens, as though he already knows their story but wants to hear them tell it anyway. He glances up and catches my eye. Just a flicker, then the smallest incline of his head: a silent question.

I sigh and flick ash into the tray before weaving through the room to his side. 'I know that look,' I murmur.

He smirks, offering me his glass. 'You've been watching from the corner like a woman deciding whether to join the living.'

'Perhaps I'm deciding whether the living are worth joining.' I take a sip of his wine, hand it back, and don't wait for his reply.

'Come outside,' he says, the faintest challenge in his smile.

'I've a house full of people,' I counter, reaching for my own coat before he can. I slip it on, deliberately. 'But if you want air, I'll allow it.'

Priscilla's eyes catch mine. I tip my head slightly – a quiet reassurance – before I lead David down the hall, past the soft spill of voices and the scent of pine from the Christmas tree.

'I've not seen you since July,' I say once the door closes behind us. 'I didn't think you'd come.'

'I'm here now.'

Outside, the cold air cuts my lungs clean. Mist drapes the fields, and frost glitters faintly on the terrace stone. Behind us, Pratts glows like a lantern with the movement of guests flickering at the windows.

David leans against the balustrade, resting one hand on the cold stone. His breath curls white in the air. 'The house is breathing again,' he says quietly.

I look back through the glass, seeing the blur of colour and life within. 'Yes. It is.'

He studies me in the silence, and the night settles around us. For the first time in years, I feel the air move through me without catching on splinters. After a pause, I say, 'There's something I want to show you.'

We walk along the gravel path, our boots crunching softly over the frost. The greenhouse looms, its repaired panes clouded with condensation. Beyond it, in the farthest corner of the garden, a young tree rises stark against the winter sky. Its bare branches are etched like ink.

David stops. His brow furrows. 'That wasn't here before.'

'No.'

'You planted it?'

'In the spring. You rarely visited. A Dawn Redwood.'

He steps closer, brushing gloved fingers along the rough bark. 'They thought these were extinct.'

'And yet … here it is.'

We stand in silence, watching the mist cling to the tree's thin trunk, the frost glinting like scattered glass across the lawn.

'Kew offered saplings,' I say.

'You've brought something back.' His voice is soft but certain.

I rest my hand on the trunk, feeling the cold seep through the leather of my glove. 'It felt necessary. To plant something that would outlast us. To remind myself that some things endure.'

Not love, not grief, not even this strange tether between us – but roots, branches, a future that asks nothing of me.

He exhales slowly. 'We're not meant to carry each other forever, Melville.'

I look at him, then at the glow of the house, where Priscilla leans into John and laughs at something I'll never hear.

'Perhaps that's the point,' I say.

We walk back toward the terrace. The music and voices spill out, warm and alive. When I open the door, the scent of pine and mulled wine wraps around me. I hesitate for a heartbeat on the threshold of my home, then step inside.

A Glass of Sherry

August 1947

England feels lighter tonight, though the war still lingers in the frayed edges of things: in the careful mending of dresses, in the once rationed sugar of the cakes stacked on the trestle table. The village hall hums with warmth, laughter threading the air like a tune we thought we'd forgotten.

I stand just inside the doorway, watching Priscilla move through the crowd. She's wearing her blue dress again. A habit of quiet frugality not inherited from me. My daughter moves easily. She greets neighbours with a touch to the elbow, a warm smile, a soft word. I think of that small hand that once clutched mine in the garden parties at Bellecroft. Marriage suits her. She's grown into herself. She's grown into the kind of grace that doesn't ask to be noticed but is felt all the same.

By the fireplace, John speaks with a man from the council, nodding politely, but there's a looseness in his stance. A quiet contentment that betrays where his thoughts rest. He has built his calm around her. How rare it is to love without fear, to live without the shadow of loss pressing too close. Something tightens in my chest. Not grief, not fear, not even nostalgia. Gratitude, sharp and startling. She has what I once wished for myself: a life lit from within. I've not always known how to love softly. My own mother was steel: firm and unyielding. Her affections were measured out in duty rather than warmth. I wanted more for Priscilla. I wanted her to feel held, to feel known, to feel worthy. Still, now, as I watch her – head tilted back in laughter, hand finding her husband and resting lightly on his sleeve – perhaps I succeeded.

A presence at my side shifts. I turn to find Lady Hargreaves offering me a glass of sherry.

'A lovely evening,' she remarks, her sharp eyes scanning the room.

'The village needed it,' I reply, taking the glass. A sip. The sherry is warm, and smooth against my throat.

Lady Hargreaves' gaze lingers on Priscilla. 'She looks happy.'

'She truly is.'

'And no children yet?' she asks, with the smug entitlement of someone mistaking gossip for duty.

I don't bristle. I've had this conversation before this evening, and I'll have it again. 'In time.'

Lady Hargreaves hums. She's either satisfied or unwilling to press further. She moves away and her silk gown rustles as she goes. She patrols the village's hopes for heirs as faithfully as others patrol the hedgerows for weeds. Priscilla appears beside me. She plucks the sherry glass from my hand and takes the last sip without hesitation.

'She asked when I'd reproduce?'

I nod.

She rolls her eyes but smiles, tucking a stray strand of hair behind her ear. 'I've been questioned four times this evening.'

'It's their duty to ask,' I say dryly. 'They'd wither without a proper inquiry.'

She grins, but there is a softness in her expression. 'You never ask.'

I study her for a moment, seeing not just my daughter, but the woman she has become. A woman who has held grief in both hands and still dares to build something of her own. My love for her is fierce, but I'd never seek to own her decisions.

'I don't need to.' I have loved her enough to let her be. That's the only answer that matters.

She leans into me slightly, her shoulder pressing against mine. Her weight against me is as familiar as her first cry in my arms. It's a small thing, but it roots me. I adore her. She'll always be my child, but in moments like this, she's my friend, too. *How lucky am I?*

'I'll miss this place,' she says suddenly.

The words catch me off guard.

'It's not as if Scotland is the other side of the world,' I say, though already I feel the distance pressing at the edges of her words.

'No, but it'll be different.' Her voice carries both the girl she was and the woman she's become. She exhales softly, her eyes tracking the movement of John across the room. 'I think I'm ready for that.'

She was always more cautious than Simon, slower to leap into things. Still, there's something certain in the way she speaks tonight. It's a quiet conviction that settles into my chest.

'You'll like Scotland,' I say after a pause. 'The air will suit you. You and your brother were always happiest outside.'

'John says there's a lake just beyond the house. I can already see it in my mind… Early mornings, mist rising off the water.'

I close my eyes briefly, imagining it, too. 'I wish your father could have seen you like this,' I say quietly.

'I do, too.'

For a moment, neither of us speaks. The music swells, the murmur of conversation rising and falling in waves. Somewhere, a cork pops from a bottle and a peal of laughter follows in its wake. The musicians strike up another tune – a waltz, though no one dances formally anymore. War has stripped the stiffness from things. It's left only what is essential. People move in soft sways, hands resting against shoulders, eyes searching for what still remains.

Priscilla turns to me suddenly. 'Dance with me.'

I let out a small, surprised laugh as her hand slips into mine. And so we dance. The boards creak under our steps, the air thick with candle wax and rosewater, the music looping through memory. In the middle of the village hall, among the women in their faded floral dresses and the men tugging at the collars of their best jackets, my daughter and I step into the music. It's not a formal thing, not precise or rehearsed. It's simply movement. It's the way we have always shifted together. We've danced through grief, through relocation, through the quiet moments that have shaped us. I feel the years between us, all the moments we've stitched together: the scraped knees I kissed, the nightmares I soothed, the secrets whispered in the dark. The nights when I stayed at her bedside just to hear her breathing. The mornings when I tucked a loose strand of hair behind her ear and thought, *God, how I love you.*

She twirls me suddenly, laughter escaping her lips, and I shake my head. I'm breathless.

'You've become bold,' I say.

'You taught me all I know.'

And there it is. The thing that's always tethered us to one another – not obligation, not expectation, but unconditional love and respect. It's woven through every touch, through every glance, through every moment. My daughter and I have chosen each other, and I'll continue to pick her in every lifetime. I tighten my grip on her hand.

The war is over. The music is bright.

If time could hold still for one moment, I'd choose this one.

14th September 1947

My Dearest Mama,

I hope this letter finds you well and not fussing over me more than necessary! I know you, and I can already hear the way you'd tilt your head and press your lips together if you were here, debating whether to scold or simply sigh.

It's colder in Scotland than I expected. The kind of damp that creeps into your bones, no matter how many layers you wear. John teases me that I've grown soft from too many summers in Oxfordshire, but even he admits the wind here bites. The house is grander than I thought. High ceilings and long corridors that seem to hold their breath when you pass. Some evenings it feels as though the house might swallow me whole. As if it's remembering things I haven't lived yet. I catch my own footsteps echoing and think of you in Pratts, of the hush of our house when Simon first left.

I have been trying to settle. To make it ours. The garden is hopeless. It's wild, untamed, and thoroughly unimpressed with my efforts! But I've made peace with that. I suppose everything needs time.

I can't seem to shake this confounded sniffle, though. John insists I rest, but I cannot bear to sit still when there is so much to do. It started as nothing. It was a chill after an afternoon in the rain, I think, but it lingers. My limbs ache at the end of the day, but that might be from the work of making this place a home. I am fine, though, truly. The air up here is simply sharper, and my body is slow to adjust. Mrs Fraser – the village nurse – told me it's nothing but the damp and that I ought to eat more broth.

You asked last time if I am happy. I think so. Happiness is a strange thing, isn't it? It doesn't announce itself boldly, but I feel it in the quieter moments. In the way John's hand steadies at the small of my back when we walk, or in the warmth of the kitchen when the fire is lit. And in the mornings, when I wake before the world outside has stirred, and I imagine you at home, moving through your day as I move through mine.

I miss you. I didn't think I would as much as I do, but there it is. There are moments I turn to speak to you, before I remember how far away you are. I miss our easy silences, our knowing glances over tea, the way you always managed to see through me when I tried to hide something. Mostly, I miss the comfort of you being near.

Perhaps, in time, that might ease? I don't know, though.

I hope you won't worry. I promise it's nothing. Write soon, please.

All my love always,
Pris

The Knock

October 1947

The knock is sharp. Certain. The kind of knock that knows what it brings. It doesn't belong to an ordinary evening. It cuts through the hush of the house, through the slow crackle of the fire, through the needle I have poised in my lap. My fingers still. Thread is caught mid-pull. The silence that follows is heavy. Waiting.

David looks up from his book, eyes narrowing. I hadn't known he'd be here tonight. A rare visit. He should not have been, and yet he is; it's as though the knock summoned him too, as though the house already knew I'd need a witness. 'Shall I get it?'

I shake my head. The floor is cool beneath my stockinged feet as I cross the room. My hands smooth down the creases in my skirt, as if that might steady something inside me. I'm not dressed for visitors.

The hall is dimly lit. Shadows pool at the edges. I press my palm against the door. I feel the grain of the wood beneath my fingertips, hesitating longer than I should. I know before I open it. I think of her laugh, the way she tucks her hair behind her ear, and for a heartbeat I see her at the window, waving like she did that summer day.

The man standing there is dressed for the rain. His coat is dark with damp and his hat is pulled low against the wind. A courier. He smells of cold air and wet wool, of soot and damp pavements.

'Mrs Russell Cooke?'

His voice is too steady, too practised; I nod.

He reaches into his coat, drawing out an envelope. The paper is softened at the edges where his fingers have gripped it. 'Telegram for you, ma'am. Urgent.'

I take it without a word. Without thanks. I close the door before I even hear him turn to leave.

David is watching me when I return. His book is forgotten on his lap. The firelight flickers across his face, highlighting the tension in his jaw. He doesn't need to ask. I stand in the centre of the room. I turn the envelope over once in my hands. The weight of it is nothing. A scrap of paper. And yet it presses into my palm like stone, heavier than any coffin. It's not words I hold but a verdict.

My chest tightens. Time speeds up. My breath catches in my throat.

My body knows before my mind does.

I slip my finger under the seal. I peel it back carefully, as if rushing might change the words inside.

```
       GALASHIELS INFIRMARY STOP YOUR DAUGHTER
     PRISCILLA GRAVELY ILL STOP ACUTE PARALYTIC
     POLIO STOP CONDITION CRITICAL STOP URGENT
                    YOU COME STOP
```

The letters blur. I blink, and they settle again. Stark against the yellowed background. The paper is thin; it weighs more than I can bear. The world narrows to eight words: *my daughter is dying, and I am here.*

David is on his feet now, crossing the room. Everything feels disconnected. Staccato. Offbeat. His limp is more pronounced on the uneven floorboards. He takes the telegram from my hands, reading it quickly, his lips pressing into a firm line. I'm distant from my own body, as though watching this scene from the doorway. My fingers curl into fists at my sides, my nails bite into my palms.

'I'll wake the housekeeper,' David says. His voice is calm and deliberate. 'You'll need a case packed. I'll get a car to take us.'

The words are muffled. Like they're being spoken from another room, from another life even. They take a moment to reach me.

'I'll go alone.'

David hesitates. 'Melville—'

'I'll go alone,' I repeat. My voice has an edge to it. Grief may hollow me out, but it won't drag me on a leash.

I turn for the stairs, moving slowly, and deliberately. The house seems taller. The hallway stretches out before me. It's unfamiliar and unyielding. Like the house is holding its breath, waiting to see if I'll shatter. I reach for the banister, pressing my palm against it, grounding myself in the rough grain of the wood.

Priscilla.

I see her as she was the last time she visited: her golden hair tucked behind her ears; her fingers cool in mine. She had been well. Smiling.

And now—

My foot slips on the stair. My breath catches. My body pitches forward before I grab the banister. Stopping myself. My knees weak, my stomach turning over.

Not Priscilla.

David is behind me in an instant, his good hand steady against my back. 'Let me come with you.'

I shake my head, swallowing against the rising panic in my throat. 'She's all I have left.'

His hand lingers. It's warm and certain.

∼

Outside, the wind snakes through the fields. Low and relentless. The trees along the lane are skeletal. Their branches shiver in the dark. The last of autumn's leaves skitter across the gravel drive. They catch at my boots as I step forward. Somewhere in the hedgerow, a bird stirs, rustling the brittle undergrowth before settling into uneasy silence.

The car is waiting at the foot of the drive. Its dark shape is crouched against the night. The headlights slice through the mist curling low over the road and the twin beams illuminate the frost gathering at the edges of the path. The engine hums. It's steady and patient. A thread of exhaust curling into the cold air.

David stands just behind me. He doesn't touch me, doesn't reach for my hand or brush his fingers against my sleeve, but I feel him there. He's a presence at my back.

'The roads will be clear at this hour,' he says quietly.

I nod but don't reply. My arms are wound tightly around myself beneath my coat. The telegram is still crushed in my gloved hand. The paper is more crumpled now; it's worn from the restless press of my fingers. Perhaps by holding onto it, I can will the words to change.

David shifts his weight, his cane tapping once against the gravel. 'You'll send word as soon as you arrive?'

'I'll send word when there's something to say.'

He exhales. I hear the frustration in it, the way he bites down on whatever argument he might have made. He wants to come with me. I know that. But I've never been a woman who leans, and now is not the time to start.

I step forward, feeling the drag of my own reluctance. The driver is watching me in the mirror. His face is unreadable in the dim glow of the dashboard. He doesn't speak as I climb in, doesn't offer a greeting or a reassurance. Just nods and waits for the door to close.

The latch clicks into place. Final and solid. David doesn't move from where he stands. He lifts one hand. Not enough to reach me, just enough to remind me he could.

The silence between us is its own kind of goodbye.

9th October 1947

Dear David,

Priscilla is gone. I was too late.

John was waiting outside the infirmary when I arrived. His coat soaked through, eyes red, hands clenched like he still thought he could hold her inside them. He looked older. He was older. Grief does that. It rips through you, leaves its mark in the skin, behind the eyes, in the shape of your back when you stand.

He didn't need to speak. I knew. There's a silence men carry when they must deliver that kind of news: heavy, aching, unavoidable. It settled between us, thicker than the October mist curling around the hedgerows.

She fell ill three weeks ago. It started small: sore legs, a bit of a tremble in her hands. They said fatigue. They always say fatigue. Then fever. Then paralysis. Then the word – polio. A small word, but it cuts deeper than any blade.

How can a word so slight cut so deeply?

It moved fast. They called that a mercy. Mercy? I see her fingers everywhere: ink-stained from her letters, tapping the table when she was impatient, tracing suns into window frost. Where is the mercy in losing hands that never learnt to be still?

John said she asked for me. Near the end. Her lips moved: Mama.

But she was too weak. She couldn't speak. She died trying to say my name. And I wasn't there. My daughter's last breath rose in a room that smelled of bleach and steam. Under stiff sheets in a borrowed bed.

I try to picture her before. Before this year, before Simon, before the light went out in her face. I try to see her laughing in the orchard, her skirt bunched at the thighs, arms outstretched, shouting at her brother for stealing her story endings. I try.

But all I see is her body in that hospital bed. Small. Stilled. Wrong.

She ~~is was~~ is my whole heart walking in the world, and now she is nowhere.

She never got to be a mother.

That thought crashes into me. Over and over. She would've been brilliant. She had Simon's steadiness, my sharpness, and something else – something warm and bright that neither of us ever fully understood. She ~~is~~ was so full of love. She didn't always show it, not in the easy ways, but it lived in her, quiet and fierce.

And now it's gone.

All of it.

Snatched.

She planted roses for a future that will never come.

Simon's death carved a hole, a hollow I learnt to live around. But this – this is different. Grief on grief. Losing my daughter now is losing the shape of myself. The house is still here, the rooms intact, yet nothing sounds right. The walls don't echo; they smother. There's too much of everything, and none of it is her.

I try not to believe in curses. But it's getting harder. Every time I love something, the world takes it. Both my children, David. Both.

Why am I writing to you? Perhaps because you understand what it is to carry loss. Not like a clean wound, but like something that leaks into the walls and fabric and air. You know the quiet at three in the morning, when the world holds its breath and all you can hear is absence.

If you can, come to Scotland. Bring your paints, or not. I won't ask for words. Just sit with me. Remind me I still belong to the living.

Outside the window, the last of her roses bow under the weight of the mist. I can't bring myself to cut them.

Yours,
Melville

Interruption Ten

MARCH 1973

Catherine pressed the stop button with a trembling finger. The click seemed far too small for what she felt breaking open inside her. The room blurred; her vision swam, not with tears exactly, but with a strange internal recoil – a sensation she remembered from childhood, when the body registered truth before the mind dared to.

Melville watched her, not speaking, not softening. She simply waited, in the way that made Catherine feel simultaneously seen and unbearably exposed.

'Not her,' Catherine whispered, though she wasn't sure who she meant – Priscilla? Melville? Herself? 'It's all too … sudden.'

'Loss is always sudden,' Melville said quietly. 'Even when you expect it.'

Catherine tried to breathe. It snagged in her chest, sharp and low. She pressed a hand low against her ribs, as if steadying something that wouldn't stay still – the old ache, the echo of her grandmother's warning, that childhood illness she'd outlived but never escaped. Borrowed luck. Borrowed breath. Some part of her had always expected the reckoning.

'I keep thinking…' Catherine faltered. Her voice shook. 'Living with something in your blood – knowing it might return – it changes the way time feels. I thought I'd made peace with that. But hearing Priscilla … at my age, with my health…' She swallowed hard. 'I'm hearing echoes,' she said quietly. 'Not endings – just echoes I don't know how to answer.'

'You're listening to fear,' Melville said, leaning forward. 'Not fate.'

Catherine laughed, a sound barely held together. 'Is there a difference?'

'Yes,' Melville said. 'Fear imagines patterns. Fate pretends to be inevitable. But neither has authority unless you hand it over.' Her gaze held Catherine's, steady and unflinching. 'All time is borrowed. We just choose how honestly we live inside it.'

Catherine wiped at her cheek, surprised to find it wet. 'I'm tired of pretending I'm not afraid.'

'Then stop. Say it aloud.' Melville's voice gentled but did not lose its edge. 'Fear doesn't dissolve in silence, it festers.'

The words hit Catherine with the weight of truth. She closed her eyes, inhaled, exhaled, letting the admission settle between them like something earned.

'I'm scared.' Her voice came out thin, as though it had been waiting years for permission. 'Of the results. Of … disappearing before anything I've done matters.'

Melville nodded, recognising a confession she'd once made herself. 'Then open the envelope and know what you're facing. Or don't – and choose the life you'll live without it. But stop letting a sealed envelope dictate the shape of you.'

For a moment, neither woman moved. The fire cracked softly. The house sighed around them. Catherine felt her pulse in the base of her throat, in her fingertips, in the hollow of her stomach where fear liked to settle most stubbornly.

She rose slowly from her chair. Not from resolve exactly, but from the quiet knowledge that staying seated would mean she wasn't ready to live at all.

Melville didn't stop her. Didn't offer comfort.

Catherine crossed the room, each step careful, almost measured. Her satchel waited on the table where she had placed it earlier – too close, too far. She rested her hand on the worn leather, steadying herself.

Then she slipped her fingers beneath the flap and reached for the envelope.

Dear Dr Haynes,

Thank you for attending for investigation last December. We have been trying to contact you to explain that the results of your blood tests and the accompanying chest radiograph are now available.

Several findings are within normal limits, though a small number of irregularities require clarification before a definitive conclusion can be reached. None of these are, in isolation, indicative of any acute or progressive disease. In combination, however, they warrant further assessment to exclude latent or recurrent infection.

We would therefore be grateful if you could attend the outpatient clinic for repeat tests and a brief clinical examination within the next…

Borrowed Time

MARCH 1973

'Catherine.'

A single word, soft as breath.

Catherine lowered the page. Nothing definitive. Nothing spared. Only the familiar limbo she'd pretended not to recognise. She pressed the heel of her hand to her forehead. 'I'm sorry. I just—' Her voice fractured. 'I didn't expect it to feel like this.'

'Bad news?' Melville asked.

'No. Not exactly.' Catherine shook her head – a quick, futile attempt at composure. 'Just more questions. More waiting. They want me back for more tests.'

Melville didn't reach out, but her posture changed: shoulders eased, chin lifted slightly the way a mother braces for the cry of a child she cannot soothe. 'You've lived with the feeling of borrowed time a long while,' she said quietly.

Catherine let out a sound – half laugh, half sob. 'Since I was ten. Since they told me it could return. Since people began treating me as though I were temporary.' She wiped her face with the back of her sleeve, embarrassed. 'It makes you behave strangely. You ration futures the way other people ration hope. You hold people at arm's length because you fear they'll have to relearn life without you.'

'Or because you think you'll ruin theirs,' Melville murmured.

Something in Catherine stilled. 'Yes.'

The fire hissed. Outside, a lorry changed gears on the road; the vibration passed through the floorboards, thin but grounding.

'People think survival is instinct,' Catherine whispered. 'But you … your father, Sidney, your mother, your children… Mel, you lost so much. I don't understand how anyone continues after that.'

Melville leant back, considering the academic. 'Survival isn't instinct. It's practice. A clumsy, graceless thing you relearn every morning.' She paused. 'And no one does it beautifully.'

Catherine gave a wet, broken laugh. 'That's not comforting.'

'It isn't meant to be.' Melville's gaze held hers – steady, almost stern. 'You asked me once if I felt cursed. I didn't. I felt … chosen. Not by fate. By circumstance. Someone had to live. Someone had to carry the remembering. I stayed because someone must.'

Catherine felt the words settle – not as instruction, but as possibility. She swallowed hard. 'Then after Priscilla, what did you do?'

'Nothing heroic,' Mel said. 'I lived quietly. They called it reclusion because they needed a name for what they couldn't bear to look at.' A beat. 'But living is not the same as disappearing.'

Catherine nodded slowly, her breath evening out. She reached down, fingers fumbling at the record button. 'And what happened between you and Mr Rolt?'

A Recluse

ARCHIVE: REEL TEN

From 1957

There are women who are seen, and women who are remembered. Mrs Melville Russell Cooke appears rarely in public now, yet her presence lingers in Mayfair drawing rooms and West End galleries alike. Once the centre of society, she now seems to circle its edges in a dark green Jaguar, a figure of poise, solitude, and something darker – an elegy in motion.

Tatler magazine, April 1957

Driving Dark Roads

April 1957

They call it solitude, as if it were elegance. The truth is plainer: it is retreat. Since she died, I've let the world pass in other people's voices, other people's rooms. I've not bothered with company, not really. A motorcar isn't freedom, it's flight – but tonight, at least, it's taking me somewhere instead of nowhere.

The Jaguar growls beneath me now, eager, impatient. Britain is busy laying new motorways, smooth ribbons of promise, but the magazines still print recipes and apron patterns and call that modernity. This one though feels closer to the future: built for speed, for clean lines and risk.

I shift into third and she answers before I've thought to ask.

The road is slick from earlier rain; the low sun strikes it in streaks of gold. I drive fast. Too fast. Tyres hiss through puddles; wind tugs at the half-open window. The sharp air carries wet earth, petrol, cut grass. It keeps me present. It keeps me from slipping under.

I haven't seen David in months. I don't count the weeks anymore. What we are – occasional – suits me. A thread left untied: still attached, but loose enough not to choke. He doesn't write often. I rarely reply. The distance between us stays tidy. The seat is warm beneath me and my blouse clings to my back. My hands are steady on the wheel, though I glance down to check. Once there was a tremor. Now there's only habit.

I shift gear again and she leaps forward, as if hungry for permission.

The hedgerows lean close. They're wet and swollen with spring. On a sharp bend something slips from the glovebox, landing near my foot. A sachet of lavender. Priscilla put it there many years ago, in another car. Said it sweetened the journeys. The scent is faint now, hardly more than a whisper, but I keep it. Proof that something of her still lingers in my every day. I move it to each car I drive. Ten years on, grief has learnt new disguises. It lingers in the joints on damp mornings, in the quiet corners of the house, in the silence when no letter arrives.

It lives in objects beyond scale or sense: a sachet of lavender, worn thin as breath.

David's studio appears through the trees. Its half-concealed windows dull against the last light. I picture him inside: sleeves pushed up, jaw clenched, paint on his wrist where it shouldn't be. Probably lost in someone else's face. That thought used to hurt. Now it simply tells me he's alive. A familiar ache, like cold pressing against old bone.

I pull into the drive. Gravel crunches under the tyres. Sharp and final. Beyond it: stillness. A field humming with frogs. My headlights stretch the shape of the building, drag the shadows longer than they should be. I sit with the engine ticking down. For a moment, I almost turn back. I've lived too long inside my own walls; it would be easier to keep them standing. But I came here for a reason; though I couldn't name it if pressed.

The studio door is open, spilling jazz into the night. I leave my gloves on the seat. Smooth my skirt. Breathe. Then, I cross the threshold. I don't knock. I never do.

Inside, the studio presses inwardly. Turpentine. Oil. Smoke. All of it familiar. All of it him. The place smells like work and loss. The two things he's always known how to live alongside. I breathe in. Hold it. Let it settle. He's at the far end, back turned. Hair darker than it should be at his age, jaw tense. He leans in close to the canvas, brush moving slowly. His body relaxed, but not quite – somewhat held back in the shoulders, like he's waiting for something to crack.

'You're late,' he says. Doesn't turn to me.

'I didn't know I was expected.' I stay near the door.

'You always are.'

He lays the brush down. Turns. Studies me like I'm a problem he hasn't yet decided how to solve.

'Months,' he says. 'No letters. No calls. I thought maybe this time you weren't coming back.'

'I wasn't sure either.' My voice is steadier than I expected. 'But I came.'

He doesn't smile. Doesn't frown. Just watches.

I move towards the easel, slowly. The canvas is a riot of ochres and green, but there's no gentleness in it. The trees crowd in, their trunks thick, their shadows dark, the path between them half-swallowed by shade. Sunlight spears through the branches in broken shards. Dazzling and disorienting. It's Provence, perhaps, but not an idyll. It's a place you could lose yourself.

'It's raw,' I say.

'Is that a compliment?'

'It's a fact.'

For a moment I feel myself drawn in to the painting, as if the avenue might swallow me too; light ahead, but the shadows pulling closer. David wipes his hands on a rag, streaked with ochre and blue, as though even sunlight has weight.

'You look tired,' he says.

I glance over my shoulder at him. 'I always do.'

'No,' he says. 'This is different.'

I ignore that. I move to the shelf. Pick up a brush, turn it in my hand.

'You're getting smoother,' I murmur.

He raises an eyebrow. 'Smoother?'

'The edges. They're less guarded. As if you've stopped fighting the paint.'

'You sound disappointed.'

I shake my head, slow. 'Surprised. I didn't think either of us would allow smoothing.'

He watches me. That long, unreadable look. The one I used to crave. The one I learnt to live without.

'And you?' he asks.

'I'm either a recluse or still running. I've not decided yet.'

'You think that's strength?'

'I think it's survival.'

He walks past me, closer now, but not close enough to touch. 'You could stop, you know.'

'I wouldn't know how.'

A silence opens. The kind with history in it. 'You think if you move fast enough,' he says, 'grief won't catch you again.'

I shake my head. 'I know it will. That's why I don't wait for it.'

Another pause. Longer. The gramophone crackles. The woman's voice falters.

'I drive,' I say, quieter now, 'because it's the one place I can't think too long. The road doesn't give you time.'

I don't tell him that sometimes, on certain stretches, I hear her voice. That she's still young and full of chatter. That she's still alive. That she giggles when I drive faster. I don't tell him that.

He nods. Just once. Looks away. Picks up another brush. The moment passes. 'Do you want a drink?'

'No.'

'I didn't think you'd stay long.'

I don't answer. I drift toward the far side of the studio. Touch a cracked ceramic jar. Let my fingers rest in the dried pigment.

'I'll stay longer next time,' I say. Not a promise to him, but to myself.

He doesn't turn. Doesn't say a word.

I close my eyes for a beat. The scent of paint, of turpentine, of something long lost, fills my chest. I turn, walk back through the door I never knocked on. The lavender sachet is still in the footwell. I'll leave it there.

Smith on Screen

August 1957

The air reeks of varnish and paint. Not sea air, not even close. A sharp, synthetic sweetness meant to pass for old wood and salt-worn steel. It's a scent pretending to be something it's not. The sea doesn't smell like this. It smells like brine and rust, coal smoke and oil. This is the smell of performance, of something made to look real.

I keep my world small by design. Crowds drain me; even dinners feel staged. But I came today. Not for them, not even for the film, for myself. To see if I could stand in a room full of pretence and not vanish. I light a cigarette with steady hands, inhale until it burns a little, and step up onto the wooden platform. The smoke drifts upward. Slow and pale. It dissolves near the rafters. A ghost, if I were in the mood for symbols; I'm not.

The set is a story pretending to be history; I've lived long enough to know the cost of that lie. Before me stands the *Titanic*'s bridge. Or someone's idea of it. Gleaming brass. Freshly polished dials. A spotless wheel. The set designers have scrubbed every inch of history off it. No rust. No splinters. No blood. The illusion is almost complete, except it's wrong. Real ships don't stay new. They weather fast. They're softened by salt and time until they belong to the sea. I take a step. My heels click too neatly on the boards. Wrong sound. Wrong weight. Real deck should groan underfoot, soaked in cold. This one doesn't creak. My mother would have hated this: the pretence, the press, the fuss of it all.

And then, I see him.

From a distance, the likeness is uncanny. My breath catches, sharp and unwelcome.

A man, in full uniform, stands at the wheel. Back turned, posture perfect. His hands rest on the rail just so. Relaxed, composed. Exactly like my father in that photograph. The one they printed in every paper. The one they used until it became myth. Noble. Untouchable. Time folds, just for a second.

I think of my mother, how she bent under grief but never broke. How, later, the twins watched her with wide eyes. They were too young to understand but old enough to feel it. We all lived in the aftermath of that stance, of that photograph. It wasn't only mine to carry.

Now, the sight is a blade. My body wants to believe what my mind can't. But I refuse the trick. Memory may ambush, but it won't command me.

I force myself closer, each step deliberate. And I study him the way I once studied my father: searching for what was human, not what was heroic. Laurence Naismith turns, and the moment collapses. His face is older. Softer around the eyes. A kind mouth, which already sets him apart. He studies me with a flicker of interest. Curiosity, maybe. Or worse, recognition. I take a long drag from my cigarette. Hold it. Let it go.

'Mrs Russell Cooke?'

'Melville,' I reply. 'Unless you're here to sell me insurance.'

A smile twitches at the corner of his mouth. His gaze doesn't waver.

'It's an honour to meet you,' he says.

'Is it?'

'It is.'

His politeness is oddly steady. Not the showy kind. Not the careful patronising tone I've come to expect from men in period costume.

I narrow my eyes. 'You look more like him than the last one did.'

'Brian Aherne?' There's a flicker of humour.

'Yes. He smoked a pipe.' My father hated pipes. I don't mean to say that, but it comes out anyway. 'And he looked nothing like the man,' I add. 'Yours is better.'

He nods once. 'Thank you.'

I flick ash from my cigarette. The floor is too clean for ash. For anything.

'I used to stand in the doorway of his study while he smoked cigars,' I murmur. 'Didn't dare move. The smoke above his head hung still. Like a halo. If I shifted, it disappeared.'

I feel Naismith watching me. Not intrusively. Just steady.

'What did he smoke?' he asks.

'Partagás. The strong ones. Smelt like tar and burnt citrus. Stuck to your clothes for days.'

I glance at the set again. The brass is gleaming. The wheel looks unused. The deck could double as a ballroom.

'Too clean,' I say. 'Too neat. This ship sank in freezing water. It cracked open. It split. This'—I wave the cigarette vaguely—'this is theatre.'

He nods, slowly. 'Yes. But we try to make it honest.'

I laugh – short, sharp. 'Good luck with that.'

He doesn't bristle. 'I don't pretend to know what it is to stand here as you do,' he says quietly. 'But I've tried to do him justice.'

That stops me. He doesn't offer sympathy. He just gives me a truth, then waits.

'You were Navy, weren't you?'

'Merchant,' he says. 'Before acting.'

'Then you know uniform's the least of it. Command's in the eyes. In the voice. My father didn't wear it. He was it.'

'I can believe that.'

A silence settles. The hum of the studio sounds thin beneath it. I drop my cigarette to the floor and grind it out with my shoe.

'I hope you get it right.'

'I hope so, too.'

We stand there, both of us quiet, and I feel the ghost of salt in the air, though it's not real.

A voice calls from behind us. 'Laurence! Mrs Russell Cooke! Press shot?'

I stiffen. Of course, there's always a camera. Laurence looks to me – not for permission, but something close to it.

'Go on.' I sigh. 'It's all part of the show.'

We move together. Not close, just near enough for the frame. His hand hovers at my elbow. Uncertain. I don't move. The flash pops. Harsh and fast. The photographer steps back. I know how they'll use this: my face beside his, the dutiful daughter lending legitimacy to their fiction. Let them. They'll print their myth. I'll carry my truth.

'For what it's worth, I hope this film honours him,' Laurence says.

I study him again. The costume. The set. The eerie resemblance. 'Don't make him a saint,' I say. 'He hated being admired.'

'I won't. He deserves better than that.'

I nod once, not quite approval, but close enough, and I turn to leave.

Outside, the studio doors hang open. Rain needles down in thin lines. Sharp and cleansing. The air is cold and wet and real. I breathe it in like medicine. Behind me, their *Titanic* still stands. It's untouched, untarnished, waiting for its next scene. My father isn't there, though. He's in the silt and the silence, in the weight of absence that lives beneath polished re-creations and morbid tribute films.

The rain soaks my hair flat, streaks my powder, and for once I don't care. I light another cigarette.

Suitably Exhilarating

August 1958

The Mercedes-Benz purrs beneath me, low and sleek, a machine that knows it's meant to be admired. MEL 108 catches the fading light like a wink. I never intended to keep the car. Davenport smirked when he handed me the keys – something about needing 'a suitably exhilarating ride'. I'd refused and then taken it anyway. Grief makes you stop asking for permission.

I hit the next bend fast. Deliberate, clean. The tyres grip with a satisfying bite. The lanes are wet from earlier rain, but I don't slow. The faster I go, the less room there is for the past to slide in.

In the mirror, a motorbike appears – lean, purposeful, gaining. Not a boy showing off. A man who rides like he knows exactly what he's doing. His approach is effortless. Confident.

I press the accelerator. The Mercedes responds with a low growl that feels almost like pleasure. Speed isn't flight anymore; it's something sharper – a claiming of space I'd abandoned.

He overtakes in one smooth motion. No swagger. No show. Just precision. He doesn't pull away, simply keeps pace ahead, a silent challenge.

When he signals toward a lay-by, I nearly ignore him. Curiosity wins. It usually does.

I ease onto the gravel. The engine idles like it resents stopping. He dismounts smoothly, his leathers worn in ways that suggest he's lived through a few storms of his own. Older than I expected. Not aged – tempered.

'You drive like a woman with something to prove,' he says, grinning.

I take a drag of my cigarette. 'I drive like a woman who doesn't have to prove anything to a man on a motorbike.'

He laughs, low and feral. 'Fair enough.' He nods toward the car. 'It suits you.'

'Thanks.'

The wind carries woodsmoke and the faintest breath of lavender. My fingers twitch but I don't reach for the glovebox.

'Out for anything particular?' he asks.

'The road.'

He accepts that without comment. Some men always want more. He doesn't. That's new. Silence settles – not awkward, just alert. Like the pause before a race starts.

'Funny thing about roads,' he says. 'Most people think they're taking them somewhere. Usually, they just bring you back to yourself.'

It hits harder than I expect. I hide it by grinding my cigarette into the gravel.

'Sometimes the noise is enough,' I say.

He smiles. Approving, not predatory. 'That's honest.'

For a moment, something balances between us – curiosity, possibility, and the unspoken knowledge that neither of us is here to be saved.

'Where are you headed?' he asks.

I slide behind the wheel. 'Anywhere I like.'

He watches me go but doesn't follow. That, more than anything, makes me drive faster.

The Final Strokes

October 1959

My boots track damp across the floor. I pause. David doesn't look up. He hunches over the easel, one hand guiding the brush, the other braced on the table. His pipe rests warm in the dish, the smoke still clinging. That smell – Cavendish, paint, something darker – is the closest thing I've ever known to permanence.

'David,' I say and he turns to me.

'You came.'

'You asked,' I say, taking off my gloves. 'That seemed reason enough.'

I've lost count of how many months it's been since I last saw him. I read about his New York exhibition in July. He makes a low sound – half a breath, half something else – and steps aside from the easel.

The painting hits me like a blow.

Not a likeness. Not a portrait. A reckoning.

My headscarf flares from the canvas in a streak of vermillion. The only red in the storm of greys and slabbed whites behind it. The painted eyes are sharp, unsmiling, unwilling to bend. A woman carved by loss – Father, Mother, Sidney, then Simon and Priscilla – not defined by it. A woman still standing when everything else had fallen.

'You've gone bold again,' I murmur.

'It's the only way I know you,' he says. 'It's nearly finished.'

I move closer. The paint is still tacky in places. The strokes are fierce, almost violent. Yet there's tenderness folded inside them – the kind he'd never say aloud.

'Why capture that version of me?' I ask softly. 'Why now?'

He set the brush down. Wipes his hands. His shoulders change shape – not slumped, not tense, but resolved. 'I needed to remember. Before I tell you.'

I don't sit. Neither does he. The room holds its breath. He taps his pipe against the dish. The sound is soft, deliberate. 'Melville,' he says. 'We need to talk.'

I lean back slightly against a stool. 'So, talk.'

He picks up the tobacco pouch. Holds it like something to anchor him. 'I've met someone,' he says. His tone is steady, but I hear the catch beneath it. 'Her name is Penelope. But everyone calls her Minnie.'

The name drifts between us, fragile as steam in the cold air. I let it hang, then taste it slowly. 'Minnie.' The syllables are soft, untested.

Rain needles at the tall windows. The fire pops behind me. I stay where I am, one hand on the chair back, grounding myself in the rough grain.

'She's younger,' David says. His gaze doesn't shift.

'Of course she is.'

'Much younger.'

I tilt my head, let a smile ghost my mouth. 'Youth's not a crime. You wanted light. You've chosen it.'

He gives a sound – part laugh, part regret – and finally sets the tobacco pouch aside. 'We're getting married.'

The word lands like a dropped stone. I breathe out. 'Married.' The echo tastes bitter and sweet together. 'And that?' I point at the portrait.

'A need.'

He won't meet my eye.

'I once loved a man who gave his heart elsewhere. It taught me that possession is a myth. Timing, though … timing is the only truth. And this is yours.'

The air shifts. Not tense, but heavier. The truth has finally rooted itself, and neither of us can move it.

'It's not about leaving you behind,' he says. His fingers tighten around the edge of the table. 'It's not about that at all.'

I shake my head; we both know he's lying. 'But you will. For all of us.' I step closer to the easel. The smell of linseed oil rises, sharp, unyielding. My fingertips skim the canvas where the paint is still tacky. My own painted eyes stare back at me. They're defiant, unsmiling, unafraid. 'You're right to be drawn to beginnings. To spark. I was that, once.'

'You still are.'

'No.' I look him square in the face. 'I'm what spark becomes when it survives the fire. Smoke. Ash. Memory. None of it young, but all of it strong.'

He steps toward me. The floorboards protest under his weight. His hand brushes mine, briefly.

'I didn't know how to say it,' he says. 'You mean more to me than anyone.'

'That doesn't mean you're mine to keep.'

He looks down. Paint stains his fingertips. A streak of crimson smudges near his temple. I don't tell him. He never did like to be tidied.

'I'm not angry,' I say. 'I've mourned too many people I love. I won't mourn the living. I won't add you to the list of ghosts.'

'You always speak like a woman who's already survived the ending.'

'Because I have.'

He nods. There's no argument. 'I want you to have the painting, when it's finished,' he says.

I smile; it's not sad, not bitter. 'You keep it.'

'I'll miss you,' he says.

'You'll have her.'

'It's not the same.'

'No,' I agree. 'It isn't.'

I walk to the door. The rain meets me, soft but persistent. He stays behind.

Interruption Eleven

MARCH 1973

(The recording clicks back into life. A chair scrapes; Catherine is already on her feet. There's a brightness in her voice that hasn't been there for weeks — an urgency she hasn't bothered to hide.)

Dr Catherine Haynes: that's it. The painting — David's portrait from fifty-nine. The cool grey, the vermillion slash … God, it's the same brushwork, the same eye-line. He caught you exactly as you described: unguarded, uncompromising. (A rustle of paper. Possibly notebook pages turning). The file said 'private collection', no provenance, no sitter. Just … a woman refusing to look away.

Melville Russell Cooke: I didn't think of it for years, Then I read some article — nonsense, really — about the collector who thought the painting was cursed.

DCH: did you keep the clipping?

MRC: (A beat. A soft intake of breath), I'm sure I did. At the time. I remember the collector was named. It'll be in the suitcase with the others.

DCH: The suitcase. The one you said—

MRC: (Lightly, too lightly), lost, yes. These things wander. I wouldn't know where to begin looking. (A brief silence. Movement: a chair leg catching on the floor).

DCH: (Catherine registers the tone — the kind that masks more than it reveals, but lets it pass.) That painting is the thread that pulled me to you. All of this started there — the paper, the archives, the first letter I sent you. (Breathing hard) And David — did you ever see him again?

MRC: Of course I did. I'm a stubbornly fortunate woman, Doctor Haynes. And women like me always find their way back to what matters.

DCH: (A click. She sits — or drops — back into her chair), I'd best start a new reel.

A Fortunate Woman

ARCHIVE: REEL ELEVEN

From 1971

This year's Royal Academy Summer Exhibition includes a quietly commanding portrait by David Rolt, now aged 56. Titled simply, *Portrait of a Lady*, the work shows a silver-haired woman seated amid long grass and an open sky, as if she has turned her back on both spectacle and memory.

Rolt, who first exhibited at the RA in the 1940s and became known for his vivid society portraits, declined to name the sitter. In the subdued chatter of the preview, however, she is identified as a once familiar figure now living a largely private life in Oxfordshire.

'A good portrait tells you how someone was,' Rolt said quietly. 'A better one tells you what they have carried.'

The Observer, 18 November 1971

White Tinged with Lavender

November 1971

The gallery is warm, but it's a staged warmth. Like a hostess who smiles with her mouth and not her eyes. Pools of light fall just so, parquet polished to a shine, champagne bubbling in coupes as if the fizz might distract from the chatter. Even the hush feels rehearsed.

David's canvases cut against all that. They're weather, not decoration: skies clawed open, faces that don't pose but stare back until you blink first. He's always known how to strip people bare. People think they come to look. Instead they leave feeling looked at.

I peel off my gloves, fingers slower than they used to be, and snap open my umbrella hard enough to make a few patrons startle. Good. Let them. I've always preferred a room that isn't quite ready for me. The champagne's passable. Celebration in a glass, pretending it means more than it does. I take one anyway.

'Melville,' comes the gravel-warm voice at my left. 'You're late.'

And there he is. Pushing through a clump of overdressed people who part without thinking. Older, of course. We both are. His limp's deeper now, the brass tip of his cane catching the light each time it hits the floor; it's a steady counterpoint to silk hems and nervous laughter.

'Mr Rolt,' I say, tugging at my mouth. 'Still desperate for attention, I see.'

'Still arriving like you've bought the deed to the building,' he fires back.

We meet in the centre of the room like weather fronts colliding. Familiar storm. He kisses my cheek. I catch turpentine and pipe smoke, and beneath that a note of linseed – and loneliness. Since his marriage ended, he's carried it like an aftershave no one chose.

'You wrote to me,' I say, sliding an arm through his. 'Said I "would regret not seeing my old self framed".'

'I did. And you came. I wasn't sure you would.'

'Curiosity got the better of me. That, and the fact I've outlived most of your collectors.'

He laughs, properly. The kind that comes from somewhere lower than the ribs. 'The divorce helped. No more permission slips.'

I nod. It explains the softness around him. There's something looser in the way he stands now. Less defended.

We move through the crowd, and then I see her.

Me.

There I am: hair silvered and coarser, swept back as if speeded off by the wind; seated in profile, shoulders honest, mouth shut the way mine does when I have finished explaining myself. The canvas flatters nothing.

'I didn't sit for that.'

'You did,' David replies. 'You just didn't know it. One afternoon last summer. You were watching birds in your garden and telling me to stop fussing.'

I step a little closer. The blouse I'm wearing is pale – white tinged with lavender – creased in the way linen creases honestly. The brushwork isn't kind, but it's true. The neck is thicker than I remember, the jaw softening, but not yielding. The lines around the eyes have been painted deliberately. Without vanity. Without apology. There's a familiarity to the posture. The sort that only comes when someone knows your silences as well as your speeches. And behind me, barely there in the grass, an empty deckchair leans off-balance. I can't tell if it's waiting or if I've left it that way.

'You didn't paint me looking out,' I murmur. 'You painted me inward.'

'You always gave the best of yourself sideways.'

I snort. 'That sounds poetic.'

'It's the truth.'

We fall quiet again. The room shifts around us: art handlers in black polo-necks pretending not to hover, champagne being replenished like it matters.

'I remember being told that portraits are about likeness,' I say.

David shakes his head. 'That's what amateurs think. Likeness flatters. A true portrait keeps the ledger of a life. What it held, what it gave away. That's what this is.'

We turn away together and pass a seascape. His familiar angry brushstrokes, the canvas thick with it. Sea gone wrong. Wind against the tide.

'Still painting storms?' I ask, lifting a glass of something dry and overpriced.

'I watch them now. From the cliffs. Let the waves do what they will.'

'You're suddenly lyrical. Should I be worried?'

He gives me a sideways look. 'I painted a seascape this summer. The sea looked like your sneeze.'

I bark a laugh. 'That's either deeply flattering or unhinged.'

'Is there a difference?'

We pause by a window. Outside, the rain has turned to that shiny London mist. Not quite rain, not quite over. Taxicabs wink in puddles like sullen little eyes.

'Catherine's nearly eleven now,' he says. 'Toby's nine next month. She writes poems about ponies, and he still builds trains out of toast crusts.'

'Madness clearly runs in the family.'

He smiles. 'They ask about you. "Mel with the silver rings," they say. "Mel who makes the rules."'

I feel the flicker of an old ache, but it passes. 'They'll grow out of it. Become sensible. Dreadful.'

'I hope not.'

I glance back at the portrait – at the woman in the chair: older, composed, whole. I made my peace with this long ago. His life carried on. So did mine.

There's a silence.

'Did you ever think we'd end up here?' he asks. 'Alive. Civilised. Almost dignified.'

'Speak for yourself,' I say. 'I arrived drenched and wearing a dress from nineteen-forty-nine.'

'I painted that dress once.'

He grins and I nod.

'Do you regret any of it?' he asks, and this time the question lands differently. Not banter. Not nostalgia. It's the kind of question people only ask when they think the end might be close enough to matter.

'No,' I say. 'I loved and I lost. I drove too fast, drank too much, smoked too often. And I turned every bit of wreckage into something that was mine. That's the job, isn't it? Not just to survive, but to make survival mean something.'

He watches me. Something sharp behind the quiet of it. 'You did that,' he says. 'More than anyone.'

'I'm a fortunate woman,' I say. Not smugly, not bravely – simply true. 'Mostly because I kept choosing to go on. That's luck enough.'

'I'll raise my glass to that.'

'And, for now, I'm a gallery feature again. Next stop … catalogue storage. Or taxidermy, if they're feeling cruel.'

He finishes his drink and sets the glass on the sill.

'I'll walk you out?'

'You'll hobble me out, more like.'

We go out together, slow and deliberate. His gait is different now. Less urgency, more agreement. I let him take my hand. Not for old times. For the fact we're still here. Not owning. Not pleading. Just steady.

Interruption Twelve

MARCH 1973

Catherine stopped the recorder before the click had fully settled. She rose at once, pushing back her chair too sharply for the room's stillness. The fire had sunk to a low, exhausted glow; the air tasted faintly of cooled ash and old dust. She pressed her palms hard against her eyes – not crying, simply steadying the pressure behind them, clearing the blur.

She began to pace. Slow at first, then in measured strides that betrayed how quickly her mind had outpaced her body.

'So that's everything,' she said, half under her breath, half to Melville. 'Your whole ... your whole life.'

Melville, propped on the sofa with a shawl pulled around her shoulders, watched her with a small, wry curve of the mouth. 'Not everything,' she said. 'Just the parts I thought you could carry.'

Catherine let out a short breath that nearly passed for a laugh. 'It was more than enough. More than I ever expected. I think...' She stopped by the mantel, fingers brushing the brass clock as though testing whether time had steadied or accelerated. 'I think I finally understand the shape of it. And I have everything I need for the paper. Absolutely everything.'

'Good,' Melville replied. 'Then you won't have an excuse to hide behind drafts any longer.'

Catherine glanced back. 'I'm not. Not anymore,' she said, surprising herself with the truth of it.

'Scholarship is a very respectable form of hiding,' Melville said mildly. 'I've done it myself. Letters. Lists. Commentaries. Anything rather than live a thing directly.'

Catherine didn't argue. Her throat tightened. 'I'll go next week,' she said. 'To the hospital. I'll have their tests. No more postponing.'

Melville's gaze held hers with the same unnervingly accurate perception she'd shown in every recording. Catherine swallowed. The room felt too full, and yet she knew she would remember this exact quiet, this exact light, for years.

'I'll write the paper,' she said softly. 'And I'll go to the appointments. And I'll—' She faltered. 'I don't know what comes after. I've never planned a life beyond maybe.'

'Living,' Melville said. 'It isn't a riddle. You keep going until you can't. And even then, you find a little more – an hour, a day, a reason. You take what you're given.'

The clock ticked: thin, insistent, the room's smallest metronome.

Catherine crossed to the table with a steadying breath. She gathered the cassettes into a neat stack. She checked each label twice – not from doubt, but from wanting the story to stay intact, before slipping the final one into her satchel.

'You've been generous,' she said. 'More than I had any right to expect.'

'Don't be absurd,' Melville said briskly. 'I've enjoyed your questions. It's been...' She hesitated, the briefest flicker softening her tone. 'Company.'

Catherine stopped mid-stride. Something pressed in her chest – not sorrow, not quite relief. Something settled. A recognition that the companionship had been mutual. 'We don't have to stop seeing each other, just because the recordings have.'

Lamb on Sundays

APRIL 1973

The light spilled across the parlour in long, honeyed sheets, catching the edges of the silver tray and the polished sherry glasses Melville had insisted on using, despite Mrs Atkinson's muttering. The housekeeper, stiff as starch, had complained about fingerprints and waste, but Melville still preferred to polish the glasses herself. It wasn't cleanliness she cared about – it was ownership. Proof that the house was still hers to command.

The lamb rested in the oven, rosemary softening in the heat. The scent curled through the hallway and into the old timbers like a benediction. Her appetite, at seventy-five, still surprised her; she took it as a sign she wasn't done yet. Sunday lunches had become a ritual again – a suggestion from Mrs Atkinson that had sounded like an order.

'The house likes company,' she'd said, stacking plates without meeting Melville's eye. 'And that woman from the university looks like she needs a good meal.'

It had been three Sundays so far.

From the window, Melville saw them now: Catherine and her Canadian colleague, Marianne, coats flapping, hair whipped about by the Oxfordshire wind, boots somehow muddied from the walk up the driveway. They were laughing.

Melville got to the door before their knock landed. Slower than she once would have been, but still on her own terms.

'Another minute and I'd have poured your sherry down the drain,' she said, sweeping them inside. 'Mrs Atkinson's already accused me of drinking before noon.'

'It's half past,' Catherine said, cheeks pink from the cold.

'Which makes it scandalously late,' Melville replied. 'Boots off, coats abandoned, sherry immediately. House rules.'

They obeyed, now familiar with the choreography of her Sundays. Catherine's movements were careful today – less stiff than the week before – and Melville noticed. She noticed everything.

'It's so quiet here,' Marianne murmured, settling by the fire. 'Like a place that remembers things on purpose.'

'It does,' Mel said, pouring generously. 'Pratts forgets nothing. Though it rarely gives the whole truth either.'

Marianne looked up at the framed map above the mantel. 'You have a map of Atlantic Canada? How haven't I noticed that before?'

'Halifax,' Melville said. 'My father's connection to the place was an unfortunate one.'

Marianne blinked, realisation dawning. 'The *Titanic* recovery … the ships that brought—'

'The survivors,' Mel finished. 'And the bodies. Yes. That's where the story of my family became the world's property.' She said it without bitterness, only certainty. 'Though I didn't bring you here to give lectures on maritime tragedy.'

They moved to the table when the oven chimed – a modern intrusion that Melville tolerated only because she liked the precision. The lamb carved easily, the fat crisping along its edges.

'This looks wonderful,' Catherine said, though her voice was softer than usual. She'd lost weight recently; her collarbones showed more sharply beneath her blouse.

'It *is* wonderful,' Melville replied. 'Eat more than three forkfuls and I might even let you return next week.'

Catherine smiled – a real one – and served herself obediently. After a few minutes, Melville glanced at her.

'Marianne tells me you finally said yes to coffee with that young research fellow.' She spoke as casually as if she were noting the forecast. 'Michael, isn't it? About time. A woman can't live on archives alone.'

Catherine froze mid-movement, fork poised near her mouth. A flush rose quickly, betraying her before she could summon any academic neutrality. Marianne's grin widened – unrepentant, delighted.

'It's only coffee,' Catherine managed, though the defensive note in her voice undermined the claim.

'Of course,' Melville said, entirely unconvinced. 'Most things worth beginning start with an *only*.'

Marianne nudged Catherine's arm, a small conspiratorial gesture that said she was proud of her – and perhaps a little relieved.

'Now,' Melville said briskly, 'let's see if either of you can pour without making a mess of my carpet.' She turned towards the sherry glasses with the satisfied air of a woman who had been waiting for precisely this moment.

Marianne stepped forward to oblige, lifting a glass with theatrical care before passing it to Catherine.

'How were the latest tests?' Melville asked quietly.

Catherine swallowed, dabbed with her napkin. 'The same. Not worse,' she said. 'They're … monitoring things closely. Weekly for now. And I'm letting them.' She laughed softly. 'They think it might be nothing. Or something. They're not sure yet.'

Melville said nothing at first – just reached for the mint sauce as if the conversation were weightless. 'Doctors love uncertainty,' she said finally. 'Makes them feel important. You'll tell me next Sunday what they've invented for you.'

Catherine gave a breath of laughter, shaky but grateful.

'And stop pretending your appetite's vanished,' Melville added. 'Eat, or I'll feed you myself.'

Lunch eased after that – the rhythm of the food, the fire, the shared warmth doing its quiet work. They spoke of lectures, archives, bicycle punctures, and Marianne's perpetual astonishment at British weather. Catherine brightened across the meal; colour returned to her cheeks, and the crease between her brows faded. She ate without thinking about proving anything to anyone. It was the closest she had felt to ease in months.

Later, over more sherry and the last of the roast potatoes, Marianne nodded towards the map over the mantel.

'Will you ever write it all down?' she asked. 'Your life?'

Mel snorted. 'Absolutely not. I've been written down before. Newspapers, memorials, myths. Once you let people pin you to a page, you become whatever they need you to be. I prefer being inconvenient.'

Catherine watched her with quiet intensity – the same look she had the first time she'd asked for a recording.

'Then I'll write carefully,' she said.

'You'd better,' Melville replied. 'Or I'll come back and haunt you. I've lived through worse than death; I can manage a haunting.'

∽

When the meal was over, Melville walked them to the door. Catherine's steps wavered only once, and her host pretended not to notice when she steadied herself against the frame.

'Next Sunday,' Melville asked, though it wasn't a question.

'Next Sunday,' Catherine said firmly. 'I'll bring test results.'

'Bring an appetite and news of your coffee date,' Melville corrected. 'The rest we'll deal with as it comes.'

The academics walked back along the driveway, Marianne linking her arm through Catherine's, both heads bowed against the wind. Melville watched them until the gate clanged shut behind them, the map of Halifax glowing faintly behind her in the dying light.

Finding Polaris

MAY 1973

Pratts House had its own weather. Floorboards sighed. Wind pressed the chimneys like a warning. The day had been close, the air thick enough to taste. By evening, the house felt watchful – not hostile, but alert, as if it knew something was coming to an end.

Melville had read Catherine's draft paper twice. Slowly the first time, warily the second. When she set the pages down, her hands were perfectly still.

It was a good paper. Sharp, perceptive, braver than Catherine realised. It understood Melville – not completely, but enough. Enough to make something in Melville contract with an old, private startle.

The young woman had found her way to the truth: that *unlucky* had been a language used on her, not for her. That the world had shaped her story in its own image. That she had survived, not because of some inherited curse but because she kept choosing to.

And yet—

Catherine's pages had also done what scholarship always did: fixed her in place. Neatened her. Turned a life of raw edges into something that could be cited, footnoted, held up as evidence. A story someone else could now claim. She didn't blame Catherine. That was the danger of being seen clearly: the world always wanted to keep the image.

She stood abruptly, joints protesting, and climbed the stairs. In her bedroom, she knelt – slowly, but without hesitation – and reached beneath the bed. Her fingers found the handle exactly where she had left it.

The suitcase slid forward like an old animal returning to light.

E.J.S.

The initials caught the low lamplight. Her father's case. And all her ghosts inside it.

She had lied to Catherine, of course. Lied with the ease of someone who had spent a lifetime defending the territory of her own past. The suitcase had never been lost. She had kept it hidden because she had not known, until today, what she meant to do with it.

The clasps groaned open. The lid lifted.

There it all was.

The glove Priscilla had worn at five.

Sidney's toy plane, bent wing crooked like a broken promise.

The wedding band that had outlived its finger.

Newspaper cuttings – yellowed, brittle – shouting *Daughter of the Titanic*, *Widow*, *Unlucky Woman*, *Recluse*.

And letters. So many letters. Some written in her hand, others in the hands of people who had wanted to claim pieces of her, of her father, of her mother, of her husband, of her children too.

Their words still smelled faintly of damp stone, sea air, and the ink of public appetite.

Melville read slowly. She let each scrap sting once more, and once only. She traced her younger handwriting on a torn Lichfield newspaper margin:

Find Polaris.

A note to herself from a time when she still believed direction was something granted, not chosen.

She closed the suitcase.

Downstairs, the fire waited. Flames knotted impatiently in the grate. She carried the suitcase down, step by careful step. Pratts House did not resist. It opened around her like a silent witness.

In the parlour, she set the suitcase on the hearthrug and eased herself to the floor, as if negotiating with her knees.

Her breath did not tremble.

One by one, she fed the contents to the fire.

The past curled, hissed, blackened. Headlines folded into themselves. Photographs blistered into ash. The glove shrank into nothing. The toy plane glowed briefly, then subsided into a soft red surrender.

Nothing would be left behind for others to claim.

Smoke rose, carrying decades with it. The room smelled of char, turpentine, and an unexpected sweetness – freedom.

Only one thing remained: the postcard.

The tiny bird in the corner. Her father's handwriting steady and sure.

I could not catch a little bunny to send you in my letter, so send you a card by this little bird.

She pressed it to her chest. The paper, thin as breath, warmed beneath her hand. This, she would keep. Not because it was evidence, not because it was story, but because it was hers.

Mel slipped the postcard into her pocket, straightened with care, and crossed to the hall table. The telephone gleamed under the lamplight, black Bakelite catching the room's glow.

She lifted the receiver.

'Davenport,' she said, when he answered.

'Melville!'

'I've decided it's time for something faster.'

A crackle of delighted laughter. 'I wondered when you'd come back to me.'

'Tomorrow,' she replied, and replaced the receiver before sentiment could find a foothold.

At the front door, the night air struck her like a tide – sharp, bracing, real. Polaris glimmered high above the orchard, steady and faithful. She no longer needed its guidance, but she was glad it was there.

Horizon Opens Wide

JUNE 1973

The Aston Martin V8 growled beneath her, smooth as ever, as if it, too, refused to acknowledge the years. The road unfurled ahead in a series of generous curves, and Melville took them without hesitation. The wind tugged at her scarf until the knot loosened; wisps of grey hair whipped across her cheeks like fine threads caught in motion. She let it happen. She had earned every knot, every wild strand.

At the crest of the next rise stood a small, independent petrol station – a single pump beneath a lean wooden overhang. A boy, no more than twenty, leaned against it with the easy slouch of someone waiting for the day to start behaving.

Melville pulled in. Gravel spat under the tyres. The boy straightened, brushing his hands on his overalls.

'Afternoon, Mrs. Lovely motor.'

'She is,' Melville said, easing herself out. Her knees objected, but she ignored them. 'Fill her, please.'

He took the keys reverently. 'How's she on the corners?'

'Glued to the road,' she replied.

While he worked, she glanced toward the station window. A noticeboard sagged under curling papers – adverts, lost dogs, bulb sales. One photograph caught her eye: a line of RAF pilots, all bright-eyed bravado and brittle youth.

'That yours?' she asked, nodding.

The boy followed her gaze. 'My granddad's squadron. Put it up years back. Said someone had to remember them.'

'He was right.' Her voice stayed level, though her chest tightened. They looked Simon's age. Youth that never learnt to grow old.

He replaced the petrol cap. 'All done. Three pounds forty-five, please.'

Mel handed him more than necessary. 'Keep the change.'

He blinked, then accepted. 'Thank you, Mrs. Drive safe.'

'Spend it on something reckless,' she said, already slipping back into the driver's seat.

The engine answered her touch with a low, eager snarl. She pulled out, the photograph lingering in her mind a moment longer – before the wind tore it away.

Russell Cooke, Helen Melville (née Smith) passed away suddenly on 18 August 1973, while preparing for a bath, in Oxford, aged 75. Beloved widow of Sidney Russell Cooke. Dearly missed by friends. Funeral service to be held at Brookwood Cemetery, Surrey. No flowers by request.

Helen Melville Russell Cooke

EPILOGUE

From April 2013

OPINION – THE LETTER THAT LIVED

Last weekend, a modest cream postcard – the kind a child might tuck into a pocket and forget – sold at auction for £10,000. It was written by Captain Edward Smith of the *Titanic* to his young daughter, Helen Melville Smith: '*I could not catch a little bunny to send you in my letter, so send you a card by this little bird.*'

Headlines pounced. Daughter of the Titanic. A relic of tragedy. Commentators treated the postcard as proof of a curse, a symbol of misfortune handed down from father to daughter like an unwanted heirloom.

But the woman who kept that card for more than sixty years was no relic.

She was [Helen] Melville Russell Cooke: a woman whose gravestone, shared with her husband in a quiet Surrey churchyard, reduces her to two words – *his wife* – and omits even the year she died. As if her extraordinary life could be folded away.

It can't.

Ask anyone who knew her: my mother, Dr Catherine Haynes, did. Early in her career she spent long Sundays at Pratts, eating lamb at the table while Melville smoked, teased, argued, and revelled in every sharp, small joy the world still offered. When Mel spoke of the curse others believed had shadowed her life, she pressed my mother to confront a fear she had long buried.

That insistence – that single, immovable demand that she keep her hospital appointment – kept my mother alive. It also gave her the courage to stop running from the future she wanted, and to say yes at last to Michael, the research fellow, who would become my father.

I exist because of her.

Melville Russell Cooke laughed loudly. She lived stubbornly. She survived more than most – and still insisted on joy.

And the postcard? It was the only thing from her personal archive that she kept.

Everything else – clippings, pity, headlines, the world's claim to her story – she burnt in the fireplace one May evening in 1973. My mother never included that detail in her university paper; she kept Melville's secret until the end. But I understand it now.

The postcard was never an artefact of disaster.

It was the one piece of her childhood untouched by myth: a private kindness from a father, unclaimed by anyone else's story.

The price it fetched is beside the point.

What mattered was her choice – to keep it, to claim it, to believe that a life could be shaped by love rather than loss.

Emily Haynes-Williams

∼

THANK YOU FOR READING
DAUGHTER OF THE TITANIC

IT WOULD MEAN SO MUCH IF YOU COULD LEAVE A REVIEW ON ALL YOUR PREFERRED PLATFORMS AND SOCIAL MEDIA TO HELP SPREAD THE WORD!

YOU CAN ALSO FOLLOW ME ON INSTAGRAM @CAROLINE.CAUCHI, ON X @CAROLINE_S, AND CHECK OUT MY WEBSITE WWW.CAROLINECAUCHI.CO.UK FOR UPDATES ON MY LATEST WORK.

∼

READ ON FOR AN EXTRACT FROM MY NOVEL
THE WOMAN WHO WENT OVER NIAGARA FALLS IN A BARREL

Author's Note

Helen Melville Smith – known to those closest to her simply as Mel – was born into privilege, shadowed early by seismic loss. Her father, Captain Edward John Smith, went down with the *Titanic* in April 1912. Her mother, Sarah Eleanor, died in a road accident less than two decades later. Mel married Sidney Russell Cooke in 1922, only to lose him in 1930. Their twin children, Simon and Priscilla, died young; Simon in the war, Priscilla from polio soon after. After her death in 1973, her ashes were placed in her husband's grave.

These are the fixed points.

Between them lies a life shaped by grief, yes, but also by speed, eccentricity, wit, and a fiercely private sort of courage. She learnt to fly. She drove fast cars. She collected art with certainty. She gave generously and formed intimate bonds outside traditional structures. She remains, even now, partly unknowable – glimpsed through portraits, auction records, stray recollections, biographies of others – and photographs in which she meets the camera with a direct, almost challenging gaze, as if insisting, *I am here. Look properly.*

This novel is written against that quiet erasure. It is not a biography – that would be false. What it offers instead is an imagined portrait shaped by what survives, and by all that the archive neglected to keep.

~

I came to Mel's story through fragments: photographs, newspaper clippings, shipping ledgers, sales catalogues, and one remark from Anthony Coleridge that the contents of her home 'form a major portion of our collection. She had great taste, and we shall forever be in her debt.'

David Rolt's portraits were my first anchor. Across the years he painted her in different guises, yet always with the same alertness – an unmistakable presence. Those images offered what the historical record could not: the sense of a woman who knew how easily a life might be misread, and who held the gaze anyway.

Around these visual traces, the silence presses in. There is no consistent record of her schooling, her friendships, her private rituals, or her thoughts during the long winters at Pratts. These absences are not unique to her; they reflect how women's lives have so often been documented – or not documented at all. What the archive preserves tends to be their losses, their marriages, their relation to men. Their inner worlds, their ambitions, their contradictions: these fall away.

Fiction enters where the record fails. Every imagined moment risks intrusion, yet I hope it is also an act of regard – a way of returning dimension to a life allowed to thin to almost nothing on the page.

Mel's life, rendered publicly as a sequence of tragedies, defines fatalistic framing. A woman who endured losses becomes a woman destined for them. A life with sharp turns becomes a life defined by them. Once such a narrative takes hold, it can be astonishingly durable; people look only for the evidence that supports it.

But in her portraits – the clear gaze, the wit at the corner of her mouth – I found a life that refused that story. Mel did not move through the world as someone cursed. She chose speed, beauty, generosity, appetite. The more I sat with her image, the more the label of 'unlucky' felt not only reductive, but wrong – a misreading of what it means to respond to the world with vitality despite what has been lost.

Her gravestone reads:

Sidney Russell Cooke, 12 Dec 1892–3 July 1930,
and Melville, his wife.

To have lived with such force and be remembered only in relation to another feels like a final injustice. This book is an attempt to offer her more than that narrow line. Not a corrected account, but a richer possibility: attentive rather than definitive, imagined rather than claimed.

We live in a moment increasingly alert to the lives history has overlooked, especially the lives of women whose voices were denied space in the record. Mel's story – or the traces of it – belongs among them. Re-examining her is not nostalgia; it is part of a larger act of recovery, a refusal to accept that a woman with such presence should disappear into silence or superstition.

I have listened carefully in the quiet rooms she left behind. In doing so, I have learnt something about how stories endure, how quickly they vanish, and how urgently we must reclaim them. To stand before her portraits is to feel that insistence still. *Look properly.*

I am grateful to Helen Melville Russell Cooke for the time spent in her imagined company, and for the reminder that choosing beauty, even after loss, is a legacy in itself.

—*Dr Caroline Cauchi*

Thanking

Writing this novel meant spending time in the company of a woman history insisted on calling unlucky. Melville Russell Cooke survived her father's loss, a nation's myth-making, and the long shadow of a story she never asked to inherit. To learn about her – patiently, slowly – was a privilege. What stayed with me was not her proximity to disaster and tragedy but her refusal to be defined by it. She chose something brighter. To endure grief and still turn towards joy is, I now realise, its own form of luck – the kind we make, the kind that remakes us.

To Charlotte Ledger, editor of my dreams and glorious human, who steered this book with vision, verve, and an unfailing instinct for where the truth of a story lies. Thank you for encouraging me to write into the gaps, for trusting me with Melville's life, and for offering the kind of permission that feels like being handed a lifeboat and told, firmly, to row. I am endlessly grateful (and in awe) that I get to work with you.

To HarperCollins UK and the brilliant team at One More Chapter, my heartfelt appreciation. from editorial to production, from digital to the foreign rights team, your collective brilliance brings my novels into readers' hands. Amongst many others, thank you personally to Grace Edwards, Chloe Cummings, Kara Daniel, Lucy Bennett, Katie Sadler, Francesca Tuzzeo, Sofia Salazar Studer, Caroline Scott-Bowden and Emily Thomas. Your belief in my work means more than I can say.

To the wonderful HarperCollins Canada team – this is a chance to thank you for your unwavering enthusiasm for *Queen of the Mist*, and for welcoming me to Canada with such warmth and generosity. Special love and thanks to Dave Knox, Kristina Jagger and Lauren Morocco for steering me around GNR. I am so excited to see what you will do with *Daughter of the Titanic*, and to meet more Canadian readers who have embraced my writing with such open-hearted kindness.

To my colleagues at the University of Hull – thank you for your encouragement, patience, and for creating a working environment in which research and imagination can thrive. Particular thanks to Drs Catherine Wynne, Jo Metcalf, Jenny Macleod, Laura Birkinshaw, and Edmund Hurst, whose support extended well beyond office hours.

My gratitude also to Robert Eagle for early guidance on David Rolt's work, and to Toby Rolt for generously sharing insight into his father's artistic life. This novel is stronger for your contributions.

To Jackie Jardine – thank you, for more than I can write here, and more than you'd suggest I say aloud.

To my friends, extended and new family – Pauline Williams, Ellie Williams, Jacob Williams, The Ruddicks, The Bevans (special mention to Becky, my steadfast pen pal from 1989 and now new sister), Ramon Azzopardi Fiott, Matty Busuttil, Steve Spiteri Fiteni, Alex Brown, Anne Cater, Keith Rice, Emily Hills, Charlie Rice, Wendi Surtees-Smith, Rachael Lucas, Paula Groves, Richard Wells, Margaret Coombs, Ryan Groves, Elsa Williams, Mark Zarb, Clare Christian, Kat Nokes, Catherine Cole, and Johnny Vegas – thank you for your humour, advice, encouragement, and your refusal to let me take myself too seriously. You make the world feel less sharp at its edges.

To my beloved Cauchis – Jacob, Ben, Poppy and Lauren. Thank you for loving me with such noisy, stubborn bigheartedness. I am lucky – truly, ridiculously, endlessly lucky – to belong with you.

And finally, to Nathan – my then and my now. Thank you for returning to my life exactly when I was ready to meet you properly, for the love that is constant without ever being still, and for building a future with me that feels both entirely new and long overdue. This novel is for you, my darling.

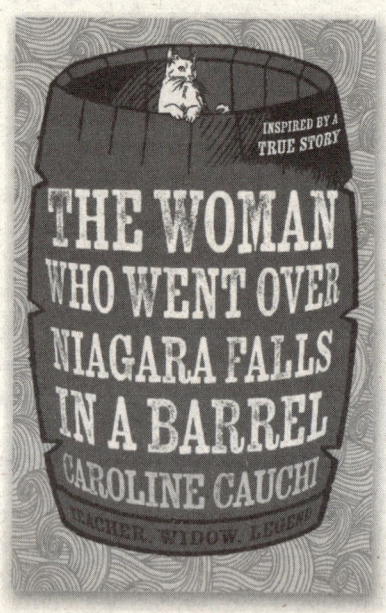

READ ON FOR AN EXTRACT!

Teacher. Widow. Legend.

It's 1901 and the mists of change are swirling. Queen Victoria's reign is about to come to an end, and an obscure widow in Buffalo, New York, is about to attempt the impossible.

Meet the courageous Mrs Annie Edson Taylor. The bravest woman you've never heard of and the first person to go over Niagara Falls in a barrel – over a decade before any man dared to do the same.

Enter a world of lost fortunes and friendship, as Annie, grieving the past and determined to change the lives of the women around her, attempts to alter the course of history.

With a single jump, that is.

AVAILABLE TODAY IN PAPERBACK, EBOOK AND AUDIO!

Annie

PROLOGUE

24th October 1901

The barrel creaks and groans around me, its wooden walls whispering secrets of the mighty Niagara. Each breath I take feels heavier, laden with the roar of the Falls. My heart pounds, echoing the thunderous cascade outside. Louder and louder. I clutch the leather harness, knuckles white, palms slick with perspiration.

'Can't back out now,' I whisper.

Memories flood my mind: Tilda and Nora, the quiet moments at home with Mrs Lapointe. I picture Samuel, my dear husband, and David, our baby boy; his tiny face is forever etched in my heart.

'Can you hear me?' I call out, hoping their spirits linger close.

The barrel tilts and bobs a wild dance with the river. Every jolt and shudder's a test, a challenge from nature itself. The dark confines of this wooden cocoon press in on me. Every sorrow, every fear, is amplified. That weight pushes down on me.

The barrel pitches violently. Throwing me against its sides. My head strikes the wood. Dizzying pain shoots through my skull. The roar of the Falls deafens. A primal scream from the depths of the earth. I squeeze my eyes shut, bracing for the inevitable.

A sudden drop. My breath catches. The world spins. I'm weightless. Suspended in a terrifying freefall.

'Help.'

The word is swallowed by the thunderous water. Impact. The jolt is brutal. Bones rattling. Teeth clenching. Water floods in, filling the barrel, threatening to drag me down into oblivion.

I struggle to breathe, to hold on, but the darkness presses closer, consuming.

How in God's name did I end up here?

Part I: Adrift

DECEMBER 1900

Annie

31st December 1900

'What I'd give to be in my parlour with a cup of warm milk and comfortable footwear...' I say, shifting awkwardly.

Instead, I'm stuck in these torture devices for women with feet as dainty as their sensibilities, which clearly isn't me. With a slight pivot on the heel, I tap the sole lightly against the ground, hoping to alleviate some of the discomfort. It doesn't. They're Mrs Lapointe's dead husband's sister's shoes, and they're a size too small.

Whispers of a grand salon gathering hosted by Mrs Winthrop – a prominent figure known for her love of literature and the arts – had spread like wildfire through Bay City. The invite list boasted esteemed members of the community, and anyone with a spark of talent deemed worthy of recognition. The woman had a knack for finding artists, writers, and anyone who could hold a quill without poking their eye out. Naturally, she invited everyone except those she actually liked. My friend and boarding house owner, Mrs Lapointe, was always on the lookout for such opportunities. I've no idea how she secured an invitation for us, but she did. I was informed that it was an occasion I couldn't miss.

That's why I find myself standing in Mrs Winthrop's grand estate. My feet have been planted firmly on this spot for ten minutes already; I must resemble one of her weathered, stone statues. The imposing mansion looms and a muddle of annoyance and nerves stream through me. Its windows are aglow with warmth and invitation, but still I'm overly keen to flee back to the boarding house for a butter tart.

Letting out an exasperated sigh, I smooth the fabric of my dress nervously. I hate feeling out of place. I'm no stranger to opulence, but this world isn't mine. I'm literally in someone else's clothing.

'Are you knocking, or should I?' he says, stepping next to me. His tall frame's imposing against the wooden door. He gestures to it.

'I'd rather not,' I say.

'Let me.' He stretches his right arm across me, his fingers slightly curled and ready to rap against the door. With the move, his arm inadvertently rebounds off my bosom.

'Sir, this is neither the time nor the place,' I say, and I see horror leap across his face.

'I didn't ... I wasn't,' he stutters, palms held up in surrender.

With a raised eyebrow and a smirk, I challenge him to question my authority or opinion. I see his fear. I'm wild and old; he enjoys his women young and tamed. The turn of the century may have brought us electric lights, but it hasn't yet cured the fear of a woman with opinions. He takes a step or two backwards.

My knuckles knock lightly on the door, and it creaks open within seconds.

'Welcome, Madam,' the butler intones with practised formality. 'If I could ask your name…' His voice is both crisp and professional. No-nonsense. I like him.

'Annie,' I say. 'Annie Edson Taylor.'

'Please, come in, Mrs Taylor.' He smiles and I step forward. 'Through there,' he says, pointing across the hallway before turning his attention back to the man who touched my bosom.

Ten short steps and I push my body against the mahogany door. It's heavy on my shoulder. A blast of laughter and chatter gushes as it edges open.

'Thank you,' someone says. 'Looks like I need to lay off pie if I'm going to squeeze through here!' A burly man, with a jovial demeanour; his presence fills the space with warmth as he wriggles past me and through the gap.

'Allow me,' a different guest says. A hint of grey streaks his dark hair. His pushing on the door appears effortless and the room opens before us.

The noise and vibrant atmosphere overwhelm instantly. Too many people, too much to see. I don't know where to look first. The room's a kaleidoscope of laughter, swirling gowns, and the kind of joy that feels almost tangible; like you could reach out and pocket a piece for later. Smoothing my eyebrow with the tip of my finger, I step into the ballroom. The room's abuzz with activity. I scan the crowds for a familiar face but see none. Mrs Lapointe was feeling a little under the weather, said she'd meet me here; I'll kill her if she doesn't arrive soon. I pat the skirts of my dress, keen to appear busy and to detract from how alone I suddenly feel. Indeed, this dress – Mrs Lapointe once wore it for an end-of-season ball – is tight and uncomfortable in its corset; a nagging reminder of the ageing I attempt to hide.

I risk a peek around, jumping my stare from person to person. My aim is to avoid eye contact at all costs. Women are adorned in jewels that glitter and materials that flow. Scarlet and emerald gowns shimmer. The men sport tailored suits in shades of navy or burgundy. Mrs Lapointe was right in her choice of dress for me; red and bejewelled. I'd told her I'd hate every minute of wearing it, yet here I am, blending in. The light from the chandeliers above reflects off the polished marble floor. A flicker of worry that I'll slip, but I push that thought away. Instead, I consider what it'd feel like to bend and stroke my fingers across its surface. This setting is beautiful, these people are beautiful, and maybe, tonight, I'm one of those people, too. I'm invisible because I'm merging and not because I'm ancient or lacking good looks. I shake my head to dislodge those thoughts; I find this relentless need for youth and femininity jarring.

I make my way to the refreshment table. One of the impeccably dressed servers points to bottles and says words I can't quite hear over the hustle and bustle and chatter.

'Dr-ink.' The server articulates the word as if I'm deaf. He gestures in front of him. 'Champagne, wine…' He pauses and then points to a bowl. His mouth twists as if he's having to force words through a pipe.

I shrug. 'What's in there?' My curiosity is piqued.

'Punch.' His tone almost apologetic. I open my mouth to speak—

'Been saying for years that something needs to be done about the alcohol problem.' I turn to two men behind me, their voices carrying over the ambient noise of the party.

'Absolutely,' the second man chimes in. Solidly built with salt-and-pepper hair; his voice has authority. 'It's high time we put an end to the excessive drinking that's plaguing our society.' Their words linger in the air, mingling with the clinking of glasses and the murmur of conversation.

I move to the glass bowl of punch, picking up a cup and turning to smile at the server. 'Punch, please. Do fill my glass to the brim.' I hear a tut behind me. I straighten up and pull my shoulders back, turning to face the men. They've already walked away, indicating in my direction.

'Can I offer you something to eat?' the server asks. He points at the grand array of serving plates. They're all perfectly positioned on a table that's adorned with ornate porcelain plates and silver utensils. This is luxury.

I shake my head, but he isn't looking at me.

'There's an assortment of small appetisers and hors d'oeuvres on offer. Perhaps crackers with cheese and slices of cured meat.' His speech is polished. He smiles. He's proud of his delivery. He pauses to walk to a plate and point, before moving to another. 'As well as larger dishes. Roast beef, salmon.' He looks at me then. There's not a hint of affection or concern. He cares neither if I eat five full platters nor starve myself to death.

'Thank you, but I'm really not—'

'Perhaps a little something from the selection of sweet treats. Cakes, pastries...'

He glances for a response. I shake my head, apologising. My stomach rumbles in protest. 'Just the punch,' I say. I smile. I hear his tut this time – he's offended – as he spots another guest and walks to her. A smile and then he attempts to convince her to try his food.

I shake my head, not quite sure why I said no. I'm hungry, there's free food and I'm trying to ignore the tempting aromas surrounding me. It's as if to eat would be a sensory overload too many. I can't trust myself to walk, to drink punch and to eat. I move with purpose and determination, then recall that I don't know another soul here. The room is filled with young, well-dressed people, laughing and chatting as they don't question their surroundings. It all feels excessive: excessively flamboyant, excessively loud, excessively articulated. I watch as they wolf the food and drink on offer. Perhaps I could be more like them, but the effort feels tedious and unnecessary. This isn't the adventure I crave. Yet, I can't shake a growing unease that accompanies the scene. I'm as guilty as they are. The extremeness of it all, the lack of restraint and moderation, it's as if this society is losing its balance, on the verge of spiralling into a frenzy of indulgence and extravagance. What are the consequences of such unrestrained behaviour? How is that shaping their values and priorities? What impact is that having on the very fabric of our society? I won't find my answers here. Times and social expectations are changing, though. My stomach grumbles in protest as I stand still, perspiring in a too-tight dress.

My eyes are drawn back to the large platters of food on the table. My mouth waters at the sight of the juicy roast beef and the perfectly cooked salmon. With a confident smile and unwavering gaze, I gulp down my drink, in a way that's entirely not ladylike. I savour the sweet taste on my tongue, then walk further into the room. Where are you, Mrs Lapointe?

Movement from the corner of my eye. I turn. I see a curious couple. He's leaning against a pillar deep in conversation with a truly elegant woman. His presence feels dwarfed by hers, even though she's clearly trying to make herself appear smaller. His dark hair's slicked back in a modern style, and his eyes seem to both study and devour his companion. She looks uncomfortable, while he exudes an air of entitlement.

He glances at me and I panic. I wave confidently. I don't even know why. I see his confusion and fast recovery as he waves back and feigns recognition. The entire encounter is over in a blink. He's impeccably dressed in a suit that hugs his lean frame. I can tell by the way he stands, or rather inclines, that he displays confidence. It's not earned confidence from his appearance or height, though, so it must have been bought with money. Excessive amounts of it. The woman he's devouring takes her chance and seemingly ducks into the shadows. I watch him look to the floor at the exact spot where she was standing, as if she's disappeared into thin air. His face contorts and he squints as he swivels, searching for her.

'That's Henry Hills. Mrs Winthrop's younger brother.'

I turn and Mrs Lapointe is here. 'Better late than not at all,' I say, but then pause. She's the vision of refined elegance in a floor-length silk gown with a high collar and fitted bodice that's adorned with intricate lace detailing.

'Was that in your chest of clothes?' I ask and she nods.

'It's a little loose here.' She pulls at the material in the pit of her arm. 'I must have been larger five years ago.'

'You're wasting away.' I pinch at her waist. She looks considerably paler than she did this morning. Still, her hair's elegantly coiffed, and a feathered hairpiece perches gracefully atop her head. Elbow-length gloves made of delicate lace complete her ensemble, adding a touch of sophistication to her appearance.

'Stunning,' I say and her cheeks blush red.

'What do you think?' She nods towards Henry, and I laugh. I try to study his face and demeanour objectively. The lighting is flattering, emphasising his bone structure, larger-than-average eyes and pimple-covered skin – though his condescending expression overshadows any physical features.

'Do you want to eat? Are you starving?' I gesture towards the server and food.

'Come,' she whispers, looking concerned. She pulls my hand and strides towards him. 'Let me introduce you. He's desperate for a wife, and we need money.'

'What?'

I'm about to shake my hand free and run for the ballroom doors when I hear, 'Mr Hills. So wonderful to see you again.'

I bang into Mrs Lapointe, causing her to stumble forward into Mr Hills. In an instant, he's not leaning on the pillar, and he attempts to catch her. It's an odd embrace as she's both taller and wider than him. That's quite something as my friend's leanness could be considered an asset. Mrs Lapointe appears to melt into a giggle in his embrace. It's entirely fake but Mr Hills laps it up. His desperation for female attention is palpable. I roll my eyes, marvelling at how someone could be so obnoxious and self-absorbed, but then realise that he's staring at me.

'Henry Hills, this is my closest, oldest and very dear friend,' Mrs Lapointe says. 'Annie Edson Taylor.'

'Hello,' I say. She's attempting humour; I'm slightly older than her. I laugh. I'm the ageing aunt respectable mothers would hate.

'Charmed to make your acquaintance,' he says. His eyebrows are too thick and too bushy. I'm convinced I could flick at them and they'd wiggle away.

'Mrs Taylor was once on a stagecoach that was held up by *the* Jesse James and his gang.' I turn as Mrs Lapointe waves and walks off into the crowd.

'Who is this *lady*?' That's the original woman. She's back. She pulls her furs around her shoulders and stands at her full height beside me. 'Has her hair ever been brushed?' She must have reconsidered or recalculated the financial gain from being with Mr Hills. She's not happy that I've distracted her prey. It seems that he has something the women here desire. But it's certainly not his personality.

'Really?' Mr Hills says. 'And you lived to tell the tale?'

For a second, I must look confused.

He sighs. 'Jesse James?' He looks concerned. 'Are you unwell?'

I shake my head. I smile, pushing up my dress sleeves in readiness for story time. 'I lived, and I kept my eight-hundred dollars, too.'

Mr Hills laughs, and that spurs me on.

'How old are you?' says his original prey.

I turn to her. Her mouth is pinched and I'm waiting for her to waggle a finger in my direction. 'Forty-three,' I say, my eyes daring her to question the fact.

She laughs. Mr Hills waves her away. He's dismissing her. He clearly likes what he sees, or he's detected something in my persona and considers it an indication that I desire him. His arrogance is astonishing. Does it matter? This could provide entertainment to distract from the fact that these shoes are strangling my toes.

'You don't believe me?' I ask, looking at him through my eyelashes. I used to flirt with my Samuel in that way, but now I possibly look like I've got a squint or am hovering on hysterical.

'I think you're a talented storyteller,' he says. I pause. Not sure if that's a comment on my encounter with Jessie James or on my age.

'I had almost a thousand dollars hidden in the hem of my skirts,' I say. 'It went undetected because the gang had no desire to explore me further.' I speak with animated gestures, punctuating my words with hand movements.

'Mrs Taylor.' He says my name as if it were sugar on his tongue. It sounds sickly and makes my stomach flip in a bad way. He stretches out a hand and I do the same. Our palms are a similar size. Despite his unimposing stature, he carries himself with an overblown sense of self-importance. 'Annie.' A nod and a wide smile. 'I'm thrilled to make your acquaintance. You really are funny for a woman.'

Rolling my eyes dramatically I say, 'Thank you.' The words are soaked in sarcasm. 'And you are rather full of yourself for a man.'

Funny, unusual, difficult – that desire to label women bothers me. My wild hair will be confusing him, though. Men like Mr Hills fear women like me; they can't predict our next moves. They like us tamed and docile. Society demands it. Still, I'll never fear life in the way that he does, and I'll never be restrained. My grasp of impermanence makes me terrifying.

He bats away my words as he doubles over with laughter. Perhaps not terrifying, then. This man really does consider me hilarious. 'I'm intrigued as to why you would believe Mr James to not wish to know you…' he looks around, before leaning in, '…intimately.'

I point my right index finger at my face and paint a circle in the air that is wider than my hair. I maintain eye contact with him as I do. This man is the pot to my kettle.

He roars with laughter, and I wait for that to stop. 'I would like to know you better,' he says. He's still holding my left hand.

'You would?' I ask, letting out an exasperated sigh. He nods.

I assume this is where women are expected to swoon. My fluttering is deep in my abdomen. It feels more like a stomach bug or the impact of too much punch than anything remotely positive. He'll know that my palms are sweaty, but I imagine he'll consider it an attraction.

'Tell me about the stagecoach.'

'It was making its way through rugged terrain when, quite suddenly, it was stopped by a group of armed men on horseback.'

I feel his thumb making circles on my palm. It causes me to pause. To look at our hands and then to his face. He shows no emotion. I'm holding my breath as if that'll stop me from vomiting on his polished boots. He perhaps interprets that as a nervous desire. He nods for me to continue.

'The door to the stagecoach was flung open and a man stepped aboard.' I fling my arms out wide. Mr Hills' entire body moves with the force of my movement and with his hand still being in mine. Everyone takes a step back.

'Mr James?' Mr Hills draws himself up to his full five feet and two inches. He rubs at his shoulder socket. The yank hurt him.

I nod a yes. 'He was tall, with piercing blue eyes and the wildest mane of hair I'd ever seen.' A small crowd has gathered nearer about me. Mr Hills has noticed this, too. He stretches his neck and pushes back his slender shoulders. A cock amongst hens.

'I heard he was handsome,' one of the women says, but I don't turn to look at her. My eyes are stuck on this odd man, whose every action seems to demand attention. The fact that he's reached out and is attempting to hold my hand again must be a curious sight for others. Are we equals? Is his ugliness matched by my old age? Who is the more desperate?

'Did he speak to you?' a different woman asks.

'At first he stared at me,' I say. I nod to Mr Hills. Like you are doing now. 'There was kindness in his eyes, though.'

'Perhaps you reminded him of his mother,' one of the women says. The others laugh.

'I am no one's mother,' I say, squaring my shoulders. The harshness in my voice shocks me.

'Yet,' Mr Hills says.

I bat his hand away. I don't mean to, but that thought. Five, four, three, two, one—

'Then what happened?' one of the women asks.

'I told him, "Blow me away. I'd as soon be without brains than without money."'

'Then what happened?' Mr Hills asks, his voice breathy. Is this exciting him?

'Jesse James spoke to me.' A pause for dramatic effect. 'Said, "We're just after the strongbox under the driver's seat. You won't come to no harm."'

A collective gasp.

'Astonishing.' That's Mr Hills.

'What did you do?'

'Nothing.' I spin slowly, making eye contact with each of the listeners. 'I nodded, my heart racing. Watched the strongbox being handed over. Watched a group of men, with bandanas covering their faces and guns in their hands, ride off into the sunset.'

The laughter and applause are like music to my ears. I bow flamboyantly.

'And he never asked you to hand over your fortune?'

'Guess I looked poor,' I say. 'Or maybe he recognised that we shared the same intentions.'

'The same intentions?' Mr Hills asks, his eyes dancing, his pimple-covered face glowing.

'Yes.' A smirk plays at the corner of my lips. 'We both had nothing left to lose.'

∼

Want to find out what happens next?
GET YOUR COPY TODAY!
Available in paperback, ebook and audio!

The author and One More Chapter would like to thank everyone who contributed to the publication of this story...

Analytics
Imogen Wolstencroft

Audio
Fionnuala Barrett
Ciara Briggs

Design
Lucy Bennett
Fiona Greenway
Liane Payne
Dean Russell

Digital Sales
Laura Daley
Lydia Grainge
Hannah Lismore

eCommerce
Laura Carpenter
Madeline ODonovan
Charlotte Stevens
Christina Storey
Rachel Ward

Editorial
Rosie Best
Kara Daniel
Charlotte Ledger
Lydia Mason
Jennie Rothwell
Sofia Salazar Studer
Caroline Scott-Bowden
Emily Thomas
Helen Williams

Harper360
Emily Gerbner
Ariana Juarez
Jean Marie Kelly
emma sullivan
Sophia Wilhelm

International Sales
Ruth Burrow
Bethan Moore
Colleen Simpson

Inventory
Sarah Callaghan
Kirsty Norman

Marketing & Publicity
Chloe Cummings
Grace Edwards
Katie Sadler

Operations
Melissa Okusanya
Vanessa Coubrough

Production
Denis Manson
Simon Moore
Francesca Tuzzeo

Rights
Ashton Mucha
Alisah Saghir
Zoe Shine
Aisling Smyth

Trade Marketing
Ben Hurd
Eleanor Slater

The HarperCollins Contracts Team

The HarperCollins Distribution Team

The HarperCollins Finance & Royalties Team

The HarperCollins Legal Team

The HarperCollins Technology Team

UK Sales
Isabel Coburn
Jay Cochrane
Leah Woods

And every other essential link in the chain from delivery drivers to booksellers to librarians and beyond!

One More Chapter is an award-winning global division of HarperCollins.

Subscribe to our newsletter to get our latest eBook deals and stay up to date with all our new releases!

signup.harpercollins.co.uk/join/signup-omc

Meet the team at
www.onemorechapter.com

Follow us!
@onemorechapterhc

Do you write unputdownable fiction?
We love to hear from new voices.
Find out how to submit your novel at
www.onemorechapter.com/submissions